Praise for *Risk*

Brock Eastman is a writer with a passion that ignites his pen and drives the reader to burn through each page. These action-packed books will keep you desiring more of the adventure as you untangle the mysteries within and become friends with the characters.

—**Wayne Thomas Batson**, best-selling author of
The Door Within Trilogy, The Berinfell Prophecies,
and The Dark Sea Annals

The journey you are about to go on is filled with detail, wonder, and surprise. After reading this book, you will only wish you could go to the jungle-filled basin of Ero Doeht. Enjoy the ride, and good luck trying to put this book down.

—**Brian Stewart**, father of two, Colorado

Sit back and let Brock take you on an exciting journey to the far reaches of the galaxy that explores the meaning of family and friends.

—**Mark Redekop**, the Adventures in Odyssey Wiki

There are two things that you can always count on with Brock Eastman's writing: thrilling adventure and characters who grow in the Lord. Here is a storyteller who refuses to play it safe by simplifying his message. Prayer and faith are an integral part of his storytelling. Bravo! The world needs more authors like Brock.

—**The Miller Brothers**, authors of the multi-award-winning Codebearers Series and *Mech Mice: Genesis Strike*

Praise for The Quest for Truth series

I'm constantly on the lookout for books that are exciting, but not too scary for my school-aged children. Eastman consistently delivers action-packed page-turners that are not only a joy for the whole family to read, but also strengthen our spiritual walks.

—**Elissa Peterson**, mother of four, creator of
Don't Let Life Pass You By blog

I cannot wait for *Risk* to come out. I loved *Taken*. I read it over and over again when I can.

—**Caleb Frey**, age 11

RISK

THE QUEST FOR TRUTH

RISK

THE SECOND ADVENTURE IN
THE QUEST FOR TRUTH

BROCK EASTMAN

P&R
PUBLISHING

P.O. BOX 817 • PHILLIPSBURG • NEW JERSEY 08865-0817

Printed in the United States of America

Library of Congress Control Number: 2012937613

To my mom:

You let me dream big,
and you selflessly helped me along the way to those dreams.
Thank you for helping me to get where I am.

P.S. Thanks for always making me Russian Tea.

Contents

Acknowledgments

A few well-deserved thanks.

Ashley, none of my books would be possible without your loving support. I'm so in awe that God would give me such an amazing woman to be at my side and to grow old with me.

My beautiful girls, Kinley and Elsie, I can't help but smile when I think of you. To see the gifts God has given your mom and me in your little ever-growing lives is humbling—that he would entrust you two to us. We love you both very much.

Mom and Dad, thanks for your continued support in my family's life and mine. It's an honor to call you my parents.

Ty, Tiff, Autumn, Maddie, and Hadley, thank you for encouraging us and believing in our work here in Colorado.

My family: grandparents, aunts, uncles, cousins, and in-laws, your support of my writing and encouragement at my book launch party was overwhelming. I thank you all for your love and laughter.

Eli K., thanks for helping me to get a website up and running. I appreciate the time and effort you took to work on it and give me a better presence on the web.

Darlene A. and Nathaniel R., thank you for the nearly twenty-four-hour speed review of *Taken*. Thank you too for your hard work to make The Quest for Truth the best it can be!

Larry W., thanks for reading *Taken* and deciding that it fit in the Focus on the Family family of books. I know you want to provide only the highest quality of literature to Focus' constituents, so it means a lot that you would choose The Quest for Truth. Thank you!

Sheila S., thanks for all your encouragement about the book and about writing. Thanks for encouraging me with the review from *Thriving Family*. Even if we didn't get to end up using it.

Jesse F., you didn't hesitate for a second to offer me the chance to put a story from The Quest for Truth in *Clubhouse* magazine. The story came out awesome!

Peg M., thank you for your hard work on the amazing art for the "Coming Storm" story. The art and poster made the story come alive.

The anonymous Focus orthodoxy reviewer and *Thriving Family* magazine reviewer, I've never met either of you, but your honest and glowing reviews helped The Quest for Truth become cobranded by Focus on the Family.

Ian T. and Tara M., thanks for responding to my one million one-word emails so quickly all the time. You guys are a great team.

Melissa C. and Aaron G., again you guys made writing, editing, and finishing the book so easy. Your tireless efforts are what make The Quest for Truth what it is.

Leslie P., your thorough editing and wonderful feedback made *Risk* so much better.

Tim P., I enjoy the technological and scientific insight you add to the series. You've made me seriously stop and think, "Well, duh, Brock" several times.

Calvin K., you were my first Obbin in Atlanta, and I thank you for becoming blue and green. The pictures were great.

All the team at P&R Publishing, you guys have put out so much for the series, and you took a chance on a young unknown author. Thank you, thank you, thank you!

All the team at Focus on the Family, Bob, Anita, Barb, Chris, Bruce, Allison, Matt, your support for the series and for me have been such an encouragement. You make working in Product Marketing a joy.

Michael W., your fan art is awesome, and it's cool to get a new piece of art in my email when I wake up. I can't wait to see your first book cover. It's fun to have a friend half a world away.

Ryan M., thanks for being so encouraging to my writing. Your mini videos are awesome and an encouragement to my work.

Brian S., you gave me great encouragement for my writing. You read *Risk* in thirty hours! Wow! Thanks for being such a great friend.

Chris F., thanks for supporting my books and for getting them in the hands of students. You're a great friend.

Most important, thank you to the One who inspired this series. You speak to me at the times when I need it most. You are the Creator and the one who inspires creativity. I pray these books are an encouragement to the Kingdom.

2.0

Prologue

Nine Years Ago

The man wore a grey suit and a black tie with a skull-shaped pin holding it in place. His coal-black hair belied his true age. However, his cold blue eyes revealed his power and focus.

He looked out on the new cadets from behind the darkly tinted windows of the tower. There were nearly a hundred fresh recruits, most of them older than he'd liked, but they would have to do. Their age made it more difficult to conduct the sort of intense reeducation necessary. But again, he had to work with the hand he'd been dealt.

The cold, wintery weather of the planet made the training intense but further served to separate the weak from the strong. For too long they had been letting their standards slip, and their observer was determined to change that.

"Sir, your son is third from the left in the front row," a soldier in a black trench coat pointed out.

"Silence!" the older man hissed, his blue eyes narrowing. "Do not mention my son. No one is to know." The man's chin rose, and he glared at the soldier. "Speak of it again and you'll never speak thereafter."

The soldier nervously swallowed the lump in his throat. "Yes, sir."

"I've seen enough. See to it that his training"—he pointed a gloved hand at the cadet identified to be his son—"is extra hard, and be sure that he does not suspect anything."

"Yes, sir." The soldier saluted.

"Have my ship prepared. I'm leaving," the suited man said harshly.

"Yes, sir," the soldier repeated and opened the door for his commander to exit. "When shall we expect you back?"

"You shan't," the man said without a second look back, the soles of his shiny black shoes clanking with every step down.

As he reached the bottom of the stairs, he fingered something in his pocket. The information on the paper in his hand wasn't exactly useful, but it did bring confirmation of what he'd always believed to be true. Finally, after years of hard work, it was within reach. Now he just had to be patient and put things into motion. It might take years yet, but he would be the one to find it. He would finally have the power to control his own fate. And, if he chose, control the fates of others.

Turning the handle to the exit, he stepped out onto a landing pad and surveyed his prized black ship, the *Raven*. It would take him on the final leg of this journey, possibly his longest assignment yet. He straightened his suit with a shift of his shoulders, then started toward the transport.

A narrow side hatch slid open, and a soldier greeted him with a salute. "Sir!"

The man in the suit shook his head and grumbled. "Tone it down."

"Yes, sir," the soldier responded.

He liked regimented order, but he would not miss the constant "yes, sirs" that accompanied his rank. No, the next few years would be quite a change for him. But if the intelligence report was correct—which it had better be, or the men responsible would suffer his wrath—then this was indeed the most rational move to make. Without a doubt, it had the greatest probability of furthering his goals.

He took the stairs and avoided the bridge of the ship. Instead he walked to his cabin and shut the door. The engines rumbled as they ignited and prepared for takeoff. He and his men would arrive at the GenTexic facility within the next two hours. Either the results of the experiment would be successful, or he'd be looking for the twelfth program director in as many months. He was growing weary of incompetent scientists and inaccurate deadlines. It was fortunate that he had access to limitless funds or the constantly ballooning budget would have killed these experiments years ago. If the program wasn't on track now, he might as well shut the entire operation down. Why allow GenTexic to continue failing and squandering resources while he was out of touch for the next few years?

He grunted. The genetics program was the backup plan. In the end, it'd be more costly and take longer to restart it upon his return than to let the fools continue trying.

His body quivered with anger at the uselessness of those around him.

He thought of the one the soldier had called his son. He'd met the man just twice, both times when the soldier was a boy. Neither time had the boy known their relationship, only that he was meeting the supreme commander. The question remained: would the boy have the same drive he did? Time would tell, and quicker than the cadet expected.

Hanging his suit jacket in the small clothes locker, he next removed his gloves, followed by his tie and pin. He held the pin out before him. It was a reminder of what he sought to avoid. He'd also have to leave the symbol behind during his mission. He could take no risks with his identity being revealed.

He pulled the paper from his pants' pocket and read the contents. "Very soon. Patience," he muttered to himself. A dark scowl came over his face as he looked at himself in a nearby mirror. "Eternity is mine."

SKULL
COMMAND CRUISER

SKULL
COMMAND CRUISER

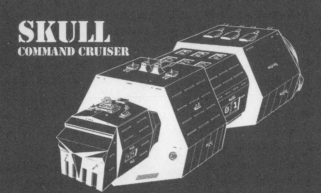

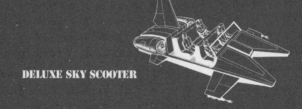

DELUXE SKY SCOOTER

STAR FIGHTER

SKY SCOOTER

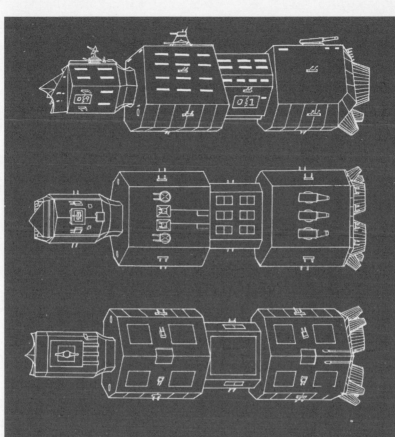

AND I GIVE UNTO THEM ETERNAL LIFE;
AND THEY SHALL NEVER PERISH.

ORDER: 36-202012

SKULL
COMMAND CRUISER

Priceless

The word *priceless* echoed in Oliver's mind as he sat alone on the bridge of the *Phoenix*, pondering the last days' events. Running his fingers through his spiky brown hair, he felt his chest rise and fall as he took a long, soothing breath. It felt like the first real gulp of oxygen he'd taken since the quest had begun. The last few days had been both an adventure and a nightmare.

His parents were gone, snatched by the ruthless Captain Vedrik and his Übel soldiers. Oliver had fled at his dad's orders, taking his sister, Tiffany, and two twin brothers, Mason and Austin, with him. It was the first of three getaways they'd made. The second had separated them from Phelan O'Farrell, a wealthy benefactor of his parents' archeological work who had gifted them with the very star cruiser he now sat in. The third escape had been from an army of blue soldiers.

He shook his head. Blue men—how could that be? It hadn't been paint, and it wasn't some sort of body art; it was their actual skin color. Regardless, Oliver couldn't shake the sight of over a hundred of them with spears and torches, surrounding the ship, ready to attack.

And now here they were on course for the planet Evad. Oliver was certain that the Übel would take his parents, Elliot and Laura Wikk, there. That's where the clues led.

He pondered those facts. At the start of this whole adventure, Tiffany had discovered an entry in their mom's journal describing a recent excavation at Dabnis Castle. At the castle, their parents had uncovered several significant finds. The first was a small green globe with two inscriptions etched across its surface: the name of a planet, *Evad*, and two coordinates, neither of which were Evad's galactic location but which were possibly coordinates on the planet itself.

Alone, this discovery didn't warrant an immediate trip to the planet. However, when coupled with the next discovery, it suggested something significant awaited them there.

On the last day at Dabnis Castle, their parents had discovered an ancient book bound in crimson leather, the contents of which were unknown to Oliver. It was this very book the Übel Captain Vedrik had taken when he had abducted Oliver's parents. The captain had somehow known of the Wikks' discovery and called the book "priceless."

Priceless.

Mr. O'Farrell had said the Übel were "the wealthiest organization, save the Federation." So for something to be priceless to the Übel captain was significant. This only deepened Oliver's intrigue in what information the book might hold.

Rescuing his parents was Oliver's top priority, but how he would accomplish this goal was still in question. Without knowing much of their destination or how large Vedrik's contingent of soldiers was, Oliver couldn't conceive a thorough plan.

A lump formed in his throat. Of course, if his parents didn't go to Evad, or had already been and left, he had no idea how he'd find them. That fact, however, he could not and would not share with his sister and brothers. They clung to the hope of finding their parents.

Since the *Phoenix* was currently zipping through space in hyper flight, contacting Mr. O'Farrell was out of the question. At least Oliver and his siblings were safe, even if for just that moment.

Oliver tapped the screen to see the time remaining in hyper flight, and his mouth curled into a frown. Two hours might not seem like much, but under the circumstances it felt like an eternity. He involuntarily yawned and stretched as he stood from the pilot's seat. His sister and twin brothers had headed to the galley a few minutes ago and were waiting for him.

He stepped into the lavatory on his way and splashed a few handfuls of cool water onto his face. The mirror reflected a very different Oliver from the one who'd left to be a cadet at the Federal Academy nearly a year prior. He'd just turned seventeen but already dark stubble grew like moss on his squared chin by the end of each day. His brown eyes had dark rims from previous near-sleepless nights. His biceps were sore from the past days' trials, the last of which had taken place a mere half-hour before when he'd scrambled up the rope ladder to escape the horde of blue soldiers.

Looking in the mirror was like seeing his father.

He sighed and nodded. Oliver not only looked like an adult, he had to act like one.

Refuse-Cycler

In the galley, Tiffany was cooking, her long brown hair pulled back in a ponytail. She was a couple of years younger than Oliver but arguably the smartest of the four Wikk children.

Mason, the elder of the twins, was setting utensils at four of the twelve seats. Mason scratched his head of sandy blond hair and sighed as he took in the empty seats, a reminder to them all that their parents were not with them.

Austin rested his head on the table, a lively tune humming from his lips. Oliver knew that Austin wanted so badly to prove himself. He wanted to be in command and lead the rescue of their parents, but the twins were just eleven years old.

Oliver walked to the cryostore and opened it. "Tiffany, what do you want to drink?"

"I'll have an H_2O, thanks."

"Mason? Austin?"

"Energen!" they replied in near unison.

Oliver grabbed the requested beverages and set them on the table.

"You're having Energen too?" asked Mason snidely. "I thought you said this stuff wasn't healthy enough for a Star Fleet Academy cadet."

"I did. But I need the energy more than ever," Oliver retorted teasingly. "Besides, I just had one on our trip to Brighton, and it's hard to turn down the crisp, cool jolt it gives you."

Austin lifted his head from the table and laughed.

Mason smiled and raised his bottle. "To success."

The boys lifted their drinks and toasted. "To success!"

Steam poured from the dishes Tiffany had prepared, and the smell of grilled chicken and broccoli filled the galley as everyone dug into their meals.

Oliver popped the top on his bottle of Energen and took a long draft from it. "Wow, that hits the spot!" he said at the crisp taste.

"How can you drink that stuff?" Tiffany stuck her fork into her chicken.

The twins popped the tops to their Energens simultaneously, taking long swigs and slamming the bottles down with satisfaction. Austin smacked his lips. "Because—it's awesome!" The energy poured from his voice.

Mason nodded his head vigorously. "And one hundred percent natural!"

"Boys . . ." Tiffany sighed. "You guys should be spokeskids."

"Love to," Austin said, as if to accept an actual offer.

"In fact, we'll take payment in a lifetime supply of Energen," Mason added with a laugh.

The twins grinned and tapped their bottles together with a clank.

"To us," Mason said.

"To Energen," Austin corrected.

Again they chugged more of the energy drink.

"So," Oliver began and sighed. "It seems that you two have a lot to tell us." He eyed a piece of broccoli on his fork. Not exactly his favorite vegetable.

The twins' jovial looks were quickly replaced with ones that mirrored cornered animals'.

"Uh, well, not really," Austin stammered.

"Yeah. You were only gone for a couple of days," Mason added in an it-was-no-big-deal tone.

Oliver raised an eyebrow, speaking sarcastically. "So the blue warriors surrounding the ship had nothing to do with you two?"

For a moment, the only sound was the soft hum of electricity running through the overhead lights. Oliver looked back and forth between the twins. One of them would crack, but who first? He glared at Mason, then Austin, then back to Mason, putting the pressure on. "Mason, tell me." He spoke in a stern voice.

Still silence.

"Fine, no more Energen."

Austin gasped. "You can't!"

Oliver nodded to Tiffany. His sister walked to the cryo-store and opened the door. She slipped a full case of Energen from the refrigeration unit and set it on the counter. She then touched a small button, and an opening appeared in the countertop.

The twins eyes widened in disbelief. "You wouldn't," Austin challenged.

"Tiffany, activate the refuse-cycler."

Tiffany touched a second button and a bone-tingling grinding noise echoed out from the hole. Oliver nodded, and Tiffany slid the case of energy drinks toward the hole.

The edge of the case hung over the refuse-cycler just as Mason burst out. "All right!" The twin broke down. "They were here for the prince."

"And probably us too," Austin added. "We met this boy, and he took our stuff. Next thing we knew, we were captured."

"Explain," Oliver commanded.

Austin looked at Mason and whispered, "We swore an oath not to tell about them."

"I know, but Oliver and Tiffany saw them with their own eyes," reminded Mason.

"That's true," agreed Austin. "Do they need to take the oath? We don't have a weapon from the gorge."

Oliver took a deep breath and tapped his fingers on the table. The twins were still whispering, though he could hear them. He looked at Tiffany, who shrugged.

"You mean like the sword on the statue?" Mason asked.

Austin nodded. "Exactly. Remember Obbin took us to that room just to take the oath."

Mason agreed. "I don't think we need to do the whole ritual thing Obbin had us do, though. Dad always said, 'Your yes should be yes, and your no should be no.'"

Austin didn't look convinced.

"At least for now," Mason said. "They already saw them anyway."

Oliver looked at Tiffany.

"They're stalling," she mouthed. He nodded, and Tiffany activated the refuse-cycler again. The grinding sound burst forth.

The twins started. "Wait!" Mason shouted.

"No more stalling, boys," Oliver ordered.

"Okay." Austin cleared his throat.

Tiffany took a seat, and the story spilled from Austin's lips. Mason filled in holes that Austin missed and added extra details. Slowly, they revealed the specifics of their day inside the blue city—Obbin, the twins' capture, the king of the Blauwe Mensen, Mr. Thule, Crown Prince Voltan, and the twins' eventual escape. In less than an hour, the twins had provided Oliver and Tiffany with a detailed account of their adventure with the mysterious Blauwe Mensen.

Oliver looked at each of the boys. They were waiting for his verdict, for their sentence. He could tell they expected it to be harsh and heavy. He leaned back in his chair and stroked the stubble on his chin, hiding what nearly broke into a smile. The twins' whole story had been exciting, and he was rather impressed by not only their escape, but also their courage in trying to reclaim the stolen supplies.

He looked at his now empty Energen can as he contemplated his position as the one in charge. The twins had been given clear instructions not to leave the ship. Oliver had learned at the Academy that insubordination could not be tolerated. The boys had really left him no choice but to be tough, to show he was a strong leader for his family.

Oliver forced a frown and placed his hands on the table. "It was wrong to leave the safety of the *Phoenix*. I gave strict instructions not to exit the ship." He paused. "Boys, this is a matter of trust. There are consequences for your actions. You endangered yourselves as well as Tiffany and me. Further—"

Should he finish? Yes, instead of rehashing all this later, he had to lay it out clearly and truthfully for them now.

"Further, you endangered our chances of rescuing our parents."

Oliver looked at his brothers. Tears filled Mason's eyes, and Austin laid his head on the table again, but this time he was not humming a gleeful tune. A guilty feeling thrashed in the pit of Oliver's stomach. They were too young. His accusation that the twins had possibly doomed their parents had gone too far. He needed to regroup.

"With that said, I also want to congratulate you," he started.

Austin lifted his head in wonder. Tiffany looked at her older brother in confusion.

Oliver continued. "While what you did was wrong, you overcame the dangers you got into and did so by working as a team. You got back our supplies instead of leaving us with nothing. For that, I thank you."

No one spoke.

Tiffany cleared her throat, and each of the twins looked at her. Oliver wondered if she would support his closing praise for the twins.

"The two of you were given one rule to follow: do not to leave the ship under any circumstances." Tiffany took a deep breath and exhaled. "We were—" She stopped. "We are in a . . . perilous situation."

"What does that mean?" Austin interrupted. He sounded annoyed by his sister's uppity vocabulary.

"Dangerous," she explained.

Oliver smiled at his sister the teacher, but she did not smile back. He knew then she hadn't approved of his commendation of the twins.

"The last thing we needed was for the two of you to be lost in some remote valley. How do you think Oliver and I would ever have found you?" Tiffany looked from Mason to Austin.

"I don't know—" Austin responded, his tone like the edge of a sword.

Tiffany's voice rose to match Austin's response. "We might not have ever found you!"

Austin laid his head back down. Oliver waited as Tiffany let the gravity of the twins' actions sink in. She'd driven home the point by making it relevant to their personal safety. *That* they could understand without feeling an unfair level of guilt. Or at least Mason could. He wasn't sure about Austin yet.

"I think the first step is for each of you to apologize to Oliver and me and promise to obey us in the future."

Nearly without delay, Mason spoke. "Oliver, Tiffany, I am sorry"—his voice cracked as he choked up for a moment—"and I promise I'll follow your orders from now on."

Quiet ensued. Everyone looked at Austin, waiting for his apology. His head lay on the table, turned away, leaving only his shaggy hair visible. When he finally looked up, his face was bright red. Wet streaks traced down his cheeks. He scowled, eyebrows meeting and nostrils flaring. "No! I won't apologize. You're not Mom"—he pointed at Tiffany—"and you're not Dad."

He stood up, his face contorted with anger. "Don't treat me like a little kid. Neither of you are much older than me. What Mason and I went through was far more dangerous than your adventure." He took a deep breath. "Oliver had his chance. He failed. He didn't save Dad and Mom when he could have. He blew it!"

"Now wait a minute—" Tiffany started, but Oliver interrupted her.

"No, let him finish." While his tone was calm, it felt like lava boiled within. He clenched his fists. He had to control his temper.

"If I'd been at the compound, Dad and Mom would be safe!" Austin nearly screamed. And with that, he stormed out of the galley.

Mason stood to go after him.

"No, Mason, stay here. Give him some time to cool off," Oliver said, but wondered if he should have followed the rules of the Academy and laid down strict punishment. Time would tell.

Mason sat back down. "All right."

"Oliver, he can't talk to you like that!" Tiffany exclaimed.

"I think the best thing for everyone to do at this point is to get some rest."

"I'm not tired," Mason said. He and Austin had just awoken from a long nap when Oliver and Tiffany arrived back at the *Phoenix*.

"That's fine, but it's better you let Austin chill alone in your cabin for a while," Oliver suggested.

"Maybe I'll go to the library, then," Mason said. "You want to come with me, Tiffany?"

"Yeah, that sounds good." She looked at Oliver. "I still don't think you should—"

"Why don't we all go to the library?" Oliver interrupted. "I just need to check the flight systems to see that we're on course and everything is running as it should be. Then I'll be down."

2.3

Library

Oliver entered the bridge to find one of the storage compartments open, items scattered on the floor. Confident Austin was responsible for the mess, he stuffed a spare harness and several safety straps back into the compartment and closed the hatch tightly. As he looked around, he saw that several other compartments had been opened, but unlike the first, nothing had been pulled out. He shut each one and wondered what Austin was up to.

Oliver sat down at the flight computer. All was running as designed, except for one generator that was at eighty-seven percent. It was possible that something had malfunctioned during the rough flight through the cavern on Tragiws or maybe the storm on Jahr des Eises. Regardless of the culprit, fixing the problem would have to wait until they'd safely landed again. He couldn't risk shutting it down to work on it during hyper flight. This being only his second such flight, he wasn't exactly sure what sort of catastrophe might await such an action.

Tiffany and Mason were sitting comfortably on a couch against the wall when Oliver entered the library. It was called the library, but the room functioned as an office and laboratory as well. On the wall opposite the door sat a couch with a porthole above. On either side of the couch were drawers containing tools, artifacts, and ancient manuscripts. The wall to the left had a desk, two chairs, and a hologram bay. A long counter with a sink set into it and several compartments where gadgets were stored stretched the length of the right wall. Several cushy chairs and a round table sat in the center of the room.

Oliver chose a desk chair and swiveled around to face his sister and brother. "So what did I miss?"

"I was telling Mason some information I had read regarding the blue warriors who captured them," Tiffany answered excitedly.

"They're called the Blauwe Mensen," Mason explained.

Their mom's journal sat open on Tiffany's lap, its dual screens glowing.

"Oh, is that so? What do you know?" Oliver asked.

"Well, the Blauwe Mensen, as they are called, are part of a myth that's been around for centuries. I found an entry titled 'The Blauwe Mensen Myth' on our way to Brighton but didn't think anything of it until Mason and I were discussing it. Let me bring up the entry."

Once the information was uploaded, Tiffany began to read.

A people called the Blauwe Mensen, meaning "blue people," has been rumored to exist on the planet for several hundred years.

Early settlers of Brighton and inhabitants of a small outpost called Mudo have all claimed that the woods of Jahr des Eises are haunted by mysterious blue humanoid creatures. Over the last hundred years, several people have gone missing in these woods with no trace. All the disappearances have been attributed to the "blue ghosts."

Although the mayor of Brighton ordered extensive searches of the surrounding woods, no settlement has ever been found, causing people to believe that the rumors are just myths.

Further, the Blauwe Mensen are believed to have descended from a line that originated on Ursprung. A book found in 1259 BE by a man named Wyndham Flizzerby is the only thing that provides any credence to this theory. The book was said to contain a printing date of AD 2559 and mentions a planet in its last days and a subsequent exodus of its people.

The book was purportedly stolen several weeks after it was discovered. For that reason, only Mr. Flizzerby ever saw or read the book. Eventually, for lack of evidence, people have come to believe the claim was false and the entire story fabricated. To this day, there is no solid evidence proving the existence of the Blauwe Mensen or the book.

"You see, Mason? You and Austin found the Blauwe Mensen. You proved they exist," Tiffany explained. "You escaped."

Mason blushed.

Tiffany's shoulders drooped disappointedly. "I sure wish I could have seen the city."

Mason patted his sister's shoulder. "We know how to get there now. Maybe when we rescue Dad and Mom, we can go back. After all, we do owe Obbin a ride in the *Phoenix*."

A moment of silence passed as the three imagined going back into the hidden city.

"That would be amazing," Tiffany said.

"I don't know, guys, but I have a feeling that this adventure is going to take us to places we never before imagined existed," Oliver chimed in. "Places as amazing as—or even more than—the Blauwe Mensen's city."

"Speaking of adventures, you haven't told about yours and about this Mr. O'Farrell," Mason said.

"Honestly, there isn't much to tell," Oliver asserted.

"Yes, there is. You saved our lives," Tiffany interrupted.

"He did?"

Oliver blushed. "No, I really didn't."

"Yes, you did," Tiffany interrupted again.

"Tell me," Mason pleaded, looking intently at his sister.

"Well, for starters, our road into the city came in the form of a maglev rail. We'd only been following it for a few minutes, though, when a maglev train came out of nowhere, barreling right for us like an angry hornet."

"It didn't come out of nowhere. I just wasn't paying attention," Oliver added sheepishly.

"Fine, but it did come screaming into view." Tiffany shook her head. "He pulled back on the scooter controls and we cleared the train by inches. If not for him, we would have been pulverized!"

"Wow!" said Mason, impressed. Oliver looked away with embarrassment.

"We decided to pull off for the night and set up camp. That's where Oliver made a friend." Tiffany giggled.

"You made a friend in the middle of the woods?" Mason asked.

" 'Friend,' ha. More like I was attacked by a crazed monkey," Oliver clarified.

Mason looked dumbfounded. "A monkey?"

"Yeah, a monkey. The thing was in an argument with a squirrel over who owned my backpack. It jumped me," grumbled Oliver.

Tiffany laughed. "If only I'd captured it on video," she teased.

Mason smiled. "That would have been one for the e-journal."

"Ha-ha." Oliver laughed sarcastically, then cleared his throat. "So, the next morning, we continued to Brighton. We almost ran into trouble, but an older gentleman helped us out. The man happened to be Mr. O'Farrell."

"Really?" Mason asked.

Oliver nodded. "I know. What are the odds? Mr. O'Farrell helped us get into Brighton. He told us about his quest for Ursprung."

"So that's why he supports Dad and Mom?" questioned Mason. "His search for Ursprung?"

"Exactly," Oliver said. "He took us to find the parts to fix the *Phoenix*. We didn't find anything in Brighton, but we did meet an interesting man named—" Oliver suddenly remembered. "The package! Mr. Krank gave me a sort of gadget—a silver ball and remote thing."

Tiffany's eyes lit up. "Where is it?"

"In my pack on the bridge. I'll go get it. Go ahead and finish telling Mason the story."

Leaving Tiffany to continue the tale, Oliver jogged to the bridge. One of the cabinets was open again, and items were scattered over the floor. Oliver was disappointed Austin would act like this and decided it was time to go say something to him. If he didn't curtail the behavior, Austin might continue to rebel, finding strength in his ability to get away with disruptive actions.

Grabbing the pack with Mr. Krank's gift, Oliver started for the twins' cabin. It was peculiar that he hadn't heard Austin slip past him and his siblings in the library, but Austin could be rather sneaky if he wanted.

He stepped quietly to the hatch of the twins' room and looked in, hoping to catch the youngest Wikk red handed, maybe tinkering with something he'd stolen from the cabinets. Instead, he found Austin, one arm hanging over the side of the bunk, sound asleep and snoring.

That's weird. Must be a faulty latch.

Oliver shrugged and headed back to the library. He sat in a cushy orange chair and pulled out the brown-paper package, setting it on the round table before him. Tiffany and Mason left the comfortable couch near the window to join Oliver. He unwrapped the packaging, freeing a small silver ball that rolled across the table. A second object sat on the wrappings. Oliver lifted it up and looked it over.

"What are they?" Mason asked.

"I don't know exactly," Oliver admitted.

"Look, there's a note written on the packaging," said Tiffany, picking up the crumpled brown paper.

"I didn't see that the first time I opened it," Oliver acknowledged. "But the tent was dark."

Tiffany began to read. "This device will mask your presence. Sync the device with the ship's flight systems. Do not lose the remote; it will make things visible again should you be away from the ship. Most of all, keep safe. I will contact you soon."

Oliver turned the remote over. He held the flat silver square out for Mason and Tiffany to see, then took it back and slid his fingers over the buttons.

" 'Mask your presence'?" asked Mason. "Is it a cloaking device?"

"It must be . . ." Oliver confirmed. "To keep us hidden from the Übel."

Tiffany handed the note to Mason and picked up the small silver ball. "But Mr. O'Farrell never mentioned our parents or the Übel. How would he know?"

"Mhmmm. No, he didn't," Oliver said.

"Will it work?" asked Mason.

"We can't be sure until we connect the uplink," Oliver said. A cloaking device would give them an extra level of protection for their landing on Evad: a way to remain hidden from the Übel, should they already be on the planet.

Tiffany's eyebrows rose. "You're actually going to use it, Oliver?"

"Why wouldn't we?" Mason asked. He'd begun folding the wrapping into some sort of shape.

"Because we don't know anything about the man who gave it to us," Tiffany retorted. "I mean, we only just met him."

"That's a good point," Mason admitted, still folding the paper. It had begun to look like a small bird.

"Yes, but remember Mr. Krank's warning? He said to open it after we were rid of O'Farrell," Oliver said. "I'd say he was trying to help us."

"He did tell us to keep safe," Mason offered.

"Maybe, but he could have been trying to trick us too," Tiffany suggested. "He might have wanted us to separate ourselves from the only adult around." She set the device back on the table as if not wanting to have anything to do with it.

"I didn't get the feeling that he was some sort of con artist." Oliver rubbed his chin. This argument couldn't be won at the moment. "We should get back to the bridge; we'll be landing in about twenty minutes," he said, looking at his mTalk. Still holding the remote, he also picked up the silver sphere.

Mason set a small paper crane, made of the cloaking device wrappings, on the table before him.

"If you need to go to the bathroom, do it now. And Mason, wake Austin. Tell him to come to the bridge for the landing."

2.4

Evad

Oliver had already brought the *Phoenix* out of hyper flight, and he and Tiffany were awaiting the twins' arrival for landing. His sister sat at the navigation console with the e-journal at her fingertips. Oliver was impressed with how quickly her fingers swept across the screen. She was trying to update the device with the twins' story and their narrow escape from the blue soldiers before they landed.

In preparation for their descent, Oliver scanned over the information his parents had acquired about Evad. The kids would venture into the mysterious jungles of the planet, and he hoped the information would assist in the mission.

He loaded a 3-D terrain map from his parents' previous expedition and then entered the coordinates discovered at Dabnis Castle. The coordinates centered on a large basin shrouded in clouds or fog. The images weren't in real time, so he couldn't see past the haze. They wouldn't know what was hidden beneath the grayish distortion until the *Phoenix* passed into Evad's atmosphere. The ship's scanners weren't powerful enough to be accurate at this distance.

The *Phoenix*'s systems had proven to be rudimentary, his training at the Academy sufficient to operate the controls.

And after the near crash on Jahr des Eises and his masterful evasion on Tragiws, he felt quite confident in his abilities to pilot the ship.

The clanking footfalls of the twins announced the boys' arrival. They'd changed into utility slacks and long-sleeve shirts—Austin's green, Mason's blue, mirroring their eyes.

The utility pants were their grandfather's invention. With extra pockets and titanium-flex fabric, they were a must for exploring. Water resistant, flame retardant, and temperature controlled, the pants were great for the adverse conditions the Wikks sometimes found themselves in on expeditions. Conditions that might change at a moment's notice.

Better yet were the Ultra-Wear shirts the twins wore. These too had been invented by their grandfather. Like the pants, the shirts maintained a consistent temperature, kept the wearer dry, and were inflammable. But they had several additional advances, including electric-shock protection and puncture protection in the case of sharp branches or animal bites. And if the shirt was pulled over one's head, it could filter poisonous gases.

Most of all, the twins liked the clothing because it was from their grandpa, Theodore William Wikk. They'd not donned the clothes on Jahr des Eises because they'd only planned on getting a breath of fresh air, not being swept away into a blue city.

There was no greeting from Oliver as the twins entered the bridge. He wasn't in the mood to rehash the previous argument with Austin. It was time to land. "Everything's ready for entry into Evad's atmosphere. So take your seats," he warned them over his shoulder.

"This isn't going to be like our landing on Jahr des Eises, is it?" Mason asked.

"No, not at all. There are no storms, and the ship isn't damaged anymore," Oliver said reassuringly and hoped it was the truth. The generator that was running at a lower capacity was cause for some concern, but not so much as to abort the landing or mention it to the twins.

Mason passed his hand through his shaggy hair and sighed in relief.

Oliver saw Tiffany adjust the harness on her seat tighter and slip the e-journal into her pack, which she then tucked under her seat. "I'm all set, Oliver. You're going to do great," she encouraged.

A series of clicks let Oliver know the twins were getting themselves situated.

"Good to go," Mason confirmed.

There was an awkward pause while Oliver waited for Austin to concur. "Austin?" he asked firmly.

"Locked," Austin said, the sharp edge still in his voice.

Oliver turned to his sister. "Tiffany, I know you have reservations, but I want to plug in the cloaking device Mr. Krank gave us."

"I don't know, Oliver. It could be a—"

"The Übel could already have landed. If they're here, they'll be scanning the sky for threats," Oliver said. "If this device can make us invisible, it'll be a huge advantage."

"But—" Tiffany tried again.

"It's worth the risk," Oliver said sternly. "I feel strongly that Samu—Mr. Krank—is on our side."

Tiffany sighed.

"He's right," agreed Austin. Everyone looked at the youngest twin, each surprised at the boy's sudden contribution to the conversation. The sharpness in his voice had disappeared. "If those nasty men are here—" He stopped. "We won't have a chance to rescue Dad and Mom if we can't get past their surveillance."

Tiffany nodded. "Okay." But it was clear she was not a hundred percent convinced.

Oliver took the silver sphere from where it sat on the console. His hand quivered as he held it. Was he nervous? He shook off this foreign feeling and plugged the device into a port on the console before him.

So far, so good.

He clicked a button on the remote, the word *Activate* inscribed on it.

No flicker of the lights, no hum, no explosion. Nothing seemed to have happened.

"Did it work?" asked Austin.

Oliver squinted in wonder. "I don't—" He clapped his hands together and smiled as a message appeared on the screen. "It sure did. An application popped open, and it's displaying all sorts of blocking methods. I don't see how any system or device would have a chance to track us now."

"Awesome," Mason said.

Oliver angled the *Phoenix* into the proper trajectory for entry into Evad's atmosphere. "Tiffany, can you do a new 3-D terrain scan so we can locate a suitable landing spot as soon as we're in range?"

"Yep." Her fingers swiped and tapped the screen before her. "I'll be ready."

"Great. Once it's complete, send it to me." Tiffany nodded. "And be sure to download the info into the journal. It'll be useful once we land," Oliver suggested.

"No problem."

"Here we go." Oliver tapped the screen before him. The *Phoenix* gave a little jerk as the nose pitched down from the decrease in thrust as Oliver prepared for entry. He quickly ran through the final checklist as the ship neared Evad. Once satisfied that everything appeared in order, he activated the computer's automated-entry application.

The computer's voice spoke. "Commencing entry in fifteen seconds."

The titanium heat shields still blocked the view ahead. Oliver's only visual on the planet was an image rotating on the screen before him. Everything appeared to be working fine, and he felt a sense of hope as he realized his parents might be on the planet below waiting to be rescued.

"Twelve seconds . . . eleven . . . ten . . . nine . . ." the computer voice said over the speakers.

"Here we go again!" Mason shouted.

". . . seven . . ."

"Hold on, everyone," Oliver commanded.

". . . five . . ."

"No one unstrap until Oliver gives the all clear," Tiffany said loudly.

Austin frowned. The remark was clearly directed at him.

". . . two . . . one . . ."

A thundering noise vibrated through the ship. Oliver tensed. Could the sonic boom have been heard below? He hoped their altitude would give the sound time to diminish before it reached the planet's surface.

Oliver looked around. His sister's eyes were shut tight, her knuckles white as she fiercely gripped the straps across her body. He knew it wasn't from a lack of experience with atmospheric entries but a consequence of the most recent flights undertaken by him. He'd done his best, but he wasn't sure his sister was completely confident in his abilities.

"Ju-st a lit-tle lon-ger," Oliver's voice vibrated. He watched the *Phoenix*'s progress on the screen. The shaking lasted a few more seconds, then ceased.

"Entry complete," the computer voice said.

Oliver gave it just a moment, then tapped the screen, and the titanium heat shields slid up to reveal a lush green planet below.

He heard a soft tapping come from the copilot's console. Tiffany was activating the scan.

Oliver pulled back on the controls, and the angle of descent decreased. The *Phoenix* curved into a long, calm, spiraling descent. Unlike the tornadic purple scene of Jahr des Eises rushing up to meet them, the landscape of Evad picturesquely stretched out before them. The sky was spotted with fluffy white clouds casting large shadows on the terrain below. Ridges and valleys carpeted in green foliage spread out across the land like a garden maze. A large blue spot shimmered below with long scraggly blue lines stretching out from it in all directions. From his brief reading about Evad, Oliver knew the landmark was Lake Josiah. It was nearly a thousand miles from the basin, but at this altitude, it looked only a few hundred feet away. According to the e-journal, his parents had been to Lake Josiah not all that long ago, and he wondered why they had not ventured into the basin.

"Do you see that?" Austin called out.

In the distance a large black thunderhead darkened the horizon.

"Tiffany, can you check the path of that storm?" Oliver asked.

"Will do," she said. "I just sent results from the terrain scan to you."

The data flooded his screen, and a map began rasterizing. Oliver checked the estimated time and distance against the coordinates from Dabnis Castle. He turned the *Phoenix* a few degrees and aimed it for a large basin encircled by a continuous ridge. This was their destination.

The map was complete. Oliver swiped his fingers across the screen, moving the newly created image until it was centered over his target basin. Something was wrong—a distortion in the map. He tapped the screen, but it didn't fix the problem. Instead, it only showed him more clearly what he didn't want to see: the imagery for the basin was a mess of indistinct, zigzagged lines. The area surrounding the basin was perfectly rendered, with altitudes and sharp definition to the terrain features, but the details of their destination remained a mystery.

"Tiffany, can you scan again?"

"Of course." She went to work.

Oliver looked out the windshield at the mysterious basin. A thick tangle of jungle encroached against the very edge of the ridge, leaving no clear landing spot within at least a couple of miles. The basin itself was cloaked under a seemingly impenetrable layer of grey fog that swirled like a giant vortex above.

"I sent you the second scan," Tiffany said.

Oliver checked as a new map began to render. "Got it."

"Oliver, I've also got info on the storm. It's moving at twenty miles an hour and is just shy of a hundred miles away. It looks like our coordinates are in the storm's path."

"Oh, great, not another one," Mason started. "I had my fill of climactic weather when we were running in the woods on Jahr des Eises."

Austin nodded in agreement. "And when we landed and got flung through the sky."

"We'll take cover when needed, but it does mean we'll have to hurry," Oliver said.

He turned back to the nearly finished terrain map. A second later, he had the same results. There was no way to see what was inside the basin. Oliver didn't have any choice. Between the distorted scan results and the inability to visually search for a landing spot, the only safe option was to land outside the basin. It had crossed Oliver's mind to fly into the cloud cover and hope it would clear enough for him to see, but there was a very real possibility that the fog was thick all the way to the ground, and there could also be any number of rock formations or buildings within.

Oliver groaned. No, it was safer just to land outside the basin. They'd be walking to their destination.

This also meant he wouldn't be able to see if the Übel had landed in the basin. He'd run a cursory scan for ships or other mechanical equipment, but it hadn't found anything. So either they were in the basin or they'd not come yet.

A worse fear crossed his mind. The Übel might have already been to Evad and left. It was a very real possibility and one he would keep to himself.

Regardless, Oliver needed to find a suitable location to land. He scanned the on-screen terrain map, which revealed a spot to the east only a couple of miles outside the basin. It wasn't as large as the clearing on Tragiws, but wider than the one on Jahr des Eises. Judging by the thick jungle canopy, he'd already figured that sky scooters were out of the question. Besides, after the twins' incident, the Wikks had been left with only one working scooter.

Landing outside the basin would also put the *Phoenix* in an unexpected location, one even more unlikely to be discovered. A good thing, since if the *Phoenix* was discovered and fell into the Übel's hands, there would be no escape. The Wikks would either be marooned on an empty planet or taken prisoner.

Oliver lowered the *Phoenix*'s gear and changed the thrust vector to ninety degrees. He decreased the power to the engines, and the ship steadily lowered to the ground, landing in near silence.

"That was a much better landing than last time!" Austin offered this compliment with no hint of sarcasm in his voice.

"Sure was." Oliver smiled. Maybe Austin was over his anger and frustration.

His sweaty hands slid from the controls. Although he knew it, he wouldn't admit to his sister and brothers that he'd been nervous.

He tapped the screen, and the ship's flight system shut down. "Well, we're here. We're on Evad."

"We did it," Mason commended his siblings.

"Yes, together we did," Oliver agreed. The four Wikks stretched their arms and legs. "Since you've all changed into exploration apparel, I'd better too."

Oliver left with a grin on his face. They were safe. Well, they were on the ground, anyway.

Tiffany's pants were similar to the twins'—blue and with fewer pockets, but just as protective. She wore a light-pink Ultra-Wear hooded shirt. She grabbed her pack from under the seat, slung it over her shoulders, and eyed the twins. "Get your packs, and let's meet in the galley. We're going to need supplies," she instructed.

"Are we camping out?" Mason asked inquisitively.

"I believe so," Tiffany answered.

"Better than being *left* on the ship again," Austin said as he and Mason headed from the bridge. His contentious attitude had returned.

Tiffany walked to the console and studied the pilot's screens. The application for the cloaking device was still open. Tiffany confirmed what Oliver had said—the gadget indeed appeared to be doing its job. She nodded her head. Mr. Krank had seemed nice. Odd, but nice. She had a good feeling about him. But why had he said to wait until they were rid of Mr. O'Farrell?

Speaking of which, she should try and contact their missing companion. She crossed back to the copilot screens and loaded the communications application. The old man's number was still programmed from when they'd escaped Jahr des Eises and tried to contact him. She reached out . . . then hesitated. Should she ask Oliver first?

She shook her head, answering her own question. No, she wasn't a baby; she had every right to make a call.

She tapped the screen, and the communications application opened the connection. But for some reason her stomach felt suddenly unsettled. Quickly, she tapped the screen again, ending the call. She wasn't sure why she'd changed her mind, but somehow it didn't feel right to place the call to Mr. O'Farrell.

She took a deep breath and decided to join her brothers in the galley.

Upside-Down Snowman

s Oliver opened the *Phoenix*'s small side hatch, a burst of warm, humid air enveloped the kids, accompanied by the fragrant smell of flowers after a fresh rain. The scene was entirely different from the last planet they'd been on. Jahr des Eises had been turning into an ice prison as they had escaped; Evad felt like a sauna. Oliver could only imagine what it must be like on Jahr des Eises now. The thought caused his body to shiver, as if the icy winds were blasting around him.

A step out from the ship and Oliver looked back at his siblings. He jumped at the shock of seeing his sister and brothers floating a short way up in the air. The *Phoenix* was invisible.

"What is it?" Tiffany asked.

Oliver took a deep breath. "The *Phoenix* is gone. . . . Well, cloaked, anyway. You guys are hovering in midair."

Austin pushed past Tiffany and turned to look at the ship as he exited. "Cool!"

Oliver retrieved the remote from his pocket and pressed a button labeled *Reveal*. The silver ship instantly flashed into view. Reassured, he quickly hit the *Activate* button again. The *Phoenix* disappeared.

"Well, it works," Oliver said proudly.

"We should mark this location on the LOCATOR app," Mason suggested.

"Good point." Oliver tapped his mTalk a few times. "Done."

"Me too," Austin said. "Backup."

Tiffany walked a few paces from the ship. "Smells amazing," she said after a long sniff of the natural perfume.

"It sure does," agreed Mason, looking around at the wet plants and flowers.

"Is this a jungle?" Mason asked, "Or a rainforest?"

"Not sure, honestly. We'd need to evaluate several—"

"Either way, it's going to be difficult to get through. All these large plants and snaking vines. We'd best get started," Oliver interrupted. He looked at the mTalk on his wrist. The device not only helped him communicate with his siblings but had a suite of other helpful applications. Some of which he'd not even explored yet. "We're a couple of linear miles from the basin."

" 'Linear'?" Austin asked.

"Straight or direct," explained Tiffany.

"It means if we have to go over or around the ridges, we're considerably farther away," Oliver finished.

"We can't go around," Tiffany said. "I looked at the terrain map. The ridge is a continuous loop around the basin; the area is a bit like a crater."

"Looks like we'll have to go over, then," Oliver admitted. "I've got a grappling launcher for when we need it. But first we have to get through this tangle of green."

"I just hope there aren't any mean animals," Mason said. "I've read a lot about some of the animals that are found in jungles."

"Actually, Mom noted that there are several large animals on Evad," Tiffany said.

"Are they dangerous?" Mason asked.

"She didn't say."

Oliver instinctively felt for the Zapp-It in his pocket. He took it out and looked it over, unconvinced. Could it handle a large, hungry animal?

He noticed his siblings looking at him. "This should keep us protected," he said, trying to sound confident, and pressed the trigger. A small sizzle of blue electricity zipped between the two prongs on the end. He felt a twinge of guilt at the half lie.

The twins didn't look scared; they looked excited and ready for the adventure ahead. Oliver's confidence bumped up a notch. Tiffany was looking at the e-journal; she too seemed unworried. Were his words enough to make them feel safe? He had, after all, proven himself several times already. A proud feeling coursed through his body, and his chin lifted slightly.

Oliver looked around at the trees. Though the canopy above reached over them, he could still see sky. As he stepped gingerly ahead, a ragtag chorus of birds filled the air.

Tiffany and the twins followed Oliver into the jungle. Tall palm trees and massive ferns with leaves as big as the twins blocked any clear path. Vines laced and wrapped around the trunks of the trees and hung from branches high in the canopy. Three bright-red birds sitting on branches covered with purple blossoms suddenly let out a series of loud chirps, warning others of the kids' intrusion into their world. Small green-and-brown birds darted around the undergrowth in a frenzy, flying from one flower to the next, hovering momentarily, and then moving on. They didn't seem to mind the arrival of the Wikks.

Oliver tapped his mTalk and found the direction they needed to go. He hacked at the large green leaves and vines ahead of them with the machete. After making a short inroad, he motioned for his sister and brothers to follow.

It only took seconds for the jungle to swallow them whole . . . and for thousands of little bugs to start swarming over them.

Tiffany stopped and dug in her pack. She pulled out a small bottle, which she pumped, sending a squirt of cream into her palm. She rubbed the white cream on areas of exposed skin.

"Here, guys, put this wherever your skin isn't covered. It will help with the bugs," she promised.

"How long does it last?" Mason asked, taking a squirt into his hand.

"A few hours or so. But we'll need to reapply it every so often."

Oliver applied the cream as well. "Tiffany, can you scan the forward terrain? Maybe we can find a way through the ridge instead of going over." He swung the machete in large arcs, forging his way ahead.

Three soft pings sounded from the journal.

"What was that?" Austin asked and heaved his pack higher on his back.

"Just the pulse from the sonar mapping," Tiffany said as she watched the three-dimensional map build on the journal screen. "It'll take a moment."

The twins' packs were laden with tools and other supplies. The twins clung to the path, immediately following Oliver and Tiffany, nudging each other aside if one got ahead. Howls, screeches, and clucks sounded from the dense growth.

A moment later, Tiffany spoke up. "Oliver, there does appear to be some sort of tunnel passing through the ridge."

Her voice told Oliver that getting to it wasn't going to be easy. "But there's something wrong?" He turned back to look at his sister.

Tiffany gave a weak smile. "Maybe." She flipped the e-journal around so Oliver could see the screen.

Tiffany had zoomed in on the section of the ridge where the tunnel drove through. A wide arc swept out from the ridge and then back again, like a hedge around the tunnel entrance.

"What is that?" Oliver asked. The twins had moved around to see the screen as well.

"That is a crevice of some sort. See here." She pointed to some negative numbers stamped over the arc. "These are the depths of the crevice."

Austin looked at the numbers and scoffed. "Ten feet. That's not so bad. You wouldn't even break—"

"The measurement is in miles," Tiffany interrupted.

Austin's mouth dropped open, and Mason's eyes were as big as his fists. "Whoa!" they each exclaimed.

"Yep." Tiffany's voice cracked.

Oliver frowned and put his hand to his chin. "What's the lowest section of ridge?"

Tiffany flipped the screen back around. "Give me a second."

"Ten miles?" Austin asked.

"It seems far, but it isn't in comparison to the deepest gorge in the Federation," Mason explained. He swallowed.

"And how far is that?" Austin asked.

"Oh, about seventeen hundred miles," Mason said, bobbing his head.

"Wow!"

Tiffany had an answer. "Oliver, it looks like the lowest ridge is about eight thousand feet, so about a mile and a half."

Oliver shook his head. "We don't have enough wire for that. We'd have to do it in sections."

"How far across is the crevice?" Austin asked.

"Not more than twenty feet," Tiffany said.

"Well, we could use the grapple to get across that," Austin proposed. "You know, like a zip line."

"That's not a bad idea at all," Oliver praised. "We just need to launch the grapple from a nearby tree and get it hooked on the other side. Shouldn't be that difficult."

"Well, if we're going to make for the tunnel, we need to go that way." Tiffany pointed to their left. "It's about a mile away."

"Then let's get going," Oliver said and began the work of blazing a trail through the thick vegetation. Branches and vines fell to the ground at each swipe of his machete. His muscles ached, but he persisted. The prospect of rescuing his parents was a powerful motivator.

Oliver could envision their faces. Were his dad and mom somewhere over the ridge? Sure, it was possible they'd come and gone under Übel escort, but if they had, Oliver would find a clue to lead them on. He had to. It was his time to be the explorer and take up the mantle of his parents' work. He had the skills and knowledge he needed; now he just had to put them to work.

After what felt like hours, Tiffany said the words Oliver had been hoping to hear. "We're very close. The jungle should open up in another thirty or so feet."

Oliver certainly didn't see how. The thick overgrowth of vines and large, fan-shaped leaves seemed to blot out the light overhead and any path before them. "We'll have to find a tree easy enough for all of us to climb with all our gear," he said. "Then we can rig the zip line toward the tunnel entrance."

As Oliver swept his blade down across a large leaf that looked like an umbrella, sparks exploded and a loud clang resounded. The machete had struck stone.

"I think we found something," Oliver said, rubbing his machete-wielding hand.

Mason stepped around Tiffany and pulled back the rest of the umbrella leaf and some vines. "What is it?" he asked.

Standing before them was a tall stone pillar. It didn't look like the ones in the images their parents had taken at Dabnis Castle. It looked like a vertical stack of spheres, each larger than the one below it. The pillar looked like an upside-down snowman, but with many more sections.

Tiffany shook her head. "I'm not exactly sure."

Mason was just touching the stone with his right hand when Austin shouted. "Look, it's glowing." Mason jumped back.

Austin pointed at the bottom sphere. A yellow light was glowing from within the globe, which was no larger than Oliver's head.

"Everyone step back," Oliver warned. "It could be some sort of defensive device. The distortion over the basin was unnatural. Something is at work to protect the secrets of this place."

The kids backtracked a dozen feet on their newly blazed trail. Mason lifted up his mTalk and started to record the cone. The lighting had progressed to the second and third sphere. Each glowed yellow.

Tiffany was furiously tapping on the e-journal screen. "I didn't see anything about this in Mom and Dad's notes."

"Remember, we don't think they were ever at this basin," Oliver reminded her.

"I know, I know, but surely they'd have come across some sort of glowing tower before," she said, her voice almost frantic.

Austin was edging forward; he held a long stick in his hand.

"Austin, stay back," Oliver commanded.

Austin turned and scowled at Oliver, then bucked his chin. "No!"

Oliver lurched toward the youngest twin, but Austin broke for the glowing inverse cone, just out of his older brother's reach.

All the globes were now lit.

"Austin, stop!" Oliver yelled, but it was too late. Austin thrust his stick at the cone. The wood hit the stone.

A second passed, and nothing happened.

"What are you afraid of?" Austin accosted his older brother.

A half-second later, Austin flinched as the lights in the cone went from yellow to blue, but the boy quickly recovered his tough demeanor.

The change in light had revealed a word on each of the spheres. The message only partially diffused the tension.

Mason began to read the words from the top to the bottom. "'Sight by not faith by walk we for.'" His eyes lit up. "A riddle?"

"You are right that it's a riddle," Tiffany said. "But I think we're supposed to read it from the bottom up. It's a bit clearer, at least grammatically."

" 'For we walk by faith not by sight,' " Mason read.

The cone flashed and now glowed green. Ahead and out of sight came a grinding noise of some sort.

"Something's happening," Mason called anxiously.

Austin held his ground, and although Oliver was angry that his little brother had not listened to him, he stepped to his side. He knew that he still had to protect him.

Oliver pointed in the direction of the sound. "You all wait here while I check it out."

Austin shook his head. "Yeah, right. I'm coming with you."

Oliver let out a deep breath. "Fine, but this time you *will* listen to me." Although he said it as firmly as he could, he doubted it had any effect on Austin. What was he going to do about his disobedience? If they were at the Academy, he'd either be assigned five lashes or be locked in a detention cell for a few days on survival rations. Neither was an option for Oliver to use. He had no choice but to impress in other ways the importance of respecting his orders.

Oliver moved passed Austin and then the ambient cone. He didn't chop through the underbrush this time, and even though he knew he shouldn't, he let more than one branch snap back and catch Austin in the chest before the twin got wise and left some distance between them.

As Oliver neared the crevice, he could see the hint of an opening through the trees. A few more steps and he stood on a narrow ledge hanging over the ten-mile-deep barrier. Across the gap was a wider stone outcropping butted up to the base of the ridge. A grove of trees crowded the rocky space. The ones at the very edge quivered as if they were fearful of falling into the void, but Oliver knew it was just the wind. He couldn't see past them, so any tunnel entrance was unexposed.

"I don't see anything to cross on," Austin said as he stood side by side with his brother.

"Me neither." Oliver repeated the words from the cone. " 'For we walk by faith not by sight.' " He looked out over the chasm as a draft of cold, earthy-smelling air billowed upward. "*Faith* means to believe in something, sometimes without proof," he mumbled to himself as he mulled the line over in his mind.

"What'd you say?" asked Austin.

"*Faith* is to believe in something."

"No, the second part?"

"Sometimes you do so without any proof," Tiffany added from behind them.

Austin jumped, and Oliver reached out to balance him. Their sister's arrival had surprised both of them.

"Tiffany, you can't do that," Oliver scolded. "We're standing right at the edge of a cliff."

"Sorry," Tiffany apologized.

"Besides, I asked for you two to remain back."

"We heard a strange noise," Mason explained from behind Tiffany.

"A growl of some sort," Tiffany added.

"And you have the Zapp-It," reminded Mason.

Oliver shook his head and patted the shocking device. "Well, all right, but be careful."

"What'd you find, anyway?" Mason asked.

Austin pointed out across the void. "There's no way across, see? The riddle was pointless."

"Austin, you're a genius!" Mason said.

Austin stepped back. No one had ever called him a genius.

"Seeing *is* proof. The riddle said to walk by faith and specifically mentioned 'not by sight,'" Mason clarified.

Oliver shook his head. He wasn't sure how Mason's conclusion made Austin a *genius*, but he wasn't going to mention it at the moment. Everyone seemed to have briefly forgotten about the argument back at the cone, and they needed to work together to figure this out.

"The mechanical sound that made you and Oliver investigate must mean something happened," Mason continued.

"Interesting," Tiffany said. She held up the e-journal and looked at the screen, tapping it. Three soft pings sounded from the journal.

Everyone peered at the glowing screen as a new map rendered. This time, the image of a narrow bridge stretched out across the chasm. Oliver did a second take of the real chasm but saw no structure.

"Well, I see it on the screen, but it certainly doesn't appear to be there," Austin said.

"That's where faith comes in," Mason assured everyone. "It's like the cloaking device on the *Phoenix*. The bridge is there, but it's invisible."

The logic seemed sound. "Tiffany, can I see the e-journal?" Oliver asked. She handed him the journal, and he stepped to the edge of the canyon again. He knelt down and glanced back at the screen, then reached out his hand. It struck something solid. He slid his palm around. The bridge did exist. "It's here!" he shouted. "Mason, Austin, grab some leaves or dirt."

The twins worked quickly and returned with their hands and arms full.

"Toss it right there," Oliver suggested.

The boys obeyed. A flurry of leaves and cloud of debris fell out over the chasm. Much of it continued to drop into the ten-mile depth, but several leaves and some dirt found the structure. A good seven-foot section was now highlighted before them.

"Whoa!" Austin exclaimed. "That's pretty cool."

"Sure is," Mason agreed.

Oliver took a deep breath. "I'll test it first."

"Wait," Tiffany said. "Use the grapple as a safety line. . . . Just in case."

Oliver felt an embarrassed warmth spread across his cheeks. He'd just about made a very boneheaded move. "Good idea, Tiff."

Oliver slipped the device from its holster at his side. The grapple launcher looked like a small gun and could launch a hook and line over a hundred feet. At the moment, he wouldn't be firing, but instead using it as a lifeline in case he slipped.

He clicked a red button and released the hook and line without firing, then quickly wrapped it around a wide tree trunk and tied a knot. He tested it with all his might. Satisfied he was secure, he clipped himself to the line and slipped the grappling launcher back into its holster, locking it in place.

With the grapple attached, Oliver prepared to step out. His heart was racing, and his palms were sweaty. Even though he could now actually see something lying out before him and he was attached to a tree by a strong line, he was still uncertain. "Okay," he whispered to himself. "You can do this."

Tiffany must have overheard because she chimed in, "Yes, you can. Oliver, the bridge is there." He looked at her, but her face didn't show the confidence he'd hoped for.

"Yeah, Oliver, you've got this," Mason encouraged.

"I'll do it if you don't want to." This from Austin. Oliver didn't know if the comment was meant as a barb or if the boy was seriously offering. Even if it were meant legitimately, Oliver could never let his youngest brother take the risk. No, as the leader, this was something he had to do.

He swallowed the knot in his throat and stretched his right leg out. Brought his foot down and . . .

It struck something solid. He took another step and stood firmly on the beam that crossed out over the chasm.

Two of Oliver's siblings cheered. He let out a huge sigh of relief and carefully turned to face them. In a couple of steps, he was back, embraced by Tiffany and Mason. Austin glowered to the side, confirming his recent statement had been a jab at Oliver's courage. But now was not the time to approach him.

"Everyone gather dirt." Oliver squatted and emptied one of the pockets on his pants. "I need to fill this pocket so I can highlight our path across." He moved the discarded contents to his pack.

The kids worked quickly, and Oliver's pocket was soon filled. "I'm going to cross and secure the other end of the grappling hook to the other side. Then, one by one, you will all cross, using these clips." Oliver handed Tiffany and Mason each one of the security hooks.

Austin wasn't paying any attention, or so it seemed. "Austin, you too," Oliver commanded. The twin took it and looked away.

Oliver sighed and started back out over the chasm. He slowly sprinkled dirt as he walked. The wind continued to whip around him.

About midway, he almost slipped. "Be careful when you cross; the dirt makes the surface slick." He looked down into the center of the chasm; there was nothing but pure blackness. "And don't look down." This, of course, was common knowledge when crossing over something at a great height.

Once across, he secured the loose end of the grapple around a thick tree trunk. At least if his sister or brothers slipped, they wouldn't fall far. Had he fallen, he could have dropped at least the length of the wire—nearly a hundred feet—and slammed into the rock walls of the crevasse. A deadly mishap.

Oliver tugged on the line several times, putting all the force he could muster behind each yank. He felt confident it would hold. He cupped his hands and shouted, "All right, it's secure."

He wanted to proceed through the trees to find the tunnel entrance, but he knew he needed to keep an eye on his siblings. They were his responsibility.

Mason was first to attach himself to the wire. He started across, keeping his eyes glued on Oliver. The crossing was slow, but he arrived on the other side without incident.

Oliver saw Tiffany and Austin arguing, but the roar of the wind had increased in volume, and he couldn't hear what was being said. Tiffany shook her head and clipped herself to the line, then started across. Austin stood with his back to the bridge as Tiffany crossed the dirt-covered beam with impressive speed, getting to the other side in half the time it had taken Mason. For someone Oliver knew had a fear of heights, she'd been awesome.

Tiffany quickly unclipped and yelled over to Austin. "Okay, I'm clear. Hurry!"

Austin spun around and attached himself to the safety line.

"What's wrong?" Mason asked, alarmed at her and Austin's urgency.

"There was something in the bushes. That growl we heard belongs to something quite large."

Oliver was switching back and forth between scanning the tree line for a glimpse of the creature and watching Austin literally run across. As if escaping from the creature wasn't enough, there was a loud grinding underfoot. Something was happening with the bridge.

"Austin!" cried Tiffany. Oliver saw it a second later. The dirt and leaves were moving, which meant the bridge was as well.

Austin was close enough to jump. He tried, but there wasn't enough slack in the safety line, and it let off a loud *twang* as it snapped taut. Austin floated in midair; the only thing between him and the ten-mile drop was the clip.

"Austin, hold on!" Oliver yelled. "Use your hands to slide along!"

It was then that Oliver noticed that Austin did not look scared. He looked excited.

Austin leaned back and made quick work of crossing the final nine feet of line. He set his feet down and smiled. "What a rush!"

Tiffany and Mason were pale. Clearly, they'd not gotten the adrenaline rush Austin had.

Angry or not, Oliver couldn't resist patting his little brother on the back. "Nice job."

Tiffany had other words, but they weren't for Austin. "Oliver! He could have been killed. We have to be more careful," she shouted. It was rare that this side of Tiffany was exposed, but when it surfaced, everyone knew to watch out. "You need to come up with a better plan. We didn't all go to the Academy like you!"

Oliver stepped back. "Like I planned any of this. Look, I didn't know the bridge was going to retract. Did you?" he shot back.

Tiffany shook her head. "No." Her voice had softened considerably.

"Stop!" Mason said. "We can't do this. We have to be on the same side and work together."

No one spoke for a few moments. Oliver knew it was up to him to make it right. "I'm sorry, Tiffany."

"I'm sorry too. Mason's right." She gave her older brother a hug. "This is all so much."

Austin sighed. "Look, I'm all right, so we should probably get going."

Mason had his mTalk up. "I figure it was about thirty minutes from when we heard the grinding to the bridge retracting. There must be some sort of timer or something."

"At least the line is still secured to the other side. Otherwise we would be stuck," Austin said.

"But it's also draws attention to the tunnel," Mason said.

"Speaking of, it should be just through these trees." Tiffany pointed.

Oliver led the way through the grove. They stopped at a wall of vine and stone. The long tendrils of green twisted their way down the cliff face of the ridge, obscuring any entrance.

"We should be there. The e-journal shows we're directly in front of the opening," Tiffany explained.

The thick foliage made it difficult, but the kids spread out along the stone wall to search.

Mason put his hands into the vines and started stroking the stone. "It's really cold and damp."

"Yuck." Tiffany's fingers ran across something gooey on the wall. She pulled back and came away with brownish-green gunk stretching from fingers to wall in long, slimy strings.

Austin looked at her and laughed, but continued feeling the stone. He stumbled forward as his hand disappeared into the side of the ridge. "It's here. I think I found it!"

Oliver, Tiffany, and Mason came to his side.

"Stand back," Oliver said and sliced away some remaining vines with his blade.

Austin raised his chin. "I found it!"

"Step aside," Oliver said.

"No!"

"I don't know what the deal is, but you've been nothing but a problem," Oliver yelled. "Don't make me restrain you."

Tiffany gasped.

"You wouldn't," Austin challenged.

"I would." Oliver slipped off his belt. "This will do nicely."

Austin inhaled through his nose. A second passed, but the youngest Wikk backed down and rolled to the side, his back against the leafy ridge.

Oliver ignored his brother and began chopping away at the vines cloaking the entrance. Every stroke of the machete seemed to make him feel a little better. A few minutes later, the smell of cold, musty air seeped past the remaining foliage. They'd found the tunnel.

Soon the opening was clear and large enough for Oliver to fit through. He removed his pack and switched on his mTalk's light. "Wait here for a moment," he ordered. He ducked under a web of knotted roots and stepped into the mouth of the tunnel.

Tiffany patted Oliver's arm. "Be careful."

He nodded and disappeared into the darkness.

Several minutes passed and Tiffany grew concerned. Why hadn't Oliver returned yet? She poked her head into the tunnel. "Oliver?" Her voice sounded dull and muffled, absorbed by the black void.

"I'm going in after him," Austin stated matter-of-factly, pushing past Tiffany.

"No, you aren't." She grabbed his shoulder to pull him back. "Just wait."

"You're not in charge," Austin argued as he looked into the darkness.

"And neither are you." Tiffany ushered him away from the opening.

The younger twin leaned against the stone wall, his face red with anger, but Tiffany didn't care. She'd hit her boiling point with him; she wasn't sure how much more she could take. She huffed and ducked her head into the tunnel.

"Why can't you just listen," Mason reprimanded in a hushed tone behind her. "Quit trying to be a hero."

"Somebody has to be!" Tiffany turned around as Austin shot his twin a nasty expression and looked the opposite way.

A few more moments passed with no sign of Oliver. Maybe something had happened. What should she do? She could go herself, leaving the twins alone in the jungle. But no—she remembered what'd happened the last time the twins had been left alone and decided against that option.

She could let Austin go, but he was rash and didn't have the same level of training as Oliver; Tiffany feared he'd only become a casualty and need rescue.

She might lead the twins into the tunnel herself, but this too put them at risk. At the same time, it seemed the only remaining option besides waiting. At least they'd be together.

Dark, dank air seeping from the mouth of the tunnel sent a chill up Tiffany's back. She hesitated. Closing her eyes, she listened to the creepy chirps and shrill cries of unidentified jungle critters. The noise was deafening.

A few more minutes passed and still no sign of Oliver. Tiffany sighed in desperation and turned to lead the twins into the tunnel. To her relief, Oliver's head poked through the opening.

She exhaled heavily. "I was about to come after you."

Oliver smiled. "Well, the tunnel is clear," he said encouragingly. Tiffany lifted Oliver's pack and handed it back to him. "Just watch your head." He patted the roof of the cave opening. "You're not going to believe what's on the other side of this ridge."

"Tell us," Mason said with excitement as he stepped closer to the opening.

"You'll see in just a few minutes. It'll be worth the wait." Oliver smiled.

"It better be!" Tiffany declared.

"C'mon, then." Oliver turned back toward the cave interior. "Let's go! Everyone turn your lights on and keep them focused on the ground. I'll tell you if you need to duck. Watch out for potholes in the tunnel floor; the last thing we need is for someone to twist an ankle." He started in. "Mason, you and Austin stay close together."

Tiffany and Mason both looked for Austin. He wasn't there. "Where'd he go?" asked Mason.

Everyone looked around the small clearing Oliver had created with the machete, but Austin was nowhere in sight. Tiffany hadn't expected him to be angry enough to venture off on his own. How had he slipped away so quickly? One thing was for sure: Austin was sneaky.

Tiffany looked at Mason. "What direction did he go?"

"I didn't see him leave. I was listening to Oliver," Mason explained. "In fact, I haven't seen him for a few minutes."

"Well, he can't have gone far," Tiffany began. "We're on an outcropping."

"You saw how much he enjoyed sliding the last few feet across the line," Mason said. "I doubt he'd hesitate to go back across."

"I don't think so. I've got his clip," Oliver said, digging the clip out of his pocket as proof. "Why can't he just—"

Oliver stopped. Tiffany and Mason followed his gaze up into a nearby tree as something screeched. Leaves rustled. Twenty feet up the tree sat Austin, pulling a bunch of crescent-shaped yellow things from a neighboring pole-trunked tree.

"Austin, what are you doing?" Tiffany cried.

Austin looked down at them, a devious smile on his face. "I saw a monkey eating one of these and figured the fruit must be edible, so I climbed up here to get one, or some. I haven't decided if the three of you deserve any," he said mockingly. Tiffany recognized that Austin often resorted to mockery when he didn't get his way.

"Austin, come down," Oliver ordered.

A smirk crossed Austin's face. "Why don't you make me?" he said defiantly.

Oliver turned to Tiffany. "I don't know what to do with him. You were right—I shouldn't have let him talk to me like that before. Now he thinks he can get away with it."

"You did what you thought was best," Tiffany whispered. "But he can't stay here; he has to come with us."

No one said anything for a moment. Austin sat down on a branch and peeled back the skin from whatever it was he had found.

Mason stared up. "I don't see a monkey!"

"Over there." Austin pointed up to his left.

Oliver nudged Tiffany, "I say we leave—"

"We can't," Tiffany argued. "He's our responsibility."

"Not leave all the way. Just to the end of the tunnel and wait. He'll come."

"Are you sure?" she asked.

"Yes. Besides, where is he going to go? The bridge is gone. I've got his clip," Oliver assured her. "And the tunnel isn't horribly long."

Tiffany nodded. "But you said it was difficult."

Oliver scoffed. "A couple bumps on the head might knock some sense into him."

"Is it good?" asked Mason as he watched Austin take a second bite.

"Yeah, it's . . . well . . ." Austin chewed. "It's different. I haven't dropped dead yet," he joked.

"That's true." Mason nodded. "Can you toss me one?"

Tiffany nudged Mason in the ribs. "We're going, Mason."

"But Austin's in the tree."

"Austin's a big boy. He'll be fine; he's made that apparent," Oliver said loudly enough for the youngest Wikk to hear.

Oliver waved goodbye to Austin and then ducked into the dark cavern. Mason shrugged and followed.

Tiffany shivered as she stepped through the remaining vines and into the dampness.

2.6

Ziggurat

Austin didn't like the snide tone in Oliver's remarks, but what his eldest brother had said was correct: Austin had proven he was old enough to care for himself. Why, he'd single-handedly saved himself and Mason from the Cobalt Gorge.

Austin stared at the monkey across from him. It was still howling at the injustice of the stolen fruit, if that's what the yellow thing was. It was tasty—not overly sweet, and more pasty and creamy than juicy. Austin threw the peel at the monkey out of sheer spite. The creature hopped a bit higher in the tree and squealed back at Austin.

Austin slowly made his way down from the tree. The path back to the *Phoenix* was gone now. He really had no choice but to stay where he was or follow. He might as well make his siblings sweat for a while, worrying about him. Even if they acted like they didn't care, he knew they did. There was one thing he'd learned about being the baby of the family: everyone was always trying to protect him. That was also what irked him so much. Clearly he could take care of himself. Obviously he was stronger, smarter, and more courageous than any of them.

He leaned against a tree trunk and slid to the ground. The gap between him and the forest reminded him of the cavern he and Mason had crossed to enter the Blauwe Mensen's gorge—

He flinched, then shook his head. He was having flash-backs—for a second he'd thought he'd seen a blue face among the leaves. But Obbin had been left behind on Jahr des Eises, and he doubted very much that there were blue people on Evad too.

Something else was tugging at his mind, though. An eerie croaking was growing steadily louder, as if something were approaching him. A dark memory of a rather vicious tree frog came to mind. Austin swallowed the lump that had formed in his throat. Maybe he'd better check on his siblings; they might need him to rescue them. He climbed to his feet.

Something screeched in the jungle to his left and caught him off guard. He stumbled backward, tripping over a root, and fell flat. The deep green canopy above him barely let any light through as it was, but it suddenly seemed even darker.

Austin scrambled to his feet and darted for the cave opening, where he was swallowed in darkness. He'd given Mason back his mTalk, but Austin was still prepared. He'd worn his inventor's pouch and had had the foresight to slip a small light into one of the pouches before he'd left. He dug around until his fingers clasped the light. With a quick click, the tunnel was illuminated around him.

The walls were slimy and grey. Puddles of icy water pooled at his feet and flowed down the tunnel. If not for his water-proof shoes, his toes would be frozen. A frigid, foul-smelling air swirled around him, its howling noise joined by a watery *plink*, *plunk*, *plop*.

A few yards into the tunnel, Austin came to a fork in the path. He nearly called out for Oliver but caught himself. He didn't need Oliver's help, and he wouldn't give his brother the satisfaction of thinking he did.

Austin noticed that a stream flowed from one side of the fork and into the other along a bank. The bank looked like a walkway of sorts, while the tunnel with the water had no such trail. Using his explorer knowledge, he decided to follow the flow of the water and walk along the bank. Clearly it was the smartest choice. Besides, he'd noticed a glowing orb set on the trail to the right. It was a LuminOrb, and it glowed yellow, which meant to proceed, but with caution. Mason must have left it for him. His twin was the only one that Austin could trust anyway.

The ceiling got lower and the path narrower. Several times, he nearly slipped into the stream. Inching along, chest to the cave wall, he worked hard to keep his balance. His heavy pack dangled precariously from his shoulders, threatening to topple him backward into the water.

As he went, other streams emptied into the one he followed, and the water grew deeper and wider, quickly turning into a river. If he fell now, he'd be swept away in the current. Austin would have to take off the pack, removing the danger it posed. What he couldn't figure out was how Oliver, Tiffany, and Mason had made it out okay. They too were laden with baggage and certainly none were as nimble as him.

But the pack wasn't worth the risk of falling into the ice-cold water. After a moment's consideration, Austin lifted it and balanced it behind him on the ever-narrowing embankment. He then continued on, precariously measuring each step. Somehow he'd have to come back for the supplies.

With his focus on the ground in front of him, Austin didn't see the rock outcropping until it was too late. The side of his face smacked against the cold stone like a solid right hook. Stunned, he stepped back, and before he realized it, his foot slid off the ledge. "Whoa!" he yelped as he teetered back and forth in an attempt to regain his balance. It was too late. With a last desperate scrabble, his arms waving frantically in the air, he slid off the embankment and into the water. His head submerged beneath the icy water before he bobbed to the surface, gasping for a breath.

The river's current pulled at him, but it wasn't too strong to fight. He doggy paddled to the edge of the embankment and grasped at the bank. His fingers slipped along the slimy rock as he continued to float along; there were no roots or vines to cling to. How much longer would he be stuck in the cold water? His legs and arms already felt numb; water had seeped through the gaps of his clothes at his ankles, waist, wrists, and neck. His body quaked involuntarily.

Something glimmered ahead. A light of some sort. Was it the end of the tunnel? He remembered Oliver mentioning that the view was awesome. He only hoped it wasn't an awesome waterfall that dropped a few hundred feet. Austin increased his efforts to find a hold on the embankment.

"Help!" he called out. He hoped his siblings would hear him before it was too late.

He neared the light and saw that it wasn't the end, but a lantern illuminating the cave. His brothers and sister were just ahead. Austin was getting closer to them. "Help!" he shouted again.

There was a splash ahead, and he realized Oliver had leapt into the water. Oliver held his ground against the current and soon Austin was floating to him. Oliver locked one arm around him and pulled them both toward the bank. The current had moved them a short way downstream, but they were met by the extended arms of Mason and Tiffany, who pulled Austin, then Oliver, out of the water. They sat on the edge, soaking wet, shivering, and heaving deep breaths.

Austin was the first to speak. "I thought these clothes were supposed to be waterproof."

"Yeah, for rain, not for being submerged in ice-cold river water," Oliver said.

Austin swallowed. He thought about apologizing; it seemed the right thing. But for some reason he couldn't bring himself to do it. He couldn't easily wave off the last few hours of arguing.

There were no more words for the moment. Mason offered Austin a hand up as the kids got to their feet. Austin watched as his siblings clipped their packs to segments of rope that hung between each of them. This was how they'd safely carried the packs through the very narrow sections of tunnel, he now understood. He probably would've thought of this method too, if Oliver hadn't taken all the rope. Austin felt his mood darkening.

"Hey, my pack is a ways back down the tunnel. Shouldn't we go get it?" Austin asked.

"No, I'll get it later," Oliver said. "Besides, we need to get out of this chilly tunnel and get changed."

Why did Oliver always assume he was the one who got to make all the decisions? After all, it was Austin's pack.

The tunnel curved and dipped, slanting downward. The slick surface of the embankment remained an issue, and every so often the rope became taut as one of the party nearly plunged into the dark river lapping at their feet. The few minutes seemed like hours to Austin, wet, cold, and bringing up the rear.

"Are we almost there?" he called.

"Yes," Oliver said, shining his light back on his family.

"Hey," Tiffany called. Oliver's beam had shone directly in her eyes. "Lower it."

"Sorry. Is everyone all right so far?"

"I'm all right as long as I don't think about being in a narrow tunnel. I think I'm claustrophobic," Mason said.

"It's true. He had an attack when we were escaping from the Blauwe Mensen," Austin added. "And I'd be better if I could get out of these clothes and get dry."

"I know what you mean," Oliver said and pulled his wet shirt away from his chest. He looked ahead. "We're close." He continued down the stone slope. "Watch your footing."

A few more minutes of careful steps and the tunnel curved. Once the group stepped around the bend, a faint light glimmered ahead.

Sunlight.

"There's the opening," Oliver explained.

The light grew larger and brighter.

"There's a small ledge to the right of the opening. It leads to an outcropping that overlooks the basin. But be careful. We're high on the side of a ridge."

The kids crept out of the tunnel and slunk along the lip of rock on the cliff face. The air was warmer than in the cave, but the strong breeze still made Austin shiver.

Finally, all four were safely on the ledge. It seemed the immediate danger was behind them as they surveyed the large basin ahead. This place was where they might find and rescue their parents.

The basin was spotted with patches of light. The dense fog that had made scanning impossible before had cleared. The water that flowed along the tunnel now formed a small canal and poured into an aqueduct that stretched a little more than a hundred feet from the cliff to a large, tiered stone structure, where the water disappeared into a black hole. Austin counted three of these towers of stone spread out across the basin. One stood straight across from them, with a second farther in the distance, and a third way off to the left.

A rocky ridge jutted out, blocking the view to the rest of the basin. Austin imagined many more of these pyramidlike structures dotting the unseen portion of the crater.

More than a hundred feet below and spread throughout the basin were many other buildings much smaller than the tower before him. Only the roofs of these structures were visible, with the remainder of the buildings hidden within the dense foliage.

"It's going to be a pain chopping through all those plants," Austin griped.

"Sure is." Oliver squeezed Austin's bicep. "But at least I've got your strong arms," he said with a smile.

Mad or not, Austin couldn't stop a grin from slipping across his face at his brother's praise, which he quickly tried to hide behind a mask of disinterest.

"So how do we get down?" Mason asked.

"I think we'll have to balance on the edge of the aqueduct until we reach that ziggurat." Oliver pointed to the nearest tower of stones.

"A zigga what?" asked Austin.

"A ziggurat is what you call these pyramidal towers of stone. See how they're tiered, like steps?" Tiffany pointed out the different levels of stone.

"Oh, neat," replied Austin carelessly. His sister's constant know-it-all attitude was really annoying.

"Everyone be careful; it's a long way down. Take your time. We aren't in a rush," said Oliver seriously. He held a section of his rope up. "This will again act as our lifeline. Should someone fall, I'll shout 'drop,' and everyone should get low and brace against the stone. Use your clips from earlier to secure yourself to the rope."

"I don't have mine," Austin said.

Oliver swept it from his pocket and tossed it to him. "Here you go."

Austin looked out over the aqueduct thing as he clipped himself to the rope. This would be no more difficult than crossing the many fallen logs that bridged the gorge behind their home on Tragiws. Or the vine-made toe bridge Obbin had led him across. Of course, Mason had almost fallen there. Austin sighed and wished he could cross on his own. He didn't need one of his siblings getting him killed.

Tiffany looked at the twins nervously. Mason grimaced at Austin. Austin shrugged his shoulders; he'd already cheated death several times, and it certainly wouldn't catch him now.

"I'll go last so I can keep an eye on everyone, just in case." Tiffany's eyes grew wide, so Oliver quickly added to his statement. "Of course, no one is going to fall."

Linked together by rope just as they were in the tunnel, the kids slowly inched their way along the side wall of the aqueduct. The chill wind blowing around them made Austin shiver as his wet clothes pressed against his goose-bumped skin. He tried to watch Mason by looking straight ahead, but his curiosity coaxed him into glancing downward, and he saw how high they were. Even the tops of the trees were far below them. A fall from this height would be the end of him.

Austin shivered again, but not from the cold this time. Where did people go when they died? If he fell, would he feel it? Would he know? Maybe cheating death wasn't a fun game.

He was pulled from his thoughts as Tiffany and Mason cheered at their safe arrival on the zigga thing. He soon followed. Oliver was last to step onto the second-most tier and Austin caught his brother's heavy sigh of relief.

Oliver wound up the rope, and everyone minus Austin hefted their packs onto their backs. They'd made it. Now what?

2.7

Entry

The waterway continued from the aqueduct via a canal into a structure at the top of the ziggurat. A small gap of not more than a few inches was visible between the surface of the water and the top of the hole into which it flowed. Oliver leaned over and tried to see in. But the gap revealed only darkness within.

On the outside of the structure there were no windows, only a single metal door. Oliver attempted to push it open. It didn't move. There was no handle or keyhole to be seen, which was peculiar.

"Well, that's no good," Oliver said. "Maybe we'll just have to climb down on the outside."

Mason shook his head. "At the chasm, the bridge was activated when Austin touched the stone cone." He started rubbing his hand on the door. Nothing seemed to happen. A minute passed. No yellow, blue, or green light.

"Looks like we're headed down the outside," Oliver said.

Mason moved to the side of the door and started rubbing the stone wall. Austin mimicked him on the other side of the door.

"Look!" Austin called as two rows of intersecting stones lit up—twelve stones in all.

"Wow!" Mason shouted as the glowing yellow stones rapidly turned blue, then green. Before anyone could react further, the metallic door suddenly slid left and disappeared into the doorframe.

"We did it," Austin said, emphasizing *we* specifically to Mason. "Never give up!"

Mason nodded. "Let's go."

Tiffany gave Oliver a look before they proceeded. But he wasn't sure if it was a here-we-go-again-with-Austin look or a lay-off-him-for-the-moment look. He shrugged and kept his mouth shut.

He was leery of how easily the door had opened. Why have a light-up keypad in place of a door handle if not to deny access to trespassers? Yet they were granted access. The same question existed for the cone and the bridge. Clearly the cone was meant as a gatekeeper to the bridge, otherwise why have it retract? Why not have the bridge permanently in place and visible? No, something was at work here; otherwise there was no way a bunch of kids could have so easily gained clearance.

Should he pull his sister and brothers back and proceed with more caution? Was this some sort of trap? The questions raced across his mind, one after the other.

Quit thinking conspiracy, Oliver warned himself. *You have to keep your head and not jump to so many conclusions. "Doubt is a weakness."* The words weren't his own. They were ones he'd heard often at the Academy. *"Caution, but not cowardice."*

Oliver shook off his concern and followed his siblings into the chamber. He didn't want them out of his sight. If something was going to happen, he'd just have to be ready to deal with it.

The room was not devoid of light, as the outside ambience entered through the open door. Nevertheless, Austin took out his small light to use. Its beam was severely weakened from its earlier soaking in the river. The rest of them each flipped on their mTalk lights to assist.

Several pillars held up the roof to the room; metal crates were stacked around them and in corners of the room. The water flowed into the dark room through a hole in the wall and poured into a curious contraption in the middle of the floor. A circular pool carved into the granite housed a small float that rose as water entered. When the float reached a certain height, a lever clicked and released the water through a drain at the bottom of the pool. They watched the process of the water filling and draining a couple of times.

"We should get going," Tiffany suggested with a glance at her mTalk.

Mason's light flickered across another door. Walking along the ledge around the pool, he approached it. Again, there was no handle to be seen.

"Kind of weird that none of these doors have handles, isn't it?" Mason said. He found the activation stones and tapped each with his fingers. The door zipped open, revealing a dark stairwell.

"Looks like we have our way out," Austin said.

"Maybe," Tiffany cautioned. "It may not lead out at all but deep into a labyrinth designed to get us lost and eternally trapped."

"Way to be encouraging." Mason shrugged.

"It's the only option I see," Austin said and shone his light around the room to clarify his point.

"I agree," Oliver said. "Is everyone ready?"

"I'd like to change first." Austin turned to Mason. "But I'll need to borrow some clothes." His voice sounded more demanding than needy.

"Right, because you left your stuff in the tunnel," Mason retorted. He unslung his pack and set it on the stone floor above the pool. "And fell into the river."

"I didn't have a rope to use, like you guys," Austin countered.

It was time for Oliver to step in. "Enough! You two just chill."

Austin looked away and grunted.

"I think I'll change as well; it's rather cold in here," Oliver said.

"We'll start heading down the stairwell," Mason suggested.

"Maybe we should just wait over here. I'll turn my back," Tiffany said.

"It's okay. We'll catch up in a minute." Oliver truthfully wished to be out of his wet clothes, but he also hoped changing would give him an opportunity to speak to Austin alone. It was time to rein him in. He hoped Austin would respond better to the admonishment if Tiffany and Mason weren't there to listen.

"What if the Übel—" Tiffany began.

"Proceed with caution. If you hear anything, just come back up," Oliver suggested.

Mason was still digging in his pack for the clothes. He pulled out a shirt and some pants and tossed them at Austin. "There ya go."

The clothes landed at Austin's feet. "Thanks," he said unenthusiastically.

"We'll head into the stairwell, then," Tiffany said. She and Mason disappeared through the doorway, their lights quickly fading as they descended.

Oliver started to undress, but Austin did not. "I'm changing outside," he said abruptly.

Oliver shrugged. "Suit yourself." He'd give the kid his privacy, but not a pass on the lecture.

Austin exited and then must have moved his hand back across the stones outside, because the door slid shut. Oliver wrapped his wet clothes in a small canvas sack and dressed in a set of camouflage. He had packed light—only what he had been wearing and some camo for sneaking through the jungle. He would need to dry his clothes by the fire tonight.

Not wanting to disturb Austin, he waited inside the chamber. The water streamed in, splattering into the stone pool, and then gurgled as the water grew deeper. After watching the pool fill and empty several times, Oliver decided it was time to hurry Austin along. He'd called Mason and Tiffany to see if they were okay. They were, so he told them to proceed, but reminded them to be cautious of traps.

He located a set of twelve stones on the inside wall and lit them up. The metal door slid open. The light from outside was brighter than he'd expected, and he shielded his eyes until they could adjust.

Austin was nowhere in sight, but his wet clothes lay scattered on the stone ledge.

Oliver sighed angrily. *Where is he?* "Austin!" he called out. "Austin, where are you?"

Nothing. His brother was either not around or being difficult. He'd already proven to be the latter, so Oliver started to search the upper tier of the ziggurat on which he stood. He made it all the way to the front and looked out over the valley. He now saw a fourth and final ziggurat to the south. It looked much larger than the other three and was set farther from the rest. A large blood-red pool stretched across the center of the basin, and sections of it extended out from the center to each of the four pyramids. The longest segment led to the remotest ziggurat. Apart from the four ziggurats, there were only a handful of other buildings of significant size.

"Tiffany," Oliver called into his mTalk.

A moment passed. "Here. What do you need?"

"Well, Austin has gone missing," he explained.

"Find him, Oliver." Tiffany's voice betrayed her concern. "We can't lose him . . . again."

"I'll keep looking for a bit longer. Of all times for someone not to have an mTalk."

He could hear Tiffany sigh on the other end. "Do you need us to come back?"

"No, I'll be fine. Go ahead and turn your homing signals on. Each mTalk has a unique one."

"How?" asked Tiffany. "Never mind. I'm sure Mason can figure it out. You just keep looking."

Oliver could tell Tiffany was getting worried. "Will do. I'm sure he's right around here. Probably trying to prove a point."

"Mason and I will keep going, then," Tiffany said. "There are many rooms off the staircase. We've checked them all, but so far the rooms have been empty except some bedroom-type furniture. This place might have been like a dormitory or apartments or something."

"Well, tell me when you reach the bottom or find the way out," Oliver requested. "Talk to you in a bit."

"Bye."

Oliver continued to search for Austin and looked over the lower tiers of the ziggurat. Furry green patches of moss spotted the stone blocks, while long, thick vines spiderwebbed in every direction like green tendrils waiting to capture their prey. He was about to hop down, but decided against it, but not because of the hungry-looking vines. Austin was not invisible, so he'd either made his way down the outside of the ziggurat with astonishing speed and disappeared into the jungle below, or he'd gone around the opposite way from Oliver in a one-sided game of hide and seek. Oliver hoped it was one of these scenarios and not that Austin had headed back for his pack to prove a point. He knew Austin's game—better than the youngest Wikk suspected.

Oliver headed around the other side of the ziggurat and quietly called for Austin a few more times. Nearly twenty minutes had passed since he'd last seen his brother, and he needed to give up.

Then Oliver saw Austin.

Again his little brother had found his way into the river, but this time he hadn't gotten out, and the water had carried him out of the tunnel. He was now floating along halfway across the aqueduct, his arms flailing as he attempted to grab hold of something. His pack bobbed ahead of him.

Oliver couldn't contain himself and broke into a fit of laughter that forced him to bend over, hands on his knees.

A moment later, Austin bobbed under the water and disappeared through the black hole that led into the ziggurat. Oliver gathered Austin's discarded wet clothes and went back through the door with an odd sense of satisfaction. The youngest twin stood up to his waist in water as it continued to fill the pool. Oliver leaned over and grabbed Austin's pack that floated next to the pool's edge.

Austin glowered at Oliver, clearly embarrassed.

Then the water emptied, and Oliver fought back laughter as the escaping water pulled Austin to his back. The twin floundered against the sucking drain like a fish out of water. When he'd regained his composure, Oliver offered his hand to his little brother and pulled him onto the ledge.

No words were spoken or needed; Austin had messed up again of his own volition. He was sopping wet, and this time there were no new clothes to change into. Oliver tossed the previously discarded clothes at his brother as a reminder.

Books

Tiffany cautiously proceeded down the steps, Mason close behind. They'd kept track and descended five hundred ninety-four steps in a long spiral. Unlit light fixtures and doors lined the staircase, and, at first, each time they had opened a door it had been like unwrapping a Christmas present. What might be inside? Of course, this had quickly worn off after the twelfth room that contained only a wooden desk, bed frame, and chair. Tiffany thought it odd that wood had still survived the moist climate of the basin and mentioned it to Mason.

He shrugged. "Probably some hybrid plant material."

Either way, their curiosity and hope continued to drive them to explore the rooms in the off chance they might discover something. It was pretty clear that the staircase was the main route through the ziggurat and that the doors were just self-contained apartments of sorts.

Several times, the sister and brother halted their exploration at eerie noises—scratching, thumping, and squealing. Tiffany told herself they were small animals, but the truth was she didn't know what they were. And she didn't really want to find out.

Finally, they came to a landing at the end of the staircase. The ceiling was higher, the walls farther apart, and a door about three times the size of any of the others blocked their way.

They had just begun their search for the stones that had unlocked the doors in the past, when a noise behind them caught them off guard. Tiffany and Mason backed against the door. Was this the answer to the creepy noises? Or was it Übel soldiers? They didn't have anything to defend themselves with.

Soon the glow from a light illuminated the stairs above. It was coming close. Tiffany lifted her mTalk to call for Oliver, but that was exactly who came into view. Somehow, all the searching of the rooms had delayed her and Mason's arrival at what appeared to be the bottom of the stairs until the same time as Oliver and Austin's.

"I'm glad to see you," Tiffany said. "I wasn't sure who was—"

Mason let out a laugh. "I thought you changed out of your wet clothes!"

Austin was wet again and sulking, his shoes making a squishy noise with each step. He glared at his twin.

Tiffany poked Mason in the side. "I don't think now is a good time to tease him," she whispered.

"Austin retrieved his pack from the tunnel," Oliver said chidingly.

Tiffany tried to look impressed. "Good job." But, in truth, she wasn't awed by his actions or attitude.

"So what's the holdup?" Oliver asked.

"We haven't found the stones to open the door yet," Mason explained.

"Did you try the walls?" Austin asked.

"Not yet," Tiffany said. "We just got here."

The twins were first to start brushing their hands over the walls alongside the metal door. After nothing happened, Oliver joined the effort.

"Why isn't anything happening?" Mason asked, his voice carrying a nervous tone.

After learning of Mason's fear of tight spaces, Tiffany could tell this was the onset of claustrophobia. "Mason, we can always go back up the stairs and out."

But even Tiffany was becoming discouraged by their delay. Progress into and through the ziggurat had gone quickly. Why were they stuck now?

A flash out of the corner of her eye caught her attention. She looked to the side wall of the stairwell, but nothing was lit up. Had the flash just been a figment of her imagination?

She backed up and started to examine the left wall. There it was: a pattern of stones identical to the ones used to first access the ziggurat from the outside. But since the stones blended in by color and the stairway was dark, no one would notice them unless he or she was looking.

Tiffany quickly touched the stones. They began to glow, flashing from yellow to blue to . . . red.

"Oh, no!" Tiffany shouted, getting her brothers' attention.

Before, the stones had glowed yellow, blue, and green. Red was known to represent stopping, danger, or fire.

Tiffany, Oliver, and Mason backed away up the staircase. Austin held his ground. "Just wait."

But the red color remained glowing like a beacon to signal danger. A buzzing noise echoed in the passage.

"Everyone back up," Oliver commanded. Again Austin waited. "Austin, you too!" Oliver wrapped an arm around the youngest twin's chest and pulled him back.

Clink! The red light changed suddenly to green. The huge door slid to the left, disappearing into a hidden recess in the doorframe.

Pfft. The sound was like popping the top on an Energen drink, releasing pent-up pressure.

Austin shook off Oliver's arm. "See? Nothing. You just need a little faith. Just like the bridge." Austin's comment did not carry a positive tone.

With no more discussion, the four kids stepped toward the opening. Tiffany's mTalk light illuminated the room as she walked in. Mason located a light switch next to the door, but even after a couple of tries nothing happened. Which didn't make any sense. Something was powering the lighted stones and doors.

From what Tiffany could see, they were in a large room. Remnants of wooden furniture and several bookcases lined the walls. Oddly, the shelves were filled with books.

"I thought Mom and Dad had been here before?" Mason asked Oliver. "Why would they have left so many books behind?"

"As I mentioned before, they have been to Evad," Oliver said. The beam of light from his mTalk circled the room. "But they were on an expedition near Lake Josiah."

"So we discovered this place?" Austin asked, walking toward a set of wooden chairs and a round table covered with several items. He left a trail of damp footprints behind him. Then he started draping his original set of clothes over the sides of the chair.

"Sort of," replied Tiffany as she moved to one of the bookcases. "It doesn't look like anyone has been here for decades, if not centuries." She pulled a book off a shelf. "Well, maybe not as long as centuries."

"Still, this is really cool," Mason said, following her to the bookshelves. "Everything looks ancient."

"We need to look around outside a bit more before it gets too dark." Oliver shone his light around the room.

"And before the storm gets here," Mason added. He was looking at his mTalk. "I discovered a weather-tracking application, and the storm seems to be moving more quickly than before."

"Then we'd best get out of here. Does anyone see the exit?" Oliver asked.

"Why don't we set up camp first?" Tiffany asked. She put the book she'd been holding back on the shelf. "There's lots of information here. We might discover something for the quest." The room presented a once-in-a-lifetime opportunity for her. She'd never seen so many books in such good condition. Not even the artifact library at Archeos had this many books.

Oliver shook his head. "No, I want to see if there are any signs that Dad and Mom have arrived yet. If they have, we're wasting our time here."

"You just said they hadn't been here before," said Mason, shining his light on Oliver.

"Not on a prior dig, but possibly with the Übel in the last few days," Oliver explained, his light still scanning the room for an exit. "If they're on Evad with the Übel, they probably haven't looked in every building. The Übel don't seem like the type to collect or catalogue artifacts."

No one spoke for a few moments. The mention of this mysterious and dark society brought a chill to Tiffany's very heart. From what Oliver had said, this Vedrik was an awful guy.

"Maybe that book Mom and Dad had contained better clues than we have?" Austin suggested with curiosity.

Austin had a point. The book might have contained information that bypassed this place altogether. That thought made Tiffany shiver. If her parents had gone somewhere else, how would they ever find them? She didn't want to think about that.

Tiffany watched Austin move aside several trinkets on a nearby table. He pulled out a small lantern from his pack and set it on the cleared surface. Although it'd gotten wet, it still worked, casting the room in a dull yellow glow, revealing its complete size and shape. Bookshelves covered the curved walls, stretching to the very top of the two-story room. The shelves were crammed with tome after tome of information. Remnants of furniture sat neglected in the middle of the room; scraps of the original fabric still clung to the wooden frames, and one of the pieces—a couch—looked relatively comfortable.

"Thanks for the light," Tiffany said as she walked around the circle of bookcases. She stopped and pulled a different book from the shelf.

"To answer your question, Austin, it is possible that their book has better guidance, maps, and coordinates. But I think it was more of a guide to history or a timeline of sorts," Oliver said. "Either way, Mom and Dad might still be here, and we need to scout out as much of the basin as we can before it gets too dark."

"You're right," agreed Tiffany, setting down the book she'd taken.

"Bring it along, Tiffany. It's your first find," Oliver said, smiling at her. He walked over to her and gripped her shoulder. "Dad and Mom will be proud."

Tiffany blushed. "Thanks." She grabbed the book and the one next to it and put them in her pack. "Just in case we don't make it back." They were random picks, but they were something.

Mason's voice caught Oliver and Tiffany's attention. "I think I found the door." He shone his light into an alcove.

"Great job, Mason. Second time in a row." Oliver slapped him on the back as he stepped next to him.

"Third, actually, at least with Tiffany," Mason joked.

"Fair enough," Oliver agreed. "Now let's get it open."

"There's so much to read here," Tiffany said, looking forlorn. She glanced around at the shelves of books. "It's hard to leave."

"Tiffany, if we're still here at dark, we'll set up camp in this ziggurat. You'll have some time then to browse," Oliver promised. "But for now, we need to trek through the basin."

Tiffany joined Mason and Oliver at the doorway. This door was similar to the one at the base of the staircase, so naturally Oliver, Mason, and Austin began searching the wall. "Tiffany, what did you look for last time?" asked Oliver.

Tiffany examined the wall with her mTalk light but could see nothing. They searched every inch of the walls nearest the door for more than a half-hour. Mason even climbed onto Oliver's shoulders to search higher up. In the end, none of the stones lit up.

Austin had abandoned the search ten minutes prior and was loitering near one of two pillars supporting the ceiling over the alcove. The sound of small stones bouncing on the floor caused Tiffany to turn and look for him. Austin was now climbing. He had a strap from his backpack looped around the pillar and his feet braced against it.

"Austin!"

Mason and Oliver were watching as well. Up he went until he was against the ceiling. They now saw what he'd been aiming for—a door of sorts, set into the ceiling. Austin slipped out a tool and began working on it. A second later, the cover to a panel dropped open on hinges.

"Austin, be careful," Oliver said.

"What's he doing?" Tiffany asked Mason. She didn't want to distract her brother, who was, in her mind, hanging precariously high in the air.

"Looks like he found some sort of control panel," Mason explained. "He must be trying to open the door."

There was a splash of blue sparks that fell from the ceiling like fireworks.

"Austin!" Tiffany shouted.

The twin looked down at her. "I'm fine. I'm wearing protection." He displayed one of his hands, which was covered with a glove, then went back to work. There was a loud groan, then a screech like an eerie siren rang out. The door rose into the air. It seemed whatever mechanism was lifting the door was old and needed some oil.

Tiffany cringed. "That sounded horrible."

"If the Übel are anywhere nearby, they know we're here now." Oliver frowned and stalked slowly forward. He looked out through the door.

There was a thump as Austin jumped down from his perch. He brushed his hands and stepped over to Tiffany and Mason. "Taken care of."

"Nice work," Tiffany congratulated him.

"Yeah, impressive," Mason said and gave his brother knuckles.

Oliver looked back at his family with a warning: "Stay here."

Blood

Tiffany and the twins waited for Oliver to give the all clear.

"All right, come on," Oliver's voice called from outside.

Passing the door, now tucked into a recess above the threshold, the kids stepped outside and found themselves standing on the remnants of an old stone plaza. Several paths trailed off into the foliage before them, each in a different direction. Probably, at one time, the paths had been clear and the forest nicely groomed by the residents of this city. Tiffany could imagine villagers walking along the roads, carrying their wares, while others trimmed back the ever-growing jungle.

Now the city sat empty and covered in years of uncontrolled plant growth. The flora had flourished and started reclaiming what man had borrowed. Bushes encroached on the path, grass and moss poked through the seams between each stone. Vines hung from tree branches like the tails of snakes. The trees grew wildly, their branches intertwined, creating a basket weave of limbs and leaves.

Tiffany watched as Mason started taking pictures of their surroundings. That was a good idea. It'd be nice to have evidence of the basin as they found it.

Austin was shivering from his wet clothes, but he seemed not to have as heavy a chip on his shoulder as before. Probably his success at opening the doors had helped.

Tiffany joined Oliver. He had the e-journal out and was trying to use the sonar function to create a map of the basin. They'd not been able to get one as they flew in the *Phoenix*, but the ship's systems relied on different mapping technology. The sonar feature relied on a very basic method: sound. It was worth a try.

Tiffany looked at the pyramid behind her. Moss spotted the large grey stones and vines sprouted from cracks that seemingly nothing should have been able to grow from. She pulled herself onto the first level of stones, then up another, and walked toward the corner. She nearly fell off the tier when she saw something move out of the corner of her eye, causing her to startle and jump back. Mason hopped up next to her, but this didn't comfort Tiffany. Mason wasn't exactly a protector in her mind. Besides, what she saw had looked like a snake, and she knew very well her younger brother had a phobia of snakes. She looked around for the green serpentine thing, but decided not to mention it to Mason.

She turned and looked out. What she saw next nearly made her throw up. A long pool filled with blood lay before her. The crimson liquid glistened in the low sunlight.

"What's wrong?" asked Mason.

She could only point.

Her brother shrugged. He was looking directly at the blood-filled pool. "I don't see anything."

Tiffany forced out a single word. "Blood!"

Mason shook his head. "I don't think so." He hopped down the two levels to the ground and stepped to the edge of the pool to look at the red liquid. He was just about to plunge his finger into the blood when Tiffany screamed. "Stop! That's disgusting!"

At that moment, a blast of liquid rushed out from a hole halfway up the ziggurat, catching Tiffany and Mason's attention. Water surged along a wide gutter that ran down the center of the stone structure, where it splashed into the pool below. The spilling liquid was clear, not red.

Tiffany exhaled in relief; the pool was apparently not filled with blood. She hopped down to join Mason just as Oliver and Austin dashed around the corner of the ziggurat.

"Is something wrong? We heard shouting," Oliver said.

"We're fine," Tiffany admitted. "Sorry."

Oliver exhaled and turned back to Austin, who was at his side. "I'm just not sure which direction to head. There are no clear instructions."

"Maybe Tiffany read something in the journal?" Austin suggested.

Tiffany went to Oliver's side. "It worked?" she asked, noticing the newly created map on the e-journal.

"Yeah," Oliver said. "This will really help."

The basin was longer than it was wide, like an oval. The kids were on the west side. A pool stretched from north to south down the center of the basin, with shorter segments branching east and west a third of the way down from the most northern ziggurat. At each end of the pools sat one of the tall stone ziggurats, capping the ends of the pool and dumping fresh water from aqueducts into the cross-shaped form.

"Hey, you guys, look at this," Mason called to the other three. He was still squatting by the red water. "The pool is lined with jewels. Rubies, by the looks of it."

They left their review of the map and joined Mason, bending over the pool. Austin reached in and tried to pull one loose. He yanked his hand back. "It's really cold water—like freezing."

"But the air is so warm. We're in a jungle," Mason countered, then stuck his hand into the pool. "Brrr. It is cold."

"The water is the same as in the tunnel and aqueduct," Tiffany said and pointed up toward the top of the ziggurat just as another burst of water gushed free.

Austin sank his hand back into the pool. "They're stuck really good," he said as he tried to yank a stone free. "Maybe if I use a knife."

He started sifting through his pack while Oliver handed Tiffany the e-journal.

"Did you read anything in the notes that might clue us in to where we should go?" he asked.

"I'll bring up the Dabnis Castle entry. I think there was something." Tiffany tapped the screen as Oliver watched. Mason crouched next to Austin, who had recovered his pocketknife and was wiggling it around in the water.

"All right, I found it," Tiffany said. " 'At life's highest point, you are going nowhere unless you glimpse the symbol of Truth among the trinity.' That was inscribed at the base of the statue Dad found in the room beneath the courtyard."

Oliver ran his hand through his hair. "Hmmm."

"According to the map on the journal, the ziggurat at the southern tip of the pool is larger in size than the other three. That might mean it is also taller," Tiffany suggested.

She tapped the screen while Oliver looked over her shoulder. "I'm bringing up an altitude scanner." Ten red dots appeared on the screen, labeled with heights, marking the tallest structures.

"The south ziggurat is almost three times taller than any of the other pyramids," Oliver noted.

"Then that is where we should go," Mason said, rejoining his older siblings.

"Wait, there's another building not too far from here; it has a tower that is higher than the other three ziggurats and only twenty feet shorter than the largest."

"But the inscription says the highest point," Mason argued.

"You're right, it does," Oliver acknowledged. "So we're going to split up. Two of us will go to the ziggurat and two of us will head to the tower." He checked his mTalk. "We only have two hours before sunset."

"How do you know that?" Austin asked.

"It was in the notes on Evad. I set my mTalk to the planetary time sequence," Oliver explained.

"We might have even less time before the storm hits," Mason cautioned, looking at the device on his own wrist. "The storm is now moving at forty miles an hour."

"Austin, you and Tiffany head for the tower while Mason and I go to the ziggurat." Oliver looked at Austin; he was still leaning over the pool, working the knife back and forth. "Austin?"

Austin looked up from the pool. He wiped the knife across his still damp pants. "What'd you say?"

"You and Tiffany are going to search a nearby tower."

Austin sighed and slipped the knife into his pack. "Sure."

Oliver nodded. "Tiffany, can you send the coordinates of the ziggurat to my mTalk? I don't want to get lost in this jungle."

"Will you send them to me also?" Mason asked.

Tiffany sent the information and noticed Austin frown. His mTalk was still damaged. That made her think: Austin loved tinkering, so why hadn't he fixed it, or at least attempted to?

"We meet back here in two hours," Oliver instructed. "If anything suspicious happens, or you see anyone, contact us immediately and get back here as soon as you can. If for some reason you can't talk, send two quick beeps."

"Couldn't the Übel intercept our transmissions?" Austin asked.

Oliver shook his head, but Mason spoke up. "I'm not positive, but what I've seen of the encryption so far is impressive. The Übel might know *someone* else is here, but it'd take them a while to intercept and decipher our transmission."

Everyone stared at the elder twin. "Well, then," Austin said. "Aren't we smart?"

"Quiet, Austin," Oliver warned. "Good observation. Limit our transmissions, and if you make contact with someone, anyone, send two quick beeps and get back to the ziggurat."

Mason gulped fearfully as Oliver finished.

Oliver swept his pack around and set it on the ground. He slipped a second machete from it and removed the blade's protective sheath. The blade glinted in the spotty sunlight. "Austin, you'll need this," he said and slid the sheath back on the blade before giving it to the youngest of the brothers. "But be careful with it."

A scowl revealed that Austin's pride had taken a hit from Oliver's reminder, but the boy didn't say anything as he took the machete.

Oliver lifted his mTalk and tapped it. "Okay, I'm tracking your homing signal, Tiffany. Mason and mine are active too, and you should be able to find them in the LOCATOR app."

Tiffany checked and nodded. "Got it."

"The LOCATOR signal is even more highly encrypted," Mason added. "So it'd be even harder for the Übel to break into and find out locations."

"Good. Now, since everyone has their orders—I mean, knows what they're doing—let's go." Oliver forced a smile and added, "When we get back we'll make a big fire and have dinner."

"Ready, Aus?" Tiffany asked. Austin nodded and they headed off in the opposite direction from Oliver and Mason.

Truth

Oliver and Mason hacked through the encroaching branches as they fought to find their target: the largest ziggurat in the valley. Using a machete worked, but was slow and tiring. The brothers switched off and on, one chopping away at the path, the other keeping an eye on their heading, providing slight changes left or right. They decided not to follow one of the stone trails, as Oliver insisted on making a beeline for the structure.

"Oliver, do you think they've been here already?" asked Mason. "Dad and Mom, I mean."

"Naw, not yet."

However, Oliver's voice didn't sound certain, so Mason pressed further. "Why not?" There'd been plenty of time since the capture on Tragiws. It was highly possible that their parents had been here with the Übel, found the clue, and were well on their way to the next destination. Assuming, of course, there was one.

Mason waited for Oliver to answer.

Oliver stopped mid-swing at a knee-high limb. "They wouldn't have left by now if they had come here."

"Why?" Mason persisted. It was clear Oliver either didn't have a good answer or wasn't ready to face the reality that they were falling behind in the race.

"Well," Oliver started. He gave the branch three hard strikes with the machete, severing it in half. The end no longer attached to the tree fell away. "It's unlikely they would have discovered the next clue already," he said. "It can take days or weeks to uncover the puzzle pieces."

Mason nodded. That was logical. All the archeological dig sites he'd visited with his parents had consisted of weeks and months of onsite digging, sometimes even tedious hand-brushing of dirt particles. "And if they did discover the clue?"

"Dad would have stalled. He wouldn't have let them leave."

"How does Dad know we're coming?"

Mason knew Oliver was still stalling when his older brother took out his H_2O bottle and took a long draft. He tossed the bottle at Mason. "Keep yourself hydrated."

Mason took a swig and closed the lid. He drilled his eyes into Oliver as he handed him back the bottle. Oliver wasn't going to outmaneuver him. Mason could be very persistent when necessary.

"Dad knows. He's the one who told me to save you guys. He knew that the coordinates were all plotted into the navigation system."

Mason wasn't buying it, and he hoped his expression made that clear to Oliver.

"He would expect me to formulate a rescue plan," Oliver added reassuringly.

It wasn't a laser-proof defense. Nevertheless, it was all they had, and he could tell Oliver was becoming irritated with the questioning. Mason had learned a few things about Oliver during eleven years of being his brother, and one of them was how to tell if he had pushed him too far. Mason was close, but hadn't crossed that line quite yet.

"I suppose the best thing we can do is find that clue first and stop the Übel from getting it," he suggested.

"That is precisely what I am hoping we can do."

Austin led Tiffany toward their destination, cutting any branches and vines blocking the rugged stone path. Although he was the youngest Wikk, his determination and strength were second only to Oliver. Tiffany knew this, and although she was highly irritated with him at the moment, his fearlessness might come in handy should they face the Übel or an animal.

The jungle was thick and the air heavy with moisture and fragrance. Tiffany inhaled a long breath through her nose. The air smelled of flowers and rain. There was something about it—something tranquil—that refreshed her deep inside.

Several buildings made of stone blocks covered in thick leafy vines still claimed residence on the path. Some were quite run-down, with trees protruding through their broken roofs or entire walls collapsed into piles of rubble and littered onto the path.

Twenty minutes had disappeared, and they were nearing their destination. Austin hadn't complained once about the work of clearing the path, but he hadn't spoken at all, for that matter. Tiffany guessed he was still pretty frustrated.

He hacked away a large green leaf twice his size. It floated to the ground, revealing a courtyard and a set of doors about a hundred feet ahead.

Tiffany and Austin stepped out from under the cover of the jungle canopy and onto a wide stone courtyard that lay in a state of slow decay. A building several stories in height sat on the far end of the plaza, flanked by a tall cylindrical tower on its right side. The tower rose nearly three times higher than the rest of the building; it looked out of place topped with its bright blue dome.

What might be in the tower? Would it hold the clue to unlock the secret to Ursprung? Would this be the last stop before they left for their final destination?

Though Tiffany enjoyed exploration and solving mysteries, she wished this particular quest were over. She wanted desperately to find her parents.

The brother-sister duo walked to the entrance, marked by a set of metal doors, both of which had been inlayed with red rubies and engraved with scrolling flourishes. Next to the door was a pattern of twelve stones, and Tiffany knew immediately what to do. Austin didn't hesitate to help, and the two had an unspoken race to see who could activate the most. Austin won, seven to five.

The stones glowed yellow, blue, then green and the doors slid apart, disappearing into the building. Tiffany switched on her mTalk's light, and Austin took out his own small flashlight. He clicked it, but the light was still dim. With a sigh, he leaned the machete against a wall. He slid his pack off one shoulder and around to the front so he could access it, then took out a small container. Opening it to reveal several small bulbs, he unscrewed the top of the light and replaced the dimming bulb, then unscrewed the bottom and replaced the power pack as well. He put everything back together, returned the extra supplies to his pack, and clicked on the light. Its brightness washed over them.

"Nice," Tiffany said.

"Just a quick fix," Austin admitted.

A room with a high ceiling greeted them, and a long, darkened hearth stood directly across from the entrance. A thick layer of dust covered the floor, and pieces of furniture were strewn throughout the room. It was as if the people who had once lived there had just vanished. An old staircase curved from the left side of the room to a balcony above the hearth. It was beautiful, but it was wooden, which made Tiffany leery of its sturdiness. She didn't imagine the integrity of the wood would survive very well in the humid jungle climate. She thought about the books in the ziggurat—how had they survived? Then she recalled the *pffft* that had resounded upon their entrance. Had it been sealed airtight?

Austin investigated the staircase while Tiffany walked over to a bookcase on the opposite wall. "Be careful," she instructed, eyeing the hundreds of dusty volumes lining the shelves.

Austin nodded his head smugly. "Of course."

Tiffany watched him hop onto the first step and bounce several times. He continued this test for the first six steps, at which point he must have gained enough confidence to continue to the balcony. She sighed and looked back at the spines on the bookshelf, illuminating each one with her light. A frown overtook her face. These tomes were in a state of deterioration. She looked around and saw several broken windows along the far wall.

Although some of the spines were covered in slime or mold or just blank, a scan of the legible ones revealed a wide breadth of topics and languages. If only there were enough time to look through them and rescue the knowledge within before it vanished forever. She paused when she noticed several titles written in a language she didn't recognize.

Her browsing was interrupted by Austin calling for her.

"Tiffany, look above the door. There's something inscribed there," Austin called, shining his light on the wall.

She turned from the books and walked to the door to get a closer view. There was an inscription etched into the stone.

"Can you read what it says?" Austin leaned against the rail in anticipation.

An old metal chair, covered in orangish rust, provided a makeshift ladder for Tiffany. It groaned under her weight. She read aloud. "Remember those who gave us hope, and honor them in all you do."

"What does it mean?"

She traced her finger over the carved letters. "It must have been important to these people, to remember their past." Tiffany took a picture of the engraving with her mTalk. And then it hit her. "Books! Of course." She looked around the room. "A library . . . books!"

Austin looked at her with confusion. "Clarify, please."

"Books, as in history books. We're in a library, and the saying is referring to a written-recorded past. These books might contain the history of the people who lived here before," she said excitedly. "If that's true, then maybe there's information on Ursprung or a clue to where these people came from."

"You really think so?"

"It makes sense," she said.

"It seems too easy."

Tiffany had an odd feeling that she and her siblings were being looked out for in some greater way than she could explain. "Maybe," she said. "Either way, come help me look for the ones about history. They might be categorized by genre."

Austin frowned. "I wanted to investigate the tower."

"Well—"

"This way you'll have time to look at the library, and I'll look for the tallest point," he bargained.

It was a fair deal. "Sure," she agreed happily. It was her deepest desire to hold these treasures in her hand and leaf—delicately, of course—through the pages. Possibly even save some of the fading history.

"I'm going to try and gain entrance into the tower," Austin explained, still leaning on the old railing.

"Let me know if you need my help," she called over her shoulder, the books consuming her attention. "And be careful."

"Of course. I always am," Austin said heartily.

Crack!

"Whoa!" Austin shouted as the balcony railing in front of him gave way and he scrambled to hold onto something. His hands grasped a nearby stone pillar just as the wooden rail fell to the floor below.

Tiffany had whirled around. Her mouth dropped open as she looked at the rail and then at Austin clinging to the pillar. He released his hold on the column and stepped back, wiping his hand across his forehead. "That was close."

Tiffany frowned. "Be careful. We can't have you breaking something! And I mean on *you*, like your leg or an arm."

"I know. I'm fine—really," he protested, but his voice cracked, revealing the close call had indeed frightened him. He cleared his throat and turned to leave. "I'll just be down this hall," he hollered over his shoulder.

Tiffany returned to browsing the spines that lined the shelves, looking for the right book to start with. With limited time, it was important to make it count. She might not get another chance like this. Her first selection was a dark-brown leather book with the odd title *XII*. Dusty and old-looking as it was, she was cautious as she opened it. To her surprise, the pages were still in rather crisp condition, so she flipped through the book with her conscience at ease.

The words in the book were unfamiliar to her as well. None of the ancient tongues she had mastered matched the text of this book.

A shout from Austin caught her attention. "Tiffany, come up here quickly. You have to see this."

Tiffany groaned; she'd just gotten started. Did he really need her at that moment, or could it wait? After all, he sounded just fine, not hurt or anything.

"Tiffany, come here," Austin's voice called again.

"All right, I'll be right there." Tiffany regretfully put the book into her pack and heaved it onto her shoulder. The weight of her pack had already increased considerably from the previous two book additions.

As she headed up the staircase, she took each step cautiously. Each might be the cause for collapse. She even contemplated what she might grab to support herself, but there was nothing solid looking within reach. She spied a couple of unlit sconces on the wall. She doubted those would hold her for very long, if at all.

To her gratification, the staircase remained intact.

Just a few feet down the hallway, she found Austin in a pentagon-shaped room filled with star maps. She loved books, but she also loved information. And in regard to their quest, this was an even greater find.

Three of the five walls of the pentagonal room were covered with floor-to-ceiling maps of star systems and their planets. Containers of scrolls and globes were stacked on shelves along the other two walls bordering the entryway. In the center of the room loomed a large, odd-looking metal table the same shape as the room. Above it, a monitor hung from the ceiling.

Tiffany put her hand on Austin's head, ruffling his hair. "Good find, Aus."

"What do you think it is?" Austin asked as he pointed at the pentagonal table.

"I'm not sure."

2.11

Highest Point

Oliver and Mason had blazed a path through the jungle for over a mile. Their arms were tired from hacking through the underbrush and foliage. But Oliver continued to drive them to their destination, unwilling to rest. Their time was limited; any moment the Übel could arrive. He couldn't risk being on top of the southern ziggurat exposed to the soldiers if they invaded the basin by ship or on foot. Furthermore, this mysterious jungle would be an imposing enemy in the dark. Arms aching, and soaked with sweat, Oliver pushed forward.

His little brother was a good sport, not complaining once. Mason did his best to assist with removing the thick plants and, when he wasn't using the machete, encouraged Oliver to keep going.

The dense jungle eventually ended at the edge of a large stone courtyard, much like the one surrounding the first ziggurat. Before them, the large grey stones of the southern ziggurat were stacked higher and higher, reaching into the sky.

"Wow," exclaimed Mason, craning his neck to see the top. "It's really tall, especially when you're standing so close."

"Yes, it is," Oliver agreed. "We better get climbing if we want to reach the top and return to camp before nightfall."

"The top?" Mason asked.

"Well, of course," Oliver said with a smile at his little brother. "The clue said the highest point."

Mason took a deep breath and exhaled. "I'm right behind you," he said encouragingly.

Oliver knew his little brother meant it. He was quickly realizing that Mason was willing to do his part to rescue their parents.

"Before we start, let's contact Tiffany to get a progress report." Oliver pressed a button and lifted the mTalk to his mouth. "Tiffany, come in." His sister and brother's safety rested on his shoulders, and a desire to know their status had continually nagged on him while they moved through the forest. With no sign of the Übel's presence, he felt at ease contacting them.

A second passed. "Oliver, I'm here. What do you need?"

"Have you and Austin found anything interesting yet?"

"Yes, Austin discovered a room filled with star maps. I'm not sure if any of them are useful yet, but we're going to spend some time looking through them. I'll let you know if we find anything of value," Tiffany replied over the speaker.

"Have you found anything that might be related to the inscription?"

"Not yet."

Oliver sighed, slightly frustrated. "That should be your first priority."

No response for a moment; he knew he'd come across as irritated with her.

"I'm sorry," she apologized.

"It's all right. Just keep looking. We need to find it before the Übel arrive," he reminded her, more compassionately this time.

"We will," she said softly.

"Have you found anything else?"

"Yeah, the building with the tower appears to be a library. More books than the ziggurat we were in before. I'm hoping that one of them might provide insight into the former residents' origins."

"I wish I were there," Mason said quietly, clearly jealous.

Oliver knew that the two discoveries their sister and brother had made had a lot of appeal to Mason, far more than hacking through a jungle with bugs nipping at their skin. Oliver looked at him and smiled. "We'll have our chance for discovery, I promise. If we have time, we'll check the library out too. The books and maps may be of use on our quest. And it'll take all of us to scour through them," he added encouragingly. He swatted his arm. "I thought this cream was supposed to last for a while."

"Maybe it wore off when you got wet," Mason suggested.

"I would have noticed before, don't you think?" Oliver said.

Mason shrugged. "Too bad Tiffany is the only one with the cream."

Oliver nodded and looked up at the ziggurat looming over them, then spoke into the mTalk. "We're heading up the southern ziggurat. We'll call you if we find anything."

"All right. Bye," Tiffany responded. "Be careful."

"Of course." Oliver lowered his arm and started around the base of the ziggurat, Mason following.

They found a set of stairs. Oliver stopped and removed his backpack, then tucked the machete inside. "Up we go. Onward to the highest point."

"Don't you mean 'upward,'" Mason joked with a smile.

Oliver laughed and patted Mason on the back. "Yeah." He looked over the mountainous monument before them. To climb it would be a task for sure. Thankfully, the staircase remained clear for the most part; the moss and vines didn't seem to overlap the steps too much.

Oliver suddenly jumped backward and shook his head. The heat must have been getting to him, because he thought he saw one of the vines move. He took out his H_2O bottle, downed a long swig, and then squirted some on his head. He looked back at the stairs; nothing was moving. It had probably just been a snake or a mirage.

He looked at his little brother. The front of Mason's shirt was soaked with sweat; locks of the boy's sandy-colored hair were matted to his forehead. "Be sure to keep hydrated, Mason," he instructed, then slung his pack onto his back. "Here we go." And with that, they began their ascent.

At first, it was fun. Oliver took two steps at a time. He was filled with energy and wonder at what they might find at the top, especially at the prospect of finding the answer to the Dabnis Castle riddle. He called out inspiring words to Mason to keep him going.

They were only a quarter of the way up the staircase when the steps started to take their toll on his little brother. Mason lagged behind. The twin's legs were shorter and his muscles were less developed than his cadet brother's.

"Are you all right?" Oliver asked.

"I'm tired," admitted Mason in an achy voice.

"You're doing great, Mason," Oliver encouraged, pulling out his H_2O again. He took a swig and splashed some on his forehead. The cold liquid was refreshing, and his hair was so wet from sweat that a little more moisture didn't hurt. "We don't have much more time before we need to turn back."

"I'm trying," Mason panted. "Why don't you go on ahead, and I'll catch up?"

Oliver didn't like leaving his little brother behind, but if he didn't go ahead, neither of them would reach the summit before dark. He smiled. "Just shout if you need me. You're doing great, Mason."

Mason nodded in agreement and Oliver turned to continue his ascent to the top. As he climbed, he thought about the inscription from Dabnis Castle. *"At life's highest point, you are going nowhere unless you glimpse the symbol of Truth among the trinity."*

What did it mean? He looked around; he could see the three other ziggurats. Perhaps they signified "the trinity" the inscription mentioned. In addition, if this pyramid was the tallest point in the basin, was it "life's highest point"? But what was the "symbol of Truth"?

There was one way to find out, and that was to reach the top of the ziggurat.

Pentagonal

The pentagonal table in the center of the room had many buttons and knobs, although it was not as high tech as the *Phoenix* and the other gadgets the Wikks had. Nothing happened when Tiffany and Austin tried the knobs and buttons. Perhaps it was just too old.

"If only we could figure out how to turn it on," Austin suggested.

"Is there power to it?" asked Tiffany.

"I don't know."

"None of the lights work, but those stones light up and the doors are running on something," Tiffany said.

"Yeah, true." Austin continued to survey the table. "I did have to open the door to the room."

"That explains why these maps are still in such good condition." Tiffany walked around the room, taking pictures of the wall-size maps. "I think these will be of use. These maps appear very old. They may have clues to where these people previously lived, which would be one step further along the path toward Ursprung." She took another picture. "Assuming, of course, these people indeed came from Ursprung."

Austin was now on his back under the table; he had several of his tools out as he investigated the wires and circuitry. Tiffany started unrolling scrolls across the floor and taking pictures. Map after map was unrolled while she captured its picture on her mTalk, then transferred it to the e-journal for cataloging. As she worked, Austin kept fiddling with things but finally gave up and pushed himself out from underneath the table.

"Well, it's no use," he said. "The table seems to be dead, and unless we can figure out how to power it up, it's not going to work."

Tiffany shrugged. "That's okay. I've found several amazing maps. One shows the layout of a large city named *Salguod*. Streets and even some buildings are labeled. I also found one for a group of several islands called The Washed Stones."

"Is that where we need to go next?" Austin asked with excitement.

Tiffany smiled. "Not necessarily. I mean, I don't know. But—"

"I'm going to keep looking for how to reach the top of the tower." Austin wasn't interested in researching the past; he wanted to blast through the present to rescue his dad and mom.

"Just be careful," she said absently, clearly preoccupied with the treasure trove of maps they had discovered. "I'll be up in a minute. A few more maps," she promised.

Austin looked around the room. There were dozens of maps left. She'd be a while for sure—there was no way she'd skip any. She was such a perfectionist and couldn't miss anything.

"I'll be back," he said and left the map room.

Down a narrow hall, up some stairs, and around a corner he found an arched opening. Beyond it, a staircase spiraled upward, tracing along the stone walls of a tower.

Austin had found the entrance to the tower and possibly the answer his family sought.

The tower was for the most part dark with the exception of a few dusty windows that allowed some scattered rays of light to illuminate portions of the stone walls. He kept his flashlight trained on the winding wooden path ahead of him. The staircase creaked with every step, reminding him of the close call he'd had a few minutes before.

He climbed one story after another with no exit.

Finally at the top, Austin found a trapdoor in the ceiling. When he pushed on it, nothing happened. He backtracked and searched the side of the tower's stone wall. A second later, he'd activated the cross of stones, and the door slid open.

He climbed the last few stairs up into a room. He'd found the top of the tower.

A weak beam of light streamed down through a skylight in the domed roof above. The ray landed on a large silver cylinder, angling from the floor to the top of the cracked dome. Austin shone his light on the enormous device in front of him, looking it over in amazement. What was it? He circled around it in wonder. It reminded him of the gadget in Obbin's room.

A telescope, that's what it is. It was bigger than Obbin's, but it looked very similar otherwise. It sat on a large platform that appeared to rotate if the correct wheels turned. Austin noticed there were certainly plenty of cranks and gears around.

Now, if only he could figure out how to make it work.

Austin climbed into a seat and looked through a small eyepiece. There was nothing but blackness. Of course, he needed to find a way to open the dome to see out. He started to search a desk of controls, looking for a switch, crank, button, or something. There were a lot of options, but the control panel was dead like the table in the star map room. It seemed everything here relied on energy; how could anyone survive without it?

Then he remembered Obbin's home in Cobalt Gorge. They did not have electricity there. But unlike the Blauwe Mensen's palace, this city was built to run on electricity. There had to be a power source somewhere. After all, the stones were lighting up to unlock the doors, and the doors weren't opening without the assistance of power.

Austin started to search the large room. His eyes spotted several cables running down the stone walls from the ceiling and leading to a grey box tucked into the wall. He went to it and pulled its hinged door open. Inside were circuits and breakers, along with at least twenty black switches and a large red one. The red switch had two words on either side of it: *Close* and *Open*. And currently the switch leaned toward *Open*.

Austin knew enough about circuitry to realize the term *Open* meant the circuit was incomplete and therefore the flow of energy was cut off. By changing the switch to *Close*, he would complete the circuit and allow the electricity to flow. Maybe then the telescope controls would work. He took a deep breath and slid the switch over.

Nothing happened, or so it seemed at first. Then he heard it: a faint buzzing sound. It was the hum of electricity running through the wires. All of the black switches were set to *On*, including one labeled *Observatory Lights*, but he was still in darkness.

Maybe the switches needed to be reset, he thought.

As he cycled each switch off and then on again, the lights around him started coming on. Something on the telescope beeped. The massive contraption was alive with power.

Now, if he could just open the dome.

Austin spied a knob labeled *Dome*, with *Open* to the right and *Close* to the left. He turned the knob to the right. The sound of old gears creaking awake resounded overhead. An opening appeared and grew wider. It halted three quarters of the way, and Austin released the knob.

With the storm moving in, there was little sunlight left to illuminate the upper floor of the observatory. It was a good thing the lights worked.

And now, with the barrier of the metal roof removed, Austin was ready to see what he might through the telescope.

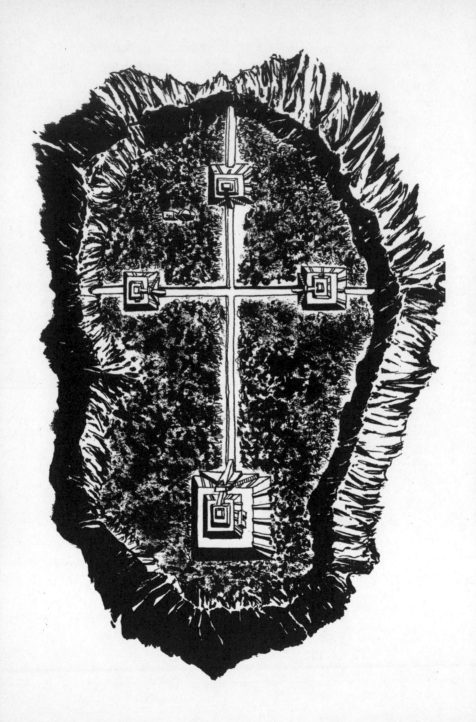

2.13

Creepy Crawlies

"Hey, Tiff, can you look up something for me?" Oliver said into the mTalk.

A moment later, his sister responded, but she sounded distracted. "Of course."

"Look up symbols that represent *truth* or *honesty*," Oliver said.

"Will do," she answered vacantly.

"What are you working on? You seem preoccupied."

"Sorry, Oliver," apologized Tiffany. "I'm still in the map room trying to capture pictures of all of the old star maps and enter them into the journal."

"Tiffany, you really should be looking for—"

"Austin's looking for it now," she interrupted with irritation. "These maps very likely are of places the inhabitants of this city once lived in or explored."

Oliver hesitated. He didn't want to get in a drawn-out argument with her over the mTalk. At the same time, it was frustrating to have the one sibling he relied on contesting his commands. She was supposed to be mature and reliable. He needed that from her.

Oliver looked toward the sky and closed his eyes, trying to keep himself calm. "Hopefully that stuff will be helpful in the future," he finally said.

"It will," Tiffany promised. "Anyway, I'll look for the information you requested and get back to you in a minute."

"I'll be waiting."

What was happening to his family? Why couldn't they all just work together and take orders? It was like he was a babysitter instead of the commander of a rescue mission. Only Mason hadn't contradicted him in the last few hours. Sure, he'd disobeyed and gotten taken by those blue people, but he'd given a sincere apology and changed his ways.

Oliver took another drink from his bottle and looked back at his soldier. Mason was still working on climbing the stone steps. Like a good leader, Oliver shouted something encouraging to his little brother, but the twin just shook his head and put his hand to his ear.

That was the first time Oliver noticed the wind sweeping around him. It had not been as obvious under the protection of the dense jungle. Now that he was exposed on the face of the stone pyramid, the powerful breeze tugged on his clothing like grasping hands.

Oliver paused to look out over the basin again. The green canopy shivered in the wind. He looked toward the ziggurat directly across from the pool and then toward the horizon. A line of dark grey clouds was rolling forward like a wall. The storm was moving in, and fast. They were running out of time. The last remains of the thick gray fog that had hung over the basin had dissipated. Most likely, the cold front of the storm was lowering the temperature in the basin, cooling the humid air and removing the cloud covering.

Oliver shouted to Mason again, but the boy still couldn't hear him. Mason looked up, but Oliver couldn't see the expression on his face at this distance. Oliver nodded and raised his right hand. He gave Mason a thumbs-up, then a thumbs-down, hoping his brother would get the gesture.

Mason seemed to be nodding; he held his hands high and gave Oliver two thumbs-up. That was a good sign. Mason was far more resilient than Oliver had given him credit for. Mason might be the weakest physically, but right now he was the strongest in heart.

Anxious to look for the clue, Oliver continued up the side of the ziggurat. A hundred steps and several minutes later, he reached the top. He set his pack down and made for an open-air structure. The dome-topped pillars sheltered a small fountain. Water shot up and poured into a small trough, where it flowed to the edge of the pavilion and down the front of the ziggurat. The smaller trio of ziggurats did not have a similar open-air structure.

The other three ziggurats sat in a cluster, close together in comparison to the one Oliver stood on. Surely that was what the inscription meant by "trinity." The deep crimson hue from the rubies was even more visible from this height. The pool's hue stood out against the luscious green jungle foliage.

"Oliver?" Tiffany's voice came over the mTalk. "I've found several entries for what might symbolize *truth*. The first entry says, 'Truth was symbolized and confirmed for the two or more parties involved by exchanging a ring with the family's signet on it. It was common for people to have collections of signet rings displayed for guests that visited their household to see. It was believed that this showed the amount of integrity and honor a family had. This custom was primarily used by the Raggud Empire before its annexation into the Federation.'"

"Nope. Next," said Oliver.

"The second journal entry says that 'Truth was often symbolized by a cross and was the main symbol of a group of a people called *Veritas Nachfolger*.'"

"That's it. It's right in front of me," interrupted Oliver.

"What is?"

"A cross. I'm looking right down the center of a large cross. From this vantage point, I can see everything in the basin. The pool is in the shape of a cross, each segment flanked by one of the four ziggurats."

"I wish I could see."

"I'll stream some video from up here," Oliver promised. He lifted his mTalk and began to capture the basin and the symbolic pool below.

"Wow, you're right, though. That seems like a match to me," she said.

"Well, I'd better go check on Mason; make sure he hasn't fainted."

"Thanks," Tiffany replied. "I'm going to—" Static fizzled on the speaker of Oliver's mTalk as a low growl of thunder echoed in the distance. Oliver looked toward the boiling grey clouds as they continued to roll forward. A flash illuminated the imposing storm front from within. The sky had grown considerably darker, partly from the onset of night and partly from the storm.

"Tiffany, I didn't hear what you said. It's getting darker, and the storm must be causing some interference. You and Austin should head back to base camp. We'll be there soon," Oliver said.

"I was just saying—" Tiffany's voice cut out again. Oliver heard another rumble.

Tiffany spoke again. "Wow, I heard that one. I'll find Austin, and we'll see you soon. Over and out."

Oliver couldn't head back without finding the clue.

" 'At life's highest point, you are going nowhere unless you glimpse the symbol of Truth among the trinity,' " Oliver repeated aloud. "So, we're at the highest point in the valley. We can see the trinity and a symbol of truth. What next?"

He wasn't that great at puzzles, but Mason was. Where was his little brother anyhow? Oliver ran back to the side of the ziggurat he'd ascended. Looking over the edge, he spied Mason below. But something was very wrong. Mason was thrashing around in a horde of green snakes below him.

Oliver leaped down two steps at a time. He pulled the Zapp-It from a holster on his belt, but he wasn't sure it'd do much good. The machete remained in his pack at the top of the ziggurat, and Oliver couldn't turn back for it.

The attackers were not snakes but long green vines. The thick plant tendrils were curling around Mason and pulling his legs in opposite directions. For the moment, his arms were still free. A vine grasped his elbow for a brief moment before Mason shoved it aside.

As Oliver got closer, he could hear his brother's frantic cries for help. A surge of adrenaline shot through him as he charged forward. He would not allow his brother to die!

Mason's hands were quickly losing the battle to keep the vines from wrapping around his neck.

Suddenly, Oliver's body flew forward; he had tripped in his mad dash downward. His hands crashed against the stone stairs, and he felt the skin on his palms tear. He'd barely stopped his face from smacking against the stone. The Zapp-It slipped loose from his hand and bounced several stairs below.

Oliver felt his right leg jerk back up the stairs from where he'd come. Something was latched around his ankle. He turned over and looked to see a green vine curling around his pant leg. He curled into a sit-up and locked his hands on the creeper, then wrenched it free. The second he did, five more vines seemed to come from nowhere and clasped onto his arms, legs, and around his torso. Immediately, the vines started to pull away in opposite directions. It was as if the plants' efforts were coordinated.

Oliver's hands were no longer free to loosen the vines from his limbs. And what was worse, he no longer heard the agonizing cries of his brother. His heart sank, and his breathing became agitated as he tried to guess his brother's fate below.

"Ahhh!" cried Mason, but not in agony. Instead, it sounded like an attack. To Oliver's relief, he saw his brother's form dash into view. The twin shoved the end of the black Zapp-It against one of the long green tendrils of plant. A sickening sound sizzled from the vine, and the plant's skin crackled and spurted boiling blue balls of sap in all directions. Mason jerked back as they splattered against his exposed skin. Oliver felt the hot bubbles of liquid land on his arm too. They burned like hot wax.

The vine's grip loosened, and Oliver yanked his arm free. A thick blue goo continued to ooze from the wound created by Mason's attack.

The vine around Oliver's torso tightened as the plant tried to crush his ribcage. "Quick, zap the others," he called.

Mason moved to each of the attacking creepers and plunged the device against them one by one. Spurts of hot blue jelly erupted each time, and, by the end, Oliver and Mason looked like they had had a blueberry fight.

Oliver breathed in a deep sigh of relief and pulled himself to a sitting position on the nearest step. Mason stood vigilantly prepared for another attack. Other vines were snaking around below only a few yards away. But none seemed brave enough to advance.

"This isn't right," Mason said. "Plants aren't supposed to act like this."

"No, they aren't," Oliver admitted. He climbed to his feet, and Mason offered him the Zapp-It. "No, you keep it; you used it well."

Mason smiled at his older brother.

A roar of thunder boomed in the sky overhead. Oliver looked up and saw the dark black clouds masking the sky from view. The storm had stretched over the entire basin during the brothers' battle with the vines.

There was no time to linger on the vines. They had to go.

"We have to hurry," Oliver said. "My pack is at the top, and we have to figure out what the clue is before that storm hits."

Mason nodded, and the brothers ran the rest of the way back to the top of the ziggurat with a renewed burst of energy.

Oliver led Mason to the fountain. "'At life's highest point, you are going nowhere unless you glimpse the symbol of Truth among the trinity,'" Oliver repeated, nearly breathless, and pointed out over the basin. "It seems we are at the highest point in the valley. We can see the trinity and a symbol of truth. What next?"

"Symbol of truth?" Mason asked.

"I called Tiffany. It turns out that a cross represents truth," Oliver explained and pointed at the red pool. "The pool is in the shape of a cross."

Mason nodded.

"But I don't get it. We see everything the inscription mentions, but that's it. There is nothing more," Oliver said.

Mason scoured the pillared structure and fountain. "Oliver, look at this," he said and knelt next to the stream of water pouring out. "There is an inscription etched into the stone floor of the trough."

"What does it say?" Oliver walked to where Mason was kneeling.

"'When you find the Truth, you have found your way. At the foot of the cross, your path home begins. Dive into the Truth, so you too may find the way.'" Mason stood and looked at Oliver. "What does it mean?"

"I don't know," replied Oliver thoughtfully. "I'll get a picture, and we can have Tiffany cross-reference the phrase in the journal."

Oliver angled his mTalk over the engraving and zoomed in. The image was blurry from the running water, but he could still make out the letters.

A peal of thunder reminded him of their need to leave. "Let's head toward the edge of the pool on our way out."

Mason stretched his legs. "Down is easier, right?"

"Right," Oliver agreed. "Unless, of course, those vines attack again."

Mason lifted the Zapp-It. "I'm ready for that."

"Yes, you are!" Oliver cheered.

2.14

Arrival

Tiffany had started into the hall to search for Austin when she noticed several wall fixtures illuminated along the wall. She looked back into the star map room to see if she'd been so absorbed in her work that she had missed a light in there as well. She hadn't.

She felt a switch and pressed it. Several overhead lights glowed to life. Had Austin somehow turned the power on? She called for him, hoping she wouldn't have to search the entire building. But he didn't answer. She left her pack next to her brother's in the star map room. They'd get them on their way back through.

Eventually, she located the tower stairs and looked at them with caution. If the railing in the lobby was any indicator, the staircase might be near collapse. Several lights illuminated fixtures running along the stairs.

A faint glow emanated through a trapdoor high above. Clearly, Austin was up there looking around with his light.

"Austin!" she shouted up the tower. "Austin! Are you up there?" She lifted her mTalk to call him and then sighed. "I can't call him; he doesn't have one," she said to herself. She looked again at the rickety stairs before her.

The wood creaked and wiggled beneath her every step. *I don't weigh that much*, she thought. Keeping close to the wall, she slunk along step after step. There was no way she'd trust the handrail.

A ripple of thunder accentuated the danger.

Calling Austin's name as she climbed, Tiffany felt her frustration mount when no replies came. It wasn't until she was nearly halfway up that Austin's head finally poked down through a hole in the ceiling. "Tiff, I'm up here. Hurry, you have to see this!" Austin demanded excitedly. Had he been ignoring her, or could he really just not hear her?

Tiffany sped up her pace, but slowed back down as the creaking grew louder and the railing before her began to wobble visibly. A shiver ran down her spine. This thing was going to collapse any minute, and she was a long way up. The stone walls were free of any handholds, and she would not survive the fall.

A deep sense of relief flooded over her once she climbed through the hole atop the staircase. The opening was a trapdoor into some sort of attic. But this was no ordinary household attic: Austin was standing next to a large telescope, a smile beaming on his face. She knew this was *his* discovery.

Austin spread his arms, displaying the find. "What do you think?" he asked proudly.

Tiffany didn't answer immediately. The telescope looked old; she'd never seen one so mechanical. "Does it work?" was all she could ask.

"Yes, and it's amazing. I can see Evad's moon," Austin said as he sat in a chair beneath the eyepiece.

Tiffany remembered her purpose for seeking out Austin. "How can you see through the storm clouds?" she asked with curiosity.

"I didn't even notice them."

"I suppose the telescope could be looking through a gap in the clouds." Tiffany admired the silver body of the telescope as she walked to meet Austin.

"Would you like to look?" Austin asked.

"Absolutely," said Tiffany. She ruffled Austin's hair with her hand. "This whole library is turning out to be a great find."

She looked around the lit room. "Austin, how did you turn on the lights?"

"I found a circuit breaker box. One quick flick and the power came on."

"And how did you open the roof?" she asked.

"Once the power was on, it was just a matter of figuring out which lever or button controlled the roof. It was actually a knob that did the trick."

"This place is more than just a library; it's an observatory too. I wonder if this building functioned sort of like a science lab for the citizens. It makes sense—the star maps, the domed roof, the telescope. I've been in an observatory before, but its equipment was computerized. This one must be very old." Tiffany nodded decisively. "Time to take a look. I'm surprised the metal hasn't corroded in the humid air."

"It might be old, but it's made of some sort of weather-resistant alloy. It's the only way to explain it," Austin said. "The wiring probably is too. Otherwise, it would have decomposed by now."

Austin helped Tiffany into the telescope's attached viewing seat.

It took a fifth of the time to reach the bottom that it had taken to climb up the stone ziggurat. And this time, Oliver and Mason didn't suffer from any attacking vines. Mason patted the holster he'd borrowed from Oliver. It held the Zapp-It safely and made it quickly accessible. Apparently his earlier escapade against the plants had been enough to make them hesitant to strike again.

Oliver and Mason stood at the edge of the pool, looking out over the dark crimson waters. The clouds' shadows had made the water look even thicker, more like blood.

"You know, the jewels that Dad and Mom took from Dabnis Castle were also rubies," Mason recalled. "It seems clear to me that Evad and this basin are the right place for us to be—the two tied together although light years apart. What did the inscription at the top of the ziggurat say again?"

Oliver loaded the picture of the engraving and read it aloud. " 'When you find the Truth, you are no longer lost. At the foot of the cross, your path home begins. Dive into the Truth, so you too may find the way.' " Oliver shrugged. "There must be something more here, something else to tell us how, or where to get on that path."

Oliver and Mason surveyed the cracked stone pavers covering the area between the great ziggurat and the edge of the pool. They hopped over the canal that allowed the water from the ziggurat to flow into the pool.

Suddenly, Mason thought of something. He turned to Oliver. "The cross represents truth," he said excitedly.

Oliver gave Mason a blank stare and said, "We already know that," not having made the connection that Mason had.

"Don't you find it interesting that the truth is a pool of water? A pool that was very important to the people who lived here. I mean, they paved it with rubies, so it must have been significant," Mason explained. "We have to *dive* into the water to find the *path*," Mason emphasized. "The path is in the pool!"

A flash of lightning flashed off the pool's surface, causing the rubies to glitter brightly. A roll of thunder echoed across the basin in response.

"However, I don't think we should get into the pool at the moment," Mason said. "Lightning and water don't mix."

"I agree. Let's start heading back. We'll need to get our diving gear from the *Phoenix* anyway. I'm not about to climb back into that cold water. We'll meet up with Tiffany and Austin and then return."

Tiffany sat in the telescope's seat and looked out into space. No storm clouds had passed into view, but she didn't think this odd. Evad's moon was bright against the black night; several craters and steam vents pocked the satellite's surface.

"I wonder what the range of the telescope is." She looked at the controls in front of her and noticed one labeled *Zoom*. She pressed it up, and her view tightened in on a crater. She swept it down, and the telescope hummed as it began to retract.

"Great. I can get it to zoom in and out, but I don't see anything to rotate it."

Austin looked at a set of controls near him. "There's a wheel here for rotating. It's a two-man job to operate, apparently." He turned the wheel to the right, and the base of the telescope creaked.

Tiffany's face tightened. It sounded like the whole thing might tear itself free of the floor.

With a violent shudder, the telescope began moving to the right. The moon disappeared from sight, and several bright stars came into view. A feeling of sadness slipped into her heart. Somewhere out there was her home. Would she ever return?

Tiffany was pulled from her thoughts as a small flash erupted in the sky. Something metallic flew from the bright point of eruption and out of her line of vision.

"Austin, quick, turn me back the other way!" she exclaimed.

"What, why?" Austin asked.

"Just do it, quick. I saw something."

Austin turned the wheel the other way. The telescope jerked and moved in the other direction. Tiffany scoured the view in front of her. "Can you make it go quicker?"

"No, I can only control where it points," Austin explained.

"Stop!" shouted Tiffany.

Austin stopped turning the wheel, but the telescope continued to rotate.

"Go back, go back!" Tiffany said in a panic.

Austin moved the telescope in the other direction but stopped after a small turn. "Is that better?" The telescope jerked and moved back the other way.

Tiffany said nothing for a moment as she searched the black space. "Yes, there it is."

"What is it?" asked Austin.

"I'm not sure. It's still too small to make out, but it's moving toward us, almost directly."

Tiffany slid the zoom lever up; the telescope began to extend, and her view focused on the object.

The room remained silent for a full minute.

"Oh, no!" Tiffany shouted, startling Austin. "It's a ship! It's huge. It must be the Übel." She quickly climbed down from the telescope. "We have to get back to camp."

A flash of lightning lit the inside of the dome, overwhelming the glow from the manmade lights. The storm had fallen across the basin, and Tiffany had failed to get her and Austin back to base camp. Now they'd be running through a forest of lightning rods while trying to avoid the soldiers who were sure to be swarming the basin like an army of ants at any moment.

"We have to go," she said and led Austin to the stairs. He stepped down into the tower.

With one last look at the telescope, Tiffany started to follow.

There was a loud creak, and the staircase began to rock back and forth. She stepped back onto the observatory floor as the wooden stair beneath Austin dropped away.

"Ahh!" he screamed as he began to fall. Tiffany's hand instinctively darted out to save her brother. As their fingers, then hands, interlocked, his weight pulled her hard to the floor, slamming her elbows and chin against its surface.

"I've got you," she yelled. She braced herself with her free hand and began to pull Austin up.

The resounding crash of wood planks snapping and slamming into the hard stone walls and floor below was frightening at the least. It sounded as if everything around them would fall apart at any moment. Lights flickered, and blue sparks burst as the wooden planks tore the fixtures from the wall. It looked as if a dozen flares were exploding.

Austin's feet dangled into the pit below. The void seemed to be waiting to swallow him as it had the staircase.

"Don't let me go, please!" he cried. "I'm not ready to die."

The words hit Tiffany like a ton of bricks. She held her little brother's life in her hands. She couldn't fail.

She heaved and pulled with all her might. Beads of sweat formed on her forehead. Her muscles quickly began to burn; he was far heavier than anything she'd ever tried to lift with just her arms.

With a final grunt, she pulled his arms above the opening. Austin used his own strength to lift the lower half of his body out of the now dark and hollow tower. Sister and brother fell backward onto the floor, breathing heavily.

Tiffany wasted no time, taking immediate action. The Übel were on their way to the planet, and she and Austin were prisoners in a tower. She lifted her mTalk to her mouth. "Oliver, Oliver . . . Come in, Oliver!"

"What's wrong?" came Oliver's alarmed voice immediately.

"The Übel—they're here," she said between deep breaths.

"They're here?" His voice betrayed his alarm. "Where? Near you?"

"No, they haven't landed. I saw them through the telescope."

"Telescope?"

"Never mind. The point is they're here."

"Okay, then hurry and get back to camp," Oliver urgently commanded.

"We can't," Tiffany shouted. "We're stuck in the observatory tower. The staircase collapsed, and now we can't get down."

Oliver said nothing for a moment. "Can't you use some rope to climb down?" he asked indignantly.

"No, we left our packs in the map room below."

When Oliver spoke again, he sounded very annoyed. "Mason and I will be there as soon as we can. Make sure your homing signal is on."

"Hurry, Oliver!"

"We will," Oliver assured her.

Tiffany looked up through the open dome roof. She could see only ominous clouds passing over the tower. The storm had come, and so had the Übel.

2.15

Rescue

"They're here, Mason. We have to run!" Oliver shouted to his brother and waved for him to pick up his pace as they sprinted down the path they'd previously created. Although they'd had no time to recover from their ascent or descent of the ziggurat, they'd have to run.

"I know. I could hear Tiffany shouting," Mason said, trying to keep up with Oliver. "What are we going to do?"

"I've got the grappling launcher and an extra hook canister in my pack. It'll do the trick," Oliver called over his shoulder. His mTalk light bounced all over the path ahead as he ran.

"No, I mean about the Übel. How are we going to rescue Mom and Dad and avoid capture?" Mason asked. Thunder roared as if at the mention of the evil band of soldiers.

"I don't know yet," admitted Oliver. "We'll put together a plan tonight, but now we have to rescue our sister and brother."

Oliver ducked to avoid a low-hanging branch they had missed cutting down previously. For the most part, the path was easier to travel, since they'd blazed it on their way to the ziggurat, but several rogue branches and roots remained.

Oliver felt an odd sense of invigoration; he was in crisis mode. Sure, they'd been on a rescue mission all along, but this one seemed more tangible. The Übel were there, and his sister and brother were stuck. The adrenaline coursed through his veins like electricity. It was like he'd just chugged two Energen drinks in under ten seconds flat.

The light from their mTalks bounced across the stone path and against the lush green foliage as they ran. The low growl of the overhead storm echoed through the woods.

Oliver stopped and looked into the darkness of the shrouded jungle. He heard the noise again, but this time he realized it wasn't thunder. The leaves moved. Something was coming toward them, hidden by the cover of the foliage.

Mason stopped too. "Oliver, did you see that?"

Oliver started back toward his brother. "Stand still." "The leaves. They're moving." Mason started to slip the Zapp-It free from its holster.

"I know." Oliver squinted to get a better look.

Without warning, a large, furry, black creature leapt from the woods, taking Mason to the ground.

A split second passed as Oliver took in the scene. *What in the world?*

Mason's right hand pressed against the front of the beast's throat, his left hand against its eyes and nose, holding it off as best he could. It snarled at him and threw its head to the left and then to the right in an attempt to disarm Mason's only defense.

Without time to think, Oliver hurled himself at the creature. He wrapped his arms around the beast's midsection and pulled. It was too heavy. It wouldn't budge.

"Help! Get it off me!" cried Mason.

The Zapp-It lay a few feet away, having been knocked free of Mason's hand. Oliver released his hold on the beast and scrambled for the weapon, grabbed it, and pressed the charge button. Only a second passed for it to energize, and Oliver jammed it against the side of the black thing. It howled in pained surprise and jumped a foot into the air, landing off to

Mason's side. Then, with an angry growl, it sprinted off into the woods, disappearing as quickly as it had come.

Mason lay on the ground, trembling with fright. Oliver helped him to sit up. The twin rolled back his sleeves to reveal bloody elbows. There was a scrape on his cheek where the cat had swiped him in the struggle.

Oliver squatted beside his little brother. "Are you all right?" he asked, looking over Mason's arms and legs.

In a shaky voice, Mason replied, "I think so. Oliver, what was that?"

"I'm not sure."

"Is it gone?"

Oliver scanned their immediate proximity, the path, and then the woods. He should have done it first. He'd been trained at the Academy to check surroundings before attending to victims. Why had he been so negligent? He could have been blindsided by another attack, and then they'd both be dead.

"I think it is for now. The electric shock startled it, and the beast ran off." He looked in the direction that the creature had escaped. "But we shouldn't stick around here. Do you think you can walk?" he asked with slight urgency.

"I think so. It didn't get my legs."

Oliver stood and pulled his little brother to his feet, holding his arm until he seemed stable.

"I'm fine," Mason said and then held his elbows out in front of him and grimaced. "Ouch. These sting, though."

"We'll get you patched up as soon as we get back to camp," Oliver said sympathetically.

"But first we have to save Tiffany and Austin," Mason reminded him.

"That's right," Oliver said and looked at the mTalk on his wrist. He activated the LOCATOR app, and a small blip appeared on the mTalk's screen, marking Tiffany's location. "Can you run?"

"I believe so," Mason responded through gritted teeth.

"All right, let's go," Oliver said, and the brothers dashed forward.

They ran toward their siblings, but with caution in their every step. Not only were the Übel going to be there soon, but vines were out to snag them and dark creatures were now lurking in the jungle, hunting them.

After several more moments, they arrived at the ziggurat designated as their base camp, and Oliver stopped. "Do you want to wait here?" he asked Mason. A light sprinkle of rain had begun to fall, moistening the stone pavers around the tiered tower.

"No. I'm all right. I want to help," Mason said bravely.

Oliver smiled and they took off down the path toward Tiffany and Austin. This path was relatively clear of branches and vines, allowing the boys to run full speed without the fear of tripping. Austin had done a decent job of clearing it.

As they neared the blip representing their sister and brother, they passed several small, collapsed buildings that testified to the age of the city. The signal from Tiffany's mTalk revealed their location to be just ahead. The jungle cleared, and a grand building stood before him. The domed tower was spotlighted by a flash of lighting in the distance, as if marking Tiffany and Austin's location.

"They're here, Mason," Oliver said as they ran across the large plaza and through the open doorway. The room they entered was brightly lit by the glow of lamps and overhead lights.

"There's electricity?" Mason asked.

"I guess," Oliver said, paying little attention to the fact. He was on a mission. He looked down at the mTalk. "All right, we have to find the entrance to the tower."

Oliver led Mason up the stairs and down the hall. An open door required a quick peek to see if it was the entrance to the tower. What they found was the star map room, still marked by Tiffany and Austin's packs as well as several unrolled maps.

"They're not here," Oliver said and started back along the hallway.

"Wait, what's that?" asked Mason as he pointed back into the room.

Oliver looked in and saw a pentagonal table. A dim yellow light blinked on its side. He stepped forward and pressed it. A three-dimensional image glowed to life, hovering above the table's surface. Mason joined Oliver in the room.

"It's a hologram display," said Oliver matter-of-factly.

"It looks like it's an image of the basin. Those are the ziggurats, and this is the building we're in," Mason said, pointing at the glowing images. "What's that red blip floating over there?"

Oliver watched it suspiciously as it circled over the basin and then lowered to the ground near the largest ziggurat. "I think it landed."

"The Übel?" suggested Mason.

"Tiffany, Austin!" Oliver remembered with a shout. A rip of thunder echoed through the building in response.

The entrance to the tower was near. The air in the hallway grew thick with dust, making it harder to breathe the closer they got. The hallway ended at an entryway. Oliver looked through the opening. The tower was dark, and unlike the foyer, there were no lights to be seen. There on the second story of the main building, the remnants of the staircase had not blocked the hallway to the tower. Instead, they filled most of the ground floor below in a jumble of splintered planks and light sconces.

A flash of lightning glowed through several windows that lined the walls in an upward spiral. Oliver's gaze fell on a small circle of light cast from a hole high above. "This is it."

Mason stepped forward and looked up. "Austin!" His voice echoed off the walls and up the tower.

"Tiffany, are you guys up there?" Oliver called.

Austin's head popped through the hole in the ceiling above. "Yes, we're here," he said. "What took you so long?"

Mason looked at Oliver. "We were attacked by something."

"What?" cried Austin.

"Don't know. A big black beast jumped out of the woods and nearly ate me," Mason explained. "Like a cat or something."

Austin's eyes got big. "Wow! You were almost eaten alive?"

Tiffany's head suddenly popped into view. "Are you okay, Mason?"

"Yes, I'm fine now."

"Now's not the time; we need to get you guys down," Oliver called. "We haven't much—"

Tiffany cut him off. "But you're okay?" she asked Mason again.

"He's here, isn't he?" Austin said snidely.

"I'm fine," Mason replied, tucking his arms behind his back to hide his bloody elbows and quickly rolling his sleeves back down over the cuts.

Oliver cleared his throat and shouted. "Tiffany, you were right—the Übel are here."

"Did you see them?" Austin asked.

"Just on the hologram table in that map room," Oliver explained.

"The table in the star map room?" Tiffany's voice lifted in surprise.

"It must have been from turning the power on up here," Austin suggested.

"I didn't see anything when I was in there," Tiffany said.

"We had to push a button," Mason explained.

"We can discuss it later. It's time to get you down." Oliver pulled the grappling hook launcher from his pack. "Austin, I'm going to fire this grappling hook at the door. You and Tiffany get clear!" he commanded. "Once it's up there, take it and secure it to something bolted down. All right?"

"Okay."

Thunder rumbled and lightning filled the tower, followed by the sound of rain driving against the outside of the stone structure.

"Tell me when you and Tiffany are clear!"

Austin disappeared, and, a moment later, yelled back, his voice muffled. "We're clear!"

Oliver aimed the gun toward the trapdoor and pressed the trigger. The launcher gave off a soft *pfft*. The hook flew upward, trailing a long, grey wire behind. But Oliver had misjudged; the grapple smacked against the underside of the observatory floor and tumbled back down the empty tower past them to clank against the splintered remains of the staircase below.

He'd have to try again. Oliver pressed a little black button on the side of the gun, and the line started to zip back into the gadget. Abruptly, though, his arm jerked forward, and he nearly lost hold of the gun. He clicked the black button again, and the reeling stopped.

"What's wrong?" asked Mason.

"It must be stuck down there," Oliver said. He took some of the unreeled wire in his hand and started to yank. There was a clatter below, but the hook wouldn't come loose. He tried again, but he couldn't free the grapple. Mason tried to help by pulling the line, but gave up in frustration.

"I guess I'll have to climb down," Oliver said. He pressed another button, and the wire released from the canister. As he stalked down the hall, looking for a place to anchor the wire, he heard Austin call down to them.

"What's taking so long? We're getting wet up here."

Still at the tower entrance, Mason responded. "The hook is caught on the rubble below. Oliver's going to free it."

"Okay, I'm going to shut the dome! We're getting drenched." Austin disappeared and, a moment later, the sound of mechanical gears grinding reverberated above. The tower seemed to shake under the stress as well.

Oliver found a metal grate in the floor a quarter of the way down the hall. He tugged on the vent with all his might to ensure it was concretely embedded in the stone floor. It was. The launching gun would not fit between the bars of the grate, so he had to release the rest of the wire, nearly fifty more feet.

A few minutes passed as he wove the wire between the bars. As he did, he thought he heard a growling in the vent. He immediately thought of the beast that he and Mason had encountered on their way to the observatory. He took a deep breath, reminding himself to deal with one thing at a time. Right now, he had to rappel down the tower and retrieve the hook.

Finishing with the wire, he gave the line several hard tugs, then started back for the tower.

"Mason, I want you to stand on the grate where the wire is anchored. Your weight will ensure that it won't come loose," he explained. Mason obeyed. Oliver shouted back up at Austin, whose wet, shaggy head appeared in response. "It'll just be a few more minutes," he called.

Austin disappeared, and Oliver lowered himself to the ground and swung his legs over the edge of the landing. Gripping the wire with his hands, he started to climb down toward the splintery rubble below. It didn't take him long to descend the wall. He'd rappelled many times at the Academy, but this time he took the added care to avoid getting skewered by the sharply fractured planks.

Something wet landed on his head. He looked up and saw a small stream of water dripping through the opening in the ceiling high above—a consequence of the rain that had poured in through the open dome.

Oliver shook his head and gave the hook a firm yank. It jerked free, and he started back for the wall. It was then he saw another metal door tucked into the stone tower wall. Situated where it was, it would have been hidden from view under the stairway landing. But now, with the stairs gone, the door stood exposed. It drew him like a moth to light.

Oliver made his way through the debris to the door, but as with the rest, there was no handle. He slid his hand across its surface and, without waiting to see if anything would light up, he swept his hands across the area of stone wall on either side of the door. Nothing happened. A small cross-shaped indentation next to the door caught his attention. He looked at it closely and coursed the indentation with his index finger. Still no lights or opened door.

The difference in access spiked his curiosity. Maybe Austin could do as he'd done at the ground-level entrance to the ziggurat and override the door.

Speaking of Austin—"Oliver! Would you hurry it up?" Austin shouted down from the top of the tower.

The uncovered door was a mystery, but with no time to waste on exploring dead ends, Oliver hastily returned to the wall. It was time to focus. The dread of Übel soldiers swarming the basin, and a fleeting thought of their captain's sneering face, fueled his resolve. He slung the extra wire over his shoulder and used the anchored end to pull himself back up the tower wall. A swift wet breeze hit him in the side, and he looked over to see a large window, the glass shattered by one of the planks. It didn't deter him, though, and he finished his ascent, crossing over the threshold.

"Mason, start freeing the line from the grate," he commanded.

Mason went to work as Oliver started toward him. Suddenly the younger Wikk jumped backward away from the grate.

"What's wrong?" Oliver asked. The wire was nearly free, but Mason had abruptly stopped.

"There's something down there." Mason's voice was shaky as he spoke.

Oliver raced the last fifteen feet to him. "Was it like a growl?" he asked.

Mason nodded.

"I heard it earlier too."

"Do you think it's those things?" Mason asked.

"I don't know." Oliver pulled the last few feet of the rope clear of the floor grate.

Mason's back was to the wall, and he was touching his elbows gingerly at the memory.

"It'll be fine, Mason. Those things won't mess with us again." But Oliver wasn't one hundred percent convinced by his own words. "We need to get Tiff and Aus down."

Mason nodded.

Oliver reattached the wire to the holding canister, then hooked the canister back to the grappling gun. Once the line had been reeled back in, it was time to make a second attempt at freeing their sister and brother.

"Stand back, here it comes!" he called up to Austin and Tiffany.

This time, Oliver took his time lining up the shot. When he was sure he was on target, he pressed the trigger and the hook flew through the air. It sailed into the opening, and he heard footsteps above him as Austin and Tiffany dashed for it.

A second later, Tiffany called down, "We've got it. Austin is hooking it to the telescope."

The steady drum of rain had replaced the rolls of thunder and now created a lulling background noise. However, it did nothing to lower the tension.

"Good. Now you'll need to climb down. Do you still have those clips I gave you earlier?" he called up.

"Yes, I have mine," Tiffany yelled back.

"Mine too. It's still clipped to my belt loop," Austin explained.

"Okay, hook them on. They won't help your descent, but they will stop you from freefalling," Oliver explained.

The climb down would be the dangerous part; with no harness and just a clip holding them to the wire, Tiffany and Austin would have to rely on their hands. As the wire was thin, there wouldn't be a lot of area to grip. Any sweat would make it slick.

Tiffany stepped away, and Oliver heard his sister and brother having a muffled conversation. Austin appeared a moment later. "Can you feed us a little more wire?" he asked.

"Sure," Oliver said and released the remaining segment of wire. "That's the last of it."

"It'll be enough," Austin said and then disappeared again.

Oliver and Mason heard several laughs and even an "Ouch!" before they saw their sister at the opening again. Tiffany swung her legs into the tower and took hold of the wire, which Oliver saw had been run up through her pant leg and out the collar of her shirt.

The plan to use their clothes in conjunction with the safety clip was just the sort of resourceful ingeniousness that Austin would come up with.

Oliver secured the other end of the wire to the grate in the hall. "All ready!" he called, and then the descent began.

After an intense few minutes, Tiffany had climbed all the way down the wire and joined Oliver and Mason. She hadn't slipped a single time; the plan had worked.

"All clear!" Mason shouted up to his brother.

Austin had been watching his sister's descent and now disappeared, obviously stringing the wire through his own clothes.

When he returned, he was ready to make the descent. He held his tool pouch in his hands.

"I'm going to send this down first. Watch out." Austin had run the wire through the pouch and let it go. It zipped toward the kids and landed on the stone floor of the hallway.

"Glad that's not how I came down," Tiffany said.

"Did you want to break your stuff?" Oliver scolded up at Austin.

Austin glared. "No. Watch out, I'm next," he warned.

"Take your time," Tiffany called back up.

As Austin began to descend, Oliver headed back to the map room to look at the hologram table. He had to see how much time they had. The red blip still glowed, parked behind the largest ziggurat to the south. He could imagine the Übel soldiers sprinting out from the ship's lowered landing plank like a horde of hungry black scorpions. The men would secure a perimeter and then either immediately begin their quest or set up a base camp. Oliver hoped they'd do the latter; he needed more time.

He assumed Vedrik and a few of his top men would be guarding Mr. and Mrs. Wikk, making it difficult, but not impossible, to rescue them.

A howl of terror caught Oliver's ear, and he darted back down the hall as the yelling continued. Tiffany and Mason were reeling backward from the opening. A second later, Austin flew through the opening attached only by the clip, like someone riding a zip line, but uncontrolled. Oliver barely had time to take in the scene before his body became a crash pad for Austin. The oldest and youngest Wikk melded into a tangled human ball as they rolled backward down the hallway.

A moment later, Tiffany and Mason were at their side, helping to untangle the boys and assess the damage.

Austin had a few new scrapes on his arm and the same knee that'd been hurt during the descent to Jahr des Eises was bleeding again. His clothes were in worse shape. It was time for yet another set. Instead of being wet, his shirt now hung like a rag on one shoulder, a slit down one side. Austin held his pants up with one hand; the entire left leg was sliced down the seam where it'd briefly ridden the wire. The clip had been the only thing to keep him from plummeting the four stories to the shamble of the staircase below.

Oliver had fared only slightly better; both his elbows were scraped and bleeding, and he was trying to catch the breath that had been knocked out of his lungs at impact.

Tiffany had already retrieved a small medical kit from her pack and was wiping clean Austin's wounds. Once done with her younger brother, she switched to Oliver, dabbing some sort of salve on each elbow.

"Thanks for stopping me," Austin said to Oliver, half teasing.

"No problem," Oliver grumbled. "What happened?"

"Some water started dripping down from the trapdoor. Quite a bit of rain had come in before I shut the dome," Austin admitted. "Anyhow, the water made the wire too slick for my palms and fingers. If I hadn't . . . I mean . . . the clip was the only thing that saved me."

Mason handed his brother the tool belt that had preceded Austin. "Here you go."

"Thanks," Austin said as he slipped it into his belt loops and used it to keep his pants up. "That works." He next took some sort of fastener from his pouch and stapled a few spots of his shirt to hold it onto him.

"Nice," Mason teased.

"Oliver, what should we do with the wire? It's secured rather tightly to the telescope," Austin explained.

"We'll have to leave it. We have extra cartridges of wire in the *Phoenix*," Oliver said.

"But won't the Übel see it and know we've been here?" Tiffany asked.

"They might, but we don't have much choice. We'll at least untie the wire from the grate and leave it hanging freely in the tower." Oliver went to work loosening the knot of wire from the grate. "It'll be less noticeable then."

"What about the electricity?" Mason asked.

"There's power in the city; we know that from all the doors and stones. So I don't think it'll create that much suspicion pointing to us."

Oliver pulled up the last bit of wire and walked to the end of the passageway, letting it fall freely away. He wanted to be sure the next person having to use that line would have to work hard for it.

A growl echoed up from the bottom of the tower. Oliver squinted; he could see the shadowy outline of a cat. Then a second leaped through the broken window. The beast, or beasts, was back!

"Run!" he yelled. His siblings flinched but looked confused at his outburst. "The creatures! They're here!"

Tracked

The kids hurried down the stairs and out of the observatory in silence. The rain was just a drizzle now, but its scent was still strong. The sound of thunder rumbled in the distance; the storm was leaving. Wet leaves splashed the water they held onto the kids as they disturbed them in their escape.

They ran toward the ziggurat, lights off. The darkness of the jungle canopy and remaining storm clouds made it nearly impossible to see the way. Oliver remained ever vigilant to the possibility of one of the black creatures leaping out at them. He recalled that you weren't supposed to run from animals, but it was too late to stop now. These things had attacked before, and he'd seen at least two in the observatory. If they were after the kids, standing their ground or running would be the same to the creatures.

Now the beasts could be anywhere. He was also unsure how far into the basin the Übel might have advanced already, or if they had patrols in the sky. The dangers were growing every moment, and he was beginning to feel out of control.

The pace didn't let up until they were at their base camp in the original ziggurat. Oliver ushered everyone in. A quick second look around the exterior of the ziggurat revealed the area to be clear. He stepped into the stone structure.

"Austin, can you close the door?" Oliver asked. His brother had been the one to open it; now he hoped he could close it too.

"Right away." Austin climbed up the pillar like a monkey, seemingly unrestrained by the injuries of his crash. Using tools from his utility belt, he went to work. Oliver remained just inside the threshold, watching. Mason was right behind him with the Zapp-It out and charged.

The metal door lowered with painful creaking and a *thunk* as it locked into place.

"So where were the Übel?" Austin asked.

"The hologram table showed them near the southernmost ziggurat," Mason replied anxiously.

Austin looked apprehensive at the confirmation of the Übel landing. He was standing with Mason near a table in the center of the room.

Oliver started to pull a couple pieces of furniture toward the door. "Come on, we need to block the entrance." Austin and Mason ran over and helped Oliver gather the rickety furniture. "If somebody tries to enter, I want enough warning for us to climb those stairs," Oliver said as he pushed the furniture firmly against the door.

"I wondered if the table was some sort of holographic display," Austin said, nodding his head. "I just couldn't get it to turn on."

"It was on when we got there," Mason explained. "Well, Oliver had to press a button."

No one spoke for a moment. "The door won't withstand blasters," Oliver admitted. "But the furniture will act as an obstacle to slow them down."

"Oh, no!" whispered Austin.

"Austin, it's all right. I don't think—" Tiffany began to say.

"No, I'm not afraid of blasters," Austin interrupted, wide eyed. "Our packs," he said frantically.

Tiffany's expression showed confusion, then dawning dismay. "That's right, they're in the map room," she conceded. "And the e-journal is in my pack. If the Übel get a hold of that—" She gasped.

"They already have Dad and Mom," Mason chimed in. "They don't need the e-journal."

"True, they have Dad and Mom, but if they had the journal they might not have any more *use* for them," Austin said, drawing his finger across his neck.

"Austin, don't be morbid," Tiffany scolded. "I only meant there are a lot of valuable and secret bits of information in the journal. Besides, we need the information to continue our quest. Our journey would be far more difficult without it."

"Relax, everyone," Oliver broke in. This was a serious issue. He expected the Übel to suspect their presence, probably even find signs revealing the kids' trespass through the basin, what with the freshly hewn trails and wire in the tower. But the e-journal was the key to their mission. Many of their decisions had been made using information within the device. Now it sat unguarded in the observatory.

"Don't worry. I'll go get the packs and the e-journal," Oliver said as he walked back to the door and started removing the furniture. "Austin, can you open the door?"

Austin made his way back up the pillar to again override the door's mechanism as Mason and Tiffany helped Oliver clear enough furniture for him to get through.

As the door slid open, Austin hopped down. "I'm going with you," he said forcefully.

"No, it's too dangerous," Oliver said. "I trained for evasion at the Academy. It'll be easier for one person to sneak through the jungle than for two."

"But what if those creatures attack?" Austin asked. "You might need backup."

"Mason, Zapp-It!" Oliver called. Mason whipped out the self-defense weapon and flipped it to Oliver. "I have this."

"But—" Austin tried.

"My decision is final," Oliver said. Austin's shoulders dropped, and he sulked away. Oliver ignored him for the moment. "Tiffany, you'll still be able to track me on your mTalk."

Tiffany lifted her mTalk. "Yep, I've still got it loaded."

"I'll be back as soon as I can. You guys make some food and see if these books"—Oliver pointed at the shelves of books behind Tiffany and Mason—"have any valuable information in them." It was an obvious attempt to distract them, he knew. Oliver lowered his voice. "And Tiffany, try to get through to Austin somehow. He seems to have stepped back from his rebellion a bit. I'd hate for this to reignite it."

Tiffany gave a quick glance at Austin, then nodded to Mason. "We'll do our best."

"Besides, he needs to close the door and lock us inside," Mason added.

Oliver pulled on the straps to his pack, tightening them. "Tiffany, I just want to add that Mason was key to discovering the next step on our path." He gave Mason a thumbs-up. "He's the one who deciphered a riddle inscription that suggested the pool was the path to whatever it is we're looking for."

"Really?" Tiffany asked proudly. Mason blushed.

"Yep." Oliver lifted his mTalk. "I'm sending you the pictures of the inscriptions. The one from the top of, and the one you found in front of, the ziggurat. You and Tiffany should discuss them."

Oliver tapped his screen and Mason's mTalk lit up. "Received."

"Also, Mason made a connection between the ruby-lined cross-shaped pool and the rubies Mom and Dad found at the castle," Oliver explained.

"Cool," Tiffany said.

A distant rumble of thunder echoed outside. It was time to get going, but Oliver had felt it necessary to give Tiffany these last bits of information, just in case. He swallowed involuntarily.

"I'm off." He began to turn, but Mason lunged forward and wrapped his arms around his older brother in a hug.

"Thanks."

Oliver hadn't expected that, and it took him a moment to embrace his little brother back. Tiffany quickly crossed the room to join in the embrace.

After a moment, Oliver pulled away. "Don't open the door for anyone. When I return, only open the door if I say, 'the *Phoenix* has landed.' Can you remember that?"

Tiffany and Mason nodded.

"Only if I say that phrase. Just because it's my voice and my homing signal shows me outside doesn't mean it's safe for you to open the door. Or that it's me, for that matter," Oliver explained. His point was clear, and he knew Tiffany and Mason understood.

"The *Phoenix* has landed," Mason repeated

"If anyone comes here other than me, don't ask any questions—just run to the top of the ziggurat and get to the ship. Then call Archeos," Oliver commanded sternly.

"Archeos? But we aren't—" Tiffany started.

"It's a last resort, sis," Oliver said. "Now I've got to go."

"One last thing," Tiffany said. "Call us when you get there, so we know you're still safe."

Oliver nodded, waved goodbye, and left through the open door. He started down the clear path, and then thought better of it and ducked into the cover of the underbrush. It would be more difficult, but it would make him harder to spot.

As Oliver snaked his way through the still-wet vines and leaves, his clothes wicked most of the water away, but his hair and exposed arms became damp. Even without the looming storm clouds, it had now grown so dark that Oliver could hardly see ahead of him. He chose to turn his mTalk light on, but no higher than the lowest setting. He hoped the thick foliage would cloak him and the light.

He carefully listened for any noise that might be a sign of the soldiers, but he heard none. Instead, he was disturbed by the growling noise he heard somewhere to his left. The creature was near, but he had to persist. The beast probably wanted its revenge on the one who'd shocked it literally and figuratively. Oliver slipped the Zapp-It from his pocket, ready to defend himself. He continued to climb over and under branches as needed.

His body involuntarily jerked as he heard another growl ahead of him. At least two beasts, if not more, stalked him, because this time the noise had come on his right. Oliver walked steadily and looked down at his mTalk. A few hundred feet and he'd be at the courtyard again.

A growl on his left.

Closer.

No, above him. In the branches.

Oliver looked up. The branches were moving, but he couldn't see any creatures.

A few more steps and he'd be in the open. Again he wanted to run for the building, but he knew that was the worst thing someone could do when being stalked by a wild animal. Or, in his case, animals. They hadn't attacked yet, so he decided to try the walking-away strategy.

At the tree line, Oliver turned and backed away from the foliage, raising his hands high over his head to appear bigger than he was. He jumped as he saw the glowing yellow eyes of a creature in the darkness. He backed closer toward the door. The thing-in-the-woods' eyes blinked several times, but it didn't move.

As Oliver looked around he noticed more eyes—five sets, as well as a single glowing eye. Moonbeams broke through the overhead clouds and lit sections of the courtyard, but also added a surreal glow to his surroundings.

Oliver bumped against the stone wall of the observatory and slid his arm behind him to feel his way through the still-open doors. He darted in. How was he to close it? Tiffany had never explained how they'd opened it in the first place.

His eyes quickly caught the glowing green stones next to the door. He swiped his hand down the vertical strip, then across the horizontal one. The lights dimmed and flashed to blue, then turned red as the doors slipped closed. Just as the gap between them narrowed, he caught the glimpse of a black figure bounding toward him. Two glowing eyes locked on their target. He heard the thump as something crashed into the metal outside, followed by an almost mournful-sounding howl. Whatever it was had either gotten hurt or was severely disappointed in not getting dinner.

The red stones were no longer glowing, and they now matched the color of the surrounding wall. Without knowing what to look for, a person might miss the access stones altogether.

It was time for Oliver to get those packs and the e-journal, now that he was free of the creatures for the moment and had reached his destination. He ran to the star map room to get the packs. The hologram table was still on. The red dot representing the Übel ship still sat behind the southern ziggurat.

Then he noticed a screen glowing on one side of the table. He touched the left arrow button, and a message came into view: "Unknown craft has entered the area."

Below the message were several statistics about the ship, surprisingly detailed for not having a direct data link with the ship. He noticed estimations of the ship's speed, dimensions, and origin. Realizing that this was valuable data, he entered it into his mTalk. He pressed the left arrow button again, and a new message appeared. "The keep has been accessed. 691-5691-691-7582." The message was clear, but the following number made no sense. Was it an ID assigned to the trespasser? Clearly a high-tech and powerful security surveillance system monitored the basin. The system had probably assigned the number to whatever Übel soldier had broken into this place.

Oliver tapped the left arrow again.

"West ziggurat accessed. XXX-XXXX-XXX-XXXX." Why was the ID number a series of Xs instead of numerals? The west ziggurat had been the one he, his sister, and brothers had entered. They clearly had set off the security notifications there and in the observatory, but why had they not been assigned a number like the soldier? Oliver shrugged; at the moment, it wasn't exactly important.

He tapped the left arrow again.

"Observatory accessed. XXX-XXXX-XXX-XXXX. Observatory power activated."

Another arrow caught his attention, this one pointing up. He pressed it, and the display suddenly changed. The buildings disappeared and instead red, yellow, and green lines crisscrossed the map. Only one line was green, and it connected the west ziggurat to the observatory, exactly along the stone path Austin and Tiffany had cleared. Oliver figured the red and yellow must represent less traversable paths—ones that were still overgrown. It was the only explanation he could ascertain at the moment.

Oliver clicked the up arrow again, and a map of the water-works and buried power lines appeared. Again he tapped the button and more than a dozen red squares appeared on the sides of the ridge. Three marked areas where the ziggurat aqueducts attached. But there were at least twelve others. What might they represent?

He tapped the arrow again. The screen was now divided into over a hundred sectors. Several blinked red—one over the southern ziggurat, one over the western ziggurat, one over the observatory, as well as the ones linking the three sectors. The linking zones appeared to follow the paths the kids had taken when they split up to explore.

This was either good news or very bad. Either the Übel hadn't set out from their ship yet, or they were headed right down the path leading to the western ziggurat, the location where Tiffany and the twins were.

Oliver decided to try something else. He'd worked with holograms before, but how old was this one or its technology? He moved his hand through the holographic images and tapped the table in the segment that displayed the Übel's landing spot. The display blinked, and when the hologram reappeared, it was of only the area he had selected. He could clearly see the Übel ship and 3-D images of people walking around. The image was live. The people's features weren't clear enough to decipher who they were, but if he could zoom in just a bit closer . . . He tried tapping again; the display reverted to the entire basin. He tapped the segment once more and the hologram zoomed back in. Then he noticed small red boxes floating over each 3-D person.

Oliver moved his finger to a box, and the image grew. He could now clearly make out facial features on the subject. The first he selected wasn't his dad, his mom, or the evil captain. It was just a random soldier. Oliver could clearly make out his uniform, down to the skull patch on the man's sleeve.

The red box had now been joined by three others—blue, green, and yellow. He touched the red box, and the soldier shrank. The other people came back into view. There were several more soldiers, all in their black uniforms, just like the night they'd chased Oliver on Tragiws.

He noticed two men standing next to what looked like a domed tent. Could it be? Were they guarding something— his parents, or perhaps the captain? He zoomed in on the shelter and could just slightly see a figure inside the opening. The person's image was partially missing. Whatever device was creating the imagery wasn't at the right angle to see inside the tent. He knew there must be several devices in the area to create the 3-D display, but none had a clear shot into the tent.

"It's them!" he gasped aloud.

The figure leaned toward the ground; the unmistakable face of his dad, Elliot Wikk, came into view. No bruises as far as Oliver could see, no sign his dad had been hurt. That was good. Something caught in Oliver's throat, and his vision blurred. Tears welled in his eyes and ran down the side of his cheeks, but he quickly wiped them away.

If only he could see his mom. He waited a moment, hoping to catch a glimpse of her. He wanted to move the devices to get a better view, but he didn't see any controls for that.

Oliver's dad had sat up again, leaving only his legs in view. A moment later, a man approached the small domed tent. Oliver knew who it was immediately: Captain Vedrik! The ruthless Übel leader pulled aside the flap of the tent and, for half a second, Oliver saw his mom, Laura, sitting across from Mr. Wikk. Oliver saw her straighten as the captain entered. Oliver couldn't tell if their response was fear or surprise at the soldier's entrance. Maybe his dad and mom had been discussing their escape at that moment, and the captain had interrupted them.

Oliver was disappointed when the flap of the tent fell back into place. The captain reached out and pulled the other flap closed. Oliver could no longer see his parents.

But at least he knew they were okay and were on Evad, which meant they were close to him. If not for the darkness and the creatures stalking him, he might have made his way south in an attempt to see, or even free, his parents. Instead, he had to wait. It was time to complete the task at hand and get back to his siblings and tell them. Then they would plan their next move.

Oliver saw the packs and checked that the e-journal was indeed inside Tiffany's. It was. He'd acquired the package; his mission was halfway over.

"Tiffany, come in. I've got the e-journal," Oliver said. "And—"

"—Oliver, we read you," Tiffany interrupted.

"Tiffany, I saw them," Oliver said with excitement.

"The Übel? Are they close? Should we—"

Oliver cut her off, "No! Dad and Mom."

"Dad and Mom? You saw them? Where?" Tiffany asked in a rapid-fire sequence of questions.

"Not in person. They're at the Übel camp, but I saw them through the hologram table," Oliver explained. "Yes, they are okay. At least, they don't look to be hurt or anything." Oliver's definition of *okay* was by now seriously skewed; it more or less meant "alive."

There was a moment of silence. "Oliver..." Tiffany sounded choked up. "We did it. We've made it to them."

Oliver hesitated. He wanted to tell her that they were far from rescuing them, but he didn't want to crush her hopes. "We're closer to them, that's for sure. Tiffany, it's going to be okay."

"I know," Tiffany whimpered.

"We'll make plans when I get back," Oliver offered.

"Wait a moment. We discovered something interesting. I'll let Mason explain."

"Oliver, it's Mason."

"I hear you," Oliver said.

"We found a book about the observatory," Mason began.

Oliver shook his head; he didn't have time for this. "Mason, can this wait until I get back?"

"No, you need to get something from the tower," Mason explained.

The tower? Didn't they realize that there were no longer any stairs leading up? "Mason, that's impossible."

"It's not," Mason said. "You can use the wire. Didn't you have to rope climb at the Academy or something?" It came across as a challenge.

"Well, sure, but—"

"Oliver, it's important."

"At least hear us out," Tiffany interjected.

"Fine."

Mason came on again. "The telescope is also a communications transponder. It has the ability to send signals to an uplink satellite that orbits Evad."

"Wow, you guys work quickly if you've already read all this."

"We make a good team," Mason said. "We found it in a section of public works books. Apparently, this ziggurat might have functioned like a city hall or something, not so much a library."

"Anyway," Tiffany interrupted. "Back to the communications transponder."

"Tiffany and I suspect there might have been other cities or colonies that these people communicated with. Some settlements might have been newer, but some might have been older."

This wasn't making a lot of sense yet. Did they want him to try and call one of these places? The likelihood that the satellite was still in orbit was slim. Without that, there was no way the communication was going to go anywhere but into deep space.

"I highly doubt the network is operational anymore," he said.

"We agree," Mason said. "But according to this schematic, there should be some sort of recorder that logged the conversations, as well as some sort of designation of the other locations."

Oliver nodded; that could be very valuable information. "How big is this thing?"

"Not big at all. As big as the e-journal at most," Mason said.

"Does this book say that, or are you making your best guess?"

"Best guess, but we can't let the Übel get it," Tiffany interjected. "If they're intelligent at all, they'll be trying to collect that sort of thing."

Oliver sighed. "Might there be a book that talks about the other locations, if there is one about the observatory?"

"Oliver, sure," Tiffany said. "But this is what we know now."

"Fair enough." He had to at least try for it. "Okay, I'll do it."

He slung his pack off his shoulder, but removed an extra clip to secure himself to the wire. His pack now joined the two he'd come to rescue in the first place. "I'll be back."

Oliver found the tower just as they'd left it. The wire used to rescue Tiffany and Austin hung limply in the open tower, like a dead snake. Now he had to figure out how to get to it without hurting himself. He'd let the wire swing to the center of the tower in an attempt to make it difficult for the next person to use the line. He hadn't expected that person to be him.

There was a good distance from the base of the passage to the rubble-strewn floor of the tower. There was no way he could drop down and avoid injury; he would have to find another way. Since they'd not been back to the *Phoenix*, he hadn't replenished his supply of wire canisters for the grappling hook. Why he'd only brought two in the first place was beyond him.

Oliver marched back to the map room, but there was nothing he could use. He started to open other doors in the hall, hoping to find something long that he could stretch out and snag the wire with. Most of the rooms appeared to be private studies with desks and tables. Maybe the observatory had been like a school too, and these rooms belonged to the professors. That's how it had been at Bewaldeter, before he'd transferred to the Academy.

Nearly ready to give up, Oliver took a seat in a desk chair in one of the studies. He'd either have to make a running leap at the wire or turn back and not retrieve the recorder.

As he sat thinking, something peculiar about one of the bookshelves caught his eye. The case leaned forward at an odd angle, and the majority of its contents had fallen to the ground in front of it. After a closer inspection, he discovered a dark passage behind the bookshelf. Oliver wrenched the shelf forward, creating a space large enough to shimmy through.

For a moment, he struggled with himself. He wanted to explore, but he also needed to retrieve the information and get back to his siblings. But then a realization occurred to him. He remembered the door at the base of the tower. What if this passage led to it? If it did, he would be able to easily access the wire and climb up through the trapdoor into the observatory tower.

With his mTalk light on, Oliver started down the tunnel. There were light fixtures on the wall, but none were lit. This was odd considering everything else in the building seemed to have power running to it.

The air of the tunnel was rank with a musty smell and felt cool on Oliver's exposed skin. Several times, he had to keep himself from sneezing. The floor of the passage began to slant down and then cut into a series of stairs.

A growl echoed somewhere ahead, and Oliver felt for the Zapp-It. He held it before him and charged it. He was ready.

As he reached the bottom of the stairs, Oliver found himself at a *T*. There were two options, but he could only take one. He tried to remember which direction the tower had been in when he'd entered the study above, and then recalled his steps and the direction of the tunnel. He was fairly confident he needed to go left.

Just a few minutes later, Oliver arrived at a door. It didn't open, and there was no red or green illuminated stone overhead. Instead, next to the door was the same cross-shaped indentation he'd seen on the very door he was trying to find. Not a push, shoulder, or kick made the door budge. It was odd that some doors in the basin had these indents while others did not and seemed to be easy to activate by tapping the correct stones. He wondered what the logic was behind these mysterious differences. What were the people hiding behind these doors? Why the extra level of security?

Oliver gave up on opening the door and headed back in the other direction. He passed the stairs and followed the tunnel until he came to another set of stairs. He followed them up and up until he found himself stepping out onto a balcony. But the balcony wasn't on a building. Instead, it protruded from the side of the ridge that surrounded the basin. The basin was dark, but he could see the shadowy silhouette of the observatory to the right and the most northern ziggurat to his left.

A soft light broke through some thinning clouds, and the jungle below glowed with an eerie orange hue. He inhaled a deep breath through his nose and smelled the fresh rain that had fallen and released the scents of the many flowers in the jungle. This place would be a paradise to live in with his family. They'd have everything they needed to survive, and there would be so much to explore and rebuild.

Reality hit him as a small blue orb sailed high into the air. The flare burst, illuminating the jungle below while reflecting off the clouds above. It had been fired from the other side of the pool. The Übel were wasting no time in their exploration, and it was time for Oliver to complete his mission. He sprinted back the way he'd come and turned left up the stairs to the study and observatory.

Having exhausted all other possibilities, he burst into the hall and headed for the tower. Once at the entrance, he made his decision. Forgetting about the locked door and the dangers, Oliver launched himself into the hollow cylindrical column and threw himself across to grasp the loose wire hanging down the far wall. He made it.

His adrenaline pumping, Oliver felt alive as he climbed the wire, hand over hand, until he reached the trapdoor.

Sore muscles and a sweat-soaked shirt were the reward for his efforts. It seemed now all the physical training at the Academy was coming in handy. He eased himself through the trapdoor opening and into the telescope room. The size and glory of the telescope was astounding. Maybe fifty feet tall, it looked ancient and from a mechanical age for sure. He circled it. It was really something to find. Oliver knew his parents had discovered a lot in the past, but it always seemed to be really, really old, boring stuff—nothing like the telescope in front of him.

Recalling his task, he looked around the room for the panel or computer that might record the data from the telescope. Several screens made it clear where he needed to be.

"Mason, come in. I think I found it," he said.

"Wow, we were getting worried," Mason said. "We didn't want to call, though. Just in case you were hiding or something."

"No, I'm fine. But I can't quite tell what it is I need to grab," Oliver admitted.

"Eject," Mason corrected. "Well, it should be . . ."

Silence for the moment, and Oliver knew that Mason was looking at the book.

"It should be to the right of the station. It'll be like a cylinder, so you should look for a circle. That's what the end will look like to you."

"I know how a cylinder is shaped," Oliver said.

He began looking and a second later found it. Next to a crystal-blue circle was a small button with an arrow. He knew it meant *Eject* and touched it. Something whirred in the machine, and Oliver stepped back. A moment later, the blue cylinder slid out of its place about an inch.

Oliver pulled it the rest of the way out and looked it over. The exterior of the cylinder was silver, but the inside was translucent. The blue had been from a light inside the recording machine.

"Okay, I got it," Oliver said into his mTalk.

"Great," Mason said. "And hey, Austin saw some sort of flash. It was similar to the flares the night the Übel attacked our house."

"I saw one too," Oliver said. "Wait, Austin is helping?" he asked cautiously.

There was a pause. "Not so much."

Then Oliver realized: to see the flash, Austin would have been outside or atop the ziggurat.

"Did he leave the ziggurat?"

"Let's just say he delayed shutting the door."

Oliver's cheeks burned, and he grunted. "Tell him . . ." Oliver sighed; there was nothing he could do at the moment. It would have to wait. "I'm on my way back."

"Tell him you're on your way back?" Mason confirmed.

"No, I mean, I'm coming. Don't tell him anything for the moment."

"Roger. We'll see you soon."

"Over and out." Oliver sighed.

As he lowered his mTalk, he had another idea. Why not shut off the lights to the observatory? If the Übel came across this building, he didn't want them to have access to the same information he had on the hologram table. It might give them the kids' location.

Oliver spotted a grey fuse box. He flicked a red switch off and then switched all the black switches too. The lights in the room dropped, and Oliver activated the beam on his mTalk. The room was silent; there was no longer the dull hum of electricity pulsing through the breaker and wires.

He shone his light up at the telescope again. If only he'd had some time to actually look through it. But he recalled the recent flare he'd seen in the night sky. The Übel were out there, and they were searching.

Oliver walked to the trapdoor. He slipped the cylinder into his pants pocket and heard it clank against something. *The clip.* He put his hand to his head—he'd climbed all that way without locking himself to the wire, a really mindless and risky thing to do.

He attached the clip to himself and then to the wire. The descent went far quicker than the climb up. When he was level with the entry from the hall to the tower, he began to shift his body and swing the wire like a pendulum. It took him several minutes to swing fast enough and in a long enough arc to reach the threshold of the entryway. Once he was close enough, he let go and flew into the tunnel.

His feet were nimble, and he didn't trip but continued in a fluid run toward the star map room. Once there, he slipped the cylindrical memory storage into his pack and gathered up Tiffany and Austin's. The hologram table was indeed off. At least this would make the Übel's task of finding the kids that much more difficult. It'd been nice to see his parents through it, though. The thought made him want to make a beeline for them, but he knew he had to get back. Tiffany and the twins needed his protection and leadership. He could not risk being captured.

With three packs precariously shouldered, he dashed for the exit. As Oliver approached the main foyer of the observatory, he heard an unexpected noise. It sounded like purring. Then he heard something fall to the ground. Oliver crept to the end of the hall and looked out from behind one of the pillars on the balcony.

He stepped back in shock at what he saw. In that brief moment, he'd glimpsed a huge black cat lying in the middle of the floor with four little cat creatures feeding.

Oliver peeked into the room again. Several books had fallen to the floor. Two more of the small cat creatures were prowling along the tops of the bookshelves. A second large one prowled back and forth around the mother, sniffing the air.

Oliver stealthily retreated behind the pillar, barely allowing himself to breathe. What he really needed now was a cloaking device that would conceal the noticeably strong smell of sweat and dirt clinging to his shirt. He definitely needed a bath. But, at the moment, he just needed to escape.

It was odd that the creatures hadn't tracked him further into the observatory. Why had they stayed out in the foyer?

2.17

Nostri Lux Lucis

Several piles of books surrounded Tiffany and Mason. They'd created stacks of books according to priority. The stack of "must reads" was, of course, tallest.

"I think you are right that there is a connection between the rubies from Dabnis Castle and the cross-shaped pool," admitted Tiffany.

Itching for a mission, Austin jumped at the opportunity. "You're right. We'll need to go and get them." It was the first time Austin had spoken to Tiffany and Mason since their most recent argument. Ignoring Tiffany's orders to stay inside and close the door, Austin had ventured just outside the door of the ziggurat to "survey the area." The blue flare had startled Austin into coming back inside. He'd agreed to close the door and had showed Mason which wires to touch together to either open or close it, saying he was tired of being a slave to them. Since then, he'd been whittling on a small piece of wood with his knife while drying his original clothes next to a small fire he'd built. Tiffany had decided against protesting open flames amid shelves of books and had ignored the acrid smell of the smoke. After all, the fire was small and hardly produced enough heat to dry the Ultra-Wear, much less catch the room on fire. In an effort to avoid argument, she remained silent; she just wanted to surround herself with books in peace. Even now, she'd heard his suggestion but chose to continue about her and Mason's research.

"I believe the place that we're looking for is deep in the pool. If you think about two of the clues at Dabnis Castle, they were both hidden deep underground. And the inscription at the southern ziggurat said, 'When you find the Truth, you are no longer lost. At the foot of the cross, your path home begins. Dive into the Truth, so you too may find the way,'" Mason read from his mTalk. "Diving would simply mean going down."

"That's a good point," Tiffany said. "And with rubies lining the pool and rubies being discovered at Dabnis Castle, it all makes sense. I wonder how the planks will be used." Tiffany glanced at her youngest brother. Austin was slowly putting things back into his tool pouch. She knew he was preparing to undertake the mission to the *Phoenix* to gather the needed artifacts.

"Do we have diving equipment?" asked Mason.

"I'm sure Mom and Dad have it packed in the cargo bay of the *Phoenix*," answered Tiffany. "I think Oliver may have mentioned something about it."

"I'm going to the ship to get it," Austin said confidently and turned to walk up the stairs, his extra set of clothes in hand.

"I don't think so. You're not going anywhere alone, and certainly not until Oliver gets back," Tiffany said sternly and got to her feet to face Austin.

"But if the Übel are here, time is scarce. We need to multitask," Austin said as he turned and scowled at his sister. "We can't wait on Oliver."

"No! I'm sorry, but it's just not safe," she added in a tone meant to end the conversation.

"Well, Oliver—" Austin began.

"Oliver is older, and he's gone through training at the Academy. He can handle himself," she said absolutely.

"I can too," defended Austin angrily.

"Doubtful," Tiffany said. As soon as the word came out, she knew she shouldn't have said it.

Austin looked like he was boiling inside. "Well, fine, I'm going to explore more of the ziggurat then," he said defiantly. "Just try to stop me!"

Tiffany started to shake her head, but Mason stood up beside her and held her shoulder.

Austin started for the stairs and then disappeared through the doorway. Tiffany trembled with anger.

"He'll be fine," Mason consoled her.

"It's not that. It's his behavior. It has to stop; he has to start being respectful."

Mason nodded. "You're right, but what can we do?"

A desperate sigh escaped Tiffany's lips. "Why can't he be more like you?"

Mason didn't speak. Other than looking somewhat similar, he and Austin had very little in common. "Why don't we discuss the clues and see if maybe we missed something? When Oliver comes back, it would be good to have a plan for him to react to."

Tiffany knew what her brother was trying to do, and she was more than willing to go along with it. She felt powerless against her other little brother, and, while that angered her, she accepted the temporary situation. She and Oliver would deal with it at the next opportunity they had, probably tonight.

"You're right," she said, and the two of them took a seat back on the floor.

"Do you think twelve is an important number?" asked Mason. "I mean, it's surfaced several times: twelve pillars, twelve rubies, twelve planks, and now twelve stones to activate these doors."

"Probably at one time the number represented something. But like so much else of history, it was lost over time."

"Kind of like the people who used to live in this basin or the castle and the reason why they eventually abandoned their homes? There must have been thousands of people living here, and they all just up and left?" asked Mason curiously.

"Answering those sorts of questions is exactly why Mom and Dad became archeologists. They wanted to discover the truth. Who were we as a society? Where did we come from? How were so many people spread throughout the universe, but seemingly disconnected from each other? Why do we follow certain 'ancient' laws, like the number of days in a year or hours in a day? Those were all questions that drove them to search further. Eventually, they asked the same question you did: why were so many former settlements seemingly needlessly abandoned? I wish we had that book. It must contain information about the people who lived here or at least about the destination the Übel seek," said Tiffany wishfully.

"Agreed. We might still find a copy of it here," suggested Mason with a smile. He got up and went to the bookshelf.

"Be careful," warned Tiffany, "They're very old."

Mason looked at her with a grin. "I'm not a baby. I've already gathered quite a few." He motioned to the piled surrounding his sister.

She laughed as he grabbed several volumes and walked back to her, setting the collection of books between them. Brushing aside his bangs, he picked one of the books up, then blew dust from its cover. He flipped the cover open, but almost instantly offered it to Tiffany. "You'll have to read this one. It's another one in some weird language."

"Yes, sure." She reached out her free hand, not taking her eyes from a large black book in her other hand. "This appears to be written in Latin. I only recognize the title as being Latin, because *nostri* means 'our people.' I don't recognize the first part: *lux lucis*," she said thoughtfully. "All right, well, I'll look through this one next." She referred to the book Mason had handed her.

The two of them were startled from their reading by a loud banging on the door. In an instant, Mason and his sister were on their feet standing next to each other.

"It must be the Übel," whispered Tiffany. "Quick, get our stuff, and let's go up the stairs."

Mason and Tiffany had started to gather everything when a voice came over the mTalk. "Tiffany, are you guys there?"

It was Oliver. "Let me in. I'm outside."

Tiffany and Mason approached the door.

"Wait!" commanded Mason. "The password."

Tiffany lifted the mTalk to her mouth. "Oliver, we need the pass phrase."

"The *Phoenix* has landed," came his reply.

"It's him," Mason said.

"Since Austin left, it's a good thing he showed you how to open it," Tiffany said. She spoke into her mTalk. "We're opening the door."

Mason climbed up the pillar and touched the end of two wires together. There was a small spark, and the door slid up. Oliver quickly stepped in.

"Close it quickly," he ordered. He set the extra packs against the wall as Mason touched the wires and the door closed.

The trio hastily moved the furniture back into place— something they'd not done when Oliver was gone.

"Is someone coming?" asked Tiffany as she took her pack. She slipped out the e-journal and looked it over as if becoming reacquainted with it.

Oliver nodded and looked at Mason. "You remember that cat thing?"

"Yeah, how could I forget?" Mason rubbed one of his elbows.

"There are more. I was trapped in the observatory by a family of them," Oliver explained.

"A family?"

"Yeah, there were eight in all. Two adults and six cubs," Oliver said.

"How'd you escape?" Mason asked.

Oliver laughed. "That's the great part. I remembered this old trick that Grandpa taught me." He smiled at his siblings. "I used the laser pointer on the mTalk to cause a distraction. I pointed it at a wall and began moving it in circles. Soon all eight cats were standing at the wall watching it. The little ones were all taking turns jumping for it." He grinned. "I moved the point across the wall and up the stairway and the cats followed after it. He held his arm over his head and stretched it out like he was pointing the laser. "When all eight were up on the balcony and out of sight, I ran for the window."

Oliver looked at Tiffany. "Unfortunately, I couldn't keep the laser steady as I jumped, so they figured out something was going on. One of them growled and came at me. I got through the window, though, and took off in a dead sprint back here. I kept checking behind me, but never saw or heard anything," Oliver finished, his eyes wide with excitement, his eyebrows raised.

"Whoa, that was close," Tiffany said. "But I suppose there really wasn't any other option."

"I can't believe there are more of them," Mason admitted, shaking his head.

"Yeah, and the one that jumped on you wasn't nearly as large as the male that roared at me," Oliver told Mason.

"Do you think they followed you?" asked Mason nervously.

"Like I said, I didn't hear anything more from them, but I'm not sure if they tracked me. I only ran because they were already after me. Stopping would have just made their hunt easier," Oliver said, looking back at the door. "That's not who I'm worried about, now that we know the Übel are exploring or searching."

"But the flare seemed to be far away," Mason suggested.

"The squad across the pool may not be the only exploration party. There may be another squad nearby," Oliver warned.

"But the door is secure enough to keep them out, right?" Mason asked.

"Not permanently," Oliver admitted. "To be safe, we'll camp higher up in the ziggurat."

"Should we just go back to the *Phoenix* tonight?" Mason asked. "After all, it's cloaked, and it's not here where the Übel are searching."

Tiffany shook her head. "I don't want to try to cross the aqueduct, trek through the tunnel, and then walk across that chasm again tonight. It's too dark. Besides, it's getting really late."

"Tiffany's right. We need to get some rest, and it's more dangerous to make that journey at night. We'd be risking it to use our lights, as we might be seen, and it's too dark to see without them," Oliver said.

"That makes sense," Mason said.

"Where is the memory from the transponder?" Mason asked.

"I put it in my pack." Oliver slipped the silver cylinder free and handed it to Mason.

"This is great," Mason said. "When we get back to the *Phoenix*, I'll figure out how to pull the data off it."

"So what of Mom and Dad?" Tiffany asked. "Are we going to rescue them?"

Oliver shook his head and cleared his throat. "Not yet. They're heavily guarded; we're going to need a good plan to rescue them. And that's going to require some scouting," he explained. "That's what we'll do tomorrow."

Oliver looked at Tiffany and Mason and then around the room. "Where's Austin?"

"He's exploring the ziggurat," Tiffany said with frustration.

"He never should have—" Oliver began.

"We know, but he wouldn't listen to Tiffany," Mason explained.

Oliver lifted his mTalk to call Austin, but Mason stopped his hand. "Remember, his got broken."

"That's right," Oliver said. His face had a red tint, and the tension in his words was clear. He was angry with Austin again. "Well, we'll just have to search the ziggurat. Mason, can you bring Austin's pack?"

"Sure."

The three of them searched every room that would open on their way up the staircase. As Tiffany and Mason had reported before, most were empty, but some had furniture and looked like living quarters. There were no personal effects like clothes or pictures, just beds, chairs, armoires, and desks. None of the doors had the indent Oliver had encountered in the observatory. He told Tiffany and Mason about it, but neither of them had come across anything regarding it yet. They only supposed the cross-shaped indent was a keyhole of some sort.

They found the torn clothes Austin had borrowed from Mason carelessly discarded on the stairs. Once every room had been searched, Oliver, Tiffany, and Mason stood in the pool room atop the ziggurat.

"Well, this is the last room. No Austin," Mason said as he casually cast the beam of his light across the metal boxes and pillars. Shadows stretched from floor to ceiling.

"I'll slip out on top of the ziggurat and see if he's there," Oliver said. "You two stay here. We'll risk being seen if we all go out. I'll stay close to the walls and in the shadows." Oliver disappeared through the door.

Mason and Tiffany watched the water flow into the room and then drain through the floor.

"Tiffany, do you think Dad and Mom miss us?" Mason asked his sister.

She smiled. "Of course they do. And we'll be with them soon."

"I wish we could go now." Mason said. "We know right where they are."

"Yes, but Oliver is right—it's too dangerous in the dark."

"Dangerous, but also advantageous," Mason suggested. "The Übel wouldn't know we were coming."

"We have to trust Oliver's instinct," Tiffany said.

A small squeak alerted Tiffany and Mason that something was in the room with them.

"What was that?" Mason asked, training his light on the pile from where the sound seemed to come.

Tiffany shook her head. "Probably a mouse or something else very small."

Oliver reentered the chamber, distracting them from the sound. "Well, I don't see him out there. I couldn't stay long with the moon full tonight and the top of the ziggurat bathed in orange light. In fact, the entire jungle is glowing, almost like it's on fire," he said. "Looks like the Übel have quite the camp set up. The glow from their lights was very bright as well. I'm sure they've created a very secure perimeter. One that I look forward to breaching."

"You really think you can?" asked Mason.

Oliver laughed with a confidence Mason and Tiffany hadn't heard for some time. "Yes, I do. These guys might be sophisticated, but that is also their weakness. They don't account for homegrown ingenuity and seem to have forgotten about rudimentary tactics."

"What do you mean?" asked Mason.

"I escaped Vedrik by climbing the charging cable in the garage and the soldiers in the woods on Tragiws by running across the log. Even the canyon chase with the star fighters resulted in a waterfall stopping an Übel pilot," Oliver explained, his voice carrying a slight arrogance.

"Got it," Mason admitted. "You did use what you had available."

"I'm just glad you saw Mom and Dad and that they were safe," Tiffany said.

"Yeah," Mason agreed. "It makes me feel better to know that."

"I only wish we knew where Austin was," Tiffany admitted.

"Well, I don't think we should search for him any further tonight," Oliver decided, his voice weary.

"But Oliver," Tiffany started, "Austin's out there, and he could be hurt or something."

Oliver shook his head. "I know, but we can't risk it. If the soldiers are out there searching, they're probably using night vision and we could walk right into them and be captured."

"But if he's hurt . . ." Tiffany began.

"We just can't; it'll be too hard to find him in the dark jungle," Oliver said. "For all we know, he might have gone back to the *Phoenix*."

"That's right!" Mason said. "He said he wanted to go back for the diving gear."

Oliver nodded. "Well, there you have it. He's probably in the *Phoenix* tucked in and asleep, which is what we should be doing."

"How can you be so nonchalant about this?" Tiffany asked. "He's our baby brother, and there are a lot of dangers out there. The creatures, the Übel, the chasm. . . . Who knows what else?"

"Yes, but I think he can take care of himself," Oliver admitted, and he actually sounded like he meant it. "He did escape from the Blauwe whatever with Mason."

Mason spoke up. "It's true, and he was very resourceful in doing so."

Tiffany sighed nervously. "Okay, if you both say so. I don't like it, but you're right—we don't have many more options tonight."

"We'll get some rest, and then I'll head to check the *Phoenix* in the morning," Oliver said.

"I need to go too," Tiffany said to Oliver's surprise. "I want to check something in the library and also on the NavCom of the *Phoenix*."

"Okay, we'll all go," Oliver said.

"What if he comes back while we're gone?" Mason asked. "Maybe I should stay here."

"Hmmm." Oliver nodded. "That's actually a good idea," he agreed.

"Sounds like a plan," Mason said and was surprised when Tiffany didn't argue.

Oliver, Tiffany, and Mason left the chamber where the aqueduct dumped water into the ziggurat and made their way to the nearest open bedroom. Tiffany took the bed, while Oliver and Mason rolled out bedding on the floor.

"I'm so tired. Don't you think it's odd that the soldiers are out searching at this late hour?" Mason asked.

"Unless, of course, they are on a different schedule from us. Daytime and nighttime vary greatly from planet to planet," Tiffany said, looking over the top of one of the dusty books she'd brought along.

"True, and they probably are assigned shifts," Oliver added. "Either way, I doubt the Übel will get much accomplished tonight."

"Mason and I are pretty confident that the pool is the path to the next clue. It almost certainly lies somewhere among the ruby lining," Tiffany said.

Oliver nodded his head in agreement as he slipped into his sleeping bag.

Mason arranged his pack next to his bedding and then pulled out some shorts and a different shirt. "We also think there is something important about the number twelve."

"Oh, that's right," Tiffany remembered. "We're going to need the rubies and planks from the *Phoenix*. We're almost certain we'll need them."

"I guess that makes sense," Oliver said. "We'll get them when we check the *Phoenix* for Austin."

Mason stepped out of the room to change and returned a moment later. "Is anyone else hungry?"

"Yeah, I actually am." Oliver rubbed his stomach.

Mason took out two cans of soup, one of broccoli and cheese and one of beefy vegetable, and offered the choices to Oliver. "Tiffany, you want anything?"

Tiffany lowered the book she was reading. "No, I'm not all that hungry right now; maybe in the morning. I had a decent lunch."

Oliver sat up and took the can of beefy vegetable from Mason. "All right. But don't skip too many meals, Tiffany. You need to keep your strength up and your mind sharp."

Tiffany gave a light laugh and dove back into her book. Mason and Oliver quickly devoured their meals.

"Tiff, you'd better try to get some sleep. We have a big day ahead of us," advised Oliver.

Tiffany sighed. "I'll read more tomorrow." Oliver yawned. "Okay."

"What time should we get up?" Tiffany wanted to know.

"Let's head out six hours from now," Oliver suggested.

"I'll set my mTalk's alarm."

"Make sure you guys wake me. I'd rather be awake than asleep if I'm going to be alone," Mason admitted. "I'll probably go downstairs and read."

"That's a good idea," Tiffany said.

"But don't let anyone in through the doors," Oliver warned. "Even if it's Austin."

"But—" Mason started.

"Promise, Mason," Oliver said. "He didn't leave through that door, so don't expect him to come back through that door if he's alone."

"Okay, I promise."

"Now, let's all get some rest," Oliver said.

Tiffany yawned and laid her head on her pillow. "Night, Olly. Night, Mason."

"Night, Tiff," Oliver answered sleepily. "Night, Mason."

"Night, Tiff," Mason echoed. "Night, Oliver."

Egg

Austin had been the mysterious squeak. Crouching behind a pile of boxes, he'd had no intention to of going to rescue his parents that night. In fact, he had only escaped to the top room so he could be alone and think. He had known that he'd been difficult—borderline rebellious.

He was about to stand up and say, "Boo!" when Oliver came back in, giving Austin pause to listen.

Austin felt strengthened after hearing Oliver's confidence in his ability to survive on his own and the recognition of his masterful escape from the Blauwe Mensen. Now it was time to prove him right.

After receiving the confirmation that his parents were indeed here and not all that far away, he knew what he had to do. The new confidence from his brother's encouragement had given him a new plan. He would rescue his parents and bring them to his brothers and sister. He would be the hero, and he would make Oliver proud.

First, though, he needed to get his pack. Oliver had gone to get it, but where was it? He slipped out of his hiding place and started down the stairs. He slowed as he heard his brothers and sister talking. They were bunking down but were not asleep yet.

Austin sat on the stairs for what seemed like forever. A couple of times, he thought one of his siblings was coming, and he retreated up the staircase a short way until he was confident the coast was clear. Eventually, the silence continued long enough that Austin slipped to the door and peeked into the room.

He wondered why they had left the door open, and further, why no one was on guard. Oliver hadn't even set up any defenses or warnings.

A new thought came into his mind: his brother had probably not wanted to accidentally harm Austin should he return. Sure, he'd been pretty angry with Oliver before, but his older brother did care about him. It was all the more reason to make him proud.

Austin saw his pack sitting at the end of Mason's bedroll. He tiptoed over and snatched it up, then escaped the way he'd come. No one even moved.

He ran up the stairs and out of the ziggurat. The air had lost some of its warmth, and he shivered. He walked around to the front of the ziggurat and looked out over the jungle. A sense of power came over him, like he was a king looking out over his kingdom. As far as he could see, there weren't any soldiers near. He could see the lights of the Übel base camp in the distance. It was late enough that he figured most of the soldiers were asleep. He was certainly tired and, if not for his mission, he'd have gotten some shut-eye himself. Nevertheless, there was no rest for a hero, and he was about to become one again.

Austin tightened the straps on his pack and started down the tiers of the ziggurat. By the time he reached the bottom tier, a heavy cover of clouds had rolled back over the basin, making it all the darker for his sneak attack. It was as if the weather were in an alliance with him. A night attack was perfect and gave him a huge advantage.

Austin started along a stone walkway heading south, but quickly realized that Oliver and Mason hadn't taken it to get to the southern ziggurat since the stone path was still obstructed by a maze of crisscrossed branches and vines. He stepped back and found the entry to the trail his brothers had blazed directly through the jungle. It didn't seem to follow any stone pathway like the one Tiffany and he had followed to the observatory. But, at the very least, the roughly hewn trail would lead him to the southern ziggurat and the location of his parents.

Not having an mTalk was really becoming an issue. Unarmed and with only a small light for guidance, Austin trekked toward his target. The wind picked up, and nearby branches swayed back and forth. If the orange moon had still been visible, shadows would have cast eerie images around him.

Unsure of what he might encounter at the camp, Austin considered his plan of action. Austin knew that he'd be outnumbered, but he also believed that because he was younger, he was more agile than the lumbering soldiers Oliver had faced. Oliver had told Austin and Mason a bit more about the chase through the woods on their flight to Jahr des Eises a few days ago. Apparently the two soldiers that had pursued him through the woods were out of shape and not that strategic. It seemed this Vedrik's crew was a bunch of misfits.

The soldiers had also only used stun shots in their attempt to subdue him, and with poor aim as well. What was the danger, then, if they weren't trying to kill him?

All these factors were in Austin's favor . . . weren't they?

His stomach swirled a little. Maybe he should go back.

A sudden outburst of growling and snarling behind him sent him into a dead sprint. He hopped over protruding roots, ducked under branches, and even swung across a small gulley using a hanging vine. But when he attempted to leap across a low spot in the path that had become a bog of rainwater, he didn't reach the other side and instead landed face first in the thick jungle-floor mud. Pulling himself out, he saw his body and clothes were coated with the muck.

A twig snapped nearby, and Austin was off again.

He ran for quite some time before he slowed and bent over to catch his breath. He listened but didn't hear any animal noises. A few more steps down the trail and he stumbled out of the jungle and onto the stone pavers of a plaza. He'd made it, but whether he really wanted to be there was still a question.

Orange moonbeams had poked through the cloud cover again and lit the sides of the southern ziggurat. The structure reached high into the sky like a mountain. Its sheer size amazed Austin; he'd thought the western one had been big, but this ziggurat was gargantuan.

His gawking ended when he realized he stood totally exposed in the orangish light cast by the solitary moon. A few steps returned him to the cover of the jungle path. The glow of the lights in the encampment reflected off the remnants of the cloud cover, giving him a heading.

Austin remained just inside the tree line and circled the ziggurat. It didn't take long for him to hear several men speaking and the low mechanical rumbling of a generator. As he moved farther along, the soldiers came into view and stood near a large oval object that looked like a glowing egg. The reverberating hum was coming from the egglike thing, and several cords snaked away toward the camp.

"Well, I think it should be set now," Austin heard one of the soldiers say. "The captain does know I'm not an electrician, right?"

"Who knows? But he sure didn't seem too happy that half his contingent was sent off to retrieve Zebra Xavier," the second soldier responded.

"Zebra Xavier—you don't really mean *him*?" asked the first soldier with a strange, terrified emphasis on the word *him*.

"Yep, him. Haven't you heard? It's been the buzz all over camp. Plus, they took the *Raven*."

"I've been stuck over here working on the egg since we landed," growled the first soldier angrily.

Austin half laughed; the egglike thing was actually called "the egg."

He heard something like a boot strike the side of the generator. "Confounded contraptions!" the first soldier exclaimed as they turned to leave and head for camp.

"Did you hear about those plant things attacking?" the second soldier asked as the men started to move away.

Austin's eyes darted around at the encroaching jungle plants next to him. Attacking *plants*? He remembered Mason and Oliver mentioning their incident.

"I actually saw them get Sekelton," the first said with a laugh. "It was hysterical."

The two soldiers moved out of earshot, disappearing around the corner of the lowest tier of the ziggurat. The egg thing now sat in the open and alone. This would work perfectly into his plan. From what the soldiers had said, it sounded like the egg was used to power the camp. If Austin disabled it, he would be able to cut energy to the Übel, leaving them in the dark and hopefully confused.

Prior to taking this action, however, he needed to locate his parents' whereabouts; once the power was off, his small light would be of little assistance in finding them.

Austin continued to stay just inside the tree line, moving until he could see what had been set up along the back of the ziggurat. The camp before him was intimidating, to say the least. A large black cruiser sat a few hundred feet from the stone structure, having flattened an entire grove of jungle trees and plants below it. Between the ship and the ziggurat was a wide stretch of stone plaza, but it was covered with four large dome tents and a dozen or so smaller tents.

Three men patrolled separate tiers of the ziggurat and, in the moonlight, Austin could see they were armed with large weapons, probably the same kind that had been used on Oliver. The soldiers also wore goggles, and Austin knew they were likely night vision, possibly even infrared. The thought frightened him, and he stepped farther back into the woods. Had they already seen him?

Nervous, Austin squatted down. He would have to be even more careful now not to be seen; neither the darkness nor the trees were enough to cloak him from the assisted sight of the sentries. Even now, they might turn and catch a glimpse of him.

The ground at his feet was squishy from the rain, and he grimaced as his hand sank into fresh mud. He looked for somewhere to wipe it off, then shrugged and swiped it across his pant leg. The smear darkened the fabric, just like . . . camouflage!

Wait, mud would work like a cloak to the infrared, wouldn't it? Not perfectly, of course, but it would lower his heat signature. At least, that's how it had worked in one of his favorite movies.

Austin dug in the dirt, getting a generous helping of mud in each hand. He quickly caked it on his face, arms, neck, and any other exposed part of his body. He was thankful to have changed back into his Ultra-Wear clothes, having dried them by the fire. The outfit not only had temperature controls that assisted the wearer, but it would further mask Austin's body temperature. He couldn't avoid the night vision, but he could minimize his heat signature.

Feeling semi-invisible, Austin moved back toward the tree line and looked out over the camp.

A scattering of smaller vehicles that looked similar to the sky scooters sat in several rows near the cruiser. Several stacks of crates had been positioned in the center of the camp, and two large communication dishes were being set up at that very moment.

Austin jumped back into the bush as the wind picked up and swirled around him without warning. The whirlwind was followed by a swooshing, rumbling sounding that grew louder and louder. A moment later, two Übel star fighters landed just a few yards in front of Austin. Their wings began to swing outward as they vertically descended and touched down in near silence. He noticed that the ships had no tail fins. They reminded Austin of bats.

During the escape through the cavern on Tragiws, he'd not gotten a good look at these masterful machines of space and sky; now, two of the ships were right before him. He stood in awe, looking over the sleek black aircraft.

The canopies slid back, and Austin took a step away as the pilots climbed from their cockpits. A small ladder slid out from the side of each ship, providing easy access to the ground. The pilots didn't spend a moment longer near their ships and instead jogged off toward one of the large domed tents.

The canopies to the ships remained open for the moment, and a low hum was still coming from the ships' engines as if they were still on. Austin could see the fighters' heavy armament of plasma blasters and fusion torpedoes. Why had they never fired on the *Phoenix* in the chasm on Tragiws? Of course, it was likely the same reason the soldiers had only fired stuns at Oliver. The Übel didn't want the kids dead; they needed them alive. If the Übel killed any of the Wikk children, there was no way Austin's parents would continue to help them.

Of course, there was always torture. Austin shook the thought from his mind.

He looked back at the black ships, reflecting the orange moonlight. *That's it!* he thought with excitement. Suddenly, a plan began to take shape in his mind. What if he took off in one of the craft and ordered the Übel to surrender and hand over his parents? The ships were right before him, unprotected, and still running. He just had to slip the few yards from the tree line to the ladder, climb into the cockpit, and take off.

But, no. Reality set in. Oliver hadn't yet taught him how to fly. There was also the chance that the Übel would just threaten to harm his dad and mom unless he landed. Then he'd be prisoner too.

No, his plan to sabotage the egg would have to work; it was the simplest method of causing chaos. But he still needed to locate his parents before any of his plans could be enacted.

Austin continued farther around the perimeter of the base. He kept his eyes on the guards as he went. The men were still patrolling their separate tiers on the ziggurat. The rifle-type things in their hands looked powerful, and he wondered if he could get his hands on one of those; then the tides might change. Austin and his siblings had no such fire power; so far, the only thing remotely like a weapon had been a lousy Zapp-It. Not exactly equal to the Übel's arsenal.

Then again, did he have the will to fire on someone, even if it was with a stun shot?

A commotion near the large black cruiser caught Austin's attention, and he sped up his pace to get a clearer view. Three soldiers ran out from the ship and mounted scooters while two people dressed as civilians were led forward by a soldier in a long black coat and a captain's hat. Austin knew immediately who the other two people were: his parents. And the officially dressed man was probably none other than Captain Vedrik himself. Austin had never actually seen the man in person, but he had little doubt.

The captain was joined by two soldiers who escorted Austin's parents to another craft that had sat just out of view. This ship was roofless and had two rows of seats, one for a pilot and copilot and the second for passengers. Austin knew this was some sort of skiff, like a deluxe scooter.

But where were the soldiers taking his parents?

The ship lifted vertically, hovering for a moment while the other three Übel scooters rose to join it. Then they were off, the three scooters leading the way and the larger craft following. They passed right over the two star fighters and flew low over the jungle toward the trio of ziggurats.

Then it hit Austin: the soldiers were going toward his brothers and sister. Maybe the Übel had discovered Austin's siblings in the western ziggurat. His wrist was bare, a reminder that his mTalk was still broken. He had no way to warn his family of the impending danger barreling toward them.

Austin sighed. He had no choice but to run as fast as he could and try to rescue Oliver, Tiffany, and Mason. His parents were no longer in the Übel camp, so his plan to rescue them no longer had any merit. His mission had changed again.

The question was, could he get past the black creatures?

2.19

Creatures

The path had not gotten any brighter with the thinning of the clouds, but had become more eerie instead. The dull howl of the wind blowing through the large, fanlike jungle leaves covered up any sounds that might warn Austin of approaching trouble. He ran. His mission had changed, but it was still important.

He felt something heavy in the pit of his stomach, and he knew it was the thought of being alone. If Oliver, Tiffany, and Mason were captured, Austin would have to either turn himself in or continue solo, a prospect he didn't want to seriously consider. He would have handled the initial encounter with Captain Vedrik differently and probably have rescued his parents, but he still wanted his siblings' company, even if he didn't want to admit that to them.

Thunder pealed in the distance, and Austin knew another storm was approaching. He only hoped he could make it back to the ziggurat before it unleashed any more rain or lightning. He was running as fast as he could without tripping or getting decked by a branch.

The wind suddenly died down, and all around him was quiet. Then the bugs began to chirp and the birds to coo softly. And then. . . . The next sound set his nerves on edge and made his skin tingle. The growl was back. Austin recalled Mason's story of the attacking black creatures. He looked around, shining his small light this way and that. He'd read at Bewaldeter, his boarding school, that animals in general preferred to keep their distance from humans and that, by making a lot of noise, a person could advertise his presence and give an animal an opportunity to stay clear. But Austin couldn't be loud. He still had to avoid the Übel, and although he didn't know the whereabouts of any foot soldiers, he now knew they were probably out there. The captain's departure from the camp had disproved Austin's theory that the Übel might be sleeping.

A loud roar echoed overhead. Thankfully, this time, it was from no animal, but from the storm directly above him. Rainwater started to make its way down through the canopy to the jungle floor. The ground became a slimy layer of mud, easier to kick up and splatter. Having purposely coated himself in the brown goo, Austin didn't care about his clothes, but his light had gained a film of mud, and its beam had faded.

Austin slowed his pace and looked around. He'd heard something else. This time it wasn't thunder; it was organic, mammalian.

He began to mumble to himself: "I'm right here on this path. I'll stay away from you if you stay away from me." Of course, he'd happily stay away from whatever it was, regardless of its desire to get close to him. "Good creature of the night. Good creature. I'm just passing along, making my way back to my family."

A low growl echoed somewhere behind him. Austin spun around and began walking backward, but he jolted when thunder cracked overhead. The birds' and insects' noises had again quieted, and Austin felt very alone. It was as if he were now one-on-one with the creature. The storm highlighted the danger of his situation like the peak of an orchestra at a tense moment in a holo-flick.

A branch snapped nearby, causing Austin to spin around involuntarily in the other direction. "Whatever you are, be warned I'm armed," Austin lied, but then quickly made his words true as he broke off the nearest tree limb he could find. "I know how to use this, and I will if I have to!" he cautioned.

A louder growl, as if in defiance, sounded out behind him. Either there was more than one creature or it was one very quick and agile creature. The answer came just a second later.

A large, black, catlike creature leaped onto the path in front of Austin. His small light caught the animal's eyes, causing them to glow brightly. He could only stand in shock for a moment. The hair stood up on the nape of his neck, and he could nearly feel the creature's eyes scouring his body as if he were a tasty treat. He raised the branch in defense, but it would do little to stop this beast. He could either stand and try his best to fend it off or could run.

Something thumped onto the dirt path behind him, and Austin turned quickly to see another one of the black creatures. His choice was made; he darted into the nearest plants and ran. The thick leaves and vines quickly became an issue, and he tripped several times, smacking his arms, knees, and face against roots and stones. The ground was soft from the rain, but that made the running all the more difficult.

Austin's eyes burned, and tears began to stream down his face. Why had he ever left the ziggurat? Why had he been so cross to his sister and brothers? He was going to be eaten, and it was his fault.

He pushed forward and heard something splinter overhead. Without looking, he knew the cat creatures were traversing the network of branches above him. There was simply no way Austin could outrun or outmaneuver them. The beasts had planned their attack, and *they* were working as a team. But Austin hadn't been a team player with his family.

His vision blurred with tears, sweat, and dirt. He tried wiping his eyes clear, but it only made it worse. His nose was stuffy, and soon his breathing became labored. His arms and legs burned from scrapes now infiltrated by mud and sweat.

Something solid met his next footfall, and he crossed from the jungle onto a semi-cleared stone pathway. Immediately, he recognized it as similar to the one he and Tiffany had followed previously that day—or yesterday by now. He didn't have any idea what time it was, but it was late. The moon was again visible in the sky, and bright rays of orange moonlight lit the stone path.

He looked both ways but was unsure where in the basin he was. It didn't matter; he didn't have time. Those creatures were near and, as if to remind him, two independent growls cried out behind him.

Austin ran.

And ran.

And ran.

Finally, he looked back but didn't see anything chasing after him. He didn't know where the creatures were, but he knew they hadn't given up. It was like a game of cat and mouse to them, and he was clearly the mouse.

There had been several small crumbling buildings along the path so far, but since some were missing walls or doors, none would provide defensive protection. He hoped he'd be nearing either the ziggurat or the observatory soon. Either would provide a room or someplace where he could lock himself in until the danger passed.

A flash of black caught his attention, and Austin barely had time to duck as the attacking creature flew right over him. He dropped flat to his stomach and then rolled onto his back. Before the cat could recover, he launched himself back onto his feet. He saw a building nearby and dashed for it, but it was doorless. Austin ran on.

The next building had a door but also had two wide-open windows. He heard a screech and looked back to see one of the creatures tearing in his direction, fangs bared. The orange moonlight made the beast glow as if on fire.

He had no choice. Austin leaped through the entryway of the nearest building. With a powerful swing, he slammed the hinged metal door shut and remained firmly against it for a moment. A stout force collided with the exterior of the door, but Austin held steady. He heard a mournful howl as if the cat had hurt itself in its attempt at breaking through the barrier.

There was little time before the cat would recover or its counterpart would strike. Austin surveyed the room and flew into action. He tossed two chairs against the door and then shoved a large, rickety bookshelf in front of one of the open windows. The other window he blocked by flipping a long, squat table on end.

The furniture might not hold long. Austin searched the small building, which he assumed to be a house, for more, and also checked for other openings where the creatures might be able to get through. The remaining windows were shuttered, and the back door was also closed tightly. To be safe, Austin upended two bed frames he found and leaned them against the windows in their respective bedrooms, then took the chairs and placed them against both doors. The roof over the house was intact, minus a few fist-sized holes that moonlight glinted through.

Confident in his barriers, he returned to the area he supposed was the living room and sat on the floor to listen. There was no way out; he was outnumbered. The hunters had him trapped, and now all he could do was hope they would get bored and leave or find something else to hunt.

Seconds, then minutes, then hours passed with no sound of the creatures. Before he knew what had happened, he'd fallen asleep on the hard stone floor, alone, uncovered, cold, and humbled.

2.20

Aqueduct

The alarm on the mTalk went off, startling Tiffany as it buzzed in her ear. She quickly shut it off. Desiring to go back to sleep, she considered her options but realized there really weren't any. Austin was out there alone, and her parents were held captive. It was time to face another day.

She reached over the side of the bed and shook Oliver's shoulder.

"Olly, wake up," she said, her voice still sleepy. "It's time to go."

Oliver wiggled and then rolled over to face her. "What time is it?" he asked, squinting through one eye.

"It's been six hours. We need to go."

"All right," Oliver said as he pulled away the top cover of his sleeping bag and sat up, stretching his arms.

Tiffany climbed out of her sleeping bag and swung her feet over the edge of the bed. She stood, but suddenly felt lightheaded. "Maybe I should have eaten last night," she said weakly.

"Are you okay?" Oliver came to her side.

"Yeah, I'll be fine." She started to deflate her pillow.

Oliver smiled mischievously. "I'll wake Mason."

Oliver gripped Mason's shoulder and jerked it to the side. "Mason, it's the Übel! We have to go now!"

Before Tiffany could protest, Mason shot up and ripped off his sleeping bag. He was scrambling to get his shoes on before he looked at Oliver, who was now bent over, laughing hysterically. Even Tiffany sat on the side of the bed, giggling quietly. Despite the very real dangers, they still enjoyed a moment of sibling humor.

In that second, Mason clearly knew the Übel were not coming. Red-faced, he clenched his fist and socked Oliver in the shoulder.

"Ouch," Oliver said and laughed again. "That was a pretty solid punch."

Mason glared at Oliver. "Yeah, and if you don't apologize, there will be another."

"Okay, okay, I'm sorry," Oliver said, holding his hands in the air in fake defense. "I'm sorry."

Mason chuckled as he looked around the room. "You could give a guy a heart attack," he warned.

"I think you're a bit young," Oliver said.

Mason shook his head. "A feather and some cream would have been a more appropriate joke."

"Boys," was all Tiffany would say.

"Well, now that I got you awake, Tiffany and I are going to be off soon," Oliver explained.

Mason sat down and started to lace up his shoes. "Okay, but don't think this is over. Yours is coming."

Oliver chuckled. "Fair enough. Are you ready, Tiff?"

"Yep. I've got everything in my pack that I need."

"Take this," Oliver said, handing the Zapp-It to his little brother.

"Won't you need it?"

"Naw, we'll be fine," Oliver promised. "I'd rather you have it."

Oliver slung his pack to his back and motioned for Tiffany to follow him into the stairwell. "Let's go."

"Bye, Mason," Tiffany said and stooped to give Mason a hug.

"See you later," Mason said under her embrace.

Tiffany stepped out the door and followed Oliver. They headed up the stairs left between the overnight accommodations and the chamber at the top of the ziggurat. Oliver found the rope they had used to make it across the aqueduct. They'd stashed it behind a metal crate knowing that eventually they'd have to go back across. He shone the light on his mTalk around until the beam found the door leading out of the room and onto the top tier of the ziggurat, the same place they'd stood last night under the bright orange moon. The sun still had not risen, but the moon was nowhere in sight. The light glow on the horizon could have been the moon setting or the sun rising; neither Tiffany nor Oliver knew. Either way, the mission to find Austin and get the needed gear was before them.

Oliver looped the rope around himself and handed Tiffany the other end.

"Tie this around your waist," he said and added, "Just in case."

They would again be high above the jungle floor, and a missed step would be disastrous. Tiffany felt her nerves prickling under her skin, and although the jungle canopy below revealed that the breeze was light, it felt like a tornado against her exposed skin. She peered at the narrow surface of stone atop the side wall of the aqueduct. She didn't care for heights, and she certainly didn't like crossing a narrow strip of stone a hundred feet above the ground and damp from water, especially with the wind. She looked around to see the trees were still, their leaves fluttering only slightly; there was nothing more than a gentle breeze.

It was time. Oliver walked toward the aqueduct and took his first step, placing one foot in front of the other. When he was about five feet out on the wall, he motioned for Tiffany to follow him.

"Tiffany, remember to look straight ahead. Don't look down," he said encouragingly.

Tiffany started onto the wall and felt her legs begin to tremble. Her heart rate increased, and her breathing grew more rapid. "Be calm," she kept telling herself quietly. But her body didn't seem to be listening. She looked at her feet and suddenly felt like she was going to fall over. Her body wobbled; she threw her arms out wide.

Oliver's eyebrows rose in panic. "Look at me!" he called.

Tiffany looked up. Oliver had turned around and was holding his arms out toward her, motioning for her to be steady. She took a few more steps. Looking forward certainly helped her feel more balanced. She continued to walk toward Oliver with her eyes locked on him. When she got within a few steps of him, he turned and began steadily walking ahead of her again.

"You're doing great," he said, trying his best to encourage her. He continued to do so as they walked the top of the skinny stone ledge.

They reached the halfway point, and their pace quickened considerably. It was easier now that her nerves had relaxed a bit. After all, Tiffany had been in ballet since the age of eight. Balance was supposed to be easy for her; it was the height that bugged her.

Oliver kept a slight lead, maintaining a safe distance with the rope. He kept looking back at her, clearly making sure she was still steady and that he was not creating tension on the rope. But as they closed in on the three-quarter mark, a sudden gust of wind rushed against them. It happened in an instant: Oliver stumbled and the rope became taut, pulling on Tiffany's waist. The wind had already startled her, but now the rope's tension shifted her further off balance. Her mouth opened in a silent gasp as her right foot misstepped and came down on thin air.

There was nothing to grab. Tiffany fell. She let out an agonized breath as the rope around her waist tightened and jerked her body to a stop. A painful thump and groan came from Oliver as his body slammed against the stone wall. He was hanging over the side, his legs dangling and his arms hooked over the aqueduct.

They hung there a second, shocked, assessing the situation. But just as Oliver opened his mouth to speak, the rope around Tiffany's body suddenly slid up and caught under her armpits; she grabbed the lifeline with both hands and held tight. Her life literally hung around Oliver's waist.

Oliver was struggling with all his might not to lose grip. She could see the intensity in his face as he looked down at her, veins bulging in his neck and biceps. A red scrape marked the side of his face where his head had collided with the stone surface in the fall. She heard him grunt as he strained to lift her and his own weight. It was clearly too much to do in the awkward position he now lay in.

"Wait!" She knew what she had to do: she needed to climb.

Tiffany pulled on the rope and moved a few inches upward. She watched Oliver grimace. She could see the rope tighten around his waist as the knot shifted with her movements. It slid over his hips. But he couldn't let go of the wall to support the rope; he needed both hands to keep her and himself from falling. He spread his legs apart to hold the rope in place.

"You have to hurry!" he called. "I don't know how long I can keep my legs like this!"

Tiffany pulled herself up hand over hand. She was nearly to Oliver's feet when his leg spasmed. He let out a sharp yelp, and his leg involuntarily jerked inward. In that second, the rope fell away. Everything seemed to happen in slow motion as Tiffany felt herself dropping.

She heard Oliver cry out, "Tiffany!"

Tiffany plunged her hand upward and grabbed hold of Oliver's ankle. The rope now dangled limply from her waist, but she was alive.

She was not scared in this moment, but instead determined. She knew Oliver could not pull her up; she needed to continue to climb.

Oliver held tightly to the side of the aqueduct, supporting their combined weight. "Keep going," he gasped in encouragement.

After several moments of strenuous labor and difficult maneuvering, Tiffany was able to climb over Oliver and grab hold of the aqueduct. She lifted herself up and then assisted Oliver and his visibly aching arms onto the aqueduct.

Now that they were both safely on top, Tiffany and Oliver sat for a moment panting exhaustedly.

Tiffany's body shook, but she didn't cry. She was scared yet thankful. *Neither Oliver nor I should be alive*, she thought to herself. Questions began to flood her mind. How had they managed to survive such a perilous situation? How had they gotten this far in their quest?

Oliver wrapped his arms around his sister as they sat there, their legs dangling over the side of the aqueduct. "It's all right, Tiffany. We're okay now. We're safe."

"Thank you," Tiffany said, quivering. "Without you, I might not be alive. Or I might be in an Übel prison somewhere," she admitted.

"Everything is going to be okay. We're all doing our part, and we'll get through this," he said strongly.

They sat for just a few moments more, and then Tiffany knew it was time to go. It was still dark out, but they were visible should a patrol be near. "I'm ready to continue if you are," she said.

Oliver got to his feet and carefully pulled Tiffany to hers. He retied the rope, still connected to Tiffany, back around his waist. "This old rope saved us, didn't it?" he said to her. He pointed ahead. "Only a few more feet, Tiff. We can do it. Just look straight ahead."

Without hesitation, they walked the last quarter of the aqueduct. The wind still whirled around them, blowing Tiffany's hair in long streamers, but she had a new sense of strength. She didn't once look down, and her breathing remained steady.

As they reached the ledge, they kept the rope tied to them and continued through the opening of the tunnel, turning on the lights of the mTalks to guide them.

"Be careful—we don't want to slip into the river like Austin and have to start over again," Oliver cautioned.

"Speaking of which, I sure hope he is in the *Phoenix*," Tiffany said.

Brother and sister slowly inched along the narrow ledge of the canal. After several minutes of walking up and up, they began to go back down. Tiffany caught the fresh wet fragrance of flowers and plants and knew they were nearing the exit.

They saw the light and the grove of trees just outside the tunnel. But something flashed before them as well.

"Oliver, look." Tiffany pointed to twelve stones shaped in a cross that glowed yellow.

"The bridge?" Oliver asked.

Tiffany nodded.

Oliver touched the stones. They turned blue, then green. A grinding sound at the chasm beyond the grove told the kids their effort had been rewarded. The bridge was extending.

Through the grove of trees, they found the wire they'd left from before. Oliver clipped himself to the line. "This is the easy part," he said. "You've done it before."

Tiffany frowned as she gazed out over where the invisible bridge was.

"You know it's there. Just have faith," Oliver said.

The word wasn't a new concept, but its meaning was becoming very authentic to them.

Oliver was quick to cross, and Tiffany followed with as much success. She hugged her brother in relief. "Well, that's how I wish the other crossing had gone."

Oliver smiled. "Faith."

They headed back down the path they had blazed the day before; it'd become crowded with new growth already but was still clear enough to trek. If Austin had come this way, he'd not taken any time to clear it further.

Birds were singing and chirping in the early-morning air. Tiffany smiled to herself at the serenity and beauty of her surroundings. Morning sunlight slowly began to stream down through holes in the jungle canopy. It seemed a world away from the dangers that lurked on the other side of the ridge.

As they approached the clearing where the *Phoenix* was, Oliver pulled out the small remote for the cloaking device and pressed a button once. Within a split second, the shiny silver ship reappeared.

Oliver smiled at Tiffany, and she knew she had to acknowledge Oliver's intuition. "It worked," she admitted.

Oliver nodded, and they walked up to the side hatch, where he typed in the entry code and the door opened. Once inside the *Phoenix*, Oliver sealed the door behind them and switched on the lights. "You know, if Austin had come back here, how would he have seen the keypad to get into the ship?"

Tiffany put her hand to her chin. "Oliver, where is he?" She felt her heart begin to race. "He's just a little boy. What if he's hurt . . . or worse." She couldn't bring herself to actually say it.

"Tiffany, don't worry about him. He is very resourceful."

Tiffany opened her mouth to speak, but Oliver continued.

"Yes, at times he can be reckless, but he's not stupid." Oliver looked her right in the eyes. "I mean that. The kid is street smart; he might not have the book knowledge you and Mason do, but he's got survival skills."

Tiffany nodded. "If you say so, then I believe you."

2.21

Taken

Something wet landed on Austin's face, causing him to wake from his slumber. He opened his eyes and looked around. He was still inside the building he'd holed up in last night. His clothes felt damp from the humid jungle air, and he noticed a bird sitting above him on a crossbeam.

A gross realization came to him, and he confirmed it with a swipe of his hand across his forehead: bird droppings.

"Get out of here!" he shouted at the small, red bird—"Shoo! Get!"—before remembering his need for quiet. He thought over his many encounters from the night before. Between the black cat beasts and the Übel, he'd had a frightening and disappointing experience. He couldn't even remember when he'd finally fallen asleep, shivering alone in the crumbling building. In spite of his desire to warn his siblings, he'd been so tired he'd not been able to continue a moment longer.

His only goal now was to make his way back to the western ziggurat and, while doing so, avoid being captured by the Übel and being eaten by the stalking creatures. It was a tall order, especially since he'd run deep into the jungle during the previous night's escape. Without an mTalk for navigation, he had no idea where he was. If he could just get above the canopy, he would be able to see the four ziggurats and get a bearing.

Austin stood and brushed himself off, then remembered the bird droppings. He squirted some H_2O in his hands and rubbed the goop off his face. Securing his pack to his back, he cleared the furniture from the door of the building and stepped out into the jungle. He needed to find a tall, climbable tree.

After several minutes, Austin finally came across a tree with many limbs and a thick trunk, which seemed a good sign that it would be tall and reach above the canopy. He pulled himself onto the first branch, then stepped to the second. He climbed like this for the next forty branches until he found himself just about to break through the uppermost layer of leaves. The underside of these green umbrella-sized leaves glowed from what he hoped was the bright sun overhead.

As his head poked through, he was not disappointed. The morning sun had just crested the northernmost ridge of the basin. He knew it to be north from the position of the other two ziggurats close by. This cluster of three had been a symbol mentioned in the inscription his parents had found at Dabnis Castle, which said something about a trinity.

The basin, in his opinion, would be a really great place to explore, but given the dangers that lurked and the need to beat the Übel to the next clue, it was time for Austin to climb back down and find his siblings.

As he stepped back onto the ground, he immediately froze. He heard a disturbance nearby. Boots, several sets, marched across the stone pathway. Austin sidestepped into a thick bush nearby and then crouched low to the leaf-strewn ground, getting a strong earthy whiff of dirt in his nose.

The thrum of the footsteps came closer. *Thump, thump, thump.*

Austin couldn't see them, but he knew they were within twenty or so feet. Was it possible they'd seen him up in the tree? Surely not. The jungle canopy was way too—

Before he could finish the thought, a hand came around his mouth, and his body jerked back. Austin tried to fight against his attacker. Forgetting the danger posed by the soldiers, he would have cried out loudly, but his assailant's hand was tightly cupped over his mouth. Austin was about to bite the offending hand, but a voice whispered in his ear as he was dragged backward.

"My boy, do not yell, do not fight. The men approach, but I have come to save you," the gravelly voice of a man said softly.

For a reason unknown to him, Austin obeyed. He let himself be pulled back through the underbrush on a hidden trail by the mysterious voice and its corresponding hand.

A moment later, the sounds of the footsteps were gone. The hand spun him around, and Austin found himself face to face with someone in a red cloak.

Empty

Tiffany and Oliver had called for Austin throughout the entire ship, but they'd seen no sign of him and concluded that he had never come to the *Phoenix*. They agreed to head back to the ziggurat to get Mason once they'd retrieved what they'd come for. Then they could begin their search for Austin.

"You look through those crates, and I'll look over here," suggested Oliver as he and his sister stood in the expansive cargo bay. "Remember, we're looking for the artifacts, diving gear, and if you can find one, another Zapp-It."

"Why don't we check the inventory log?" Tiffany suggested.

"That's a great idea," Oliver said and crossed the cargo bay to a computer console and screen. "I'll load the Dabnis Castle entry in the e-journal. The registry numbers for the crates with the artifacts were listed in there. I'll try to find them while you search for the other things."

Oliver pulled up the cargo manifest and located several tools that he thought might come in handy. He walked over to a marked crate with a multihead screwdriver and a crowbar. Tucked in a case was a larger version of the Zapp-It called the Zinger. Oliver had trained with something similar at the Academy called the TW414. The Zinger was a toned-down civilian version. The weapon had the ability to shoot small projectiles that gave several quick shocks to its target upon impact. It was nonlethal—unlike the TW414, which had the option to be lethal or not.

Oliver had started back for the console when Tiffany let him know of her find.

"Oliver, I found the crate with the rubies and the planks!" she called from the other side of the cargo bay, where she'd already begun opening a large silver crate.

"Great job," said Oliver as he headed over to her. "I found a few tools, but I haven't found the diving equipment yet."

Tiffany set the lid on the floor and pulled out a metallic-looking briefcase. She lowered it to the floor and opened its lid. There was no security on the case, which was odd.

She knelt on the floor and took a translucent red jewel from the case. It was one of the rubies from Dabnis Castle, and it was larger than Oliver had imagined. Tiffany held it up, and it glimmered in the overhead lights of the cargo bay. "This by itself would be quite a find, but to think they found twelve. And now the entire pool appears to be lined with them as well."

"Are all twelve in there?" Oliver asked.

"I think so."

"And the planks?"

"Here too. They're in the bottom of the case," she said. "Mom and Dad must have also figured the rubies and planks would be needed together."

"You're probably right," agreed Oliver.

"This case may be difficult to dive with," she suggested.

"I'll have to manage. We don't have any other choice. I'm going to check the cargo manifest for the location of the diving gear. Will you seal this crate back up and take the artifact case to the door? We don't want to take off later and have stuff flying all over the cargo bay. Oh, and grab some extra clips from the cabinet over there." Oliver pointed to the wall nearest the doors.

"Yeah, I will," said Tiffany, getting to her feet.

Oliver scrolled through the inventory listing of all the cargo bay crates and their contents. It wasn't long before he found which crate held the diving gear. He started for the crate as Tiffany headed up the stairs to the top floor of the *Phoenix*.

"I just want to get the information I needed from the NavCom and also check for something in the library," Tiffany explained.

"Okay. I'll meet you on the bridge."

Tiffany departed into the corridor, and Oliver found the final crate they needed. He opened the lid and found all the family's underwater diving gear. He pulled out a set of flippers, a mask, a diving suit, and an Oxyverter—a small mouthpiece that separated oxygen directly out of water. Oliver looked to the side of the cargo bay where *Deep Blue*, the Wikks' two-man submarine, sat. If not for the lurking Übel, he would have flown the *Phoenix* right into the basin and used the submersible to search the pool. He shivered at the thought of entering the cold water in just a wetsuit. Even if the diving outfit kept him warm and dry, some of his skin would remain exposed.

Oliver set the gear near the briefcase containing the artifacts and then headed for the bridge. Tiffany startled him as she stepped out from her cabin, and he stumbled back against the wall with a resounding thud that echoed in the corridor.

"Sorry, I didn't mean to—" she started but stopped herself. "Did you hear that?"

"Hear what?" Oliver asked, surprised at her abrupt change in tone.

"I thought I heard footsteps up ahead," Tiffany whispered.

Oliver and Tiffany stood like statues, listening.

A dull clanking sound echoed from somewhere ahead of them, possibly from the galley.

"I heard that," said Oliver in a whisper.

"Do you think it's Austin?" Tiffany whispered in reply.

"We already looked everywhere. Plus, remember that the ship was cloaked. He couldn't possibly have found it, much less gained entry," Oliver reminded her.

"But last night you seemed to think he'd come here," Tiffany said. "You promised he was tucked in to his bed." Her voice took on an accusatory tone.

"I didn't think about that, all right," Oliver defended himself. "My mind's been a bit overwhelmed."

Tiffany looked away. "Oliver, he's out there. He's alone, and whether you're confident in him or not, he's just a little boy."

"You didn't seem hesistant to leave Mason in the ziggurat alone," Oliver shot back.

Tiffany shook her head. "That's different."

"How?"

"We know where he is, he has an mTalk, he's not as curious or adventurous as Austin, and—"

"Okay, okay, I get it. Let's finish up here and head back. We'll look for him as soon as we return. Hey, he's probably joined up with Mason again anyway."

Something clattered in the galley again. Oliver instinctively put himself before his sister like a shield. His posture slackened after nothing came into view.

"I heard that," he whispered.

"What do you think it is?"

"I don't know, but it's coming from inside the galley. You stay here; I'm going to find out."

Oliver slowly crept toward the front of the ship. If only he hadn't left the Zinger on the floor of the cargo bay or given the Zapp-It to Mason. As he slowly stepped forward, he heard several more thumps, and then the noises ceased. He approached the entrance and poked his head through the doorway. The room was dark, and he couldn't see anything. He listened but didn't hear anything. He reached his hand around the doorway and pressed a switch. Instantly, the lights came on. But there was nothing. No sign of anything, or anyone, anywhere.

He stepped into the galley and motioned back down the hall for Tiffany to join him. The two looked around the compartment, but didn't see any signs that the room had been disturbed.

"It might have been some pipes creaking," suggested Oliver.

"Pipes," Tiffany countered suspiciously. "I don't think so."

Oliver shrugged. "It's my best theory. Let's hurry up and get whatever else we need so we can get back."

"And search for Austin," Tiffany reminded him. She wasn't letting that go.

Tiffany stopped at the library while Oliver continued toward the bridge. The consoles were quiet and dark. He turned on the auxiliary power for the flight systems, as they needed a bit more energy than what the *Phoenix's* internal lights consumed. The auxiliary generators were one floor down, but Oliver could still hear their dull thrumming upon their activation. That reminded him of the generator that had been running below one hundred percent.

He started back for the corridor and the small staircase that led down to the lower level. Tiffany came out of the library just as he began to descend.

"Hey, I'm just checking one of the generators. I shouldn't be long," he said.

"No problem. I need about ten minutes at least."

Oliver made his way downstairs into the dark corridor of the lower level. Only the dim guidance lights that traced the lower half of the hallway were lit. The hum of the auxiliary generator grew louder as he approached the engine room. He switched the lights for the room on and was startled to see that several drawers were open and tools sat haphazardly on the floor.

Oliver crouched low and scanned the room. He was alone, but it appeared someone had been there. Either that or the landing had caused the mess. It was also still possible that Austin had visited the ship. Oliver still couldn't figure out how he would have accessed the *Phoenix*, but he supposed the twin might have figured out a way. The kid was rather resourceful.

Oliver started his inspection of the underperforming generator. The computer display showed that one of the plasma pods had failed and would need to be replaced. Oliver knew this was something he was not capable of doing on his own nor wanted to attempt. The ship would need a professional mechanic, and Oliver wished that Mr. O'Farrell and Mr. Krank were with them, even though he knew Mr. Krank had never planned to join them on their quest. Of course, if Oliver rescued his dad, the two of them might be able to make the repairs together. But he had to rescue him first.

For now, the generator would have to run below capacity; there were simply no other viable options.

Tiffany's voice called over his mTalk.

"Oliver, I've got everything I need. Are you ready?"

"Just a minute," he responded and started to put the tools back in the drawer. As he stooped over, he noticed that one of the ventilation exhaust covers in the room had come loose and fallen off. He stepped over to the vent and lifted it back into place.

When he reached Tiffany on the bridge, she'd already turned off the flight systems and was awaiting his arrival.

"You know I heard something again, but this time it sounded like it came from above me," she said. "Is it possible that there's some sort of rodent in here?"

Oliver shook his head. "Not likely. Possible, but not likely."

Brother and sister walked back down the corridor and into the cargo bay. Oliver found a second pack, loaded it up with the diving gear, then hoisted it into position across his chest. His other pack still remained on his back. He took the metal case of artifacts in his hand.

"Do you want me to carry something?" Tiffany asked.

"No, I'm fine."

"Do we need anything else?"

"Not that I can think of," Oliver said as he started to tap the code to open the hatch into the keypad. "Wait, I forgot I need to get a few more grapples and wire." He finished entering the code, and the hatch slid open with a *thunk*. "I'll just be a second." He set down the metal case and accessed the inventory kiosk to locate the grapple. A moment later, he had reloaded the grappling gun and stored three extra grappling hook-and-wire canisters into the pack on his back.

"Now I'm ready," he said, once again taking the case.

Tiffany followed Oliver out the doorway and into the humid air of the jungle.

Oliver sealed the hatch behind them and then took the cloaking remote in his hand and activated it once again. The *Phoenix* vanished.

Way Out

M ason had made his way down to the library, spending the last few hours searching through the shelves. Austin had left the lantern from the previous day, and it now cast a dull glow. It wasn't quite bright enough to cover the entire room, though, and although he knew he was alone, he had the strangest feeling he was being watched. Every so often, he'd quickly and suddenly swing his light around the room, trying to catch the lurker. But he never seemed to find anything. He was alone.

It didn't help that the room was cold, and there was a draft. The soft tinkling of water echoed from somewhere, but oddly there was no trace of water in the room. And the pool chamber was too high above him to be heard.

Mason might not have been able to look around the observatory bookshelves or see the telescope like Austin and Tiffany, but he'd found enough books to satisfy his appetite for discovery. As he combed through the stacks he and Tiffany had created, he found several things he couldn't wait to share with his sister. Tiffany had taken the e-journal with her in order to transfer some information to it from the *Phoenix*. By necessity, Mason became really quick at entering information on his mTalk—mainly just titles and corresponding page numbers, along with a few pictures of corresponding text.

His current book had been the most useful so far. It'd already eaten up a half-hour of the time he'd spent in the library. The book was titled *The Veritas Nachfolger on Evad: Year 1 through 50*. Because the words "Veritas Nachfolger" were foreign to him, Mason almost hadn't opened up the book. But since it said "Evad," he had decided to give it a chance. Already in the first chapter, he'd learned a considerable amount about where they were on Evad. The basin was named Ero Doeht, and the city was called Yth Orod. It had been settled in 969 BE with a population of five thousand. A factoid he had learned was that the furniture in the basin had been made of one of the local types of trees called rubbelum. The local people had needed a solution after their lighter metals had continued to rust and break down. Rubbelum's sap was rubbery and semi-moisture–resistant, slowing lumber's deterioration in the humid jungle climate. Although he knew most people wouldn't care about the ingenious discovery of a material for building furniture, it was just the sort of thing Mason found interesting. It was a question Tiffany had posed earlier about how the wood had survived in the humid climate. Now he had an answer for her.

There were many other details like this, and Mason was only a fraction of the way through. He couldn't possibly put all the information in the mTalk, so he knew this book was coming with him.

Mason checked the shelf and gathered three more volumes in the set, each covering a span of fifty years. Surely clues for their quest were buried within the text. It would probably take him and Tiffany days, if not weeks, to sort and read through all of it, but the effort would be worth it.

As Mason took the last volume from the shelf, the entire bookcase let out a groan as if it were relieved at having the four tomes removed.

Then, without warning, a worrisome noise came from just outside the ziggurat's door to the jungle. Mason froze and listened. There were several voices outside the ziggurat. The voices were low and raspy, clearly belonging to a group of men. He couldn't hear exactly what they were saying, but he didn't pick out Oliver or Tiffany's voice.

The door rattled, and Mason knew it was time to go. He ran back to his pack and shoved the four volumes into his pack. The other books would have to wait. The door vibrated as someone pushed on it, and then it shook harder. Whoever was out there was clearly determined to come in, and Mason realized he had just seconds to escape. He grabbed Austin's lantern and turned for the stairs, but something else caught his attention: the bookcase he'd taken the volumes of *The Veritas Nachfolger on Evad* from had shifted forward. A passage? Oliver had found a passage in the observatory.

"Stand back!" he heard someone command, and, in that moment, he decided to take a chance on the secret passage instead of the stairs leading up.

Three crisp *zip* sounds and then the crackling slang of shattered metal scraps bouncing off the floor and walls told Mason the men outside had blasted their way into the ziggurat. Mason sprinted to the bookcase and, with lantern in hand, slipped into a dark tunnel just behind the shelf. He reached around with one hand and gave a strong tug; the extra effort was not needed as the shelf slid back into place with ease.

He was just in time, as three soldiers charged through the door and into the library. A light coming from one of their weapons shone across the bookshelf, revealing a small hole that Mason could look through. He stepped forward and put his right eye to the peephole. The three men wore black-and-grey camo fatigues and black berets, and each was armed with long rifles painted in a scheme that matched their uniforms. The soldiers aimed their weapons in each direction they looked as they scanned the room, ready to shoot anything that might pose a threat.

Mason stepped back without thinking when the weapons pointed in his direction, his breath quickening. *They can't see me. They can't see me*, he reminded himself. He watched as one of the soldiers walked over to the pile of books and, with his free hand, signaled the other two to look around. They scoured the bookshelves closely but soon gave the all clear. The first soldier—likely the one in charge of the mission—signaled for the trio to start up the stairs, and seconds later, they were gone.

Mason was about to call and warn Oliver and Tiffany of the soldiers' presence, fearful his brother and sister could be on their way back and run into the armed men. But he realized the danger that he might be heard was too great at that very moment. He'd have to wait a bit longer.

Mason could hear the soldiers' footsteps ascending, and he was glad he hadn't chosen that route. In that regard, he was still unsure where the passage he'd chosen led. He turned and held out the lantern, but its faint glow was too little to reveal the length of the tunnel to him. When he tapped on his mTalk, a beam of light streamed from it in the direction Mason needed to go. The passageway wasn't terribly long, but it disappeared around a corner.

Mason cautiously proceeded forward. But the moment he turned the corner, he found himself at a door. A handleless, metal door at that. He shone his light around and located the same type of cross-shaped indention that had been next to the doors Oliver had described to him. In a vain attempt, he pressed on the cold metal of the door, but it didn't budge. He traced his fingers inside the metal cross indent. Still nothing. He would just have to go back to the shelf and wait until the soldiers left. At least he had a light and some books to read.

As he turned around, he heard a soft grinding noise. When he looked back, the once-sealed door had opened, revealing another hall. How had he done it? At the moment, it didn't really matter. He now had a way out that wouldn't put him into a place where the very people he needed to avoid at all cost had been just moments ago and were likely returning soon.

2.24

Soldiers of Darkness

The man wore a red cloak, leaving only his hands and the features of his face barely visible. Austin almost thought the man was smiling. A silver-laced patch was the only marking on the otherwise plain cloak. Austin did not recognize the symbol or words. The man also held an intricately carved walking staff in his hand; on its top sat a red jewel. The man bowed his head but did not remove his hood. "You must come with me. They are everywhere," he said.

"Who are they?" Austin asked.

"The soldiers of darkness," the man responded. "Now come, before they find us."

Austin's new acquaintance turned and dashed away, disappearing behind a large green leaf. Austin didn't move, unable to convince himself that he could trust the mysterious man.

The leaf that had hidden the cloaked figure was swept aside. "Aren't you coming?" the man asked.

Austin evaluated his options: there were soldiers in the woods nearby, which seemed dangerous. But who was this guy who had just sort of kidnapped him?

"They are close," the cloaked man warned again, his voice urgent but kind.

Austin shrugged. What else was he to do? So he followed.

The man took off at a run again, and to Austin's surprise it was rather hard to keep up. He was sure the cloaked guy was old, yet he ran like he was in his twenties. They traveled further and further from the stone path on some sort of other path—one that a person would have to know in order to follow. Clearly this man knew the way.

As they continued forward, the cloaked man slowed to a walk. The only sound was birds chirping. It was almost soothing in a way—the fragrance of fresh plants and the melody of a bird choir. Austin wasn't one for much reflection, but this place made him take a moment to contemplate its sheer tranquility. It nearly made him forget the loneliness he'd experienced last night, and even his anger toward his siblings.

The trail suddenly ended at the side of a tall cliff, which Austin surmised to be the side of the basin. The man slid his hand across the rock face, brushing aside some vines and, in the process, revealing an opening arched with smooth grey stones. This was not just the entrance to a cavern. This doorway had been built with purpose.

2.25

Float

Tiffany patted her mom's pack. Through the canvas material, she could feel the contour of the e-journal. The information she'd gathered would prove useful if her hunch was correct. She just needed the code to unlock the information she knew was hidden behind another flashing asterisk. Her parent's anniversary, and a myriad of other important dates and names had not worked, but she was confident she'd crack it. The only reason she wasn't telling Oliver or the twins yet was to avoid embarrassment if she were wrong. After all, her rationale was a bit silly, even in her own mind.

Tiffany nearly had to run as Oliver led them at a brisk pace through the jungle. Crossing the chasm for the third time had brought the anxiety of doing so to a new low. For that, Tiffany was thankful. They went slowly in the tunnel. This time, Oliver was not only carrying one pack but balancing a second pack and the metal artifact case. She continued to ask him if he wanted her to help, but he continued to turn her down. In fact, she quickly felt that he was too proud to take assistance. It reminded her of the first few hours of the mission when Oliver had been overconfident and reckless. She hoped he wasn't falling back into that sort of behavior.

When the duo reached the aqueduct, Oliver paused and then took out the rope in preparation to secure himself to Tiffany.

Tiffany hesitated. The memory of her near-death fall was all too fresh. She could even feel the burn in her arms from pulling herself up. It felt as if something was caught in her throat, and her breathing became shallow. The palms of her hands became slick, and a spot behind her ear itched. She knew her nerves were getting to her. "Is there another way?" she asked. She hadn't felt this way over the chasm, yet its depth was far greater. Of course, both could kill her.

Oliver's shoulder lifted slightly. "Well, we could just get wet and let the water pull us into the aqueduct. It happened to Austin, and he was fine."

Tiffany looked at the clear water coursing down the trough of the aqueduct. She remembered that Oliver and Austin had mentioned it was cold, but it'd be worth avoiding a deadly fall into the jungle below. She smiled. "Let's go for a swim."

Oliver took care to seal each of the packs, something Austin had not done before. The results had been evident in the damage to the kid's flashlight. He set the packs and the metal case into the water to let them be pulled downstream. The case floated instead of sinking and then rolling along. Tiffany let her pack slip into the stream as well.

Oliver was first; he sat down and slid his ankles into the cold water. "Brrr. Are you sure you want to do this? The clothing doesn't help much when totally submerged. It's more for wicking."

Tiffany didn't need to think about it. She nodded and resolutely shouted, "Yes!"

Oliver dropped himself in the rest of the way and let the water sweep him away toward the ziggurat. Relieved, Tiffany gladly jumped in behind him.

The water was cold, but with the warm air, it really wasn't that bad. She lay back instead of fighting the current, and her body easily floated its way along the aqueduct and toward the side of the ziggurat. Her feet, then her body, disappeared through the opening, and she found herself dumped into a half-full pool of water.

Oliver was swimming around gathering the packs, including hers, and the metal case and setting them up on the side of the tub. He pulled himself out and then offered Tiffany his hand. The moment she stepped up onto the platform, the wooden door to the upper chamber swung open. Tiffany fell back in shock at the sight of the person standing in the doorway.

Quest

The tunnel had ended at a door with no handle. These doors seemed to be blocking passages all over the basin as far as Austin could tell. He'd say it was shady craftsmanship, but clearly the lack of handles had been part of a security design, not an oversight. Next to the door was the same small cross-shaped indention that Oliver had described.

The man reached beneath the neck of his cloak and lifted a small, metal cross necklace over his head and, with his left hand, held the cross within inches of the indentation. Austin noticed his hand was lacking a couple of fingers, and this gave him the creeps. But the feeling passed as the sealed door slid to the side, revealing another hall. Using his staff, the man ushered Austin through the opening. A series of doors lined each side of the hall, and Austin immediately wondered what was behind each. But he had no time to explore.

At the end of the hall, the man stopped and again held the small silver cross up to another cross indent next to the door. The door opened. Before the man stepped through, he handed the cross necklace to Austin. "Take this; it is yours."

Austin hesitated only a moment, but seeing as it was the only way through the doors and, if needed, his only way to escape, he took it.

The cloaked man motioned for Austin to proceed before him, and they came into a room lit only by a flickering fire burning in a large hearth at the right side of the chamber. The room was filled with plush furniture and more shelves of books. A large screen covered one wall, but it was turned off at the moment. The room smelled of burned wood and wet stone and reminded Austin of camping in the forest behind their home on Tragiws.

"My boy, welcome. Make yourself at home. There is a change of clothes for you through that door and a sink for washing. When you are done, there is food on the table in case you are hungry," the man offered.

Austin touched the crusty sleeves of his shirt. The caked layer of mud had cracked and crumbled off in places, but for the most part his clothing was still covered. His face and arms were equally dirty. "Thanks."

In the bathroom, he found a set of camouflage clothes. The material didn't feel as nice as the Ultra-Wear his grandpa had created, but it did feel durable. He slipped off the mud-laden clothes and washed his arms and face. He considered the shower, but there wasn't time. He wanted to know what was going on. Who was this man?

He slipped on the fresh set of clothes and left his old set on the floor.

"Do you feel better?" the cloaked man asked as Austin stepped out.

"Much better."

"Help yourself to some food," he offered.

"Ummm, well, I suppose I am a bit hungry. I haven't eaten since . . ." Austin thought for a moment. "I don't know when," he admitted and started for the table. "Who are you, and why have you brought me here?"

"You may call me Brother Samuel, or Brother Sam for short." The man stepped closer to the hearth. "You have been brought to learn."

"What?" Austin asked as he took a moist-looking chocolate-chip cookie from the table. He flipped the baked good over in his hands, eyeing it suspiciously.

"Information you need to help you on your quest," the man said politely.

"My quest?"

"Yes. Well, your and your siblings' quest."

"How did you know about my siblings?"

"The same way I knew where you were," he said mysteriously.

"We're not really on a quest, more of a rescue mission," Austin explained as he started toward the fireplace, cookie in hand. "That's where I was headed when you grabbed me."

"Rescued you," the man corrected. "And you are on a quest."

"Sure," Austin agreed. He didn't care to argue. "So what is this cross necklace thing you gave me?" He sniffed the baked good, then let the tip of his tongue touch it for a taste. His stomach growled in response to the satisfaction his taste buds had gotten, and his mouth started to salivate. The cookie was sweet for sure, but poisoned . . . ? He didn't know.

The man seemed to be thinking, because he didn't speak. His hands were folded before him. A burning piece of wood gave off a loud pop, startling Austin, who was not only waiting for the man to speak but possibly himself to faint to the floor from the potentially poisoned cookie. The fire continued to crackle, but the tip of his tongue never started to burn. The cookie was probably safe to eat. If only the old man had been eating one as well.

He poked the cookie with his finger, and it didn't sting from any dangerous toxins that might have been lurking in the treat. He sighed and bit in. It was fantastic. Moist and fluffy, with rich chocolate morsels. Austin swallowed the bite. "So what's with the necklace?" he asked again and took another large bite.

The old man spoke. "It's a key, and it is just one of the tools I will give you in the next several hours."

"Several hours!" Austin exclaimed. "I can't stay. My parents are—"

"—are here. I know." His back still to Austin, Brother Samuel motioned to a nearby chair. Austin obeyed and sat. Only the man's hooded profile was visible, and the firelight flickered off it in an eerie way.

"The key is a physical tool, but I will provide you a *full* set of tools in time—some now and some later. You will need them all to truly find what it is you are looking for," Brother Sam explained.

Austin was intrigued by the mystery of this man and this place. Was this actually for real or had he still not awakened from his sleep? He took a bite of his cookie, swallowed, and then took a deep breath.

"When do we begin?"

The man turned, half his face still shadowed. He took a seat in a chair across from Austin and threw his hood back, revealing a tuft of grey hair and a small mustache on his face. A rubied pendant flashed in the firelight, hooked to Brother Samuel's collar. "We begin now."

Grapple

O liver leaped at the soldier who'd opened the door to the
top chamber of the ziggurat. With a swift elbow, he sent
the man backward against his two comrades, who had
just come into view. He slid his other hand across the stones
that opened and closed the door. The metal door slid shut,
and Oliver dashed to pull his sister out of the tub she'd fallen
back into.

"Take my hand!" he cried, extending it as far as he could,
and in one strong, swift pull, Tiffany flew from the tub and
landed roughly onto the stone platform beside. "Go!" was his
next command, and Tiffany started for the door leading onto
the upper tier of the ziggurat.

Oliver gathered the three packs and the artifact case and
followed his sister. It had been but seconds, and the door to
the chamber was opened again. Before the soldiers came back
into view, possibly cautious of another assault from Oliver, he
and his sister were through the exit, and the door sealed in
their wake.

Oliver looked around. They had only moments to find their
escape. Loud shouts indicating an argument echoed in the
chamber behind them. There was only one thing to do, and

his sister would hate it. But they couldn't make it down the tiers of the ziggurat in time; they'd make perfect, open targets for the soldiers.

Oliver ran to the edge of the tier and then jumped down once. Tiffany followed like a shadow.

He had to set down the metal artifact case as he retrieved the grappling hook from his pack. Knowing he couldn't hold onto the case, but not wanting it to fall into the Übel's hands, he gave it a solid kick.

Tiffany gasped. "Oliver!"

"It'll be fine," he called out, but he wasn't sure as he watched the silver case crash through the wide green jungle leaves and disappear.

Oliver took a deep breath and aimed the grappling gun at the side of the aqueduct. He'd have just one shot at this. "Tiffany, take hold of me and hold on tight."

"Oliver—"

"Just do it!" he shouted.

Tiffany jumped at his ferocity but obeyed. She wrapped her arms around him and squeezed.

Oliver's finger pressed the trigger, and the pronged grapple shot forward and over the side wall of the aqueduct. There was a resounding clink as the metal hook hit the stone.

The door behind them exploded in glowing orange shards of melted metal. The soldiers had taken no chances and used their blasters.

There was no time. Oliver gave a firm yank, and the grapple held tight. He held onto the grappling gun with one hand and with the other took hold of the wire, then launched himself and Tiffany off the tier. The wire went taut, and their bodies flew out in an arc over the jungle canopy. Oliver used his thumb to click the release button, and they began to drop lower as more wire was let loose from the canister on the gun. Tiffany's feet brushed against some leaves, and then her and Oliver's legs dipped into the top layer of the canopy.

A tree branch next to them exploded in a burst of splintered green and brown pieces. The soldiers had taken aim and were trying to blast Oliver and Tiffany out of the sky before they could escape, but the men were too late, and the oldest Wikk children dropped out of sight and into the shrouded safety of the massive green tree leaves.

The wire continued to lower them. Closer and closer they went toward solid ground.

Fifty feet.

Forty.

Thirty.

Oliver felt the wire vibrate sharply in his hands. Either they were running out of wire or, worse, the soldiers were trying to sever it with their blasters.

Twenty feet.

Ten feet.

The wire slackened and Oliver and Tiffany fell the remaining eight or so feet to the ground. They landed in a tangled heap of bodies and packs with the wire wriggling as it fell all around them. Oliver saw the singed end of the wire where one of the blasters had made its mark and split the line.

Oliver and Tiffany freed themselves from each other, and Oliver helped his sister to her feet. He heard indistinct shouting above and knew time was running short. Scouring the ground around them, he searched for the metal case.

"Tiffany, look over in that area," he commanded with a swift point of his hand. "We have to find that case and get out of here."

She started toward the spot Oliver had designated, and he took off in the other direction. He thrashed through the leaves, tearing and knocking them out of the way. The case was near, and he had to find it.

"Oliver!" Tiffany shouted. "I've got it!"

Oliver turned and ran back for his sister and, to his relief, a still-intact artifact case. "Good work!" he said as he hefted it from the ground.

"Where are we going to go?" she asked. And then her face went white.

Oliver instinctively turned around, believing she'd seen something. But there was no one or nothing behind him. "What is it?" he asked, turning back to her.

"Mason! Where is Mason?" Tiffany asked.

Oliver hadn't thought of that.

"He may still be in the ziggurat," Tiffany said. "What if he's been captured?"

Oliver said nothing. This was a real possibility. He could either run around and into the ziggurat searching for Mason, possibly getting himself caught, or he and Tiffany could find somewhere else to hide and wait. He didn't have much time; the soldiers would be down from the tower and searching the woods any moment.

He took a deep breath. He'd have to risk it; he needed to rescue Mason. Determined to fight his way through the soldiers and find his brother, he stripped the two packs from his body.

"Tiffany, I'm going after him. Make your way to the cliff face of the ridge, and I'll call you on the mTalk when I have Mason and we need to find you," he said.

"Oliver! The mTalk," she remembered. "Mason has one too, remember."

"Right!" Oliver swung his mTalk up and tapped the screen to call Mason. Holding the device close to his lips, he waited for a response. He didn't want to be first to speak in case it would put Mason in danger.

Veritas Nachfolger

Austin stared at the crackling fire in the hearth, eating his cookie. Brother Sam stretched his arms out before him and then brought them back in, folding them at his chest.

"Long before you were born, long before even I was born, a group of men attempted to wipe out the story of the Truth. Their goal, as they put it, was, to '*cleanse* mankind of its greatest weakness.'" Brother Sam let out a disappointed sigh. "These men ravenously and ruthlessly acquired power and allied themselves into a ruling elite class that was untouchable. Or so it seemed. Even the emperor himself was believed to be in the clutches of these men. They soon became known as the Übel to those who discussed their fabled existence. They were wealthy beyond measure and, in their own minds, equally wise. However, they knew from many examples in history that those who are unjust often receive a just end from those they have wronged. To maintain their control, the men believed they should rewrite history. If, by controlling the media, they could reflect a past that showed only peace, prosperity, and equality, the people would come to believe it as the only truth they'd ever known.

"Unfortunately, this was easier to do than anyone could have imagined. The Empire's information at that time was primarily stored electronically. *Written word*, as it was called, was rarely written on anything of a physical nature." Brother Sam pointed toward one of the shelves. "Books in physical form, bound pages of paper, were rare then. Now they're nearly extinct, with the exception of scattered personal or hidden libraries. The reason for this scarcity was the Empire's call for all books to be burned as treacherous propaganda."

For the first time, the old man slipped up his sleeve, revealing a small device on his wrist, much like an mTalk. Brother Sam frowned as he looked at the small screen.

"We have less time than I thought," he said. "Where was I?"

"The bad men had wiped out a bunch of information."

"Ah, yes. As the men of the inner circle of the Übel aged and time passed, they became hungry for a way to live longer, to live forever. But this was the one piece of information they had not discovered, the one secret they could not unlock with money or wisdom." Brother Sam looked toward the ceiling, then returned his gaze to the fire with a sigh. "They dumped vast chunks of their combined wealth into research and exploration, combing the galaxy for answers. But, in their determination to wipe out the past, they had hidden the very thing that could set them free."

Austin frowned at the cryptic wording but held his tongue.

"While advances in nanobiology and genetics gave the Übel leadership and their chosen followers an unnaturally long life span, one by one they eventually passed away. But their legacy still exists, and the next generation of Übel leaders are as hungry for the answer to eternal life as their predecessors. Their obsession for this information became so great they willingly abandoned their pursuit of power and control over the Empire for this sole quest. This is when and how the Federation was formed."

Brother Samuel looked at Austin with a piercing gaze, and Austin felt as if the old man could see into his mind. For some reason, his heart seemed to skip a beat. But Brother Sam looked away toward the fire. "The battle for Truth has raged since the beginning of time, but darkness seems to be gaining the upper hand in recent years. But the people to whom I belong—the Veritas Nachfolger—remain loyal to the ways of the Truth."

Austin was no fan of history, but all that Brother Samuel spoke of was nothing like what he'd learned in school at Bewaldeter. Yet the incidents of the past few days were real and gave credence to the old man's story. Austin and his family were part of some sort of Quest for Truth.

"You see, while the Übel seek something that is very real, they will not be able to find it as they pursue it now," Brother Sam continued. "But they will stop at nothing to uncover the secret to control their destiny. Several years ago, the Übel's supreme commander came across an artifact that promised to provide what the Übel sought. While not the first clue to offer this, it was the first in nearly a hundred years. It ignited an explosion of activity. They are in a desperate search. They even went so far as to clandestinely enact legislation lifting the long-standing ban on federal funding of archeology. Their reach and influence is unparalleled and saturates every corner and all entities of the Federation."

Brother Sam paused and looked back to Austin. The old man cleared his throat; his eyes glistened in the firelight. Austin had the oddest sense that Brother Samuel had been near to tears.

"My boy, I once had a friend who also sought this information. I watched him come to ruin as he drove himself mad in search of this secret. When I tried to tell him the Truth, he would not listen." Brother Samuel stopped, clearing his throat again. "I hope that you will listen and learn."

A moment passed, and the old man said nothing.

"So, you are going to teach me the real Truth?" Austin asked, feeling awkward under the man's stare.

"Not teach you the Truth as much as teach you how to *discover* the Truth." A small smile passed over Brother Sam's lips. "Those men know not what they seek, nor do your parents—or your siblings, for that matter."

"I don't think I do either," Austin admitted.

"No," the man shook his head. "Not yet, but I will give you the keys to unlock the Truth for yourself and help them."

"More keys?" Austin asked as he turned the small metal cross over in his hand.

"Oh, yes, but not like the cross pendant you hold in your hand."

"What is the Truth?" Austin asked.

"That is not the right question. The Truth is not a what but a *who*—"

Brother Sam's mTalk gave a series of rapid beeps. He looked at his exposed wrist and frowned. "I will do my best to explain further, but at the moment your siblings are in grave danger, and we must rescue them before they are captured."

Down

So far, the passage had led Mason down a series of steps that twisted and turned, soon leaving him without any sense of direction. He was deep in the catacombs when the screen on his mTalk lit up. Mason saw Oliver's name and picture. He tapped it once. "This is Mason," he whispered.

A cautious voice came over the speaker. "Are you okay?" Oliver asked.

"Yes," he started. "Well, sort of. I mean, I'm somewhere under the ziggurat."

"But you're safe?"

Mason nodded, but realized Oliver couldn't see. "Yes, I am safe. I escaped from the Übel. Did you?" As soon as he asked, the question seemed irrelevant.

"Yes, but just barely. We ran into them at the top of the tower, and we had to jump off," Oliver explained.

"Jump off?" Mason said in surprise.

"Well, I used the grapple. But Tiffany and I are safe," he assured him. "We have some gear and the artifacts."

"That's good. Any sign of Austin?"

There was no reply for a moment. "I think so. There were several things out of place on the *Phoenix*," Oliver admitted. "It looked like he'd been there at some point."

Mason sighed. His twin would never learn or grow up.

"Do you think you can get out of where you are?" Oliver asked.

That phrase—"get out"—gave Mason pause. His pulse picked up.

"Mason?" Oliver said impatiently.

"I'm not sure. I've been heading down a staircase for quite some time now. Can you see my location on your mTalk?"

Mason heard a soft beep as Oliver checked the LOCATOR app on his mTalk. "No. The message just says 'No data,'" Oliver admitted. "It's weird—the app worked before. That's how we found Tiff and Austin at the observatory."

"Right." Mason fiddled with his device. He and Oliver were talking, so clearly data was being transferred. But then he saw that somehow a location block had been switched on. He wasn't transmitting his location to anyone; in fact, he couldn't even see the coordinates for his own location. He tapped the screen to unlock the block, but five small boxes popped up and requested a pin. How had his location become blocked?

"I can't seem to turn my homing signal on. Somehow it got blocked," Mason admitted. "I can't even see where I am."

He reversed his search and checked to see if he could locate Tiffany or Oliver's signals. "Weird. I can see your location, but not Tiffany's."

There was silence for several moments. "Mason, Tiffany and I are going to make our way toward the base of the ridge and stash our stuff. Then we will come looking for you," Oliver promised.

Again Mason nodded. "Okay. Should I keep going or do you want me to turn back?"

"Keep going as long as you don't feel that you are in any danger."

Mason felt pretty safe—well, as safe as an eleven-year-old could feel all alone in a dark, dank tunnel without his siblings and while his parents were held captive by nasty soldiers. He chuckled darkly to himself at the thought and then responded to Oliver. "I'm as safe as anyone in our situation can be."

The half laugh over the mTalk speaker let Mason know Oliver understood perfectly. "If you get into any *more* danger," Oliver emphasized, "then call us and we'll start for you immediately. Otherwise, signal us as soon as you can get your bearings in the basin."

"Okay," Mason agreed.

"Over and out," Oliver finished.

"Mason out."

The mTalk screen went dark as the call ended. Mason was alone again and heading down a tunnel to a destination he did not know.

The staircase continued to turn and twist lower and lower. Time seemed to advance slowly as the bland grey-stone walls passed by on either side. His mind had remained clear and on task until he looked back into the darkness and thought of how long he'd been traveling in the passage. He hadn't seen any other doors, just a straight, narrow tunnel of stairs with no windows or exits. Oliver had asked if he could get out. Could he?

His chest tightened, and his breaths became shallow. His claustrophobia resurfaced as he thought of the distance he had traversed. He was probably surrounded by thousands of tons of dirt and stone waiting to collapse the tunnel and bury him alive. Hundreds of feet probably separated him from any fresh air. What if something blocked the other end of the tunnel? What if the door he'd come through was locked, and he couldn't get out? What if an earthquake happened?

He couldn't go back; he could only hope that there was a way out before him, and close. Mason took off in a panic-stricken sprint. He had to get out.

2.30

Seven Turns

Austin snatched a large muffin and two more cookies from the table as Brother Sam took up his staff and motioned at the door. "This way."

Austin took a bite of the soft muffin. "Wow!" he exclaimed as he indulged in the flavor and walked past Brother Sam. "Raspberry?"

"Yes, many of the berry bushes grow in the wild here," the old man answered kindly but quickly.

Man and boy stepped out from the fire-lit chamber and started back down the hall they'd traveled before. But instead of exiting back into the jungle they stopped at one of the side doors in the hall.

"Use your key," the old man instructed, his cloak now back in place, shrouding his face.

Austin obeyed, and the door opened as soon as the small pendant came within inches of the cross-shaped indent. Austin stepped through, but to his surprise the man did not follow.

Instead, Brother Sam reached out his hand and gave Austin a crinkled piece of paper. "Follow these instructions, and they will lead you to your brother."

Austin looked at the paper. "It's just a number and letter?"

"The other side," Brother Sam explained with a wink. "Hold on to those instructions. They will help you." Then he handed Austin his red-jeweled walking staff.

"What is this for?"

"You'll need all of it."

"Where are you going?"

"I must see to your brother and sister."

"Will you tell them I'm okay?" Austin said as the small door began to close.

"They will not see me. Sometimes that which sets us free is not visible to the naked eye, yet is there in our time of need," Brother Sam explained cryptically. "Faith is much that way—it is not seen, but having it leads to the Truth."

Austin's eyebrows furrowed in confusion. He held up the paper. "And what about this number? And the rest of the tools—" His voice was cut short by a loud click as the door shut tight. He shook his head and then banged the staff against the door. Realizing the vanity of his attempt, he held the cross to the small indentation, but nothing happened.

He only had one choice and that was to continue down the passage behind him. He turned and shone his small light down the unlit tunnel. The old man had said he would find his brother, but whether that was Mason or Oliver he didn't know. He only knew that one of them was at the end of this hall while the other was with his sister, and apparently everyone was in danger.

As he walked forward, staff in hand, he looked over the small piece of paper. It had just seven words on it: *left, right, left, left, left, right, left*. He followed the passage as it split several times, and each time he took the turn as directed. Most times, a door stood in his path, but each unlocked with a swipe of the cross.

Austin contemplated what the old man had told him. It really wasn't that much information. After all, he'd been with the old man less than an hour. But he did hope he could remember all that Brother Sam had told him so he could share it with his siblings. Oddly, he didn't hold a lot of resentment against them at the moment. In fact, he really wanted to be back with them.

He felt something catch in his throat and swallowed hard. He knew he'd been rotten to them, and he needed to treat them better. If he escaped from this tunnel and found them, he'd certainly try.

Now that he had a better understanding of the insurmountable heap of danger that stood before him and his family, he knew they'd all have to work together to overcome it.

As he continued walking, he thought about what Brother Sam had told him of the Übel. What would it be like to have all the power and wealth in the world? Wisdom wasn't as appealing to Austin, but still, he couldn't imagine someone having everything he could possibly desire and still being hungry for more. Eternal life—now that would be something to obtain. After all, if you had all sorts of money you'd need a lot of time to spend it and discover new ways to spend it. But was living forever really worth giving up control of an Empire? That was exactly what the Übel had done.

Austin had taken every turn as listed on the paper, save the last one. The part of the tunnel in which he walked seemed to be sloping down lower and lower, but there were no stairs. He'd walked so far, Austin imagined that there was probably as much tunnel under the basin as there were paths on the surface.

The tunnel was growing cooler, and Austin regretted that he was not wearing Ultra-Wear. In fact, he really regretted leaving it on the bathroom floor, even if it was dirty. It'd been a last link to his grandfather. The fresh set of camo Brother Sam had given him was nice, but it wasn't temperature controlled. The frigid air smelled damp, and he began to long for a fresh breeze.

He thought of Mason and was thankful his twin didn't have to suffer in the depths with him. Surely he'd be panicking with claustrophobia by now.

Austin came to his final *T* in the passage. He was supposed to go left, but to his right was a staircase that led up in a very straight path. Austin really wanted out of the passage and into open air, but Brother Sam had told him to take a left last. Had Austin missed a turn or taken one wrong? It was a frightening thought that sent shivers down his spine; the implications of wrong turns deep below the surface in catacombs like these could mean he'd be trapped forever in a maze of confusion.

As if in answer to his dark thoughts and indecision, a loud resounding thump blasted against the door to the left, followed by a desperate cry.

Stash

Tiffany followed Oliver through the thick jungle undergrowth.

They'd heard the soldiers arguing with each other as the men searched. Apparently one of the soldiers had gotten trigger-happy and was firing live shots, not stuns, at the kids. The man had been heavily reprimanded for nearly killing the archeologists' children. It gave Tiffany a small measure of peace to know that indeed the Übel were not out to carelessly take their lives. But it still didn't mean they were out of danger.

With the soldiers so close, they had gone a good distance fighting back branches, leaves, and vines with their bare hands so they would not leave an easy trail for the men to follow before Oliver rearmed himself with the machete to slice through the plants. Eventually the voices had died away, and she felt sure they had lost her and Oliver.

A few minutes later, they arrived at the cliff face of the ridge that surrounded the basin. Oliver set down the case of artifacts and removed both his packs. Tiffany removed her own pack and leaned against a slender tree trunk. The morning's events had tired her out already, yet, according to her mTalk, it was only midday.

Oliver looked over the clearing and then walked the perimeter of their location. He seemed to be evaluating their position and safety. Apparently confident, he walked back to the side of the cliff and sat down. "Shall we have some lunch?" he asked. "It'd probably be a good idea to eat and rest for just a bit. We need to reenergize."

The suggestion took Tiffany a bit by surprise; she hadn't thought of eating or resting in all the excitement. At the same time, she wondered how he could think of either with soldiers after them and their brothers missing.

She knew his answer would be something about the Academy and needing to replenish the calories they'd burned from all their efforts as well as giving their bodies rest. In the end, she was hungry too and could also use a moment to sit.

"That sounds like a good idea to me," she said, her stomach grumbling in agreement. She was famished, having not had a decent meal the previous night.

Tiffany removed a small bottle of soup and twisted the cap. The hot liquid meal coursed down her throat as she took a swig. It was good but not nearly as savory as Mr. O'Farrell's homemade stew.

Where was Mr. O'Farrell? He had not tried to contact them, as far as she could tell, and she hoped he had not been captured by Schlamm, even though his tactics for trading weren't honest. Mr. O'Farrell's help was vital for success in rescuing her parents. Without his intimate knowledge of her parents' archeological digs and future goals, she felt inadequate in deciphering information from the e-journal. There was so much information in the device. If only she had a little more insight into what her parents were doing. But that was information Mr. O'Farrell could provide. She'd just have to wait to see if he eventually contacted them. Until then, Tiffany would have to do her best to figure things out.

Oliver was sitting with his back against the vine-covered stone cliff, a bottle of Energen in one hand and soup in the other. His short brown hair was sweaty and matted against his forehead, several scrapes marred his face, and he had a nasty bruise on his left forearm. Seeing him marked with the scars of battle choked Tiffany up inside. Her brother had taken the brunt of the soldiers' abuse so far, but he continued to remain strong for her and the twins. Maybe he'd not always said or done the right things, but she knew he was doing his best. His heart seemed to be in the right place.

Tiffany's back slid against the trunk of the tree as she lowered herself into a sitting position, still holding her bottle of soup. She dug through her pack and retrieved the e-journal. She didn't have much time, but she wanted to document the events of the last hour or so.

As she entered the sequence that would unlock the journal, she heard a soft purr from somewhere overhead. Tiffany slowly looked up and caught a glimpse of a small black cat perched in a tree branch above. It stared down at her with glowing yellow eyes. It had a cute button nose and silvery whiskers sprouting out from each side of its muzzle.

Her warm fuzzy feelings toward the cat vanished as she remembered the black cat creatures that had attacked Oliver and Mason the previous day. Tiffany cleared her throat and looked back to her brother, then whispered, "Oliver. *Psst*, Oliver."

He was fiddling with his mTalk. "What?" he asked in his normal voice.

"Shhh," she stressed to him and continued to whisper. "I think it's one of those cat things." She motioned to the tree limb above her.

Oliver's gaze lifted to the leafy foliage overhead. The look in his eyes confirmed her suspicions all too clearly.

"What should we do?" she asked. "Do you think there are more?"

Oliver shrugged. "I don't know," he mouthed. His hands slipped into his pack, and he started to dig for something. Tiffany recalled the long device he'd referred to as the

Zinger. She knew it was more powerful than the Zapp-It he'd used before.

As he took out the weapon, he used his thumb to activate the charge, and it gave off a soft hum that slowly grew louder. Tiffany even saw a bluish haze of energy flashing across the tips of several points protruding from the front of the weapon. She looked back at the small cat above her.

It looked no bigger than a common house cat, and it was quite cute. She could picture it curled up in her lap as she read from the e-journal safely in the library compartment of the *Phoenix*. Tiffany looked back at Oliver and raised her hand, then mouthed, "No. Wait."

Oliver frowned, his eyebrows furrowed. "Why?" he mouthed back.

Tiffany didn't answer, but instead pushed herself up into a standing position. When she saw Oliver nervously look around the clearing, scouring the underbrush, she knew he was searching for the bigger black creatures that had attacked him before. She turned to peer at the small cub and then extended one of her hands. It was out of reach by several feet, but the gesture seemed enough, because the kitten thing hopped down to a closer branch and then leaped into Tiffany's outstretched arms.

The second she stroked its soft, somewhat matted black coat, it began to purr loudly and rub its face on the underside of her chin and neck. For Tiffany, it was an instant connection.

"What are you doing?" Oliver asked in surprise. He got to his feet and was next to Tiffany in an instant, the Zinger buzzing with electricity. He held defensively toward the perimeter of their location and moved around it in a wide arc, warding off a possible attacker. "It's one of those wild cat things' cubs. You can't hold a wild animal," he exclaimed.

"Well, I am," she said. "And it doesn't seem all that *wild* to me."

Oliver huffed. "We can't keep it, and we can't risk its parents coming to look for it. It's best we just get rid of it."

"Oliver!" Tiffany gasped.

Oliver motioned for her to keep calm. "Not rid of it like kill it. I mean send it packing," he corrected.

Tiffany nodded. "I know we can't keep it, but it clearly wanted me to hold it."

Oliver sighed and returned to his seat against the wall, but held the Zinger in his hands, his eyes continuing to search the edge of the jungle for any movement.

Tiffany held the cat loosely so as to not make it feel endangered by her, but slowly lowered herself back into a seated position. She spoke to the cat in a calm voice. "So, little kitty, are you all alone?" She knew it couldn't understand her, but speaking to the animal was soothing to her soul. The cat remained seated in her lap as she got back to what she'd started prior to hearing the purring noise. It was time to update the e-journal. There was still so much she'd not kept track of. Writing was difficult to do when life wouldn't hold still.

Something cracked in the nearby underbrush, and Oliver jumped to his feet. A few minutes passed while the kids and cat remained motionless and silent. When nothing came, Tiffany started on the journal again. Oliver, on the other hand, remained like a guard on duty.

Together

Austin stumbled back at the sound of someone or something colliding with the metal door he stood in front of, but the sound he heard removed any concern of danger. He recognized his twin brother's groan immediately.

"Mason?"

A startled and surprised voice responded, muffled by the door, "Yes. Austin? Is that you?"

"It is," Austin replied and immediately held the cross-shaped necklace against the indent to unlock the door. The door slid out toward Mason, and Austin shone his light to reflect on his twin's face. He expected a smile, but his brother's sandy hair was disheveled and wet from sweat. His blue eyes were wide with fear, and several streaks—apparently from tears—striped his soot-covered face.

"Are you okay?" Austin asked.

Mason stepped through the door and hugged his brother, then let out a long sigh.

"Better than I was. But I have to get out of here, and now. I can't stay trapped underground anymore," he explained, his voice abruptly rising to a frantic level.

Austin turned back to look at the staircase he'd not taken and pointed with Brother Sam's gifted staff. "This way," he said. He briefly considered what Brother Sam had said about sticking to the directions. The directions had said left. He had followed it and indeed found his brother, but there were no further instructions on the paper and the stairs seemed promising.

Austin led Mason back, and together they started up the staircase toward an unknown destination. At least it was up, and hopefully out. From Mason's expression, going back the way he'd come didn't seem like an option.

"Where'd you get that staff?" Mason asked. "And you're wearing camouflage. Where have you been?"

"I don't think you would believe me if I told you," Austin said.

"Try me. I didn't believe that blue people existed or that a dangerous group of soldiers would come to capture my parents, but it all happened. There is very little I won't believe these days."

"I was in the chamber atop the western ziggurat when you, Oliver, and Tiffany came looking for me. After I learned the Übel were for sure at the southern ziggurat and that Dad and Mom were there, that became my immediate destination," Austin explained. "I even retrieved my bag from the room you all were sleeping in."

"Of course. I didn't even notice it was gone. Why did you leave? You should have stayed with us," Mason said.

Austin frowned sheepishly to himself, knowing his brother couldn't see. "I was wrong to do it," he admitted.

"So you never went back to the *Phoenix*?" Mason asked.

"No, why?"

"Because Oliver and Tiffany did, and apparently they thought you might have been there at one time," Mason said.

"That's odd. No, I went to the Übel base camp to scout it out and rescue Dad and Mom," Austin said. "You can see I clearly failed in the first task. But not all was lost. I met someone."

"You met someone? Who could you have possibly met out here in the jungle?" Mason asked with a hint of disbelief in his voice.

"I told you that you wouldn't believe me," Austin scolded as he continued up the lengthy staircase.

"No, I do," Mason promised. "Continue."

"His name was Brother Sam, and he was part of the Very Knock Folder," Austin said.

"The what?"

"Verify Not Fold . . . or something like that."

"Wait, do you mean the Veritas Nachfolger?" Mason said.

"That's it," Austin realized, halting midstep. Mason nearly ran into his back but stopped just in time. Austin turned and looked down at his brother, two steps below. "How'd you—"

"I have a book on them." Mason swung his pack around and pulled out one of the volumes from the series. "See," he said and held out the spine for Austin to read.

Austin shrugged. "Their name isn't really important, but what is important is what he gave me." He held out the small cross pendant on the chain still around his neck. "It unlocks the handleless doors with the indents next to them."

Mason's eyebrows rose with interest. "It does?" He returned the book to his pack. "So, that's how you opened that door."

"Yes, and the man gave me exact instructions and said I'd find my brother," Austin explained. "Somehow, he knew you'd be coming this way and that by following his instructions I'd find you."

"That's strange, don't you think?" Mason asked.

"Really? How can anything be *strange* to you at this point?" Austin asked. "Just like nothing could surprise you. It's the same thing."

"You're right," Mason said, embarrassed. "So, where is this guy?"

"Well, he'd planned on telling me a whole bunch of stuff but then said he'd run out of time. He sent me to find you and left to help Oliver and Tiffany. Of course, at that time I didn't know if it was you or Oliver who was with Tiffany."

"How'd he know about all of us or even our locations?" Mason asked. "Oliver couldn't even find me via the mTalk locator."

Austin shrugged as an eerie howl whistled up from the lower section of the staircase, causing him and Mason to shiver.

"Why don't we keep going?" suggested Mason with a quick glance behind them.

Austin nodded, and the twins continued up the stairs. "I don't know exactly how he knew. But he knows this place inside and out."

Passenger

Oliver's nerves had finally eased over the presence of the black cat. There'd been no sign of the larger beasts that had attacked him and Mason before. Tiffany looked happier than she'd been since the beginning of the ordeal—at least, as happy as someone in their predicament could look. She sat typing away on the e-journal, the black feline curled in her lap, its purr so loud that he could hear it from several feet away.

He and his sister had agreed to rest for thirty minutes before searching for Mason. They knew he'd contact them when he figured out where he was or if he got into any danger, which was a very real possibility.

A soft beep warned Oliver that their respite was over and they'd need to head out. For where, he didn't know. Tiffany had heard the alarm as well, because she stretched her arms, and the small cat gave a soft *meow*.

"Good kitty," she praised. The black feline stood and arched its back, its fur prickling as it did. It strolled from Tiffany's lap and made its way toward Oliver.

He eyed the creature as it neared him. He wasn't exactly a cat fan. But as he stood and stretched and the cat weaved through his legs, he couldn't resist bending to stroke its back.

"See, she's a nice cat."

"She?" Oliver asked.

"I checked," Tiffany explained, tucking the e-journal into her pack.

"Oh." Oliver cleared his throat, returning to the business at hand. "I don't like it, but I think we need to hide and leave some of our stuff here. I don't think any of the buildings are going to be safe if the Übel are searching them."

Tiffany agreed, and Oliver began removing several things from the second pack and setting them against the ridge along with the artifact case. He took out a small square of camouflage-schemed plastic; it looked like his tent but was only a tarp. Unfolding it, he laid it over the objects, then sliced several branches free from nearby trees and bushes and laid them over the tarp.

It crossed his mind to launch a LOCA-drone, but he quickly dismissed the idea as foolishness. It would only attract the Übel, regardless of its encrypted access. The levitating silver disc would be like a beacon to the artifacts and supply cache. Instead, he opted to add a waypoint on his mTalk. He hoped the fact that the LOCATOR app seemed to be experiencing major issues didn't mean the waypoint would malfunction too.

Oliver kept his personal pack of supplies, the machete, the Zinger, and the grapple launcher, plus extra canisters of hook and wire. He heaved his pack over his shoulders and situated the Zinger across his chest with a strap. The grapple launcher fit well in its holster on his belt, and the machete remained in his hand.

A soft giggle from his sister caught Oliver's attention. "What?" he asked. She really was in a good mood if she was laughing. He looked to where she pointed.

The pack he'd just emptied was no longer empty. Instead, a black furry tail twitched back and forth. A hump within the canvas pack made a circle, and the cat's face and whiskers appeared at the opening. Its eyes seemed to plead with Oliver.

"Can we take it?" Tiffany asked.

Having seen the joy and comfort the cat brought to his sister, Oliver sighed and agreed. "Sure, but you have to carry the pack," he bartered.

She smiled and retrieved the cat and pack, slinging it over her shoulder and arranging the pack across her chest. The little cat stretched its neck, touching the top of its head to Tiffany's chin, and Oliver saw the delight in his sister's smile.

"Are you two ready?" he asked kindly.

The cat answered for them with a soft *meow*.

Oliver led Tiffany back through the jungle but didn't cut back the branches as they went. He did not want to leave any evidence of where they'd stashed the supplies. Every few minutes, he would stop and listen for any sound that might alert them to soldiers or even the larger black creatures. Occasionally, they heard a distant rumble in the south, and Oliver assumed the disturbance was coming from the Übel camp, as a result of the soldiers' search operations to unlock the next clue.

Oliver and Tiffany were running out of time. If they didn't find Mason and Austin soon, Oliver knew he might have to begin searching the pool without the assurance of his brothers' safety.

He looked at his mTalk. He could see where he was in correlation to his surroundings. They were just off course, so he adjusted slightly to the left based on their location in the basin. The trail they followed was not a stone-paved path, but looked to be made by some sort of animal. There was a possibility the creators were the very same black cats that had attacked him, but Oliver was more prepared this time. His assurance was strapped across his chest.

Oliver and Tiffany's goal was to reach the north ziggurat and mount its top. They would have to be very careful not to be seen, and he was considering making the climb by himself. From there, they'd look out over the valley and try to spot any Übel search parties, his parents, or even the twins. If none were to be seen, he and Tiffany would make their way back to the ridge and get a few hours' sleep. He would then enter the pool at night and seek the path referenced by the final clue Mason had found.

Oliver tapped his mTalk and looked at the image he and Mason had taken of the inscription while at the southern zig-gurat. He read it quietly to himself: "When you find the Truth, you are no longer lost. At the foot of the cross, your path home begins. Dive into the Truth, so you too may find the way."

Surely the Übel would have found this clue by now and found the path. No doubt he and Tiffany had to hurry. He looked back at his sister. "We need to pick up the pace a bit."

She nodded and gave him a thumbs-up. There was a *meow*, but a black tuft of hair was all that poked out from the pack. "Midnight agrees," she said.

Oliver shook his head and mumbled to himself, "She named the cat?"

Raft

At the top of the staircase, Mason and Austin found themselves at another door. This time, however, there was no cross-shaped indent for the key necklace, and the door was wooden. But Mason knew it must be made of the rubbelum tree he'd read about.

"What now?" Mason asked. "You said the brother guy didn't give you any more instructions?"

"Nope," Austin admitted and groaned. He pulled out the cross pendant necklace from underneath his shirt and began swiping it on all sides of the door in desperation.

Nothing happened.

"Maybe it's the light-up stones," Mason suggested.

The brothers went to work swiping their hands across the doorframe and walls. Still nothing happened.

"Looks like we're at a dead end," Austin admitted. He swallowed loudly. "We'll just have to go ba—" But his words were cut short as a squealing blast of cold air swept up from the depths of the staircase.

Armed with the light from his mTalk, Mason quickly shone the beam around. Then he saw it. "Look! Up there." He pointed to a spot nearly seven feet above the mantle over the door. Tucked between the stone bricks was the cross-shaped indentation they sought. "How do we reach it?" he asked.

"Maybe if you boost me up," Austin suggested, setting his staff against the frame of the sealed door.

"It's pretty high," Mason cautioned.

"Just try. Come on, make like a ladder."

Mason nodded and locked his fingers together, creating a foothold for Austin.

"Closer to the wall," Austin commanded.

Mason shifted so his back was against the door. Austin stepped up and then climbed to stand on Mason's shoulder. Mason couldn't see, but he heard Austin grunting and felt the pressure from his younger brother's shoes pressing into his shoulders as he tried to reach as high as he could.

Mason groaned under his twin's weight. "Can you use the mantle as a step?"

"No, it's too narrow."

"Climb back down then, because your feet are digging into my shoulder blades," Mason complained.

"All right." With that, Austin jumped down. But as he did, his foot twisted, and he stumbled toward the sharply descending stairs. Mason saw the danger, and his reflexes forced his hand forward to grip hold of Austin's camo shirt, pulling him back just in time.

Austin looked at his brother with a thankful smile and exhaled. "That was close."

Mason nodded. "We need a better way."

Austin's face scrunched into a familiar tangle of thought, one Mason had seen often. The next instant, Austin lifted the cross necklace from around his neck and then retrieved the jeweled staff from next to the door. Mason watched as his brother started winding the chain of the necklace tightly around the crest of the staff, which Mason estimated to be about five feet in length.

Once complete, he made his request. "Mason, boost me up again." Mason obeyed and lifted his brother up and onto his shoulders.

"Why," Mason began through gritted teeth, "would they place it so high up? Weren't the other ones right next to the door?"

"They were," Austin said, his voice strained as if he was reaching. Which Mason supposed he was. "Maybe it's meant to stop someone who got into the tunnels but wasn't supposed to."

"Like us?"

"No, we're supposed to be here. Brother Sam sent me," Austin said.

"Sure."

"I almost got it."

Mason couldn't see what Austin was doing, but he'd figured it out. The soft click of the door opening behind him startled him a bit, and he almost knocked Austin off balance.

Austin jumped down from Mason's shoulders, staff in hand. Mason turned round to see through an open door, but only into darkness.

With their lights on, the twins proceeded. The sound of water drops pattering alerted them to a slow trickle of water falling from a trapdoor in the ceiling. Austin walked over and shone his light up at a square rubbelum plate embedded in the ceiling.

Thunk!

The twins turned to see that the door they'd come through had just closed, sealing them inside the chamber. Mason was unworried, though; they'd been led to this place. Now they just needed to find the way out.

They continued to investigate.

"Look, there is a pulley or something attached to the door," Austin said.

Mason shone his light on the pulley and followed a short cord leading away and disappearing into the ceiling. The rope began to tighten, and he quickly knew where they were.

"Austin, quick, get back!"

Austin turned to look at his twin, but it was too late. The trapdoor swung down, knocking Austin square in the back and propelling him forward. The walking staff flew from his hand, nearly striking Mason. A deluge of water gushed from the ceiling, giving off an odd mechanical whirling sound. There wasn't time to investigate. The water was pooling at their feet, rising to their ankles, knees, and soon their hips.

Mason realized they would have just seconds and reached out for his kneeling brother, whose head was by then only inches above the water. Pulling Austin to his feet, he also retrieved the fallen staff and went to the door in an attempt to open their only way of escape. He looked for the cross indent, but there wasn't one. He couldn't open the door, and the water was still dumping through the hole in the ceiling, quickly surpassing the two boys' waistlines. It had reached above their chests when, without warning, a door in the far side of the chamber slid open. The water rushed out the new opening, boiling and surging toward its escape as if alive, giving off a thunderous growl as it did.

The water tugged at the boys, but its current wasn't strong enough to take control. Mason gasped with relief as the water level quickly dropped until only a few scattered puddles remained at their feet. Austin was soaked but standing next to Mason, who handed the staff back to the youngest Wikk.

"We must be just below the chamber or a chamber like the first one we entered when we crossed the aqueduct into the ziggurat," Mason explained. He really wasn't sure which ziggurat they were in.

Austin set the staff against the wall and shook his head and hair, sending a spray of droplets loose. "Well, how do we get out of here before we get—" He stopped.

A metal door slid open, but the sound had come from above. Several footsteps, followed by a muffled but commanding voice, alerted the twins to intruders in the chamber above. Austin raised his finger for silence, but the gesture was unnecessary. Mason was already crouching and backed tightly against the stone wall. The overhead conversation could not be understood through the wooden trapdoor or stone floor. But it sounded like a tense discussion.

Mason heard a twang and looked up to see the chord tightening on the pulley to the drain. The trapdoor dropped open and another flood of water poured into the room along with the swirling noise. The twins stood up straight, their backs against the wall. The water again reached their chests before the release door opened and the water swept from the room. Just as the water dropped below their knees, Mason noticed the staff floating on the current just a few feet ahead. Austin had forgotten to take hold of it after the distraction of the trespassers above.

"The cross!" he gasped.

Austin's eyes went wide, and he dove after the staff and cross. But he got a mouthful of water and bobbed to the surface with a loud sputtering cough. Even the sound of the exiting water could not cover the outburst as it echoed in the chamber.

A second later, Mason realized losing the staff was the least of their worries. A booming voice sent a streak of fear coursing through his body.

"Who's there?" the commanding voice of a soldier asked from above. As if there were any way he or Austin were going to answer that.

Austin had recovered the staff and was now stepping back toward Mason on tiptoe. Almost no water was left in the room. The twins didn't speak. The release door for the water slid shut with a click, and the trapdoor in the ceiling closed with a *thunk*.

Mason and Austin remained silent for a moment, hoping the soldiers would think it was just the water making the noise. Their hope was for naught, because a green explosion and brief surge of water brought the trapdoor to the stone floor in burning orange splinters. A weird cylindrical fan clanked to the stone floor, a wide hole nearly splitting it in half.

A metal drain grate remained intact, but another blast sent it to the stone floor with a loud clang and clatter. Water continued to pour through the gap in the ceiling.

"Frantivic, through the door. Now!" the original intruding voice screamed. "You next, Sekelton! Go!"

Mason and Austin didn't have a second to react before a boot appeared in the hole above.

"Quick!" Austin ordered and tugged Mason toward the door that had released the water. "It's our only chance."

The water had again begun pooling at their feet. The twins were nearly to the door when a soldier dropped through the drain. His back was to the twins, and he was dressed in grey-and-black camo fatigues and wore a black beret. The stock of a rifle of some sort protruded from his side. The man stepped forward, away from the twins. The butt of the rifle rose as the soldier began to turn, using the light on his weapon to search the room.

The second soldier, Sekelton, dropped into view quickly after; he looked no older than Oliver. Mason hardly had time to realize this before the young man spun around and faced the twins.

"There!" he shouted, getting the attention of his comrade, Frantivic. The soldier spun around, standing nearly side by side with his counterpart.

Mason felt a jerk on his waist as Austin bear hugged him and threw the entire combined weight of their bodies against the door. A loud crack resounded from behind him, and Mason felt his body falling backward as a flash of sunlight blasted into the room from the outside. He barely had time to see the soldiers throw their hands up in defense against the blinding light.

The planks of the door did nothing to cushion their impact as Mason and Austin fell back on the former gate against a stone causeway. Mason flipped onto his stomach and realized he and Austin were sliding down the face of the ziggurat on the waterway door as though it were a toboggan.

He saw Austin next to him gripping the jeweled staff, which thrust out before them like a javelin. He looked back and saw the hole in the ziggurat that they had just fallen through. It was rapidly getting farther away, which meant something else was getting nearer. He faced forward again and saw they were flying down toward the blood-red pool. The water was coming closer and closer, and the speed of their crude raft was increasing.

A green blast sent fragments of stone flying in all directions as the two soldiers began firing on the twins from their perch high up in the ziggurat. Another shot hit their makeshift raft, splintering one of the planks.

Out of the corner of his eye, Mason saw several figures in uniforms standing on the plaza surrounding the ziggurat. More soldiers—they were everywhere. One in particular stood out to Mason, although he didn't know why.

The raft hopped up a bit, and Mason looked forward again. The wind whizzed through his hair and brought a chill over his wet body. Austin shouted an unusual cry of joy at their roller-coaster ride. Mason looked to see his brother staring forward, staff now raised like a flag as they plummeted down the side of the stone structure toward the cross-shaped pool below.

Then the end of the staff lit like a crimson-colored star as a green streak struck it. Mason saw the trio of soldiers firing rapidly at the twins. He only hoped, as Oliver had said before, these were stunner shots, nothing lethal.

Another green streak came close to the kids but seemed to get zapped into the red-jeweled stone at the end of the staff. In that second, Mason realized the jewel looked the same as the ones lining the pool. And the pendant was cross-shaped like the pool. These things were not coincidences. They were part of a plan.

His moment of revelation ended as the front of the raft hit the surface of the water, launching the back half upward and projecting Austin and Mason into the air in uncontrolled somersaults. The twins each hit the water with a smack and splash.

As Mason's head bobbed above the surface, he quickly gathered his bearings and located the shore. He looked around and noticed Austin a few yards away, one hand holding the staff and the other pulling him through the water.

Mason looked back toward the ziggurat and saw only a black hole where their raft had once been a door. A chill coursed through his wet body, but it wasn't the effect of the frigid water. Long green vines had wrapped themselves around one of the soldiers, and the other was firing at it in an attempt to free his comrade. Mason knew the feeling of those plant tendrils all too well and pitied his attacker.

The trees lining the pool blocked the stone plaza and the soldiers occupying it from view. He hoped the men at the base of the ziggurat had gone to the aid of their fellow soldiers atop the ziggurat. If they had, Mason knew that he and Austin had just minutes to disappear into the thick jungle.

The escape was not complete yet. He neared the side of the pool and hefted himself out of the water onto the embankment. His pack was still securely strapped on his back. Thick green foliage crept right to the edge of the pool in this place, and several branches dipped into the water. Mason motioned for Austin to join him. His brother was standing near where the cascading stream of water had entered the pool.

His younger brother shook his head and then frowned as a man in a black trench coat stepped into view and placed a gloved hand on Austin's shoulder. He knew who the man was.

Mason stood and turned to run, but suddenly two soldiers in camo emerged from the jungle. Both were out of breath, but Mason was caught. With one stride, one of the soldiers raised his rifle and pointed directly at Mason's chest.

"Don't move!" he commanded. "Or you'll wake up with a terrible headache."

Mason raised his hands in the air in surrender.

The soldier moved forward and let go of his rifle, which hung by a strap from his chest. With both hands, he brought Mason's arms down and twisted them so his thumbs were against the small of his back. Mason felt a coil of something wrap around his wrists and knew he was bound.

Mason now wished all the soldiers had been restrained by the vines.

2.35

Protector

Tiffany and Oliver had observed the last few minutes of action unfold before their eyes. They'd set their packs aside, crawled on their stomachs across the stone-paved surface of the top tier of the northern ziggurat, and watched as a patrol of Übel, Vedrik included, scoured the eastern ziggurat, searching for the next clue to lead them to their prize. Then, without warning, the twins flew out through a hole in the side of the ziggurat on a makeshift raft. An odd sense of relief came over her at the sight of her youngest brother; at least she knew where he was, even though he was currently in danger.

She gasped as she saw green streaks zip past them and explode against the stone tiers of the ziggurat, creating a spray of stony shards. A set of soldiers appeared at the twins' point of escape and continued to fire on them. As the twins descended, Tiffany and Oliver climbed to their feet and watched their brothers' plight in horror.

The rest of the Übel soldiers had run to the waterfall and begun firing at the twins. Oliver reassured her they were just stun shots. It didn't matter to her what was being fired; she didn't like anyone shooting anything at her baby brothers.

The raft crashed into the pool, and the boys disappeared into the water. When they reappeared, Tiffany saw that the patrol of soldiers was dashing toward the pool to capture the twins while the ones atop the ziggurat were tangled in a battle with the green vines. Tiffany felt no sorrow for the evil men.

The worst thing was that neither she nor Oliver could do anything about it. They watched as Austin, then Mason, was captured by the men. Oliver lurched forward, as if to attack, but quickly halted and returned to Tiffany.

"The soldiers have them," Oliver said. "We have to go. We have to get to the next clue before the Übel."

"But what about Mason and Austin?" Tiffany asked.

Oliver shook his head. "We can't help them now; we have to get ahead of Vedrik, and that means finding the clue and stopping him from getting it. At least we know where Mason and Austin are."

"They're just little boys," Tiffany scolded.

"Tiffany, stop acting like their mom. You're not!" Oliver berated. "Listen to me: the soldiers aren't going to harm them. They can't. They need Dad and Mom to participate in their search. Killing any of their kids would seriously undermine that, don't you think?"

But Oliver's tone set Tiffany off.

"You've been nothing but irresponsible toward them—letting Mason stay alone, sending us to sleep while reassuring me that Austin was safe in the ship. It was a lie!"

Oliver stepped back. "That's uncalled for," he accused. "I'm not a liar. I'm making decisions as best as I can—"

"Decisions without any of our input!"

"Someone had to take control. Someone had to lead this family!"

Zip! Crack!

Shards of stone flew everywhere.

Zip! Splat! Zip! Crack!

Oliver flew to Tiffany, pulling her to the ground. The back of her head didn't hit; instead her tailbone and elbows took the brunt of the impact. Oliver rolled off her and glanced back toward the direction the firing had come from, even though at their height and angle they could only see the far ridge of the basin and the sky.

"They've seen us!" Oliver said. "Stay down. We've got to get into the jungle right now. We'll climb down the back."

"What about through the interior of the ziggurat? That's the way we came."

Oliver shook his head. "No, we'd be trapped inside. It'll take longer, and they'll be here before we can get out."

There he went again, making all the decisions. Not listening to her.

Zip! Crack!

"We have to go! Now!" Oliver ordered, crawling toward the back of the ziggurat where they could jump down the side, hopefully out of view of the soldiers.

"The vines!"

"I'll take care of them. Now come!"

Tiffany had to decide: would she follow him or challenge him? She decided to follow. She went after her brother to the back of the ziggurat, where they retrieved their packs. At first, Tiffany's heart sank as she pulled on the pack that had held Midnight and found it was empty. It was one more loss added to the many. She thought of the green vines that had assaulted Oliver and Mason and then the Übel soldiers. The thought choked her up.

Oliver looked at her. "Are you coming?"

She nodded and lowered herself to the next tier down, then stood.

"Meow."

Tiffany turned to see the small black cat pad casually into view as if oblivious to the danger around.

Oliver was waiting. Tiffany scooped Midnight up and shoved her into the empty pack, then slung her own pack containing the e-journal over her shoulders and onto her back. While she could no longer see the soldiers, and the barrage of firing had ended, she knew they weren't out of danger yet. A battleground of swirling vines awaited their descent. They had come up to the top of the ziggurat by climbing the staircase within and therefore avoided the plants. By going down the outside, they'd be putting themselves in the clutches of the vines. She hoped Oliver's plan to deal with them would work.

Oliver held out the Zinger and aimed it. He pressed the trigger, activating the weapon. It hummed loudly as blue streaks of energy coursed over it. Tiffany followed the direction he aimed with her eyes and noticed a spot on the ziggurat where several of the green tendrils connected.

He fired.

Whoop!

Two small projectiles flew from the weapon and plunged into the stem of the vine. An explosion of blue goo erupted, and instantly several dozen vines writhed painfully in the air and crashed against the ziggurat.

"Let's go, quick!" Oliver ordered. "Before the soldiers figure out what we're doing—and before those other plants regain their courage."

Tiffany thought that was a strange way to describe the vines, but she wasn't about to argue with him anymore. Their argument had nearly gotten them stunned and captured. They needed to work out their issues, but it'd have to wait until they were safe. Or at least safer.

The sun was bright and hot. Tiffany felt beads of sweat running down her cheeks. She used the collar of her shirt to wipe her face dry but felt the sweat droplets forming again only moments later. Oliver was nearly five tiers further down than she was. He held the Zinger ready to respond should the vines get within range of him. Oliver was on a mission, and Tiffany knew nothing could stand in his way.

At the base of the ziggurat, Oliver dashed into the jungle and disappeared. Tiffany was aghast at her brother's abandonment. Relief came a second later as Oliver poked back through the tree line and waved for her to join him. She lowered herself down from the lowest tier and, although tired, jogged to her brother and stepped into the shadowy jungle cover.

Oliver took off at a run and never slowed down. They followed the same animal trail they'd used before. Previously, Oliver had held back branches until Tiffany passed them, but this time he dashed through without regard for his sister, who was trying to keep up with him. She kept a safe distance to avoid being smacked by leaves and limbs.

As she followed, Tiffany thought of her brothers and her parents and the mess they were all in. With the latest event, she wasn't sure that she and Oliver should try to remain free any longer. She contemplated their surrender. At least then the two of them would rejoin their family. How bad could it be? Oliver had mentioned that their parents looked to be in okay shape. He had also said the Übel wouldn't harm the kids and risk their parents' anger.

As if to knock these thoughts from Tiffany, a branch swung toward her, barely giving her time to duck and avoid a smack to her head.

A heavy wind rattled the leaves overhead, and tree branches swayed; the sound of the wind was soon matched by the noise of engines. Oliver turned, dashed back to Tiffany, and nearly tackled her to the ground for the second time. They hit the jungle floor just in time as three soldiers, dressed in camo and adorned with black helmets, dropped through the jungle canopy on ropes. They touched down just fifteen feet away but dashed away immediately, not even taking time to check their surroundings. The squad took off in the same direction Tiffany and Oliver had been going.

The engines above sputtered a thunderous roar and the three ropes suddenly ascended and disappeared. Whatever the craft was, it flew away. The soldiers were already out of earshot. Oliver pulled Tiffany to her feet, apologizing as he did. "I'm sorry for shoving you. I had to act quickly."

Tiffany brushed off her knees and stomach, sending leaves and dirt particles to the ground. "No, no worries." But her brother's apology was a welcome change from his earlier hostile tone and neglectful charge through the jungle. A frightened *meow* reminded that Midnight had been in the bag. She flipped open the flap but the kitten looked fine, just startled.

"The men took off toward our stuff, and I estimate we're only a hundred feet from the ridge where we left everything," Oliver explained.

"Were they looking for us?"

"Possibly, but why didn't they search the area? They looked like they had a clear goal."

"Do you think they're going for the artifact case?"

"I don't know, but I can't think of how they would know it was there. At the same time, I can't think of any other reason to land here and head in that direction," Oliver admitted. "We just have to hope they won't find it."

Tiffany watched Oliver flip the Zinger and check it over. It hummed loudly, and a surge of energy seemed to roll over it in blue crackling streaks as Oliver compressed the trigger, instantly activating the charge. "We've got this if we need it," he promised.

Tiffany nodded, and she and Oliver crept forward on the trail. But she felt knots forming in her stomach. Was Oliver really prepared to take on that many soldiers? To shoot at them?

Several minutes of agonizingly slow movement brought them very near their destination. Oliver motioned with his hands to keep low and quiet, but Tiffany already knew that. She heard nothing; there was no sign of the soldiers except a few boot prints in the soft dirt trail.

Oliver motioned for Tiffany to stay put as he surveyed the small clearing where they'd stashed their stuff. Through gaps in the foliage, Tiffany could see no one and still heard no voices. The silence was interrupted by a low mumble overhead.

Oliver and Tiffany looked up. To their amazement, they saw the three soldiers above them wrapped in a large net. Tiffany nearly fell back in surprise. The men hung nearly twenty feet up in the tree branches, their hands bound together and mouths gagged, only a garbled set of sounds getting through the cloth gags.

How had the soldiers been captured? How had neither Tiffany nor Oliver heard any of the battle? She looked around the clearing and something crimson red caught her attention a short distance into the jungle. "Oliver?" she called to her brother, "Look over there." But when she looked back, joined by Oliver, the red thing was gone.

Eagle

Austin waited under the guarded gaze of one of the soldiers. A patch on the heavy man's left breast pocket read *Cruz*. Austin had tried to loosen the bindings that held his wrists together against his own back, but it had been no use. Every few moments he had to shift his shoulders to keep his pack from sliding out of place. They'd taken his staff from him.

Why hadn't he used it to fight back?

Mason stood near, bound and guarded by Sekelton and Frantivic, the two soldiers who'd dropped into the chamber. Sekelton's sleeve was torn and the knee of his pants ripped. Austin knew the damage has come from the vines; he'd overheard Frantivic comment on "Sekelton's run of bad luck, getting attacked twice."

Another soldier had appeared out of the ziggurat. Austin learned he was the third in the group that had ambushed Mason and Austin, and his name was Bargoz. Bargoz began speaking to the one Austin now knew to be Captain Vedrik and the other soldier, still unnamed, who had captured Mason. He heard something about the doors suddenly getting all jammed up and the soldiers having to blast through to get out.

The captain, dressed in black, was the very one who had led the raid on Austin's home and taken his parents. He knew that this Vedrik was in charge of the mission. Austin only wished he was free of his bonds. If he could take the leader out, then maybe he could cause confusion amongst the soldiers. Austin wiggled his wrists, but the restraints were solid. Each movement only brought a sting to his skin.

Austin wondered why his parents were nowhere in sight. Why would the captain dare leave the Wikk parents' sides? Wasn't the captain afraid they might escape? They could be under the escort of some other soldiers. But Austin had other hopes: one, his parents had actually escaped, or two, Oliver and Tiffany would take advantage of the captain's absence and rescue their dad and mom.

Captain Vedrik and Bargoz returned to the twins and their guards while the unnamed soldier disappeared into the jungle.

"We will wait here; the transport is on its way. You two"— the captain pointed to Sekelton and Cruz—"will head back with these boys, and I will remain with the archeologists. Frantivic and Bargoz will remain behind and guard the door to the ziggurat."

Austin's mouth dropped open, and he peeked at his brother to see if he too had heard the mention of his parents. Mason was staring at the ground, a look of defeat on his face. This put an end to Austin's hope for his parents' escape. They were here, probably just a few hundred feet away within the ziggurat. Maybe if he could just. . . . No, he couldn't possibly. . . .

But he had to try!

Austin ducked his head and then drove his left shoulder into his guard's stomach. Cruz grunted and hunched over. Austin darted forward, his goal the jungle and then the ziggurat. Hands still bound, his balance wasn't all it should have been, and he nearly tripped a couple of times. It mattered little as he careened only twenty feet before a set of pounding boots came up behind him, and someone grabbed him around the waist.

The soldier, Frantivic, was stronger than he looked and heaved eleven-year-old Austin over one shoulder. It was exactly like when the Blauwe Mensen soldiers had captured the twins. At this angle, Austin could only see the shadow of his captor and the stone pavers of the pavilion.

The rumble of engines alerted Austin to an approaching transport, the one summoned to take him and Mason back to the Übel camp. All hope was fading away with the craft's approach.

Then, without warning, Austin was unceremoniously dropped to the ground, landing painfully on his shoulders and knees. He heard soldiers shouting. Austin rolled to his back and saw Frantivic lift his rifle into the air. Austin followed the soldier's aim and saw a silver ship flying low over the jungle. It was headed right for them. Austin immediately recognized the ship as the *Phoenix*.

The soldiers took aim and began to fire. Austin saw that Mason had been shoved to the ground too. The ship slid through the air toward the ziggurat, and the soldiers trained their weapons, firing volleys of green streaks at the silver craft.

"More firepower!" commanded Vedrik. "Stuns won't do anything, you imbeciles."

The soldiers switched their weapons, and blasts of blue shot from the guns toward the ship. Still, the attack looked to have little impact on the ship.

Oliver and Tiffany had come to rescue the twins, and, if they did it right, possibly their parents as well. Of course, Austin needed to somehow alert Oliver that Mr. and Mrs. Wikk were near.

The silver ship banked, and its right wing slid toward the soldiers, just a few feet from the stone floor of the pavilion.

Austin knew Oliver could fly, but he had no idea his older brother could pilot this well.

At that moment, Austin felt the bindings around his hands slip loose. He brought his hands around to his front and looked at them. Somehow, the restraint had been sliced through. He turned around, but there was no one behind him.

Then he heard Mason's voice. "Obbin, how? But when? You're . . ." Mason stuttered.

Austin looked and, sure enough, the blue prince from Jahr des Eises had his small bone-handled knife out and had just sliced through Mason's bindings. He'd changed clothes since they'd left him in their cabin before departing Jahr des Eises. The prince again was shoeless, shirtless, and wearing only his grey-striped fur shorts. Obbin motioned for Austin to join him and Mason.

The soldiers were still distracted by the silver ship, and Austin noticed several were staggering to their feet, having dived out of the deadly path of the attacking spaceship wing. Austin spied his ruby-crested staff lying on the ground and wanted desperately to grab it. It was one of the tools he'd been given, but it was among the firing soldiers. He might be seen, trampled, or killed if he got in the fray.

Austin turned and followed Obbin and Mason into an area of nearby jungle, and then continued to charge through the low-hanging branches and vines. A million thoughts flooded through his mind. He'd thought Obbin was still on Jahr des Eises, yet the boy was with them right now. How had he come? How had he found the twins? Where was he leading them? Had Tiffany and Oliver sent him?

He heard several more *plinks* as the soldiers continued to fire on the *Phoenix*. Suddenly, a burst of engine thrust sounded, confirming that the ship was leaving. Had it been damaged? Were Oliver and Tiffany okay? Austin looked toward the sky, but there was no smoke or damage that he could see. The ship then flew from sight, and Austin turned back to look at his liberator.

Obbin and Mason were still moving deeper into the jungle at a quick pace. After several minutes of running, the blue prince stopped without warning and pulled a small cross from his pocket. He waved it over an area of turned-up ground and then yanked on a handle that looked like a gnarled root. A small trapdoor lifted free, and he motioned for Mason, followed by Austin, to enter. A ladder led down into darkness.

Obbin descended the ladder last and pulled the trapdoor shut overhead, closing out the little light that had seeped through the jungle canopy.

They climbed downward in pure darkness for just a minute. Austin heard a splash below.

"Whoa! That's cold," Mason said. "There's water down here."

Austin was next and reluctantly stepped into icy water about a few inches deep. The water splashed onto his ankles, but his shoes protected his feet.

Obbin was next and splashed into the icy water with bare feet. He didn't seem bothered by the cold at all.

Neither of the twins spoke but stood in the dimly lit chamber staring at the blue prince in astonishment. How had he gotten to Evad? How had he known where to find them in the jungle? How had he pulled off such a daring rescue? Austin hoped that Obbin was about to tell them. There were just too many questions.

Note

Oliver and Tiffany stared at the men, caught like flies in a spiderweb above, suspended in midair. Somehow, the men had not only been pulled into a trap, but they had been bound and gagged.

"Whoever did this also took all the soldiers' equipment," Oliver said, pointing to a pile of weapons and electronics a few feet away next to the bushes. He turned and looked toward the ridge, where a large bush appeared to sit undisturbed. Of course, he knew this was actually just a guise to hide their supplies. The assailant had not messed with their stuff.

"What should we do with them?" Tiffany asked.

Oliver shrugged. "Nothing at the moment. We'll leave them to be found by their comrades."

Tiffany frowned. "What if they aren't discovered?"

"Then that's just too bad. They're the bad guys anyway."

"Oliver!"

"Look, most likely, their being stuck or lost will force the Übel to search for them and hopefully that will be cause for a long delay."

"And if they don't look?"

"That's not our problem. Besides, aren't you at all interested in who put them up there? And if you and I might be the next target?"

Tiffany shook her head. "And if the same were done to us, I'd want to be set free by the next people that came across me."

"If we set them free, they'll take us captive." Oliver hesitated and then spoke quietly. "Even if we had their weapons, we can't escort all three of them. We're on a mission, remember?"

Tiffany sighed. "So, what should we do then?"

"We look for the next clue." Oliver started for the stash of supplies he and Tiffany had left earlier. As he walked toward the bushlike pile, Oliver noticed a scrap of paper attached to a small metal chain or necklace. He lifted the chain up and a cross-shaped pendant dropped into view. The paper remained attached, and Oliver pulled it free and handed it to his sister, knowing she'd be most interested.

Tiffany cleared her throat and held the note up to read it. " 'You have made it far, but there is more to go,' " she started, but stopped when Oliver motioned for her to lower her voice so that the soldiers overhead could not hear. She continued, " 'Do not give up hope or faith. The cross is the key to setting you free when you have come to a hard place. Good will defeat evil. Light will consume the dark.' " Tiffany looked over the note a second time.

"Tiff, there is something written on the back," Oliver whispered as he placed the cross and chain around his neck.

She flipped it and read. "620.2011 Z."

"Sounds like a coordinate, with the Z attached. Is there a number with a Y or X following?" Oliver asked.

"No, just the note." Tiffany handed the paper back to Oliver, who slipped it into his pack.

"Strange," Oliver mused. "Someone came here, captured and imprisoned the soldiers, by the looks of it, didn't take any of our supplies, and to top it off left us an encouraging note and a necklace."

Tiffany nodded. "It's strange, for sure, but a welcome change."

Thunder sounded in the distance, warning of an impending storm.

"If you're going into the pool, you'd better do it quick," Tiffany whispered. "These storms haven't been very friendly, and lightning seems to accompany them."

Oliver nodded and quickly began uncovering the tarp. He pulled the camouflage plastic aside, revealing the artifact case and the diving supplies he had unloaded.

"Tiffany, I'm going to need the spare pack," he said.

She nodded her head, raised the flap, and lifted a sleeping Midnight from the pack. The small cat was purring loudly as Tiffany held it up. She kept it in one arm and gave the pack to Oliver.

Oliver set the flippers, the mask, and the Oxyverter into the pack. He then took the diving suit and unfolded it. "I'm just going to step over here and change," he explained. His sister nodded and turned away from the spot where Oliver was headed.

A grumble from overhead reminded him of the prisoners, and he was sure to find a spot out of their sight as well. Oliver reluctantly stripped off his grandpa's exceptionally designed clothing and donned the wetsuit. It'd keep him dry, but it didn't have all the protective properties the Ultra-Wear stuff did.

He stepped back through the foliage that hid him, and Tiffany laughed. "Nice outfit," she jested. She'd taken out the e-journal, and its screen glowed brightly as she held it in her right hand.

Oliver pulled at a section of the waterproof material near his leg; the wetsuit was tight, but one benefit of that was it made his muscles stand out, and this he liked. He even looked toward the captured soldiers and raised an arm, flexing his bicep.

"Are you almost ready?" Tiffany chided at her brother's arrogant display. Midnight was weaving around her ankles as she looked over the e-journal.

"Yes, but we'll need to take everything with us and stash it elsewhere along with the soldiers' weapons. We can't leave anything here in case they somehow get free. I mean when they get free," he added for his sister's benefit. He stuck the remaining loose supplies from the *Phoenix* into his packs. Tiffany set the e-journal back in her own pack and gathered a few tools and supplies that she tucked in small compartments. Oliver hefted the artifact case and headed for the pile of weapons and electronics. He gave the Zinger to Tiffany, who reluctantly took it and slung it over her shoulder. He then took the three rifles and crisscrossed them over his back and chest. Several devices remained, but Oliver had no free hands. He had to carry the artifact case in one and the machete in the other.

He knew that Tiffany had grown attached to Midnight, but she would need both her hands to carry the Übels' gadgets. The cat purred loudly at her feet and then stood and stretched its front paws against Tiffany's legs. She bent down and lifted the small cat into her arms.

He felt guilty for what he was about to say. "Tiffany, you can't bring Midnight. I need you to take the remaining electronics, and there just isn't any more room in our packs." They were both overly weighed down by all the gear.

Tiffany looked as if she might cry. She held the cat out to look into its eyes. "You've been a good kitty . . ." she started, but broke off. She set the cat down and took a step toward the path she and Oliver would take to reach the pool. "Midnight, come."

The cat didn't hesitate and plodded along right after Tiffany.

"I guess she doesn't need to be carried," Oliver said, relieved that his sister wouldn't have to deal with another emotional loss.

Tiffany smiled. "Nope," she said. And then, to Midnight, "Good kitty. Stay with me."

2.38

Obbin

M ason was excited to be reunited with Obbin, but he still couldn't figure it out. Ever since Obbin had freed him and he'd turned around to look into the turquoise eyes of the blue boy, he'd been trying to unravel the enigma.

The last time he'd seen Obbin, he had been in the twins' cabin on the *Phoenix*. But the prince had disappeared, and Mason had assumed he'd abandoned his quest to fly and escaped the ship to join his people, the Blauwe Mensen.

"Where have you been?" Mason asked.

Obbin smiled sheepishly. "I've been in your ship."

"Hiding?" Austin asked.

"Well, duh," Obbin replied. "What else would I be doing?"

Austin shrugged.

"Why didn't you show yourself?" Mason asked.

"If I'd told your brother, he would have taken me back," Obbin said. "I had to be sure that he couldn't. At least, not right away." He leaned over and picked up a pack that sat against the wall.

"Well, then, why not when we landed?" Mason pried further.

"After hearing the argument between you"—Obbin looked at Austin—"and your older brother, I knew it wasn't the right time to come forward even if you had told them about me."

Austin scoffed. "He was harsh, wasn't he?"

Obbin nodded. "I've fought with my brothers before, but only Voltan ever treated me like that."

Mason decided to intercede. "It wasn't anything more than a misunderstanding, really." It was a bit more, but Austin finally seemed to be getting over all of it and he didn't want to reignite his brother's rebellion. "So, where were you hiding?"

"The ventilation shafts were big enough, and I borrowed supplies as I needed them," Obbin admitted.

"Well, why did you come out now?" Austin asked.

Mason was relieved; it seemed Austin had veered away from an outburst of temper.

Obbin sighed. "You guys were gone for an entire day. I became worried that you'd left another way or something worse had happened. When your brother and sister returned, I followed them."

"Why not reveal yourself to them?" Mason asked.

"I didn't know them. I knew you two. But I hoped they would lead me to you," Obbin explained.

"We were separated, so how did you find us?" Austin asked.

Obbin looked as if someone might be coming after them. "We might want to walk as we talk," he said. The prince lifted his arm and tapped something on his wrist, sending a beam of light ahead of them and illuminating the hall ahead.

"My mTalk!" Austin exclaimed.

Obbin, who'd started forward, stopped and glanced over his shoulder. "Oh, yeah, I fixed it. But I'm going to hold on to it," he said firmly.

"No, you're—" Austin started, but Mason, who was last in the line, grabbed his twin's shoulder.

"Let it go. Right now isn't the time. We need to find Oliver and Tiffany and our parents, and Obbin's on our side. He's helping us."

"Fine," Austin conceded, but added in a whisper, "But I'm getting it eventually."

"So, how did you find us?" Mason asked.

"I followed your brother and sister after they left the ship. Watching them from the jungle, I saw their trick to cross the chasm. I didn't have a clip, but that did not bother me. I've crossed the crevice outside our home many times before with my brother Rylin. We never used any such device," Obbin said. "After getting through the cave, I watched your brother and sister swim toward the pyramid down the water bridge—"

"Aqueduct," Austin corrected in a mumble.

"But it was just a few minutes before they came flying back out, pursued by some soldiers. Next thing I knew, they disappeared over the side on some sort of hook and wire. I waited in the tunnel entrance and watched as the soldiers fired into the trees, but eventually they gave up and started down the side of the pyramid in pursuit, dropping down level by level." The blue boy took a left at the *T* in the tunnel, after eyeing a slip of paper in his hand.

Mason switched on the light on his mTalk and shone it behind them. "So, what happened next?"

"Once the soldiers were out of sight, I was going to balance along the side of the brid—aqueduct and onto the top of the pyramid. But a man in a red cloak came up behind me and stopped me. He said, 'I have a better way,'" Obbin explained.

The twins and prince arrived at a door, and Obbin waved the cross pendant next to the usual cross-indented plate. The door slid open, revealing the next segment of the passage. Obbin started through, but Austin didn't follow.

"Red cloak!" he exclaimed. "What was his name?"

Obbin stopped and turned to look at Austin, the light from Obbin's mTalk shining over Austin's shoulder and into Mason's eyes.

"Lower it, please," Mason requested sharply.

"Sorry," Obbin apologized and then looked to Austin. "He called himself Brother Sam."

"So, you met him as well?" Austin asked as Obbin turned to continue walking. The twins followed.

Mason shook his head. "Didn't you wonder who this cloaked guy might be?" he asked. "Why didn't you run?"

"Where was I to go? I'd never left my home planet before, and now I have no idea where I am, and as far as I could tell your sister and brother were about to be captured," Obbin explained. "I certainly didn't want to be stuck here alone forever, especially since no one from my village knew I left, and you didn't know I remained on the ship. Besides that, your brother made the ship go invisible; how would I have ever found it again? And, if I did, I'd never have gotten back in."

"That makes sense," Mason said. "Our brother and sister—you mentioned them being captured. Did you see it happen?"

Obbin shook his head.

"If you don't know where they are, who was flying the *Phoenix*?" Austin asked.

"That was not the *Phoenix*, and Brother Sam was piloting it. He called it the *Eagle*," Obbin explained as he waved the pendant next to another door. The door opened and revealed a downward-spiraling staircase.

"Here I thought it was Oliver. Where could they be?" Austin wondered aloud as the trio descended the stairs.

Mason suddenly felt silly. Where had his mind been? He was supposed to contact Oliver and Tiffany to let them know where he was. And further, he should have told them he had found Austin, and about Austin's encounter with the cloaked man. He had seriously failed to keep them informed, and it might have cost them valuable time.

"I can call them," Mason said. "I should have done it earlier! We got separated, and then they couldn't use the LOCATOR application to find me, and my device wouldn't even give me my location. Something was wrong with the homing signal."

"No!" Obbin shouted. "Don't call them."

"It's fine. They know about you. They aren't going to—"

"It's not that. Brother Sam said not to use the mTalk for communication, and he is the one blocking your location," Obbin explained. "He'd have blocked Oliver's as well, but for some reason he can't. He suspects it's been tampered with."

"Oh," replied Mason. For a few minutes, the three young boys circled down the stairs. Only the soft tinkle of water dripping from the ceiling of the staircase could be heard.

The boys came to another door at the bottom of the stairs, and after a few feet there was another *T* in the path. Obbin looked at the piece of paper in his hand again. "We go right."

"Did Brother Sam give you those directions?" asked Austin.

"Yes, and that reminds me . . ." Obbin began digging in one of his fur shorts' pockets and removed a small scrap of paper. "He did tell me to give this to you."

Austin took it and then handed it to Mason, who shone his light on it. "It's just a number," Mason said. "120.1995 Y."

"I know, but he wanted one of you to have it," Obbin explained. "He said we would need it eventually."

"He didn't say anything else?" Mason asked.

Austin, who had been relatively quiet until then as if thinking, answered instead of Obbin. "No, I met this guy, and he's quite cryptic. He speaks honestly, but it's like he's giving us just what we need to believe and follow for right now."

Mason had never heard his brother speak like that, and some of his word choices surprised him. But this wasn't a time to critique his brother.

"He also gave me these," Obbin said and dug in his pack. He revealed the now clean and folded set of Austin's Ultra-Wear clothes that he had discarded on the bathroom floor in the secret chamber.

Austin took the clothes, his face beaming with excitement and thankfulness. "I'd thought I'd never see these again. Thanks, Obbin."

"Thank Brother Sam when we see him next. He's the one that gave them to me for you."

"I will," Austin replied, placing the clothes back into his own pack.

"Where are you taking us now, Obbin?" Mason asked, trying to bring his comrades back to the urgent task at hand.

"It isn't much farther," he promised. "I'm not exactly sure what is at our destination, just that I was to follow the directions on the paper to navigate the tunnel at the bottom of the ladder. Then we would come to a final door. There are no more directions on the paper, so I assume we just follow the tunnel to the next door."

The trio walked in silence for the remaining length of the tunnel and came to the assigned door. Obbin lifted the cross necklace over his head and held it near the indented shape on the wall. It gave off a soft click, followed by a painful creaking sound as the door slid open, leading into another room.

2.39

Water

Tiffany and Oliver slowly walked through the jungle, weighed down by the extra supplies. Oliver had told Tiffany they'd wait for a good spot to ditch the stuff but then decided it would be better to keep the weapons and other gear nearby. The devices and rifles might come in handy in the future. The last spot they'd seen any roaming Übel was across the pool at the eastern ziggurat, but this didn't mean other patrols like the one slung up in the tree weren't searching for them nearby. How many men were working for the Übel?

The journey was going to take a long time; they had originally planned on resting again before Oliver's swim but had never gotten a chance. Tiffany was feeling extraordinarily tired. While seeing their brothers get captured, they'd had a brief surge of adrenaline, but that had since worn off and the day was dragging on. Soon night would fall across the basin, and before that a storm would strike.

Their destination was the most dangerous location in the entire basin—the southern ziggurat. That was where Oliver and Mason had seen the clue and entry point noted in the inscription. Oliver had read it to Tiffany again: "When you find the Truth, you are no longer lost. At the foot of the cross, your path home begins. Dive into the Truth, so you too may find the way."

It was clear, and she could think of no other way: Oliver had to enter the water at the foot of the cross-shaped pool. He'd been warning her nonstop about the danger of going so close to the Übel camp and had begun coaching her on evasion tactics and occasionally scolding her for walking so loudly. Oliver even referenced Midnight's artful ability to walk gingerly as a good example for Tiffany to follow.

The plan was to locate an abandoned building near the south end of the pool and stash all their stuff there. Then Tiffany would keep the Zinger, e-journal, and artifact case with her and walk along the pool just inside the protective cover of the jungle foliage. She'd be ready to give Oliver the case once he located the path or found out where and how he needed the artifacts. Tiffany would also have the Zinger in case the black creatures appeared or attacked and the e-journal in case they needed to look something up from their parents' notes. She was running the mission intelligence and support role, while Oliver was the mission operative. Midnight's role was still undefined.

The danger of undertaking the search for this clue was high, and they knew it, but at the same time they both accepted it. The truth was their parents were securely defended; the opportunity to rescue them hadn't come. Their only hope was to find the clue and take it, or destroy it if need be, so the Übel would be unable to continue. At the least, having the knowledge of the clue would allow the kids to continue on their quest if for some reason the Übel and their parents were able to leave without them.

"We're just a few hundred feet from the southern tip of the pool. Let's find somewhere to stash our stuff and then make our way to the edge of the pool," Oliver directed.

Tiffany agreed, and after checking four buildings they found one that still had a roof, door, and all of its walls. Several of the windows were missing, but the building was in much better condition than any of the others. Once everything was in the structure, Oliver and Tiffany started to cut straight for the pool. Oliver had retained only the Oxyverter, flippers, mask, and a small knife that he'd attached to his ankle in a sheath.

Once they arrived at the edge of the jungle, just steps away from the cross-shaped pool lined with rubies, Oliver looked to see if any soldiers were in view. Seeing none, he turned to Tiffany and spoke. "If for some reason the Übel come and you have to get away, send me a message on my mTalk. I won't be able to reply, but I'll know there is danger. If the worst happens and I am captured, go to the *Phoenix* and"—Oliver hesitated—"contact Mr. O'Farrell. If you can't reach him, call Archeos."

"But—" Tiffany started; she couldn't imagine leaving her brother, especially since she'd be all alone. At the same time, if he were captured, what choice, other than surrender, did she have? "I will," she promised.

Oliver nodded and gave his sister a big hug, then gripped her shoulders and held her at arms' length. "Everything is going to be just fine. Remember, I love you."

She felt her throat tighten and tears begin to well in her eyes." I . . . I love you too," she said.

Oliver looked as if he might choke up, and he swallowed hard. Then he cleared his throat and spoke firmly. "You'll be able to track me on your mTalk. My homing signal isn't blocked like Mason's. At some point, I'll probably need the artifacts. When that happens, I'll swim to the side of the pool and get them from you. So walk alongside me as I swim, but remember to stay inside the protection of the tree line."

Tiffany nodded; she knew it was time to get to business. The sooner this quest was over, the sooner she'd be back with her family.

Oliver put his arm around Tiffany's shoulder, and they walked the remaining few hundred feet to the end of the pool with Midnight still in tow.

Swim

ustin was last to enter the dark room. Obbin and Mason had led the way with their mTalk lights. Austin planned to insist that Obbin stop using his *stolen* mTalk, but being underground in a mysterious tunnel trying to rescue his parents and siblings while staying alive himself was not the right time to fight to get it back.

The sound of water lapping against stone caused them to turn their two lights to the floor. In the center of the room was a small pool of red liquid. Austin remembered the rubies. "It's not blood, it's the rubies," he said, as much to reassure himself as the others.

"Right," Mason said and continued to shine his light around the room. "Look!" He pointed to the far wall.

There was an inscription that read: "When you find the Truth, you are no longer lost. Enter the pool to reach the Truth; there, your path home begins."

"It's nearly the same as the one Oliver and I found," Mason explained. "I mean, it's different, but a cross is a representation for truth, and the pool in the center of the basin is a cross. My guess is this pool is another way to access the larger pool."

"But how? We're underground," Austin said.

"It's like the Aqua Cathedral beneath my home," Obbin explained. "Although you guys and I didn't explore them fully, there are several underwater tunnels that lead away from the large cavern we swam in. I and my brothers have often explored them. One leads to—" But Obbin stopped abruptly as if he was about to reveal something he wasn't supposed to. "Never mind, it's not important right now."

"You can tell us," Austin reminded him. "We took the oath."

Obbin nodded, but Mason spoke up. "Maybe later. Right now, we have a quest to finish." Mason shone his light back at the pool. "I wonder how long we have to stay under water."

"I can hold my breath for quite a while," Obbin bragged.

"Yes, but we don't know how far we have to swim under-water before we reach fresh air, and 'a while' might not be long enough," Mason said.

"He's right," Austin agreed. "But those might help," he added, pointing at the wall where Obbin's light was still shining on the inscription. Just at the edge of the light, where only a dim glow remained, there were a dozen or more masks hanging from hooks, each with a mouthpiece attached. Austin knew right away that the masks were simi-lar to the Oxyverter.

Obbin trained his light to reveal several items below the inscription, including flippers. The boys gathered around the hooks, and each plucked a mask from the wall.

"It looks like they're adjustable to fit almost anyone's head," Austin said, and then laughed as he turned to look at Obbin, who had already put his on—upside down. "That is if you put it on right."

"Well, I guess we're getting wet," Mason said as he knelt down and stuck his hand into the cold water. "Brrr. I sure wish we had wetsuits."

Obbin and Austin nodded.

"But we'll just have to make do," Austin said as he started to pull his camo shirt over his head. "It's going to be cold, but somewhere at the end of this pool is the next clue, and we need it."

Mason sighed. "Yep."

The twins removed their shirts and tucked them into their packs. Obbin wasn't wearing a shirt, so he was already set to go.

Austin was happy to have been given back his Ultra-Wear shirt. Without towels, getting dry would have been hard, but the temperature controls of his Ultra-Wear shirt would warm him back up from the frigid temperature of the water.

"What about our pants? They're not as short as swim trunks," Mason said.

Obbin slipped his bone-handle knife from his pocket and approached Mason, who'd sat down to start putting on his flippers. "I'll take care of that," he said.

"Stop!" Austin exclaimed just as Obbin grabbed hold of some of the fabric and lowered his knife to cut it. "You don't need to cut them!"

Obbin fell back, and Mason looked shocked at Austin's outburst. "I . . . I was just trying to help," Obbin said.

Austin caught himself. In the very short time he'd known Obbin, he'd never seen the prince look sorry or frightened.

Mason intervened. "You're right. These are one of the last things we have that our Grandpa Wikk gave us. Obbin, I know you were just trying to help."

Austin interjected. "Besides, you won't need to cut them; you can roll them up. They are water resistant, and if you use some cord or wire, you can seal the waistline and the cuffs on each leg to keep water from getting in," he explained and then turned to rummage in his pack. A second later, he pulled out a coil of wire. "This will do just fine."

"Obbin, actually, I have an extra pair of pants. Why don't you borrow them so that you can keep warm too?" Mason offered.

Austin frowned. "Wait, you have a second set?"

Mason nodded.

"But you gave me some regular clothes the first day I got wet," Austin pouted.

"And you destroyed them," Mason retorted.

Austin couldn't argue with that, even if it hadn't really been his fault. He'd not had another choice for escaping the observatory tower.

Mason looked at Obbin. "Would you like them?"

"That'd be great. These animal-hide shorts are kind of water resistant, but I think your grandpa's pants will be better," Obbin admitted.

Mason handed him a pair, and the prince quickly changed.

Austin changed into his recovered Ultra-Wear pants as well and stuffed the camo ones into his pack. He began to wrap pieces of wire around the waistline of his pants and just above his knee, where he'd rolled the pant legs up. "I wish we could do the same with our shirts, but I don't think wrapping wires around our necks would be very safe."

"You've got that right," Mason agreed.

After all three boys had sealed their pant legs and waists, they donned flippers and put their masks on. Obbin tucked his fur shorts into his newly acquired pack, and the twins sealed each of their packs tightly so as not to let any water in. Obbin and Mason were still the only ones with lights, but Austin said nothing. Obbin was younger than him, and he felt bad about jumping on the blue boy over cutting the pant legs. After all, he had just been trying to help. And, so far, Obbin had been a far greater asset to the twins than the Wikk boys had been to him.

The three boys lowered their legs into the icy-cold water. Austin jerked his legs back at the liquid's bite on his feet. "I don't know about this," he said.

"You were the one who just said"—Obbin changed his voice to sound like Austin as he continued—" 'it's going to be cold, but somewhere at the end of this pool is the next clue, and we need it.' "

Austin shook his head, and Mason laughed. "That was a really good impression." Mason applauded.

"Thanks," Obbin said.

"Hardy-har-har," Austin said. "But you're right, I did say that," he admitted. He stood up and, without a second thought, cannonballed into the pool.

2.41

Dive

Oliver reached his bare hand into the water and felt its icy-cold bite. He knew the wetsuit would keep the majority of his body warm and dry, but his hands and head were sure to be cold. He was just happy that he had short hair that wouldn't get in his face while he dived.

It was time. Oliver looked back at his sister. He slid his legs out from under himself and slipped into the water feet first, then lowered his head below the surface. Immediately, the sting of the frigid water caused him to gasp, but the Oxyverter did its job and gave him a large supply of oxygen in return.

His hands felt as if small needles were stabbing at his skin, but the cold subsided after a few moments. Oliver was prepared to proceed. He lifted his right hand above the water and gave a thumbs-up, which he knew Tiffany would be hoping to see.

Now to swim. Oliver lowered his head and, with two pulls of his arms and several kicks of his flippered feet, propelled himself through the surprisingly clear water. Sure, from a distance, it looked like it was thick with blood, but that was just the hue given off by the sunlight reflecting on the rubies that lined the pool. The sun today had been extremely bright, but unfortunately he knew it wouldn't last much longer. Dark clouds were gathering on the northern horizon.

His first goal was to look for something that might be considered a path. Oliver plunged lower and lower into the depths of the pool. It was far deeper than he had expected, reaching by his estimate maybe twenty feet. His ears had already started to hurt from the pressure of the water.

The pool was relatively clear, and Oliver could see a fair distance ahead. He had gone just a few more feet when he noticed a white line running along the center of the pool floor below. Every ten feet, two lines projected out from the centerline at angles, like arrows. The arrows pointed toward the north, as Oliver had suspected.

Oliver soon found that he was at the center of the pool. As the walls to his right and left began to disappear, he reached the cross point of the lengths of water. The arrows he had been following also disappeared, the bottom of the pool dropped away, and Oliver assumed the path was now headed further down.

He swam downward with his mTalk light trained into the deep. Deeper and deeper he went and the hole became darker and colder. He was thankful for the wetsuit. Minutes passed, and he finally arrived at the bottom. The pool's walls and floor were still lined with rubies. Oliver shone his light around him, looking for any signs or inscriptions. He'd almost made a full circle when he saw it: a silver circle about four feet in diameter was set into the ruby wall. Around the silver circle, Oliver counted twelve rings. The innermost was red, and the rest alternated silver, red, silver, red, extending out into the final silver ring. It looked like a giant target with the silver circle as a bull's eye.

Oliver swam to the silver center and looked for a way to pull it open. There was a handle of sorts, but after pulling on it, and even bracing his legs against the rings, the silver door would not budge. Several pegs protruded from the rings, but they were small, and when Oliver tried using them to pull the door open, the rings only slid left or right. He gave the disc a push, then an underwater kick, but both efforts were useless.

Oliver remembered the cross necklace and pulled it out from underneath the neck of his wetsuit, where he'd tucked it earlier. The note that had accompanied the necklace referenced the cross as a key to getting out of a hard place, and at the moment Oliver was certainly stuck. He searched the circle, which he assumed to be a door, for somewhere where he could insert the cross. But there was no such keyhole. He next felt the sides of the pool wall to see if any of the rubies might light up and unlock the entrance.

Oliver wondered if the rings were like a screw. Might he be able to loosen the rings enough to come out of the wall?

He grabbed a peg and started to turn it; the ring moved, and he felt sure that he had figured it out. But after several moments, the silver door hadn't shifted inward or outward. It was then he noticed that the red ring directly above was spinning in the opposite direction from the way he had been turning the silver ring. In fact, all the rings were moving, each opposite the previous one. Something clicked in his brain: the pegs and the spinning rings were connected. Oliver needed leverage to get the rings to spin together, like a wrench and bolt. Then maybe the door would unscrew.

Oliver needed the twelve planks. Each plank had several holes cut out of it and he wondered if somehow they would help him open the silver door.

He needed to swim to the surface and retrieve the artifacts from his sister. Oliver tapped on his mTalk, and the screen glowed in the red-hued water. He tapped out two quick messages to Tiffany: "Is everything clear?" and "I'm coming for the case."

A second passed before a single-word message returned: "Clear."

Oliver started swimming to the surface. He'd not realized how dark it had become until he started swimming upward and noticed the sparkle of sun against water.

Inches from the top, Oliver paused with an odd sensation of anxiety. What if Tiffany hadn't looked thoroughly enough at her surroundings? What if they had a lookout watching the pool from the southern ziggurat? These were risks he'd have to take. He had to have the artifacts from Dabnis Castle.

Oliver's hands touched the orblike red jewels that made up the wall. He was amazed by the care and the expense that had gone into creating and lining this pool. The people who'd lived here must truly have treasured this body of water.

Oliver's hands slipped above the surface, followed by the top of his head and his eyes. He looked around. The surface of the pool was still, except for where he'd just broken it. Jungle plants came right to the edge of the pool at this point and several branches even hung out over the pool, providing excellent cover. The foliage moved and, for the briefest of seconds, Oliver held his breath in anticipation. He breathed a deep sigh of relief through the Oxyverter, sending a spurt of bubbles into the water, as he saw his sister's smiling face. She brought the case forward and slid it into the water, where Oliver took hold of it.

Midnight strutted into view but kept her distance from the water. Not wanting to remove the Oxyverter from his mouth, Oliver nodded his head and gave his sister a thumbs-up with his free hand.

"No problem," Tiffany said. "You're doing great."

Oliver smiled with his eyes and ducked back under the water, case in hand.

2.42

Underwater

Swimming in the underwater tunnel had been challenging for Mason. He'd not thought of how claustrophobic he would feel, and he had to keep reassuring himself with the knowledge that the mask would create a plentiful supply of oxygen.

Obbin was in the front of the pack, his light searching the path ahead, causing the ruby-lined walls to sparkle brilliantly. Austin was second and Mason last, occasionally shining his light behind him to watch for anything out of the ordinary. He'd never thought of what might live in the pool, and thus far had not seen anything. Not even a minnow. The boys had agreed not to surface but to use hand signals in order to communicate.

After several more minutes, they came to a wall. Mason started to feel a sense of panic set in. While he could always swim back, the wall before him represented an enclosure, an underwater cage. His breathing picked up, and bubbles of carbon dioxide rapidly spiraled out from his mask with every exhale.

Obbin pointed up with his right hand. There was an opening in the roof of the tunnel. Austin and Obbin were already swimming upward, and Mason quickly followed, relieved to be getting away from the supposed dead end. As he swam, he noticed another tunnel branching away, but after shining his light through the blood-red water, Mason saw a door blocking the end. He'd rather try his chances going up and hopefully out. He could always swim back down.

To Mason's relief, he surfaced through a pool set in the center of a room. The three boys bobbed in the water. The two mTalk lights revealed the room to be much larger than the one they had come through several minutes before.

Climbing onto the rock ledge, they could see the room around them wasn't just a cavern. Like the tunnels, it looked as though it had been painstakingly built stone by stone. In front of the boys were five more doors. Surrounding the gateways were several hundred small holes, as if snakes had burrowed the entrances to their dens in the wall. Mason gasped at the thought of hundreds of snakes ready to strike. That would be worse than finding the green snake in his sleeping bag back when he was five.

Austin walked closer to the doors. "Can you bring a light? There's a plaque over the middle door."

Mason didn't move closer and waited for Obbin to answer the request, which the blue boy did.

Austin read the inscription aloud: "Place each jewel into its proper hole. If you lack even one, then you shall be lost. If you misplace too many, then your fate is sealed."

Mason's blue eyes were huge, his eyebrows raised in excitement. "That does not sound—"

The water of the pool splashed as a man heaved himself out of the pool. He stood at the edge, poised to attack. His weapon was trained on Mason.

The soldier's hair clung to his face, and his grey-and-black camouflage clung to him. Water streamed to the ground, pooling at his feet. An Oyxverter lay on the floor nearby.

"I've got you," the soldier sneered. "What a prize, for sure."

Mason recognized him as the unnamed soldier who'd captured him after he and Austin had slid down the ziggurat.

This was the guy who had disappeared into the woods. Had he followed them?

Austin stepped forward.

"Freeze!" the soldier ordered.

"We already are," Austin said with a shiver. "Freezing, that is."

"Don't mock me," he warned, training his weapon toward Austin instead.

Austin stepped back. Obbin hadn't moved and neither had Mason.

"What do you want?" Mason asked, but he knew it was an unnecessary question. The soldier wanted to bring the twins and the blue prince back to his commander. Surely this would gain him some sort of commendation.

"I want the next clue," he said. "And the three of you are going to help me."

"We can't," Austin explained.

"You will!" the soldier countered.

Austin slowly moved his hand to point at the plaque. "It says we need some jewels."

"There are more than enough here in the pool," the soldier said with a shoulder nudge toward the water behind him. "You come over here," he called to Mason.

Mason tentatively stepped closer.

"Don't try anything funny," the soldier warned. "Use this to loosen the stones." He slipped a knife from a holster at his side and set it on the ground, then kicked it to Mason. "One wrong move, and you won't wake up for hours."

Mason let out a long-held breath at the realization the soldier was only going to use the stun. He was sure it wouldn't feel good to be hit with one, but at least he wasn't going to die.

2.43

Planks

Oliver fought the cold, dark water as well as the artifact case, which wanted to float back to the surface. It took greater effort to dive back down the opening in the pool since swimming with one arm wasn't easy. When he reached the bottom, he tried to stand on the floor of the pool, but his body and the case's buoyancy made it too difficult. Oliver sighed, sending a spray of carbon dioxide bubbles spiraling out through the Oxyverter. With one hand holding the case, he used the other to release the clasp. An explosion of bubbles poured from the metallic case, and it suddenly seemed nearly as heavy as it had been on dry land. Oliver let the case sink to the floor, where it landed with a soft thud. If only he'd done that earlier, it would have made the descent much easier.

Oliver carefully began to remove one of the wooden planks from the case. Knowing that they would float to the surface if given the chance, he quickly closed the case after the first wooden artifact was free. Leaving the case behind, Oliver swam to the silver circle and twelve rings, then studied the pegs for a moment. Some rings had more pegs then others, and there didn't appear to be any uniformity to their placement on each ring. Oliver knew this was why the specialized planks were needed. It would otherwise take a very long time to figure out the pattern and create something that would work to unlock the door.

The plank he'd retrieved first had three holes bored into it, so Oliver looked for three pegs in the same pattern as the plank. He found several that were close, but every time he tried to fit the planks over a set of three pegs, they were either too far apart or too close together. He began turning the rings to create new sets of three that might fit, but he soon realized this would take hours and he might never find the correct combination, especially if he had to do it with each plank.

He had to be missing something. Oliver shone the light from his mTalk onto the silver-and-red-ringed door. Engraved delicately into each ring were small symbols, the outermost having the symbol *XII* engraved on it. The next ring in had *XI*, the next *X*, then *IX, VIII, VII, VI, V, IV, III, II,* and, on the ring nearest the door, *I*.

Each hole on the plank he held also had a symbol engraved next to it. This plank had *VII, V, IX* on it. Oliver moved the three rings with corresponding engravings in position to create a combination of three pegs that looked like they might match up with the holes in the planks. He slowly fitted the plank over the pegs, and to his delight, it worked. He smiled as best he could under the Oxyverter and then retrieved another plank. He only hoped he had the initial combination correct and that he wasn't missing something. He checked the engraving by each hole and then again moved rings to make a pattern similar to the one on the piece of wood. The final symbol matched one he'd already used and, as he moved a needed peg on that ring into place, the other two rings moved as well. So far, his theory seemed to be working.

After ten minutes of matching pegs and planks, all twelve rings were connected via a series of planks. However, there was still one plank left. Oliver looked it over. The plank was short, and it had just two holes, but there was only one peg left on ring *XII*. Shining his mTalk light around the bull's eye, the beam uncovered a final peg protruding from the rubied wall itself. He floated the last plank into place and it fit perfectly, linking the rings to the wall.

There were no planks left, and it was time to try again. Oliver grabbed hold of a handle on the silver center and began to turn it left, recalling an old adage his grandpa had used: "Lefty loosey, righty tighty."

The outer twelve rings did not move, but the silver door began to wind outward toward him. After forty rotations, the long silver cylindrical door stopped moving. It stuck out into the pool on four long tracks; a space of only a few feet behind the door allowed access into a newly opened tunnel.

Oliver shone his light into the long tunnel; it appeared to be straight and clear of debris. He quickly tapped out a message to his sister and then retrieved the artifact case that still sat on the pool floor. It was time to swim into the unknown once again.

He swam only as far as the silver door was long before finding another underwater opening like the one he'd swum down in the center of the pool. It too was lined with rubies. The vertical shaft opened both upward and downward. It was time for another decision.

2.44

Coming

Tiffany sat in the jungle, holding Midnight and recording the last few days' events. It might not have seemed like the right time for journaling, but it was the only thing that was keeping her calm. She was alone in the jungle; her only free family member was now diving deep into a dark, blood-red pool. At any moment, Übel soldiers could come. She'd spent the first half-hour remaining still and vigilant, but her mind had begun to create sounds, and her anxiety had grown. Working in the journal was the best thing to distract her, the only thing she could do at the moment. Besides, it was helpful to their quest, and she'd remembered several details that needed to be added.

Tears had pooled in her brown eyes a few times as she entered information that Mason or Austin had told her. Where were her little brothers now? Were they with Mom and Dad or restrained and alone? Either way, they were captives of the Übel, and that was enough to make her worry about them.

The small black cat let out a soft *meow*, and Tiffany stroked the fur on its neck. "It's all right, Midnight. I'm sure it won't be much longer now."

Tiffany eyed the Zinger, which sat near her but not too near. She knew it was her best defense should the black creatures or the Übel come. She also knew in the back of her mind that it would be hard to use it on either, unless her life depended on it.

The cat mewed again, longingly. It pawed at her arm, then licked her hand.

Tiffany cocked her head. "I bet you are hungry and thirsty."

Midnight climbed from Tiffany's lap and began to circle her. She took out a can of chicken noodle soup; it wasn't ideal for a cat, but it would have to do. She twisted the cap, and steam rolled from the container. The food was too hot and the can too narrow for the cat. She needed something to pour the soup into to make eating easy and so she could add water to cool it. She searched her pack, but there was nothing to use.

Midnight meowed again. "I know," Tiffany whispered. "I'm working on it."

Finally, she took out a pocket knife she had in her pack and worked to cut her half-empty H_2O bottle in two. She poured just a little soup into the bottle and offered it to the cat.

"You'll like it," she promised.

The cat sniffed it tentatively. Then it poked its paw at it. Tiffany shook her head. Cats were so finicky. The food was there; now it was up to Midnight.

Thunder crackled in the distance. The storm was coming. If Oliver didn't return soon, she was going to get wet.

An idea crossed her mind. Tiffany tucked the e-journal into her pack and stood, stretching her legs and arms as she did. She'd have to be careful not to make too much noise, but she knew she was far enough from the nearest path not to be seen. After all, the jungle was very thick and the birds were extra busy today, full of noise.

She searched the jungle floor for long branches and, after she'd gathered seven, she walked back to her spot, where she built a small cone-shaped structure. She took out her small knife again. Oliver had insisted she take it, just in case. It was coming in handy for the second time in a short while. She slid the blade open and used it to cut free a long section of thin ropelike vine, then wove the vine around the top point of the structure, securing the seven sticks together.

Satisfied, she started cutting large fan-shaped leaves from the surrounding plants and placing them over the beams of her structure, tucking their loose ends under neighboring beams. It took only fifteen minutes before she had a seemingly waterproof covering over her hut. Tiffany stood back and admired her work. A little ingenuity and effort, and she hoped it would keep her dry.

Midnight had already made herself a small nest on the floor of the hut and fallen asleep. She looked back at the half bottle that had held the soup. It was empty.

Tiffany set her pack back into the cone structure but held onto the knife. She had to admit it'd been very handy. She was hungry and had come across a couple of possible fruits that were known to grow wild in jungles. One had been the yellow crescent-shaped thing Austin had been eating upon their arrival. It was curious that none of the monkeys Austin had been teasing were in the basin, but Tiffany wondered if the large black cats had anything to do with that. Speaking of which, she grabbed the Zinger and moved it into the hut. Surely rain and an electric-firing weapon were a bad combination.

As she walked through the foliage to the edge of the pool, a loud peal of thunder growled overhead. She let an unfamiliar smile cross her face at the thought of her hard work on the hut. She wasn't getting wet in this storm.

Her search for the yellow fruit hadn't been successful as of yet, but she'd come across small red berries, which she'd recognized as the same type her parents grew and made jam from. Sweet and juicy, they were called raspberries. She'd eaten several, but wanting to avoid a stomachache, stopped herself and gathered some for later. The bushes had been right next to the water's edge, and the plants location had reminded Tiffany of her top priority: keep an eye out for the Übel. She had to make sure they had neither entered the pool yet nor were nearby posing a threat to her or Oliver. How long had she spent on the hut? Sure, it'd kept her mind off things, and it would keep her dry, but it'd been a distraction. Oliver was counting on her.

She crept forward and peered out over the pool. She watched the surface of the water for a moment and saw no bubbles, which made her a little uneasy. Then she remembered Oliver's message: "I've opened a door, and I'm heading into a small tunnel."

Tiffany looked at the eastern ziggurat, which sat across from her location. She marveled at the skill and labor that must have been put into building it. Her eyes turned to the largest ziggurat, which sat at the southern foot of the pool. If it had been beside the other three, it would have dwarfed them, which was saying a lot, as the northern trio were huge themselves. Knowing the amount of rooms and tunnels that existed inside them, she was hungry for the opportunity to explore them all but knew the probability of this happening to be very low.

The sky had grown dark, and the pool was cast in shadow. Only a few remaining rays of sunlight broke through the cloud cover, each landing on the southern ziggurat. It was time to get back to her small hut. As if in confirmation, a rumble of thunder roared to the north of the basin.

As she turned to step back into the jungle, something caught her attention at the southern end of the pool. A harsh shiver of fear passed through her body.

They were coming.

2.45

Unnamed

Mason had freed at least three stones. The trio of jewels sat on the stone floor next to him. Out of the corner of his eye, he watched the soldier. He'd been trying to see the man's nametag, but hadn't been able to make it out yet.

There was something oddly familiar about him, like he'd seen him before. Mason shrugged it off, thinking it was his mind playing tricks on him, that the recognition was based on the earlier run-in.

The water was frigid as Mason plunged his hand in again to free another jewel. He worked it back and forth and pulled loose a fourth ruby. As he set it down, he looked at Obbin and Austin, who now sat with their backs against the wall, ten feet apart. The soldier had been clear that no one should talk and that if anyone tried anything, they'd get a shock from his stun rifle, which he bragged was a JC-42596. Mason didn't know or care what that meant about the weapon, but Austin had nodded as if he understood.

Mason turned back to his work. A ripple crossed the surface of the water and lapped against the edge. No more followed, so Mason began to work the fifth stone loose. How many more would he have to free?

As he set it down, he was shocked to see Austin getting to his feet. Mason glanced toward the soldier, but the man was looking out over the dark pool.

Mason looked back at his brother just as Austin threw his diving mask at the soldier. It hit the man square in the back. The soldier wheeled around and, without warning or hesitation, fired the stun rifle. A blast of green shot toward the wall, but Austin had already moved and rolled across the floor. The soldier took aim again, but his shot zipped toward the ceiling as the man plunged backward into the pool.

Mason saw arms wrap around the soldier, pulling him into the water. Waves crashed, and water splashed everywhere as a struggle erupted in the pool. Mason backed away.

Two men wrestled in the dark waves. Finally, one held the other back to his chest. A moment later, the soldier was silent. The victor, wearing a mask and Oxyverter, swam to the edge of the pool and heaved the soldier so he was half out of the water.

Their emancipator pulled himself out of the water and removed his mask and Oxyverter.

"Oliver!" cried Mason. He wrapped his bare arms around his brother in sheer excitement.

Oliver squeezed his little brother, then pulled away. "He's only asleep. We need to restrain him quickly."

Austin and Obbin were already gathered around. Austin undid the wire he'd used to seal his pants. Oliver flipped the man over and tied his wrists together.

"Where'd his weapon go?" Austin asked.

"It must have fallen into the pool," explained Oliver. "We don't need it. We have to hurry."

The reunion was short-lived. Oliver was ready to get right to business.

Oliver's head had just broken the surface to spy out the scene when he had seen the back of the camo-dressed man. He had known right away that this was a soldier. A second glance and he had seen Mason at the edge of the pool and Austin and a blue boy against the wall.

Austin had seen him, and Oliver had quickly motioned for him to make a commotion. The rest had happened very quickly, resulting in Oliver subduing the man.

A closer look at the Übel's face and Oliver was shocked. The young man's name was Drex Powers. He'd attended the Academy with Oliver, in the very same class. In fact, he'd been Oliver's biggest competition for top honors.

Why was he now here? When and how had he joined the Übel?

"Oliver, how'd you find us?" Austin asked, interrupting his thoughts.

Oliver broke from his stare at Drex. "We were following the clues," he admitted. He caught sight of the infamous blue boy. "You must be Obbin."

The prince nodded. "And you are Oliver."

Oliver nodded. "Yes, I am. Came long for the ride, huh?" Obbin nodded. "We can talk about stowing away later." He looked at his brothers. "I thought you two had been captured."

"We were, and then Obbin saved us," Austin explained.

Oliver looked toward the blue boy again. "Thanks." Obbin nodded as Oliver continued. "I'd ask how, but we haven't much time if you want to avoid being recaptured." He paused. "Let me tell Tiffany I found you." He lifted his mTalk.

"Wait!" said Obbin.

Surprised, Oliver glanced up.

Obbin looked at the twins, then back to Oliver. "Brother Sam said not to use the mTalks for communication," he said quickly. "He said they were compromised."

Oliver looked at the three of them, gauging the prince's words. Austin and Mason were nodding in agreement. "Well, that may be true, but I don't see any way around it. With Tiffany up at the surface and us down here . . ." He ran through the options in his head and then made his decision. "We're just going to have to use them."

Obbin looked as though he wanted to argue. But with a sigh he shrugged, as if to say, "Well, I did my part."

Ignoring him, Oliver quickly tapped out a message to Tiffany: "Found the boys. They're safe. Have you seen the Übel?"

He looked around the room. It appeared to be a dank underground chamber. He was thankful for the wetsuit. It had indeed kept most of his body dry, with the exception of his face and hands. They were cold in the chilly underground air. He shook his head several times in an attempt to lose the water from his spiky brown hair, but not that much water had remained. He ran his fingers through the blunt strands.

"Oliver!" came Tiffany's frantic voice. She sounded out of breath. "The Übel—they're near the pool. I think they've found the clue."

Oliver was startled at the voice coming over the speaker; he had sent her a text message, and she'd responded with a call.

"Did they see you? Are you in danger?" Oliver asked. He'd expected them to come eventually.

"No, I don't think so. But they seem to be preparing to enter the pool. I couldn't see who all was there, but there was quite a large gathering," Tiffany rattled off rapidly. "You have the boys?"

"Yes. They're safe. Are you?"

"Yes. I mean, I think so. At the moment. I ran back to my hut."

"Your hut?"

"It's going to rain. I built one," she explained.

Oliver found that amusing and impressive and, even in their state of danger, he couldn't stop himself from smiling.

"Try to remain calm," he said softly. "Stay hidden for the moment in your hut." Their time was drawing short, and he and the boys needed to uncover whatever secrets were hidden in the chamber or risk the Übel getting them first.

"Tiffany, I'll call you back in a minute," Oliver said. "Out."

"Out," was her response.

Oliver looked at the scene before him. There stood five metal doors, surrounded by several hundred small holes. It was an odd-looking wall, like Swiss cheese, which had been served to Oliver several times at the Academy.

"Have you guys figured out anything yet?" he asked the twins and Obbin.

"We just found a plaque," Obbin said.

Oliver followed the three boys to the wall.

"Place each jewel into its proper hole. If you lack even one, then you shall be lost. If you misplace too many, then your fate is sealed," Austin read again.

"Why couldn't all the clues be this clear?" Oliver said aloud. He knew immediately that he needed the rubies from Dabnis Castle.

"I got some rubies from the pool already," Mason said, pointing to the small pile he'd started.

"Not necessary. I have some," Oliver explained.

"But the inscription doesn't say how many we will need," Austin said.

"We'll have to see how many are in the case," Oliver said as he crossed back to the pool. He placed his mask over his face and his Oxyverter over his mouth, then jumped back into the pool. He swam to the floor of the pool and retrieved the case. The three boys were eagerly awaiting his reappearance and helped to pull him and the metal case from the water.

He set down the metal artifact case, and they all bent over it. Oliver clicked the two latches open and lifted up a small divider that had kept the planks separate from the jewels.

The twelve rubies were dazzling indeed, but he wondered what made these different from the ones that lined the pool. The boys removed the jewels, twelve in all.

"I don't see any numbers on the rubies," Obbin said. "There are numbers on the holes in the wall."

Oliver went to the wall. He fingered one and then another; the holes' sizes and shapes were exactly alike. The symbols were much like the symbols on the planks. Tiffany had said that each ruby had a symbol etched on it.

"There should be some sort of corresponding symbol," Oliver explained. Austin tossed him a jewel.

Mason gasped. "Be careful."

Oliver looked it over.

"See, nothing," Austin pointed out.

"Mason, message Tiffany. The Übel might be near, so don't call," he warned. "Ask her to find the pictures Dad took of the pillars with the jewels. The journal had mentioned symbols, but these rubies have none."

Mason nodded and went to work on his mTalk.

"Austin, you and Obbin keep an eye on Drex over there. If he wakes up, let me know," Oliver commanded.

Oliver went back to the plaque, then looked over the hundreds of holes dotting the wall. He noticed that there were three ropes coming from a large hole near where the wall met the ceiling above. He followed the ropes with his eyes and noticed that they ran overhead and were laced over and around several beams of wood. Above these beams and snug against the ceiling was a very large boulder.

A horrible thought hit him at that moment, and he glanced at the plaque again. "If you misplace too many, then your fate is sealed." Was the inscription saying that if he put too many—his guess was three rubies—in the wrong holes, the boulder would be released and fall into the pool of water, blocking his exit forever? He decided not to explain this to the twins. If they came to the conclusion themselves, that would be another thing.

A moment passed before Mason had the results from Tiffany's search.

"Oliver, Tiffany sent a list of symbols," Mason said. He glanced at the mTalk. "The first is a *V.*"

Austin picked up a ruby and tossed it to Oliver.

Jewel in hand, Oliver walked over to the wall. He looked over the many holes and symbols until he came across the symbol *V* and then whispered to himself, "Here it goes."

Placing the ruby in the hole was like flying into a horde of Corsair star fighters—one wrong move and you'd find yourself blasted into oblivion. With a deep breath, Oliver released the jewel, and it dropped downward. A small noise tinkled on the other side of the wall as the jewel tumbled along something, maybe a track of sorts.

Everyone waited with captive breath, then jumped as two of the five doors rapidly slid upward, disappearing into the upper portion of their frames.

"Great, so which door?" Austin asked.

"We won't know until we place all twelve jewels," Oliver explained.

"That's like the dig on Eus Diane. The right passage was only revealed when the right sequence of cranks was turned," Mason remembered.

Oliver nodded. "You're right. What is the next symbol?"

"X and three *Is,*" Mason read.

Oliver picked up a second ruby from the case and searched the wall for the accordingly labeled hole. It almost seemed too easy; he located the symbol *XIII* and set the ruby into the hole. Once again, he heard a clanking and then a screech. This time, however, one new door opened and one of the already opened doors closed.

"Next, please," Oliver said.

"Two *Xs* and an *I,*" came Mason's reply.

Oliver walked over to the wall and found the symbol that matched the description. *XXI.* He placed the ruby in the hole and heard the familiar clanking noise.

However, this time a second noise followed; it sounded like the grappling-hook launcher's wire being reeled back in. The sound moved upward along the back of the wall.

Every set of eyes followed the sound and landed on the rope. It was sliding toward the boulder along several brackets. It came free of several of the wooden beams supporting the boulder. The massive rock shifted and the remaining two ropes tightened, creaking under the additional weight they now supported, as only two of the three cords remained.

Oliver jerked squarely against the wall, his shoulder blades stinging as he did. The twins and Obbin flew toward the wall, pinning themselves tightly to the wall on either side of Oliver.

The giant slab of stone rocked back and forth. How old were the ropes, and could they support the boulder?

Oliver looked to his left.

"Mason, that wasn't right. Something was wrong," he said breathlessly.

Mason looked down at the device. "No, it is right. *X, I, X*," he said.

"*X, I, X*?" Oliver scolded. "You said two *X*s and an *I*."

"That's what it is," Mason retorted.

Oliver knew he was right, but that wasn't the point and there was no sense in arguing. "Next time, *please* read me the exact order of how the symbols appear."

"I will," Mason promised.

Keeping to the wall and away from the boulder, Oliver found the symbol *XIX* and placed the ruby into it. The boys were relieved to hear just the clanking, followed by two more doors opening while one closed.

Mason carefully read Oliver the next eight symbols and he found each of the corresponding holes. All of the doors were now open.

It had all come down to the final ruby. Just as Oliver had suspected, this one would reveal the correct path to them. "All right, Mason, what is the last symbol?"

"L, I, X," he read slowly.

At that moment, Oliver realized that they were all out of rubies. The misplaced ruby had not counted toward deciphering the path, and by looking at the five possibilities, there was no way to determine which would be correct. The doorways were all exactly the same, and Oliver wasn't taking his chances crossing over the wrong threshold; there was no way to know what the misstep might set off. Surely some sort of booby trap awaited a misguided trespasser.

Oliver eyed the pile of rubies that Mason had gathered earlier.

"Quick, Austin, get me one of the jewels," he commanded.

Austin retrieved a jewel and threw it back across the chamber to Oliver, but remained by his ward, the still unconscious Drex.

"L, I, X," Oliver repeated to himself. He found the symbol and set the ruby into the hole. A rolling and clanking and then suddenly four doors slid down and shut with an echoing clink.

All the boys cheered.

A single hall now remained in front of them. Oliver approached the dark passage cautiously.

"The way looks clear. I'll go first," he said.

"All right. Be careful," Mason said anxiously.

"Let Tiffany know we're in. We'll let her know as soon as we figure something else out," Oliver said. "And find out where the Übel are. Austin, you and Obbin stay close to Drex. If he moves, call for me."

"Okay," Austin agreed.

The dark passage was straight and narrow and sloped upward. It was paved with small, white stones, and every so often a line of rubies segmented the path. Oliver had crossed twelve ruby lines when he arrived at a silver door with a knob made of ruby. The door was unlike any he'd encountered so far.

Oliver gripped the handle and turned, but the door didn't move. He searched the side walls and the frame for the light-up stones, but none illuminated for him. Then he noticed three rubies just over the lintel. He stood on his tiptoes and stretched out his hand. His fingers just brushed against the first, then two other stones. They didn't light up, however, and Oliver dropped back to his heels.

Maybe the cross pendant. It'd worked in the past. But disappointment struck Oliver as he reached for it. The cross was missing; only the chain remained. He quickly zipped down his wetsuit, but the pendant from the necklace wasn't there. He'd lost it. Had it come off in his struggle with Drex?

Oliver went back down the path. He and the boys made a cursory search around the chamber. But the cross was not to be found. They'd have to figure out something else. Perhaps Austin could hotwire it as he had done with the ziggurat.

The boys gathered their packs. After looking at the empty artifact case, Oliver shrugged and tossed it into a corner of the pool where they could find it later if need be. Drex was still out cold and restrained, so they left him where he was and gathered at the ruby-handled door.

After a quick look over the door frame and adjoining wall, Austin shook his head. "There isn't an access panel of any kind."

"What about the crosses?" Obbin asked.

Oliver stared at him. "You have one?" he asked with surprise.

"Yes, Brother Sam gave it to me."

"Brother—" Oliver started.

"That's right; I have the one he gave me too," Austin said.

Mason sighed. "Everyone got one but—"

Oliver raised his hands. "Wait, who is Brother Sam?"

"He's a guy who's been help—" Austin began.

"Is helping us," Obbin corrected.

Mason's mTalk speaker crackled. "Ub . . . half . . . fift . . . min." The mTalk went dead.

"Was that Tiffany?" Oliver asked.

Mason looked at the lit screen of his mTalk. "Yeah, but the reception is really poor."

"I think she said something about the Übel and fifty min-utes," Austin proposed.

"Fifty or fifteen," Obbin said.

"We'd better hurry then," Austin said.

Oliver stared at the door. "First, we have to get past this door."

Obbin held out his cross pendant and waved it around the door. There was a soft click as if a lock had come undone. Obbin's blue hand grasped the red handle and tried to turn it again, but the door did not open.

"Wait." Mason was looking at the rubies over the door-frame. One of them now glowed. "Austin, try using your pen-dant," he suggested.

Austin obeyed. There was another click, and a second ruby began to glow.

They all realized at the same moment: they had two cross keys, and it appeared they needed one more to unlock the door.

"Obbin, try yours again," Mason commanded. The blue boy did, but nothing happened.

"I guess I'll have to find mine," Oliver said and started back toward the pool.

"We'll all help," Mason said. "It's the only way." He turned to go.

"Wait, the door just clicked again," Austin said with sur-prise. He turned the door handle . . . and it opened.

The third ruby was lit overhead.

Mason paused. "How?"

Obbin shrugged. "Do you have a key?"

Mason shook his head.

"Brother Sam is watching," Obbin suggested. "Maybe he's able to control the security."

"Wait a second," Mason said and removed his pack. He set it on the ground and began taking things out one by one, searching them over. "When the Übel came, I was able to escape through a door just seconds before it locked."

Clothes, gadgets, and several books lay around him now. Mason lifted a final book out of the pack and read the title: "*The Veritas Nachfolger on Evad: Year 101 through 150*. This is the third book of the four volumes I took from the western ziggurat. The same four that, once removed, unlocked a secret passage behind the bookcase."

Mason leafed through a couple of pages. "Look!" He revealed a hollowed-out area within the pages of the book. The text flowed around it, uninterrupted by the key. The concealment had been planned from the inception of the tome.

Mason beamed with pride as he held up the cross. He swept the chain around his neck. "Let's find out what's through the door."

Oliver led the way as they walked into the next room.

Game

Almost immediately after Oliver crossed the threshold, lights began turning on, spreading along the walls from either side of the door and surrounding the room in a single ring of white light, bright enough to illuminate the entire room. The place was circular in shape and not much larger than the bridge of the *Phoenix*. Its ceiling was only a few feet higher than Mason was tall, and the outer wall of the chamber was no more than twelve feet away. Several alcoves were evenly spaced along the perimeter of the room, a large trunk sitting in each one. Bookshelves lined the gaps between the alcoves, but they all had been emptied.

A solitary table and chair sat in the center of the room, with a checkered board set upon the tabletop. Mason immediately recognized it as a chessboard. The game looked out of place in the room. Why would anyone have come all the way down here to play chess? Maybe it was for the guards. But then again, there was just one chair.

A screen hung on one wall between two of the alcoves. Austin approached it. "How do you think we turn this on?" he asked as he looked it over and started tapping on the screen like he would an mTalk or the consoles on the *Phoenix*. He put his ear against it. "I don't think there is any power going to it. But then again, something did illuminate the rubies and the lights in the room, so there must be power."

Oliver responded. "There has to be a switch to turn it on or something. So far, it seems everything we do sets something else into motion. We already know that this city and the clues we've discovered so far—both here and in Dabnis Castle—have been part of an intricately mapped out path."

Obbin was busy looking over the checkered board. "What is this?"

"It's a board for a game. A fun one, in fact." Mason laughed darkly to himself. "Austin and I were playing it right before we met you."

"Really?" Obbin asked.

Austin laughed. "Let's just say it's the reason we left the *Phoenix*."

Obbin jumped back, clearly startled by the threat the game might pose.

Mason shook his head. "No, no, the game didn't actually make us leave. We let our competitiveness get out of hand when we were playing, and we ended up fighting."

Oliver scowled knowingly.

Obbin nodded. "Okay. Well, then, can you teach me how to play?"

"I'd be happy to, when we get back to the ship," Mason said.

"So Brother . . . ummm?" Oliver paused.

"Brother Sam," Obbin offered.

"Brother Sam led us to find only an empty room," Oliver said, his hand to his chin. "But there must be a reason."

"Let's search the trunks. Something must be waiting for us to find it. There must be a clue somewhere," Austin suggested.

"Or a secret passage behind one of the bookshelves. That's how I escaped the soldiers in the ziggurat," Mason admitted.

"True, and I found a passage behind a bookshelf in the observatory," Oliver added.

They searched all of the trunks, but they were totally empty. In the end, they gathered back around the table, where Mason noticed something inscribed on the side of the chessboard where the white pieces would usually be set up.

"The King will reign forever; he has already defeated evil. You too must defeat the opponent that stands in your way to finding the Truth."

Austin looked at Mason curiously. "What does it mean?"

"There seems to be a lot of these riddles," Oliver said with a laugh.

"And they all seem to be important," Obbin added.

"I sure wish Tiffany were here. Is the signal any better?" Oliver asked Mason.

Mason looked. "A little better."

"Tap her out a message with the inscription," Oliver ordered.

Mason worked on sending the message and reread the inscription as he did. " 'The King will reign forever; he has already defeated evil. You too must defeat the opponent that stands in your way to finding the Truth.' " He hit *Send* and then looked for a switch on the board. "I think the inscription is challenging us to play, but there's no way to turn on the game."

Obbin had moved to the table and sat down in the chair. "I do hope you—" The boy stopped as white and black holographic images appeared on the board before him. The chessboard had come to life.

"You did it! The chair must have been the activation trigger," Mason said.

The screen on the wall glowed to life, and a video began to play. The boys turned at the sound of a gruff voice. Only the figure's shoulders and head were visible, his face masked under a shadow cast from the red hood of his cloak.

"To continue on the path before you, you must first best me," the man explained.

The full set of three-dimensional chess pieces pulsed brighter on the board as if beckoning someone to take the challenge.

Obbin still sat in the chair.

"Well, Obbin, I guess this is as good a time as any to teach you how to play," Mason said.

Austin's face darkened in disagreement. His mouth had opened as if he were about to speak when Obbin let his opposition to the plan be known as well.

"No, that's okay. It's too risky. I don't think we can afford any mistakes," the blue boy rattled off nervously.

Oliver laughed. "No, you're right, but Mason and I will coach your every move. You'll just make them."

Obbin still looked apprehensive.

Austin obviously didn't like it that Oliver hadn't mentioned his name as a coach. "I'm going to go check on Drex," he said sullenly.

Oliver shook his head. "I got caught up in this room and forgot about him. I'll come with you. I want to see if my mTalk has a better signal out there." Oliver looked at his device, then back at the game. "Mason, you get started. Chess can take a long time, and we may not have much longer before they come." Oliver and Austin turned to leave.

"Right. White moves first," Mason said.

Oliver and Austin started toward the door, but before they had taken more than a step or two, Oliver's mTalk scratched and squeaked. Tiffany's whispered voice came across, her tone tense. "Oliver, they're here. I mean, they're at the center. They're diving."

Mason turned to look at his brother. Oliver spoke into the mTalk. "Tiffany, stay safe. We'll have to hide."

"Okay," Tiffany said, and the call ended.

"The trunks?" asked Austin.

"No, they're not safe enough anyway," Oliver said. "Mason, Obbin, come back to the pool chamber."

"But what about the game, the guy on the screen?" Obbin asked.

"I have an idea." Oliver lifted his mTalk again. "Tiffany, come in."

"I'm here."

"I'm going to send you a video feed. Can you record it?"

"The signal strength is weak, but yes," Tiffany said. "I'll do my best."

"All right, we're going to use the mTalk to get the next clue," Oliver explained. "You guys go on to the pool room. I'll be right there."

Austin, Mason, and Obbin ran down the hallway and into the open chamber. There was nowhere to hide. The stone walls stretched to the ceiling and the remaining four doors were still closed.

The worst part, though, was that the soldier was gone.

2.47

Parents

Tiffany crouched in a large palm frond bush, huge fan-like leaves stretching over her. Midnight had remained asleep back in the makeshift hut. She had a fair view of the southern ziggurat and the stretch of pool leading to the center where Oliver had dived.

Several swimmers were in the water at the center of the pool. One of the men had disappeared below the surface a few minutes ago and hadn't returned yet. The other two seemed to be waiting for something.

The crowd Tiffany had seen earlier had gone—where, she didn't know—so she was listening for footsteps or talking behind her. She didn't want to be surprised by a squad of soldiers. But if the three soldiers at the pool were waiting, it was probably for the captain and more support.

A happy thought crossed her mind: it might also mean she'd get to see her parents.

A flash of lightning reflected off the pool's surface, followed by the crackle of thunder. She'd always been warned not to go into or near water during a lighting storm, as it was deadly dangerous. But below the surface was her brother. She knew he wasn't in the water anymore, but what if the storm was still striking when he needed to come back to her? She sighed. It was just another unsafe reality of their quest.

A glance at the e-journal's screen showed a large monitor on the wall with an image of a red-hooded person frozen on the display and a table in the center with glowing holographic chess pieces. She was glad the feed was working and checked to see she was still capturing it for later.

The secretly positioned mTalk also meant she was now out of contact with Oliver. Her last contact had been to warn him that the soldier-divers were coming, or so she believed. She'd tried Mason, but for some reason not even he could be reached via mTalk.

A splash of water caught Tiffany's attention, and she looked back to the two divers. They were now rejoined by the third, who had swum below. One of them was speaking into a device on his wrist; Tiffany supposed it was similar to the mTalk. If reinforcements weren't on the way already, they would be now. She knew the diver must have found whatever it was Oliver had discovered just minutes before.

Proving her suspicion correct, three small craft similar to a sky scooter zipped into view. The ships flew low over the pool, their exhaust rippling the water behind them as they went. The ships, piloted by the grey-and-black-clad soldiers, were coming toward her at an alarming rate. The craft stopped dead center of the pool, directly over the three divers, for just a moment. Then the three craft slowly started circling the perimeter. The soldiers had taken out long rifle-like weapons and were vigilantly searching the jungle and surrounding area while maintaining control of their craft.

Then, startling Tiffany, out from the bushes came a low rumble. But unlike the thunder she'd been hearing, this was mechanical. A couple of star fighters dropped out of the sky and flew low over the pool, then circled back toward the southern ziggurat and came back for a second pass.

They were on high alert, ready to defend themselves from an attack. But how could they think Oliver and Tiffany were a threat? . . . unless whoever had captured the three men earlier was still around and the Übel knew it. Maybe that was who they feared? Tiffany smirked to herself. They had an ally, and although she didn't know anything about him, she liked him if he could keep these battle-trained soldiers on edge.

A ripple of thunder echoed overhead, as if telling her that the help she was receiving truly was more powerful than these vagabond kidnappers.

The star fighters were headed back for a fourth pass when a craft larger than the sky scooters but without a canopy started down the pool from the largest ziggurat in the basin. Her dad had used a craft similar, called a skiff, on a few digs before. As the ship neared, Tiffany could see that it held several people. She wondered if the captain and her parents were among the passengers.

Then she saw a woman with long brown hair like her own. Tiffany knew she was her mom and next to her was her dad. Just seeing her parents alive, and sort of in person, sent a sense of relief over her. Tiffany had not seen them, other than in video or pictures, since their capture, and that had now been several days. She wanted to call Oliver and celebrate, let him know she'd seen them, but again she recalled that the mTalk was alone in the chamber.

She glanced at the e-journal screen again and then blinked. Someone or something had moved across the camera. She rubbed her eyes; all this adventuring, worrying, and lack of solid sleep had caused her to start seeing things. But she nearly let out a gasp as she saw the someone again. A man in a red cloak—not just the image on the screen but a real, live human being. She lifted her mTalk to call out to the person, but stopped, afraid the nearby soldiers might hear her.

Who was it? What was he doing? Did Oliver and the twins know?

"You two stay here, keep this thing running!" someone shouted, bringing Tiffany from her thoughts. She looked up to see the man she'd come to despise without ever speaking to him or meeting him. Tiffany now saw him with her own eyes.

Captain Vedrik was standing next to her parents pulling a wetsuit over his camos—a change from the long trench coat Oliver had described him as wearing. He still had his captain's hat, but he had just removed it. It looked like her parents, who were already wearing wetsuits, would be diving along with the other soldiers and the captain.

Tiffany glanced back at the e-journal screen, but the live video feed was just of the monitor on the wall of the chamber. She watched for a few seconds, but the red-cloaked person did not reappear. After a moment's thought, she took a small wireless earpiece from her pack and slipped it into one ear. She hoped if the person were still in the room, she'd be able to hear him.

A splash turned her attention back to the pool. Her mom sat on the side of the skiff, feet dangling just into the water. She had an Oxyverter in her mouth, and her hair was now up in a bun. Her dad was no longer in sight, but she saw him surface a second later, having been the cause for the splash. Tiffany could see her parents clearly now.

"Get going!" the captain ordered with annoyance.

Tiffany's mom pulled off her Oxyverter and spoke. Hearing her mom's voice sent shivers of delight down Tiffany's spine. "There is no need to be impolite, Captain. We've told you we're going as fast as we can. Archeology is not like piloting star fighters."

The captain grumbled but did not respond.

Her mom's courage made Tiffany surprised but proud.

Tiffany's mom replaced her Oxyverter and slipped gracefully into the icy red water. A second later, her parents disappeared below the surface.

The evil captain still stood on the skiff. He looked left and right. "Keep a lookout. Signal us if they come. I don't want to be caught unprepared, and we can't risk failing. Zebra Xavier will be arriving shortly. And he will not tolerate the loss of the Wikks. His anger was already significant because we lost the kids."

Vedrik grabbed the shoulder of the skiff's pilot. "You wouldn't know anything about how Zebra Xavier found out, would you?" he asked.

The soldier turned, "Sir, I already—"

"Never mind." The captain sat on the side of the craft and hung his legs over. "We'll finish this later." He donned his Oxyverter and disappeared beneath the blood-red ripples.

Tiffany had been so happy to see her parents that she hadn't thought to record the captain and the soldier's conversation. But she knew it would be important to enter into the journal, so she opened a note and began tapping in all she'd heard. Especially the mention of someone called Zebra Xavier. The video recording would continue as she did; the red-cloaked figure would have to wait.

Hide

When Oliver got to the large room with the entrance to the pool, the three younger boys were already on the move. They were quickly using the hundreds of small holes in the wall as hand- and footholds for climbing. Obbin was leading, and he was nearly to the two ropes that had not been cut during the opening of the door.

The boys can't possibly be thinking of hiding atop that huge rock, he thought. The two ropes already seemed to be under a lot of strain, and the added weight of all four of them might be just enough to unravel the cords and unleash the boulder into the pool, sealing them in forever.

"Guys, we can't go up there." Oliver called.

"We have to," Obbin shouted from the top of the wall.

Oliver realized it must have been the blue boy's plan. "The ropes won't hold our weight and the boulder."

"We're not going for the boulder," Obbin explained. "We're going for that." He pointed, and the light from his mTalk landed on a small outcropping of rock hidden behind the boulder.

Oliver watched Obbin, who was using as handholds the small brackets that the ropes were laced through. Oliver had done many pull-ups and repeatedly crossed monkey bars at the Academy, but these brackets weren't very close together. Obbin had to launch himself from ring to ring. This concerned Oliver for the twins' sake. While he was confident he could handle it, and the blue prince's capabilities seemed to meet the challenge, the twins weren't exactly athletes.

He looked around the room. Without his own mTalk, he had to rely on Mason and Obbin's lights. There was nowhere else to hide. The four other doors were still closed, and there was nothing else in the room, just solid stone walls.

Nothing else in the room?

"Where is Drex?" Oliver asked.

"We don't know. He was gone when we came back," Austin said. "He must have escaped."

"How? He was restrained."

"We don't know, but he's not here," Austin answered emphatically. "Obbin and I looked the best we could."

"They did," Mason agreed.

"At least he doesn't have his weapon," Obbin added.

Oliver nodded.

"Oliver, we have to go. The soldiers might be here any instant."

Oliver looked up at the ropes and then to the outcropping. He didn't have a choice. The blue boy's plan would have to work.

Mason was next to reach the rings, but he hesitated. Austin quickly caught up to him.

"Mason, you'll be fine. Just take it slow. It's just like gym class at Bewaldeter," Austin said.

"Ha," Mason scoffed. "At Bewaldeter, you fell just a few feet and landed on pads. I see a hard rock surface twenty feet below us."

"It won't be twenty feet when your feet hang down. Just fifteen," Austin encouraged.

"That helps a lot," Mason said sarcastically.

"Guys, you'll be fine," Oliver said. He'd started up the wall but was having more difficulty than the twins appeared to have had. His feet and hands were large; their feet and hands fit into the small holes better. The small holes also didn't reach up the entire height of the wall, so he had to start finding small pockets for his fingers and tips of his shoes.

Austin had taken to the metal rope guides and was swinging across with no problem. Mason too had started but his progress moved more slowly. Still, it looked like he'd be just fine. Oliver gave a sigh of relief at the twins' success thus far. He was almost to the top of the wall himself.

Obbin had nearly reached the outcropping when he stopped. "This last part might be the hardest," he explained. "The ropes stop, and we'll have to climb up over the boulder. It's narrow, but we *all* should be able to make it through." He slung his pack off and shoved it ahead of him through the opening.

"Narrow," Oliver heard Mason repeat.

"No turning back now," Austin called out, but Mason had stopped.

Oliver was swinging hand over hand quickly toward his younger brother and would soon run out of rings if Mason didn't get moving. He did not want to lose his momentum. "Mason, you have to go, bud. You can do it!" he encouraged.

"Yeah, you can do it!" Obbin called out, his voice muffled by the stone boulder, as only his legs were now visible.

Mason started swinging again. "How do you fit?" he asked Obbin.

"It's not that bad. I have about an inch or two to spare over my back and plenty of space on either side of me," Obbin said positively, his voice still muffled.

"Austin, don't climb onto the boulder until Obbin is through," Oliver commanded. It was enough to hope that the boulder would hold each individual person's weight.

"I won't," Austin said as he slowed his swinging. He reached the boulder and waited a moment. "Obbin, are you through?"

"Yes." Obbin's voice echoed from somewhere behind the boulder. "I'm clear."

"Coming through," Austin said, and Oliver saw his youngest brother launch himself at the boulder. Although it was difficult to manage while holding on, he too succeeded in getting his pack off and slinging it ahead of him. He followed it up through the thin space between the room's ceiling and the top surface of the boulder. It was tight, and Oliver only hoped he could squeeze himself through.

Without a problem, Austin squeezed through, going even quicker than Obbin had. "I'm clear," he cried out.

Mason had reached the boulder, and Oliver was right behind him, waiting.

"Come on, Mason, you can do it. We don't have much time," Oliver said.

"Yeah, you can do it . . . do it . . ." Austin said, providing a fake echo.

Mason looked over his shoulder at his older brother, and Oliver could see the fear in his deep-blue eyes.

"It's going to be okay," Oliver promised. "Look how far you've made it."

Mason swallowed and then nodded. The twin turned and pushed himself toward the large rock and hung on. With a trembling hand, he slowly pulled his pack off and looped it over his wrist. As he crawled near the crack, he paused and turned toward Oliver. "I can't."

"You have to!" Oliver commanded. "They could—" He stopped midsentence. A flurry of bubbles had erupted in the pool directly below him. Oliver looked down into the red pool, barely visible in the dim light. He didn't need to finish his sentence; it'd already come true.

A black object emerged out of the water.

Obbin must have heard or seen, because his light suddenly went off. Mason's, however, remained on.

"Mason," Oliver whispered. "Your mTalk. Off."

Mason obeyed, and Oliver hoped the figure below had not heard. It was pitch black in the room, and he wondered if the intruder had night vision. That would be disastrous, as he hung twenty feet up with no cover, just a black wetsuit and pack that would stand out against the grey stone walls and ceiling of the room.

Mason was still on the rock but not moving. He seemed frozen, and Oliver could no longer offer encouragement. Meanwhile, his arm muscles were growing sore, and his palms were becoming sweaty.

A bright-blue light suddenly exploded beneath him, and Oliver heard the fizzle of something igniting. He looked down, and sure enough, the figure had deployed a flare to the floor of the room. And now the soldier was being joined by two more—no, three . . . five more—people. Small light beams shot out from each of their wrists; three of the lights searching the room. One of the people not searching looked like a woman. Was it his mom? Oliver couldn't quite tell in the iridescent blue flicker of the flare, but inside he felt sure it was.

Strength had come back into his arms, but still his hands were growing slick with perspiration. "Mason, you have to go," he whispered, knowing his voice would likely be lost to the crackle of the flare below and the commotion of the new arrivals.

Oliver couldn't tell for sure, but in the blue flicker, it looked like his brother nodded. To his relief, Mason seemed to be squeezing into the gap.

"The door here is open as well," one of the soldiers shouted.

Oliver shivered at the memory the next voice evoked—the man who'd invaded his home, attacked his parents, and nearly shot him was there.

"What did you expect, Bargoz?" Vedrik hissed. "The door in the pool had been screwed open as well. Did you think that they would just abandon their quest after getting this far?" Vedrik paused as if waiting for an answer.

"No, sir," the soldier replied, and even in the dim light, Oliver could see the man's head was lowered in shame.

" 'No' is correct. Whoever is searching is staying just one step ahead. We never should have returned to that castle," the captain scolded, turning on the woman and a man beside her. Oliver felt anger burn inside him, his muscles tense. The man and woman were surely his parents, and the captain was still treating them with disrespect.

A new feeling coursed through Oliver at the next voice to speak. "You asked us to be thorough, and we wanted to be absolutely sure we did not miss anything back at Dabnis Castle," the man said. Oliver warmed at hearing his dad's voice. He also knew that his parents were fighting for the kids by stalling and drawing out their side of the quest. It was no less than Oliver had suspected.

"Ahhh, enough of this. Let us proceed," Vedrik said. "And since the door is open, I guess we did not need the artifacts you had discovered after all." Vedrik kicked the nearby flare into the pool, extinguishing the bright-blue flicker. "I told you, Pyrock, no flares! And explosives will no longer be needed, as the path is already clear."

One of the soldiers let out an odd maniacal giggle.

"Silence!" Vedrik commanded.

"Yes, sir, sorry, sir," the soldier called Pyrock said, but it sounded like another maniacal laugh escaped.

"You proceed through the door," Vedrik hissed, commanding the soldier he'd called Bargoz.

"Sir, but—" Bargoz started.

"That's an order!" Vedrik screamed. Then his voice drew to a snarl. "The Wikks are too valuable, and Pyrock is color-blind and missing a hand. Cruz is too slow to help if we have to act quickly, and I don't owe you an explanation. I will not explain myself again. You will obey without hesitation. Now, go! Pyrock, Cruz—you two guard the pool. If anyone comes, don't hesitate to use whatever force necessary."

"Yes, sir," the two soldiers said in unison.

With that, Bargoz proceeded through the door. Vedrik waited a moment. "No screams. Must be clear." He glared at

Mr. Wikk. "Don't try anything, or you'll get another nasty shock."

Without a single acknowledgement of the threat, Oliver's dad disappeared into the passage, and Vedrik detained Mrs. Wikk a moment longer. After twenty or so seconds, he motioned for her to proceed. "It appears to be safe. Ladies first."

Oliver's mom said nothing and started forward, the light from her mTalk disappearing into the tunnel. Vedrik followed her.

With his parents and the captain out of sight, Oliver nearly lost his grip. He looked toward the rock and couldn't see Mason's feet, but he wasn't sure the twin was through, and there was no way to know without asking, which he could not do. Oliver would have to risk it; he couldn't hold on any longer.

He swung his legs and then launched himself at the rock. The large boulder seemed to sway ever so slightly, and he heard a soft gasp from up ahead. Mason was still making his way through, and now the two ropes were holding an extra two hundred and fifty pounds or so—his and Mason's weight.

Oliver's feet scrambled to get a better footing, and several small stones fell loose. He heard several splashes in the pool and assumed the soldiers below had as well.

A beam of light swung around the cavern. "Did you hear that?" came the voice Oliver knew to be Cruz's.

"Uh, no. Did the captain mention? I'm a bit deaf too," Pyrock said. "The explosives, ya know."

Oliver had just shimmied his upper torso into the crevice and pulled his legs up tight when the glow from the soldier's light fell on the ceiling and the boulder. He'd barely avoided being seen. He reached his hand forward to pull himself further through, but his pack wedged in the tight space. He waited a moment until the light moved to the other side of the chamber, then slowly, silently, he pulled back just far enough to wrangle one arm out of its strap and pull the pack around to his chest and ahead of him. That had been close.

"Mason, are you there?" he asked in a whisper, the stone dampening his voice so that no one but Mason could hear.

"Yes," came a weak reply.

"Are you okay?"

"No."

"Mason, I know this is hard, but you can do this. You have to!" Oliver encouraged. "You have it inside you. I know you do."

Mason whimpered. "I can't go any farther. It's too tight."

"You can, Mason. I believe in you."

A moment passed with no response, but then Oliver heard scuffling. His brother was moving.

"Mason?" Oliver asked. He really hoped his and his brother's voices were not carrying to the soldiers below.

"He's through," came Austin's low reply.

What had happened to Mason? Inching his pack ahead of himself, Oliver slipped through the rock. It was definitely tight; he knew the wetsuit had been snagged a few times.

As he dropped off the boulder and onto the outcropping, he saw Mason on his knees, Obbin's hand on his back.

"Is he okay?" Oliver asked.

"He will be," Obbin said. "He just about lost his lunch."

"He'll be fine," Austin said. He was crouched at the edge of the outcropping.

"Mason, you did great," Oliver said.

His little brother bobbed his head in a yes, but didn't speak. Oliver joined Austin. The two guards' silhouettes were the only things visible in the weak glow from the soldiers' lights below.

"Oliver," Austin whispered. "We can take them. I have a plan."

Oliver shook his head and realized that Austin couldn't see the motion. "We can't. Not yet."

"But Oliver, those two would be easy to take. You already fought off Cruz, and this Pyrock guy looks pretty scrawny."

"Plus, he's missing a hand," Obbin added from his spot next to Mason.

"I agree, but Vedrik gave them orders to use whatever force necessary. They may need Dad and Mom, but they don't need us," Oliver explained.

"He probably meant that about Brother Samuel," Austin retorted. "He attacked the soldiers with his ship."

Oliver wanted to ask about Samuel and the other ship, but this moment wasn't the time. He had to concentrate on their next steps. "We also want to be sure we can keep our parents safe from Vedrik when we do free them. Right now, they're in a small chamber with a single entrance. Not an ideal location for rescuing them."

Austin didn't say anything, and Oliver knew he was probably disappointed. But his lack of arguing meant he might very well have agreed with Oliver.

Finally, Mason and Obbin crept to the edge, joining the surveillance detail. The four boys watched the two soldiers below. They'd apparently determined the disturbance in the pool to be nothing, which relieved Oliver. But he could tell that neither of them was exactly looking to be an overachiever or to impress the captain either. That's what Drex had been up to, probably. But where was Oliver's young classmate now?

2.49

Clue

Tiffany had just finished entering a few notes from the exchange she'd overheard. What the captain had said about someone called Zebra Xavier had been interesting. She'd even taken a few pictures of the soldiers who still remained on guard. Again, this work was essential to keeping her nerves calm while she sat alone, a few feet from the evil soldiers, the rest of her family in a subterranean chamber with the vicious Captain Vedrik.

She was still angry after the arrival of a second skiff that had passed by. It had come zipping down the pool loaded with several cages. When it had stopped, the soldiers on guard had admired the prizes. Apparently, the men were free to trap and pillage; in this case, they'd captured several animals, probably to be sold to a zoo or to private collectors. The animals were large black cats, and Tiffany realized they were probably Midnight's family. She was glad Midnight had managed to remain free. Tiffany had no choice now but to keep and care for Midnight.

To get her mind off the cruel behavior of the soldiers, she turned to the recent entry she had found with the asterisk. Still unable to break the pin, Tiffany was growing frustrated. The information behind the security could be anything, but most likely it would be helpful. Why had her parents created so many barriers without giving her the know-how to overcome them?

Her thoughts were disrupted when voices buzzed into her earpiece from the mTalk left in the chess chamber. She switched to the video screen and, sure enough, her parents, Captain Vedrik, and a single soldier had entered the chamber. Only Vedrik and the soldier were in view of the camera, but she could hear her parents talking so she knew they were there. A sense of guilt washed over her for being frustrated with them only seconds ago.

"Looks empty," her dad said to her mom.

"Whoever came into the chamber first must have cleared out any artifacts here," Tiffany's mom responded.

A sense of pride for her brothers filled Tiffany. Had they already taken stuff from the room? Oliver had only said the video would be their way to get the next clue.

"Zebra—" Bargoz started.

"Zebra Xavier will not know about the previous intruder," Vedrik hissed. "I warn you not to cross me, Bargoz."

"Yes, sir," the berated soldier answered.

"Besides, clearly this chessboard in the middle of the table and that monitor on the wall have something to do with the clue," Vedrik said. "Now, you two figure it out, or I warn you—" A sizzling noise came from just out of view of the camera, but Tiffany recognized it as a Zapp-It or something similar.

Mr. Wikk cleared his throat and stepped into view. "Yes, well, we will try to avoid that," he said. Tiffany's dad looked over the game board and began to read. " 'The King will reign forever; he has already defeated evil. You too must defeat the opponent that stands in your way to finding the Truth.' "

"An interesting clue," Tiffany's mom said. "But easy enough to figure out. We must play a game of chess and win to receive the next clue."

"Then get on with it," Vedrik ordered.

"Captain, would you really wish to provide such an opportunity for sabotage?" Tiffany's dad asked. "After all, you'd never know if I lost on purpose or if I was simply bested."

The captain's eyes narrowed, then glimmered as his mouth curled into a competitive sneer. He moved to the chair and took a seat. "I'd surely punish you if you lost, but it so happens I rather enjoy this game," he said proudly. "I've never been defeated, and today will be no different." The captain cracked his knuckles, letting out a series of pops. "Now, to begin. Knight to . . ."

And so Tiffany sat and watched the evil captain take on the mysterious hooded figure displayed on the monitor. After each of the captain's moves, the person on the screen would come on and in his gruff voice would call out his next move. The holographic pieces floated across the board as if held by invisible hands. Fifteen, then thirty minutes, then forty passed, and Tiffany was growing weary of the game. She also wondered where her brothers were and if they were okay. The one thing that kept her eyes glued to the screen was the occasional appearance of one of her parents. They weren't staying still, but instead paced around the room, examining it. Mr. Wikk seemed to be taking notes, but he wasn't using an e-journal. Instead, he was using a technique that was as rare as the books the kids had discovered on Evad. He was writing. He held a small black journal of paper and used a nonelectronic device called an ink pen. He seemed to be making marks on the paper.

Tiffany also noticed that the soldier, Bargoz, kept dozing off where he sat on the lid of a trunk set into an alcove. The captain had taken no notice of him as he seemed to be concentrating intently on the game. He kept wiping his brow free of sweat, and Tiffany was glad to see that the man was stressing over the game. Clearly, he was under a lot of pressure, and she wondered who this Zebra Xavier guy was. Probably not someone she'd actually want to meet, but she was glad he at least could strike fear into Vedrik.

One by one, the pieces on the board had dwindled, and it looked like Vedrik had finally gotten the upper hand.

"Checkmate!" Vedrik cried out, both of his fists pumping into the air like a schoolboy's. He lowered his arms as if recalling where he was and who he was with.

Mr. and Mrs. Wikk gathered around the table, and Bargoz snorted as he awoke from his slumber. "Uhhh-mhmm," the soldier wheezed and cleared his throat.

Tiffany watched as the remaining white holographic pieces glowed brightly and then the black pieces, including the king, suddenly dissipated. The screen on the wall flashed brightly, and the man in the red cloak again spoke. "The path to the Truth is not always easy, but it is always clear," the man said in his gruff, but now kindly sounding, voice. "You have been searching for the answers, yet they are hard to come by. Man has worked hard to suppress the Truth, but it cannot be contained, so it is written." The man's head rose ever so slightly to reveal a rounded nose and white beard. "Not even a stone could stand in Truth's way. The Truth brings hope, and that you still have," he continued. "Because you have come, there is hope that what man tried to silence will be found again, for Truth can never truly be lost, and all attempts to hide the Truth by those who seek it only for themselves will fail. For not even the greatest of deceivers could defeat the Truth."

The words were like a riddle, and Tiffany was relieved that she was recording all of it. It would take many times listening to it to unravel the enigma in the cloaked man's words. She looked closely at the man. Now that his hood had lifted slightly, she noticed something silver embroidered onto the upper-right corner. She couldn't read it at the current resolution, so she'd have to zoom in on the stitching later. The cloaked man was also wearing an amulet pinned to the collar of his shirt; the object contained a ruby surrounded by several smaller clear stones. That too would require a closer look when she had the chance.

Vedrik and her parents looked a bit perplexed at the man's words.

"I leave you now with these three coordinates. Go and find the way on the path to the Truth. Beware: evil lurks around many corners, and those you may trust, you cannot." The image of the man faded, and three numbers popped onto the screen: 102.580 X, 5912.23 Y, 22.0 Z. They remained for just a few moments before fading to black. The white chess pieces disappeared from sight as well.

"Did you get that?" Vedrik hurriedly asked Bargoz.

"Uh, no, it was—" Bargoz started in a panic. "I—"

"It's all right," Tiffany's mom said. "Elliot got it."

Tiffany's dad held the journal out for Vedrik, and she could see black lines where something was scribbled onto the paper. He stepped forward, and Tiffany noticed a small slip of paper on one of the shelves. Vedrik did not.

"Those had better be right," Vedrik warned Elliot Wikk. "If we squander our time somewhere—"

"They are, I promise you," Mr. Wikk interrupted. Tiffany was curious why her dad was being helpful.

"Well, if that is all," Vedrik hissed. "Bargoz, get Pyrock. His services will be needed after all."

Tiffany wanted to check where the coordinates were leading, but she couldn't stop watching the video feed yet. Something else might happen that she didn't want to miss.

Boom

The soldiers below Oliver and the boys had been carrying on a lengthy conversation. Mostly Cruz had been doing the talking, but occasionally Pyrock gave a one-word response, keeping the conversation alive.

Every so often, one or both of the soldiers' light beams would crisscross around the room, sometimes landing on the stone ledge where the four boys had hidden themselves. The boys would lie as flat as they could, scoot back, and then return to their post once the lights had moved on. At least one time, Oliver was sure they'd been seen; a light paused on the outcropping for nearly a minute, but to his relief moved to the boulder, which the two soldiers began to talk about with concern.

Oliver knew it might be some time before his parents and Vedrik returned, as they were likely playing chess. He wondered what would happen if they lost. He also hoped the mTalk was still delivering video to his sister and that she was okay. Mason had tried to contact Tiffany, but the signal for his mTalk had dropped out again.

As Oliver lay there thinking and waiting, he heard one of the soldiers say something that got his attention.

"Do you think Vedrik is right about the kids?" asked Cruz.

Pyrock didn't answer, and Oliver assumed he'd probably shrugged or nodded or used some sort of nonverbal gesture. That was fine by Oliver. The soldier's voice sounded like a high-pitched squeal to Oliver.

"Vedrik sure seemed interested in the older boy's Academy record," Cruz continued. "Apparently, the boy received high marks as a pilot and in evasion tactics. I can attest to the second, and those two star fighter pilots who crashed in the canyon on Tragiws are proof of the boy's flying skills." Cruz paused for a moment. "Boy, was Vedrik angry with those guys. I haven't seen them since. I think they were sent back to headquarters, probably cleaning toilets."

At that, Pyrock let out an eerie cackle, not quite like the giggle Vedrik had scolded him about. "Weren't you stuck cleaning the lavatory on the *Skull*?"

Cruz didn't speak. Clearly, he was embarrassed.

The *Skull*? Oliver wondered. Was it the Übel's ship that had landed in the basin? Maybe it was the one that had hovered over the Wikk compound on Tragiws on the first night of the quest.

"Can you believe those kids got to this planet?" Cruz asked. "I mean, the twins were captured . . . then the door to this chamber is open." Silence passed for nearly a minute before Cruz continued. "I wonder who they're working with. It wasn't the kids who trapped the squad in the net and hung them high in the trees. Those guys said it was a bunch of men in red cloaks," Cruz explained and then lowered his voice and half laughed. "Although I have it on good authority there was just one guy in a red cloak."

A smile crossed Oliver's face as he recalled the soldiers bound and gagged high up in the jungle canopy.

Cruz cleared his throat. "And then, of course, there's the ship that attacked us on the plaza. It couldn't have been one of the kids. We saw the oldest two on that other ziggurat just before it swept in."

Another ship had attacked? This came as a surprise to Oliver. He was eager to learn more about the twins' escape, but it'd have to wait for the moment.

He was proud to hear that the men were aware of his flight skills and that Cruz had remembered their previous encounter. It also meant that the Übel captain knew Oliver was a force to be reckoned with and capable of leading his sister and brothers. Oliver slid his body back to the ledge and peered over.

"You know, they say that the daughter can speak thirty languages," Cruz said. Oliver knew this was an exaggeration.

The sound of footsteps coming down the tunnel stopped the soldiers in their conversation. It was Bargoz.

"Pyrock, the captain wants you. He says your services will be needed. I'm supposed to stay here with Cruz."

Pyrock shouted with childish glee and gathered up a black pack that Oliver hadn't noticed before. The soldier took off through the open door and disappeared.

Bargoz and Cruz didn't speak.

"Oliver," Mason whispered, "weren't Pyrock's skills something to do with explosives?"

Oliver nodded in the dark. "Ummm, I think you're right."

"Do you think he's setting them now?" Mason asked. "Shouldn't we get out of here?"

"He might be, but Vedrik and our parents are still in there. We'll have to wait and then get out of here. I don't think they'll detonate anything until they're long clear of the pool," Oliver whispered confidently.

"Right," Mason agreed.

"Could we disarm them?" Obbin asked.

"I don't know, but it might be too risky," Oliver said.

"I bet I could do it," Austin argued. "I got those doors to work, and I've deactivated several security alarms. How much different can the wiring for a bomb be?"

"It's too dangerous. They may be set to go off if tampered with. We just don't know," Oliver explained. Pyrock didn't seem like the type of explosives expert to take any chances. He was clearly very good at what he did, even if he had suffered some injuries.

Beams of light and the sound of pattering feet told Oliver that his parents and the captain were returning. "We have all we need, including our next destination. We leave immediately," commanded Vedrik. "Cruz, you wait while Pyrock sets the charges. I want this entire chamber buried," he ordered.

"Yes, sir," Cruz replied and bowed his head slightly.

"Bargoz, you and I are taking the Wikks back to the surface."

"Yes, sir," answered Bargoz.

Oliver's heart pounded against his chest at the confirmation of the explosives. They would have very little time to escape if they had to wait for the soldiers to leave, and they couldn't go too quickly behind them without risking being seen.

Oliver's fear was overcome with anger at what he saw next. Bargoz approached Mr. Wikk and pushed him toward the pool. "Get moving, you two." The soldier moved to push Mrs. Wikk, but Mr. Wikk deflected his arm.

"Don't ever touch my wife," Mr. Wikk warned fiercely.

Bargoz raised his fist to strike. "Bargoz, restrain yourself!" Vedrik shouted. "Their skills are more valuable than yours. You will remember your place."

Bargoz shrunk back at the rebuke.

"And Cruz, I want that door closed as you exit. If anyone is still in here, I want them eternally sealed in this place," Vedrik snarled fiercely, then laughed. "I hope your boy isn't still here."

This seemed an odd twist on the captain's earlier insistence on not harming the kids. What had changed?

Vedrik looked around the chamber, then shrugged.

Had the captain hoped to draw them out, Oliver wondered, by casting fear of death upon them? That had to have been it.

Austin elbowed Oliver in the side. "We have to attack now. We can take them. We'll jump down there and free Dad and Mom."

Oliver certainly didn't want to be trapped, but a frontal assault would fail and he knew it. The boys needed patience. "Just wait. The right time will come."

"But—" Austin started.

"Wait," Oliver interrupted.

Vedrik, Bargoz, and Oliver's parents jumped into the pool and disappeared into the water. Cruz was shining his light around the chamber as Pyrock walked casually back into the room. The soldier's body language did nothing to reveal the danger and destruction that he'd just set into motion.

"I set the timer for nine minutes," Pyrock said. "I have to set a few out here." The soldier shone his light toward the two remaining ropes. "I think I'll set one up there."

"Shouldn't we get out of here?" Cruz's voice was tense. "I'm . . . I'm sure the ones you . . . you set will be enough. It's going to take some time to swim out. Come on, let's—"

"Silence, you coward!" Pyrock scolded and started up the wall with amazing speed, his black-and-grey uniform causing him to resemble a spider. "It'll only take a minute."

A minute that Oliver knew they didn't have. "Obbin, what time is it?"

"Six-forty-five pm," Obbin reported.

"Watch it and tell me when it's six-fifty pm. If the men aren't gone by then, we'll have no choice but to jump and do our best to escape," Oliver explained.

Pyrock was nearly at eye level. He never did look the boys' way, but instead set, not one, but five charges and climbed back down like a monkey who'd just downed several Energen drinks.

"Time?" Oliver asked.

"Six-forty-eight."

"We have seven minutes," Oliver said.

Pyrock didn't stop when he stepped onto the floor. Instead, he turned and ran toward the pool, letting out a maniacal laugh, and then dove into the water. Cruz looked around, almost in confusion, and then waddled as quickly as he could to the pool, where he awkwardly tried diving in. The result was resounding belly flop. Oliver couldn't stop himself from cringing at the heavier soldier's entry into the water.

He waited thirty or so seconds. "Okay, boys," he said and crouched. "Let's go. Get your packs back on." Everyone quickly complied. "Austin, you first. It's a long way, so don't try anything. Just drop straight down."

Austin sighed and swung his legs over the edge. "Light, please?" Obbin and Mason lit up the pool below them.

"The mTalk," Oliver said. "I need to get it. You guys take turns and wait for me in the pool. If you don't see me by six-fifty, leave without me."

"Oliver, there isn't time," Mason said. "We can get another one."

"There is!" Oliver said and slid off the ledge, dropping into the pool below. He surfaced and then started to climb from the pool. "Go, Austin!" he shouted.

"Here I go," Austin said, sliding through the air like a knife in butter, disappearing into the water below. He bobbed to the surface a moment later. "It's not bad at all," Oliver heard him call up to Mason and Obbin.

But Oliver couldn't wait. He had to run. He heard another splash as he ran up the corridor to the small room with the chessboard. The mTalk was still tucked back into one of the bookcases. He grabbed it and, not a second later, Tiffany's voice came over the speaker.

"Oliver, I'm glad you're—"

"There is no time," Oliver said and turned to run out. He'd seen the charges spread around the room; there were way more than necessary.

"No, Oliver, wait!" Tiffany cried. "Dad left a note!"

A short way down the hall already, Oliver skidded to a stop and turned back for the room. "What do you mean?"

"He wrote something on some paper and left it on the shelf by the monitor," Tiffany explained.

Oliver entered the room and saw it right away. He wondered how Vedrik and Pyrock had missed it. Then again, the two men were so driven—one on fulfilling his orders and the other on explosives. Oliver knew the dangers of this level of concentration and how easy it was to miss the small things.

He retrieved the note but didn't take time to look at it. He glanced at the mTalk. Six-fifty-one. He was out of time.

Just as he lurched forward to break into a dead sprint for the pool, a hand caught his shoulder. Oliver looked behind him to see a man in a red cloak. He might have found this odd, but he'd heard so much about the cloaked man and seen one on the monitor in this very room.

The man did not speak, but quickly walked to a second chest and tore the lid open, then ushered Oliver into the trunk. With no time left to run, Oliver obeyed. The second he stepped into the chest, the floor below him vanished and he found himself descending down a slide. The speed of his descent was faster than anything he'd ever experienced before.

He looked up but could not see the cloaked man.

Where had the man sent him?

2.51

Alone

Tiffany crouched in the bushes, still calling to Oliver in a whisper. Her brother had left her hanging with no information, just a clear sense of danger. She'd seen a few more seconds of video as the camera swung up and down with Oliver's every stride, but then it had gone black, the feed ending. What had happened? What was happening? Everyone she loved was down in that chamber: her brothers, her parents.

She tried to calm herself by bringing up the video again. She forwarded to the part with the coordinates and then tapped the numbers into a separate application. It took just a split second for their next destination, a planet, to appear. Tiffany recognized the name immediately.

Enaid was the most populous planet in the Federation. The entire world was one giant city, and she shuddered to think they would have to find a clue there. But, at the moment, she and her brothers didn't have a choice. They had to go.

A commotion at the pool turned her eyes from the blank screen of the e-journal. Vedrik and her parents reappeared above the water, but just one of the soldiers was with them. The copilot of the skiff rolled a rope ladder over the side of the craft into the water. Vedrik was first up, followed by

Mrs. Wikk, Mr. Wikk, and then the soldier who'd kept dozing during the chess match.

She listened, hoping to hear the results of the mission, and
then had the presence of mind to start capturing video with
her mTalk camera.

Vedrik turned to the pilot of the skiff. "Have the men tear
down camp and prepare the *Skull* for takeoff. We have no
time to waste; someone has already been to the clue and may
already be on his way to the coordinates."

"The Wikk boy?" the pilot asked.

"Yes," Vedrik hissed. "I believe so, but he appears to have
had help. It is as Zebra Xavier suspected. Now, make the call."
Vedrik stripped off the wetsuit, and the copilot of the skiff
handed him a long black coat, which he quickly wrapped over
his uniform. He motioned for the Übel scooters to come in close.
"You two, wait here for the other two men. They're setting the
charges. Once you have them, hightail it to the *Skull*. I will not
wait long. You, come with us," he said to the final scooter pilot.

Tiffany shook her head and frowned. "Charges?" she whispered to herself. She'd seen the soldier setting something
around the room. But she'd thought they were security sensors
or something. Not explosives.

The two scooter pilots saluted the captain in unison.
"Yes, sir."

"Now go!" Vedrik shouted at the skiff pilot, barely taking
his seat before the ship zipped forward. Mr. and Mrs. Wikk
had already sat down, but Bargoz was not as lucky, and he
nearly fell out of the craft. The soldier caught himself and
grimaced with pain.

The deluxe Übel scooter zipped away toward the southern
ziggurat and the Übel base camp, followed by the scooter. The
two star fighters did not return from their pass over the ziggurat but appeared to land. The Übel soldiers were clearing
out quickly. The problem was that Tiffany didn't know the
status of her brothers. She knew they were not with Oliver,

but were they alive, injured, trapped? She had no choice but to wait. Although the captain thought they'd left already, she knew they hadn't.

Seconds seemed like hours, but the water's surface rippled again as two more Übel divers appeared. They were hoisted onto the backs of the two awaiting scooters. The heavyset diver had a very difficult time getting his leg over the scooter and nearly made it fall into the water.

They'd barely started off for the Übel base when the ground shook and a loud rumble echoed somewhere below Evad's surface. A stream of large bubbles blasted to the surface right where all the diving had taken place. It looked like a plume of blood.

Tiffany's arms and legs went numb. It felt like her heart dropped to her stomach, and a chill came over her entire body. Not a second later, she became very warm, and her stomach turned over. She leaned to the side and threw up into the bushes. For at that moment, she knew her brothers had been killed in the explosion below. The rumbling had confirmed the explosive charges detonating.

As if on cue, rain began to fall from the sky. A bright flash of lightning lit the pool's surface as it had before, but this time, the water looked more blood red than it had before. Thunder roared overhead, mirroring the emotions that were screaming inside her. Tears began to stream down her face. For a moment, she sat there, incapable of thinking or moving.

The sound of engines roaring set her in motion. She had to go! She had to get to the southern ziggurat before the Übel left. If she didn't, she'd be left here all alone on this planet—something she couldn't stomach. She'd rather be held captive with her mom and dad. At least then they could comfort each other.

Frantic, she jumped up and began collecting her things. She'd have to retrieve what few supplies she'd left in the hut too, she realized. And as much as she could carry of the things from the stash she and Oliver had secured before his dive.

Stumbling around a panic, she almost didn't see the small black form coming toward her. Midnight! "Here, kitty," she called.

The cat stopped, its ears perked up. It stared intently into the foliage past her. Tiffany turned as well, listening, but she couldn't hear anything. Without warning, the small cat scampered toward the jungle and disappeared into the wet foliage.

Gasping, Tiffany quickly took the pack from her back and looked through it, searching for the Zapp-It in case the big cat creatures attacked. Her fingers closed around the weapon, and she brought it out. She would be ready for the animals, although she doubted any remained in the jungle.

She was ready.

Ready for anything . . .

Taking a deep breath, Tiffany shook her head, the wet strands of her brown hair sticking to her face. She *was* ready, she realized. What had she been thinking, losing control like that? Even knowing her brothers' fate, even knowing her parents were leaving with Vedrik, she had to keep it together. She couldn't turn herself in—couldn't give up. She was stronger than that, and she still had other options.

At that moment, she made two decisions: she was not going to turn herself in to the soldiers, and she would rescue her parents.

Tiffany dashed for the nearby jungle. "Midnight! Where are you?" she called.

The black cat's head appeared, and the animal strolled back out of the trees toward Tiffany. "There you are!"

As she bent down to pick it up, two feet appeared in front of her.

They were bare.

2.52

Time

Tiffany followed the bare feet up and saw a boy—a young man—wearing a black diving suit. It was Oliver. He was soaking wet, his brown hair matted to his forehead, small droplets dripping down his face. But standing before Tiffany was her brother, alive and unscathed.

Tiffany jumped forward and hugged him. "Oliver! I thought—" She choked with tears again. "I thought you were—" She swallowed.

"Dead?" came a second voice. Mason stepped into view. "Hey, Tiff."

Austin came out of the foliage and stood next to his older twin. Tiffany looked them over—Mason with blue eyes, Austin with green, but otherwise the same height and with sandy blond hair, now plastered in long wet strings to the sides of their heads.

More movement and the blue boy Tiffany had heard mentioned before but never seen pushed aside some shiny green leaves and stepped into view.

"But the explosion . . ." Tiffany said.

"We barely escaped," Oliver admitted. "But we mustn't talk now. We have to go. We have to get to the *Phoenix* and figure out where we're going next."

"I know," she said. "The video gave a set of coordinates, and I've already looked them up. We're headed to Enaid."

"Enaid?" asked Mason. "That place is dangerous."

"We'll be fine," Oliver assured them. He looked around cautiously. "We need to get our stuff and go."

Tiffany frowned. "Why didn't you call?"

Oliver held up his wrist. "None of the mTalks work anymore. They all went dead after the explosion."

"I thought I'd lost you all," Tiffany admitted.

Oliver shook his head but didn't say anything.

"I didn't want to be alone," she continued. Midnight seemed offended and mewed loudly at the five kids' feet.

"It's okay, Tiffany," Oliver said, embracing his sister. "It's going to be okay." The twins and even Obbin joined in and, for a moment, the five kids stood in the rain, letting it wash away their fears.

The noise of a star fighter's engines swooshing overhead got everyone moving again. The Übel were for the moment still there. But Tiffany knew they wouldn't be for long.

Moving rapidly, the kids found the supplies and distributed everything as evenly as possible before heading for the western ziggurat and then the *Phoenix*. The door to the ziggurat was nothing but charred strips of metal from the soldiers blasting it open earlier that morning; this made access to the interior of the building easier. They quickly reached the top of the ziggurat and stepped out toward the aqueduct.

"I know that none of us has had a good experience crossing this so far," Oliver said. "But we have to do it. So everyone—"

"Wait," Obbin said. "There is a better way. Brother Sam took me through a passage under the aqueduct."

Tiffany breathed a huge sigh of relief.

"Well, aren't you full of surprises," Austin joked.

"Lead the way, Obbin," Oliver ordered, and the Wikk kids followed the prince back into the ziggurat and down one flight of stairs. Obbin pulled out his cross necklace and waved it past the metal key plate. The lock clicked and Obbin pushed the door open.

"Who is Brother Sam?" Tiffany asked as they moved into the tunnel beyond the door.

"He's the guy in the red cloak," Austin said.

"You've met him?" Tiffany asked.

"And I did too," Obbin said.

"I haven't yet," Mason shrugged. "But I did get a necklace." The blue-eyed twin held up the pendant.

"Don't worry. He didn't even speak to me," Oliver admitted. "So I didn't really meet him."

"Red cloak?" Tiffany asked. "I saw him too. I mean, sort of. A red cloak flitted past the mTalk before Vedrik arrived at the chess game."

Oliver's mouth dropped. "He was right there all the time! That's how he knew to show me the slide."

"Do you think he got out?" Austin asked.

Obbin answered. "There were many secret passages and tunnels like this one all over the basin. Brother Sam was very resourceful, and he knew all of them. I would say he got out."

Moving as fast as they dared, Obbin led the party of five down the dank-smelling tunnel with only Tiffany's mTalk light for guidance.

"So, why didn't he stay to help us?" Tiffany asked.

"We don't know," Austin said. "But when we get back to the *Phoenix*, I have to tell you some of the stuff he was teaching me."

After that, they moved without conversation, racing along the corridor, through another door, and farther in. They could hear water coursing overhead, as well as drops that trickled continually down the walls on either side. But they kept going, continuing deeper and deeper into the tunnel. Tiffany watched Mason, mindful of his claustrophobia, but other than gritting his teeth, he gave no indication of fear. Perhaps they were racing too quickly for it to matter.

Finally, Obbin stopped. Opening a side door, he led them up a spiral staircase to another door. When they opened that one, they were at the edge of the river they'd first followed into the basin. Behind them lay the basin and before them the entrance to the tunnel through the ridge.

They'd made it.

"Great job, Obbin," Oliver said, giving the blue boy a clap on the shoulder. "You really gave us a head start. Now, let's get through the ridge and over the chasm and then we'll be on the *Phoenix* and on our way."

The kids started forward.

The rumble of engines pulled their attention skyward. Midnight nearly leaped from Tiffany's hands, but she clung tightly to the cat.

Oliver ordered the twins into the tunnel, and they grudgingly obeyed. "Tiffany, turn on your mTalk recorder. It's coming this way."

She obeyed and followed Oliver to the outcropping that blocked the southern area of the basin. With backs snugly against the stone ridge, they watched as a large black ship cruised into view.

"That must be the *Skull*," Tiffany and Oliver said in unison.

"How did you know?" Oliver asked.

"Vedrik ordered it prepared for takeoff," Tiffany said. "You?"

"One of the soldiers in the underwater, underground chamber teased the other about cleaning the *Skull*'s lavatory."

"Nice," Tiffany said. She was recording the ship. It was gaining altitude and heading for the dark storm clouds above. "Well, there go our parents," she said.

"You sound okay about it," Oliver noticed.

"Well, they're safe, we're safe, and so far, we've been able to keep up. Besides, I've got a feeling we've got help that the Übel do not have," Tiffany admitted.

"You mean the red-cloak guy," Oliver said.

"Not exactly," she said. "It's just a feeling, but—"

Tiffany grunted as Oliver yanked her flat to the ground. Midnight leaped free and ran into the tunnel as four sleek black star fighters zipped past and then circled the ziggurats, each firing off flares as they did. The star fighters angled sharply upward and zipped into the dark clouds, disappearing.

"We have to go!" shouted Oliver, pulling his sister to her feet.

"What . . . what is it?" she asked as he nearly dragged her into the tunnel through the ridge.

"Boys, go! Run!" Oliver screamed.

Mason scooped the cat into his arms and started into the tunnel, but Austin hesitated. "Run? The ledge is to narrow," he cried. "Last time—"

"Just go!"

Tiffany could still see the western and part of the eastern ziggurat from her position in the tunnel when a sound like metal being torn in two pierced the sky over the valley. Tiffany looked back as several missiles zipped toward the ziggurats, long trails of orange flame bursting out from the projectiles' engines. The rockets pierced the stone structures like a fork into a fresh tomato, disappearing from sight.

"Down," screamed Oliver, and everyone hit the ground.

An explosive roar thundered through the valley, followed by another, and another, and then two more. A blast of fiery-hot air blew into the tunnel, and the sound of shards of rock pummeling the side of the ridge echoed around them. The kids could do nothing but cower and hope nothing hit them.

Finally, the rush of wind settled and disappeared. Oliver pulled Tiffany to her feet. She saw the twins looking past them. Their faces looked grim. She didn't want to look, because she knew what had happened to the basin.

She knew it was gone.

With a sigh, she turned. There was little to see but black smoke and red flames. Everything in the basin was leveled. Had they taken any longer to get out of the valley, they'd have risked the weapons' ferocity being unleashed on them. . . .

Tiffany shook herself from her thoughts. But they hadn't been harmed, she told herself. They'd escaped to the ridge.

Again, they'd been spared by some unknown force.

The kids' journey through the tunnel was just as quick and as silent as the last one. This time, Oliver knew, they were all considering what might have happened to them had they delayed any longer. They made it to the end of the tunnel in record time. Activating the bridge, they stepped out of the cold, dank tunnel and into the grove, then crossed the chasm with ease.

The path Oliver had cut was only a remnant of itself, and the three younger boys each took turns leading the way, reclaiming the path with the machete. They soon made it back to the *Phoenix's* location. Oliver pulled out the small remote for the cloaking device and clicked it once. "Here we go," he said as they approached where the ship was supposed to be.

The silver ship shimmered into existence before them.

"We're home!" Austin exclaimed.

"Home," Mason scoffed. "I guess it is true enough."

The kids ran toward the now visible door. Oliver tapped the access code into the keypad, and the side hatch opened.

"Everyone to the bridge. We take off immediately," Oliver ordered. "We've got to get off this planet and on our way."

The kids raced to the bridge as Oliver sealed the ship. A moment later, Tiffany was at the NavCom and he in the pilot's seat.

"Should I bring up the course for Enaid?" Tiffany asked.

"No, we're headed to Jahr des Eises," Oliver admitted.

"What?" the three boys cried in unison.

"It's time to get Obbin home and pay a visit to someone," Oliver said. His decision was final, and although he didn't say as much, no one challenged him.

The engines fired, and the *Phoenix* lifted into the air. Oliver pulled back on the controls and the silver ship, the Wikks' current home, zipped toward outer space.

Visual Glossary

Academy, Federal Star Fleet: The Academy provides top-of-the-line education while creating future leaders for the Federal fleet. All males in the Federation must participate in the Federation's military service for at least five years. Most begin at age eighteen, but a select few are admitted early at age sixteen.

Archeos Alliance: An organization that exists to unlock the past that has been lost. Founded as nonprofit, but receiving both private and Federal funds, the organization has become a battleground for special-interest groups. Mr. and Mrs. Wikk often receive grants through this organization and are considered employees. They report their findings to Archeos, and then Archeos makes official reports available to the Federation and other groups.

Bewaldeter: A boarding school, Bewaldeter is one of the premier early-education establishments in the Federation. A majority of Archeos employees send their children to Bewaldeter. The school provides a curriculum that allows kids to focus on their interests. Tiffany, Mason, and Austin Wikk attend it, and Oliver did too until he was selected for early admittance to the Academy.

Black Cat Creatures: Resembling panthers, these large black felines roam the Ero Doeht basin on Evad. Midnight is one of these creatures.

Blauwe Mensen (*Blue People*): A mysterious group known to the people of Brighton and Mudo as "blue ghosts." No one dares enter their home in the Cobalt Gorge. Obbin belongs to the Blauwe Mensen's royal family.

Captain Fritz Vedrik: An agent and captain of the Übel forces who attended the Übel's Raven's Nest Academy on planet Babylt. Fritz Vedrik never knew his father. His mother died when he was just five years of age. He was enrolled for pre-military training in the Düsterkeit Boys School, which specialized in math, virtual war games, and endurance and survival techniques. He went missing from the school for several years and was eventually found and brought back. Shortly afterward, he was sent to the Drachen Bach colony for further training and reeducation. He excelled and quickly rose to the top of his class. At age seventeen, he was given his first secret mission. Having gained top-level security clearance, he conducts clandestine, off-record missions on behalf of the Übel high command. Capable of going rogue, he often works for himself. He is dangerous.

Cryostore: A refrigeration and freezing appliance in the galley.

Dabnis Castle: This castle has long been abandoned, but several clues and artifacts were found during the Wikks' last archeological dig. The clues, located under a pavilion, on the roof of a tower, and within a catacomb deep below a library, provide what the Wikks believe is the missing step on the path to Ursprung.

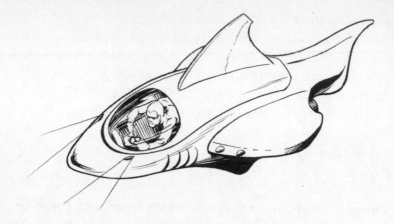

Deep Blue: A two-man submarine used by the Wikks during their exploration. It has a test depth of approximately eight hundred feet and can reach speeds of twenty-five knots.

Eagle: Another sister ship to the *Phoenix*. Piloted by Brother Samuel, it was used to help the twins escape from the Übel.

e-Journal: An electronic notebook in which Mr. and Mrs. Wikk stored all their archeological notes. The notes consist of maps, statistics, pictures, videos, reports, coordinates, contacts, and much more. The information contains clues that may help unlock the path to Ursprung via a complex tapping method that traces links and makes connections. This tapping method is known only to Mr. and Mrs. Wikk and Tiffany.

Empire: The government preceding the Federation, ruled by an emperor of unknown origin. The Empire expanded through war, annexations, and clandestine revolutions. During this time, the truth of Ursprung was lost.

Enaid: This planet was the site of the beginning of the Empire. Although it is not the capital of the Empire or the Federation, the first settlements, then cities, were built there. Located at 102.580 X, 5912.23 Y, 22.0 Z, Enaid is somewhat centrally located in the current boundaries of the Federation. The planet is small and controlled by one major city. This city is thought to be one of the most dangerous in the Federation despite its ample police force. The governor of the planet has allowed bribery and corruption to influence every facet of the planet's government.

Energen: The boys' favorite drink. It provides a jolt of energy and is 100 percent natural.

Ero Doeht: The basin on Evad in which the village of Yth Orod sits. The basin was formerly home to the Veritas Nachfolger. It is marked by four large ziggurats that sit at the ends of the four points of a cross-shaped pool. An observatory and many other buildings are spread throughout the jungle. A series of tunnels and secret passages crisscross the basin. Many plants and animals call the basin home, including the rubbelum tree, panthers, and attacking vines.

Evad: A planet previously explored by Mr. and Mrs. Wikk that became part of their search via a clue found at Dabnis Castle. The only habitable planet in the Rel Krev system, it is covered in lush green tropical plants, some of which can be deadly. The atmosphere is breathable, but hot and humid. It is home to many wild animals, some of which are unknown due to lost research.

Federal Star Fleet: The military arm of the Federation that stands to protect and serve its citizens. Half of the entire force is dedicated to the expansion of the Federation. Expansion occurs through either colonization of uninhabited planets or annexation by a vote of the inhabitants of a non-federal planet. The Federal Star Fleet has taken a peaceful approach to expansion. All males must serve five years in the federal service.

Federation: Established when the childless emperor Albert the XI ceded rule to the senate by declaring, "The people should decide their fate." The Federation consists of 1,983 planets, asteroids, and stations. Governed by a president and Senate, the Federation is enjoying a time of great wealth and expansion.

Grapple Hook Launcher and Canister: The grapple has about one hundred feet of wire and can be reloaded with spare canisters. The grapple can be holstered.

Griffin: The sister ship of the *Phoenix*, built as an identical twin. It was given to Rand and Jenn McGregor to use on the quest for Ursprung. The ship, attacked by Corsairs and traded to Schlamm, is currently stored at his warehouse in Mudo on Jahr des Eises.

Hyper Flight: Space flight navigation at extreme speeds, considered very dangerous for inexperienced pilots. The route of hyper flight must be entirely clear for the duration of the trip, or the ship will smash into another object and be obliterated.

Jahr des Eises: A small forest planet. Initially the planet was discovered and settled by the Blauwe Mensen. These people, however, remain hidden and are not officially known to the Federation. An outpost, Mudo, was established by a resource exploration company as a base for logging operations. When the planet was annexed by the Federation, the city of Brighton was established.

While covered in a thick forest of gargantuan trees, the planet suffers from ice storms called Eises every three years. In the two years of growth, the logging industry is in full operation. During the Eises, those who remain behind are sealed within the dome of Brighton. Phelan O'Farrell, a wealthy donor to Archeos and to the Wikks specifically, live on Jahr des Eises in the city of Brighton.

JC-42596: This is a model of Übel stun rifle that has been equipped with a small grenade launcher.

Krank's Parts and Service: A parts and repair shop in Brighton owned by Mr. O'Farrell's friend, Samuel Krank. Mr. Krank assisted in the refurbishing of the *Phoenix* and the *Griffin*.

Laoc Esahc IcIc System: Contains only the planet Tragiws and its two moons, Sno Srap and Nellum.

LOCA-drone: A small silver disc with a screen embedded in its top. The LOCA-drone uses magnetism and negative energy to propel itself to a position over a designated area. Often used for search and rescue, it  can also be used to mark locations and coordinates. Each device is assigned a unique encrypted access signature code.

LOCATOR: An application used to track and find LOCA-drones. The *Phoenix*, the *Griffin*, and their corresponding sky scooters are equipped with LOCATOR. It also can track other mTalks that have been linked through optional sharing.

LugerKX5: The type of stun pistol that Captain Vedrik uses. Highly specialized and custom designed, the weapon is not widely manufactured. The trigger of the gun has a fingerprint sensor, allowing only its owner to fire it. Its charge pack can provide enough energy for a thousand stuns on one charge.

LuminOrb: A small orb that glows when squeezed. LuminOrbs are often used to mark paths or designated rendezvous points. Squeeze once and the orb turns blue, representing general marking. Two squeezes for green means the path ahead is clear. Squeeze three times for red, which warns that something ahead is wrong. Squeeze four times for yellow, which signifies that caution should be used. Five squeezes causes the orb to take on a glowing blackish hue that warns others to escape immediately.

Midnight: One of the black cat creatures' cubs. Tiffany has adopted the cub as her pet.

mTalk: Worn on the wrist like a watch, the mTalk has many useful applications, including a built-in video call feature, flashlight, navigation device, video camera, and other features still unknown to the Wikks.

Nanocook: A high-speed cooking appliance.

Oxyverter: Used for diving in salt or fresh water, the Oxyverter is a small mouthpiece that separates oxygen directly from water. The filter does not need to be replaced and can provide an unlimited supply of oxygen to the wearer.

Phoenix: A spaceship donated to the Wikks to facilitate research on their quest for the origins of mankind. The ship's sleek silver skin and forward-swept wings give it a unique appearance. But those features are nothing compared with the secret capabilities of the ship that Oliver has yet to discover. The ship consists of a bridge (cockpit), four cabins (sleeping quarters), a galley (dining room/kitchen), three lavatories (bathrooms), a library/office, an engine room, an electronics suite, a two-story cargo bay, and an artifacts room.

Raven: The ship belonging to the man in the black suit.

Refuse-Cycler: A disposal device common to ship galleys.

Rel Krev System: A planetary system with seventeen small planets, one of which is Evad.

Rubbelum: A tree growing in Ero Doeht basin. The settlers of Yth Orod found the wood to be a good material for building. Rubbelum's sap is rubbery and semi-moisture-resistant, slowing the deterioration of lumber in the humid jungle climate. The local people had needed a solution after their lighter metals continued to rust and break down. This wood was used for furniture, doors, and buildings.

Skull (Übel cruiser): This cruiser is one of the primary craft in the Übel's small fleet. The communications bridge rivals the technology and power of a Star Fleet frigate. The cruiser's exterior is black and heavily armored with thick nano-carbon skin.

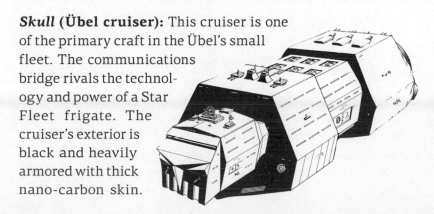

It is armed with plasma blasters, phaser torpedo canisters, and skeleton-missile launchers. Housing a full battalion of soldiers, it also carries star fighters and ground equipment.

Sky Scooter: This small craft seats two and has multiple storage compartments. It can hover up to twenty feet above the ground and can reach speeds of one hundred miles per hour. The scooter is ideal for short commutes.

StunShot Rifle SI: This rifle can use either lethal standard bullets or a stun option that fires a green orb of energy. *SI* stands for "standard-issue," as this rifle is widely man-ufactured and used among the soldiers of the federal fleet.

Thermaclean: An appliance to instantly sanitize tables and cookware.

Tragiws: The planet the Wikks call home. Its climate is arid, but it is not a desert. The Wikks' home sits on the edge of the Plains of Yrovi near a deep cavern. The planet is small and sparsely populated.

TW414: A device with the ability to shoot small projectiles at a target. Upon connecting, the projectiles deliver a series of disabling shocks. The civilian version, the Zinger, is less powerful.

Übel: A secret order/society composed of renegade forces. Captain Vedrik is an agent of the mysterious society. The society's handiwork is threaded throughout the history of the Federation and Empire but is not publicly recognized. Its reach and influence is unknown, but thought to be vast. Its financial resources are second only to the Federation.

Übel Deluxe Scooter: A roofless craft with two rows of seats, one for a pilot and copilot and one for passengers. It is also known as a *skiff* and is armed with two plasma blasters.

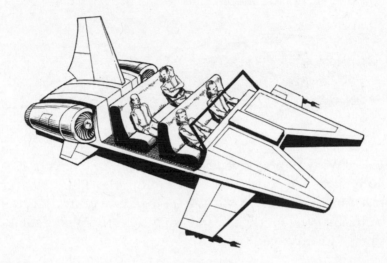

Übel Scooter: Unlike the Wikks' scooter, Übel scooters are armed with dual plasma blasters. They can carry up to two soldiers.

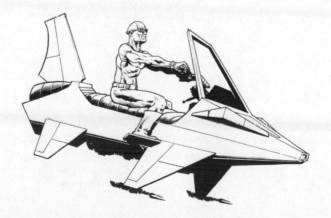

Übel Star Fighter: These sleek black fighters are single-pilot and armed with plasma blasters and phaser torpedoes. While able to jump into hyper flight, they do not carry ample supplies for their pilots and must remain close to a support ship or base. The crafts' top speed is unknown, but little has been known to outfly them. The wings on these fighters can be extended or brought into the jet.

Ultra-Wear Pants: Invented by the Wikk children's grandfather, the pants are made of titanium-flex fabric. Water resistant, flame retardant, and temperature controlled, the pants are great for the adverse conditions the Wikks sometimes face on expeditions.

Ultra-Wear Shirt: Invented by the Wikk children's grandfather, the shirts can maintain a consistent temperature, keep the wearer dry, and resist flames. Other features include electric-shock protection and puncture protection against sharp branches or animal bites. The shirt can be pulled over the wearer's head to filter poisonous gases.

Ursprung: A fabled planet believed to be the birthplace of mankind. Many seek to discover it.

Veritas Nachfolger: A group of people who guard the Truth. They remain to keep Truth alive and guide those who quest for it. The Veritas Nachfolger symbolize Truth with a cross and use it as their symbol and insignia. They integrate the cross and many other symbols into their daily lives. The Veritas Nachfolger understand the Übel to be the forces of darkness. They have been seen wearing red cloaks.

Vines on Evad: Long spidery vines that cover the ziggurats. They attack unsuspecting intruders and attempt to pull their victims apart. When wounded, they ooze a bluish goolike sap.

Wikk family: The Wikk family's core is Elliot and Laura Wikk, who married after meeting each other on an archeology internship with Archeos during the summer of their junior year at Veritatem University. Together, they trained with Dr. Craig, who excavated the moon Tygr, where thousands of artifacts were unearthed and preserved. Soon their four children were born while Mrs. Wikk took leave to be a fulltime mother.

When the youngest kids, the twins, were old enough to attend Bewaldeter, Mrs. Wikk again joined her husband in the field. Oliver, Tiffany, Mason, and Austin traveled to dig sites and explored with their parents during summer breaks. They relished their time together as a family.

Yth Orod: The city that the Veritas Nachfolger inhabited while on Evad. Set within the Ero Doeht basin, the city was surrounded by a high ridge that acted as an extra layer of protection. The city was settled in 1397 with a population of five thousand, and, within ten short years, the large ziggurats and cross-shaped pool had been completed. Meant to serve as a symbol of and beacon for the Truth, many other secrets were laid in the depths of the city in order to preserve the path back to Ursprung.

Zapp-It: A small defense device that uses an electric shock to either deter or stun an assailant.

Zinger: A larger version of the Zapp-It that shoots small projectiles at a target. Once connected, the projectiles give off a series of disabling shocks. The military has a more powerful version called the TW414.

Recipe for Veritas Nachfolger Chocolate-Chip Cookies

Thanks to Ashley Eastman for sharing this recipe with our fans.

Ingredients

- 2 1/4 cups all-purpose flour
- 1 teaspoon baking soda
- 1 cup butter, softened
- 3/4 cup packed brown sugar
- 1/4 cup white sugar
- 1 (3.4 ounce) package instant vanilla pudding mix
- 2 eggs
- 1 teaspoon vanilla extract
- 2 cups semisweet chocolate chips
- 1 cup chopped walnuts (optional)

Directions

1. Preheat oven to 350 degrees F (175 degrees C).
2. Sift together the flour and baking soda; set aside.
3. In a large bowl, cream together the butter, brown sugar, and white sugar.

4. Beat in the instant pudding mix until blended.
5. Stir in the eggs and vanilla.
6. Blend in the flour mixture.
7. Stir in the chocolate chips and nuts.
8. Drop cookies by rounded spoonfuls onto ungreased cookie sheets.
9. Bake for 10 to 12 minutes in the preheated oven. Edges should be golden brown.

Brock D. Eastman likes to write, but his focus is on his wonderful wife and two daughters. They reside at the base of America's mountain and are learning to call Colorado home, but sometimes need a visit to the comfortable cornfields and hospitality of the Midwest, especially during spring and harvest.

Brock is product marketing manager at Focus on the Family, where he has the privilege to work on the world-renowned Adventures in Odyssey brand, a show his dad got him hooked on when he was a little boy. He also makes frequent appearances on the official Adventures in Odyssey podcast and has written an article for *Thriving Family* magazine.

He started writing the Quest for Truth series in 2005 and, five years later, with his wife's encouragement, signed a publishing deal. He is always thinking of his next story and totes a thumb drive full of ideas.

To keep track of what Brock is working on, visit

www.BrockEastman.com

Or connect with Brock at

Twitter: @bdeastman
Facebook: http://www.facebook.com/eastmanbrock
Blogger: http://thequestfortruthbooks.blogspot.com/
YouTube: http://www.youtube.com/user/FictionforAll/videos

MORE FROM BROCK EASTMAN!

BOOK ONE   **THE QUEST FOR TRUTH**

> "Taken is a riveting tale of just how far mankind is willing to go . . . for the ultimate prize."
> —**Wayne Thomas Batson,** Bestselling Author of *The Door Within* Trilogy, *The Berinfell Prophecies*, and *The Dark Sea Annals*

THE QUEST FOR TRUTH series follows the four Wikk kids in their desperate race to find the mysterious planet Ursprung and stop the Übel renegades from misusing its long-lost secrets. Ancient cities, treacherous villains, high-tech gadgets, The Phoenix—encounter all of these and more on this futuristic, interplanetary adventure!

BUY *TAKEN* WHEREVER BOOKS ARE SOLD.